Destiny Has a Way

By

Stephanie Schaffer

PublishAmerica
Baltimore

First printing

All characters in this book are fictitious, and any resemblance to real persons, living or dead, is coincidental.

PublishAmerica has allowed this work to remain exactly as the author intended, verbatim, without editorial input.

ISBN: 978-1-4489-2523-0
PUBLISHED BY PUBLISHAMERICA, LLLP
www.publishamerica.com
Baltimore

Printed in the United States of America

To God

For giving me the ability

To put imagination to paper.

And to my niece Lisa,

Your input has been invaluable

Chapter 1

Sitting on her front porch swing, Shelby Russell looked out across the field in front of her. The time of the season was changing. The leaves on the trees were starting to change their colors; reds, yellows and paler greens. The farmers were taking the crops off their fields, whether it be soy beans or corn, they were hard at work harvesting the crops they had planted in the spring.

As Shelby watched them, she began to think back to another time in her life when things were so much different. Laughing softly to her self, a thought had crossed her mind. Why was it as kids, we couldn't wait to grow up and as adults, we wished we we're kids once again?

"I think we all spend quite a bit of time pondering that thought from time to time." She said out loud with a chuckle, knowing no one was around to hear her talking to her self.

She sat on the swing with an old high school year book splayed across her lap, flipping through it. She couldn't believe how long ago that seemed now. Looking at the pictures, she was having a hard time putting names with some of the faces with out looking at the directory.

She had no regrets of her high school years, but looking back now, she wished she would have paid more attention to things than she had back then. She had made it through high school on the honor roll every year but socially she didn't convey that of a book worm.

Shelby was never a trouble maker but she was a very out going person and made friends with every one. She didn't hang out with the "in crowd," she hung out with everyone. She had friends with every social crowd not just one "click" in particular. That was one of her attributes that made her unique through out high school. Some people thought she was weird for being that way, but in the end, she didn't care one bit.

Growing up in the small farming community of Timberville Indiana, there really wasn't much for any one to get into trouble for. It's a beautiful community and every one that lives there knows everyone. It's a tight knit community and the towns' people would give you the shirts off their backs if they thought you needed it.

Sitting out in the middle of no where, away from any major cities, Timberville is right around fifty miles away from Ft. Wayne Indiana; give or take a few miles. It *is* the best place in the world to grow up. Shelby had always had dreams of going off to college to become a veterinarian and starting her own practice right here in the very community she had been raised, and that's exactly what she had done.

Shelby's parents own a house in town where her and her twin brother CJ grew up. CJ stands for Carl Jasper; after he had gotten older, he liked the nick name CJ way better than being called Carl. For a young guy into sports, the sound of CJ was more masculine than just plain old Carl.

CJ was born just two minutes before Shelby and every chance he got, he reminded her about it. By two minutes, he really *is* her older brother and even though he aggravated the dickens out of her every chance he got, Shelby loves him more than anything. She teases him back by telling him that they must have been to close in the womb because he's *always* a real pain in her side.

Growing up in town had its moments. CJ was into football and Shelby was every much a tom boy. Not only did Shelby have a brother, but her neighbors on either side of her house had all boys as well. She had male testosterone all around her with the exception of the mothers. She was treated just like one of the guys all of her life.

On the right side of her house were the Parkers'. They consisted of Mr. & Mrs. Parker, the oldest Jack, Cole in the middle and the youngest was Roger. Jack is about three years older than Cole and loves baseball. Cole is the same age as CJ and Shelby, and of course like her brother, loves football. Roger being the baby of the family by about four years wasn't into *any* sports. He's the musician of the family. He loves to play the violin and he's very good at it to.

On the left side of her house live the Smiths'. They consist of Mr. & Mrs. Smith, the oldest Dallas, who is also the same age as CJ and Shelby and very much into football, and the youngest Luke. He's into any sport he can get into. He just can't get enough! When one sports season is finished, he's in line waiting for the next one.

Through out high school Cole and Dallas were Shelby's two best friends.

Of course she had a few girl-friends, but those two were her *very* best friends. They were always known as the three musketeers. The three of them always seemed to be together somewhere and if not; they always knew where the others were. Sometimes that wasn't always a good thing either. People do seem to get jealous and start rumors that shouldn't be created. That can play havoc on your life but they always managed to find a way to shut them up.

Coming back to the present, Shelby sat looking at the year book when another picture caught her eye. It was a picture of Cole, her and Dallas at the senior prom. She laughed out loud at the sight before her as she remembered that night. She was the only girl that had come with two dates. Two dates! The three of them had gotten into a huge shouting match over who was going to be going with whom. The final decision was made that the three of them would go together and that would be the end of it.

Shelby still couldn't figure out what all of the fuss had been over. It wasn't like Cole or Dallas couldn't get a date. Between Cole, Dallas, and CJ, they were the three top players on the football team! Every girl in school drooled over the three of them. Admitting it to her self now, they were also the three hottest guys in school.

Needless to say, CJ hadn't been too happy with the idea of Shelby going to the prom with his two friends but she cut him off at the pass before he could object too much. She had set him up with her best friend Leah, who she had known that CJ had had a crush on for a very long time, and then found out that Leah was very much into CJ. The match worked out perfectly for all parties involved.

As time went on, the summer after they had all graduated from high school, things started to change between Shelby and her two best guys. Shelby, CJ, Cole and Dallas spent the summer hanging out together before they all had to leave out for college in the fall. They all knew that they would be gone from each other for the better part of four years so they were trying to make up for that lost time in the few months they had left.

CJ, Cole and Dallas were going to college on football scholarships to the same university and Shelby was on her way to a top notch veterinarian school. Everything was going according to plan. So Shelby thought.

As time went on, and the summer was coming to an end, Cole and Dallas starting acting differently toward her; it was as if they were distancing themselves and Shelby didn't like it one bit. Out of the clear blue, Cole called her up one day and asked if she could meet him at the local diner where they all hung out for lunch.

"You know Shelby; I'm really going to miss high school." Cole started the conversation after Shelby had sat down and settled her self in the booth across from him.

"I know what you mean. It seems we just got out and now we're heading off in different directions. I'm going to miss you guys so much." She said as she slid her hands across the table to squeeze Cole's hands.

"You have no idea how happy I am to hear you say that." He replied looking at her hands holding his.

"Are you alright? You look worried about something." She asked as concern stated to fill her eyes.

"I'm worried about a lot of things." He answered playing with the straw in his glass not looking at her. He slowly pulled his hands back from hers.

"I don't see what you have to be worried about. You're going to college on a full football scholarship. It's what you love more than anything." She said with a gleaming smile as she took a sip of her soda.

"Football has been my life but there is one thing I love a lot more than that." He said seriously looking her dead in the eyes.

Shelby almost choked on her soda when he gave that reply. She narrowed her eyes on him for a second and a shiver coursed up her spine. She then let out a laugh and said, "What could there possibly be in this world that you would love more than football?"

She was starting to feel uncomfortable at the direction of where their conversation might be going.

"Come on Shelby, I thought after all these years, you would have figured that out by now." He said placing one hand over hers and slowly started to move his thumb in a caressing motion across the top of her hand.

She looked at him in stunned silence. She didn't know what to say or what to think about what he was saying to her. Was she really hearing what he was saying? Was he admitting at that very moment that he was in love with her? This can't be possible, she thought. Cole's my best friend! He's like a brother! This can't be real. This can't be happening!

At that moment, the waitress walked up to the table and asked if they were ready to order or if they needed refills on their drinks. Shelby shook her head at the woman as if her head was in slow motion, not taking her eyes off of Cole.

8

The woman knew something was going on and walked slowly away from the table.

"I can see from your reaction that you figured out what I'm talking about. Are you going to say anything?" Cole asked.

Shelby shrugged her shoulders up and started shaking her head, "I really don't know what to say. I'm shocked. Where is this coming from?"

"You really have no idea how I feel about you?" he asked narrowing his eyes at her in confusion.

"Cole…I…I've never thought of *you* in that way. It's never crossed my mind. I never thought you would think of *me* in that way."

"So, you're saying that you have no feelings for me at all?" he asked with a tone of disappointment.

"I do, but not in the way you're thinking. You mean the world to me, but more in a brotherly way than in a romantic way. I just don't see you like that." She tried to explain to him.

"I see. Don't I look like a complete idiot, I sure as hell feel like one." He said as he pulled his hand away and hung his head looking down at the table.

"Cole, I don't understand, where is this coming from? Why are you bringing up something like this now? If you really feel this way, why haven't you said something before now?" She asked looking for some kind of explanation.

"I'm telling you this because I've felt this way for a really long time, and in a few more weeks, we'll be going off to different colleges. I don't know when I'll see you again and I won't be around to make sure you're alright." He started explaining. "You're going to be miles away from here. What if something happens to you? This isn't like high school. I'm not going to be right next door." He said sternly with a hint of anger in his tone.

"Cole, nothing is going to happen to me. We'll all be home for holidays; we'll get to see each other then. You act like the world is coming to an end. I'm going to be fine." She said with a slight giggle about it.

Now she was starting to see the real reason why Cole was acting this way. He didn't want her going off to college by herself! He wouldn't be around to be her protector, but at the same time, that really did make his declaration of love more real. Why else would he feel he had to protect her? The more she thought about his revelation, the more confusing it was becoming.

"My world *is* coming to an end!" Shaking his head he stood from the table. "I can't believe I just told you that I was in love with you. How stupid could

I be? I have been holding this back for so long that I thought I was going to lose my mind, and you act like it's a joke!"

"I don't think it's a joke! Will you please wait? Are you *really* serious about this? *Are* you in love with me?" she asked, pulling on his shirt sleeve trying to stop him from leaving.

He stopped dead in his tracks and turned to look at her.

"Do you want to know just how serious I am?" he asked.

"Yes, I do." She answered.

Before Shelby could react, Cole pulled her to him forcefully and wrapped his arms around her. His lips smothered hers and he kissed her as if it was the last thing he would ever do. He kissed her so hard and so full of emotion, that she felt like her life was being pulled right out of her.

After a few moments, what felt like a life time, he released her and she had to suck in a deep breath to refill her lungs. She opened her eyes slowly to see Cole staring at her with anguish and tears starting to well in his eyes. He flipped some money down onto the table to pay for their drinks, but before he walked away, he had one more thing to say.

"I hope you have a good time in college. Maybe there you'll meet someone who'll make you feel the same way you've just made me. I'm trying to be honest with you and you take it as a joke." He said as started for the door once again.

"Cole, please wait! Is that what this is about? Are you afraid I'll meet someone in college? That's what it is, isn't it?" She asked him trying to keep him from leaving.

"Just wait and see. It'll happen and you'll forget all about us back here." He answered as he walked out the door.

Completely dumbfounded, Shelby sank back down onto the booth at her table. She sat with her elbows resting on the table and her hands holding her head. She was at a loss for words and rational thinking. Cole had just thrown a bomb into her lap from out of no where. He had never said or done anything in the past to make her think that he thought of her as anything else than a very close friend or that he wanted more out of their friendship than what it was. She just couldn't understand what was going on.

Then it hit her, he had kissed her! She held her fingers to her lips and slowly started to trace her lips where Cole's had just left their mark. She began to think again; maybe he had left clues in the past that he wanted to be with her. Maybe she was just too blind then to see it, or maybe she just didn't want to see it.

A few days went by and Shelby still hadn't talked to Cole. She had called and stopped by his house a dozen different times and he was never around. He was avoiding her at all costs and she knew it. She didn't know exactly but it was bothering her beyond belief. She couldn't leave for college knowing things between her and Cole were unsettled.

Deep in thought, her phone rang and almost made her jump from her bed. Maybe it was him, but as Shelby looked at the caller ID on the phone, she saw that it was Dallas. Maybe he would know where Cole's been hiding!

"Hello?" she answered the phone.

"Hey, Shelly girl, whatchya doin'?" Dallas asked in his usual upbeat happy mood.

"Nothing at the moment, what are you doing?" she asked in a half depressed tone.

"Same here; just bored. Would you want to go hang out with me at the diner?" he asked.

"Sure, why not. I need to get out of this house for awhile." She answered.

"Cool. How about I meet you there in about fifteen minutes?" he asked as his voice shook.

"That'll work. I'll see you in a bit." She said and hung up the phone.

He sounded kind of odd. I wonder what's up with him, she thought. Right now, she didn't have time to try and figure out what was wrong with Dallas, she had to find out what was going on with Cole.

She arrived at the diner and Dallas hadn't made it there yet. She walked over to the usual booth where they always sat and smiled at the waitress as she passed by. She was the same waitress that waited on her and Cole the other day.

Like clock work, Dallas came bursting through the door acting like his usual goofy self. Shelby couldn't help smiling as he walked up to the table. If she had to compare Cole and Dallas, she would have to say they were complete opposites. Cole is always serious, even though he has his moments of fun. Dallas though, he's always goofy and doesn't *ever* seem to take things seriously. He's just a happy go lucky kind of guy.

He sat down at the table beside her and the waitress came over to take their drink orders. After she walked away, he sat there for a minute drumming his fingers on the table so Shelby started out the conversation.

"I have a question for you. Have you seen Cole in the last few days?"

He turned to look at her. "No I haven't, have you? I've been trying to get a hold of him to iron out the rest of the details before we leave for school but he's never home. I don't know where he disappeared to."

"I know. I saw him a few days ago and we got into a huge argument and I haven't seen him since. He won't take any of my calls either. I really need to talk……" was all she got out when Dallas cut her off.

"Shelby, I wanted you to meet me here so that I could talk to you about something." He said as he reached over and grabbed her hand.

All of a sudden, Shelby was starting to get the feeling of de javu all over again. After a few minutes, she shrugged the thought away, thinking it couldn't be possible for a second time.

"Ok, what's wrong? You're acting kind of strange. Is there something going on that I don't know about?" She asked in a confused tone.

"Yeah, kind of, but I hope after I get this off my chest you might feel the same way." He said with a devilish grin.

"Well, spill it!" she said thinking he was going to tell her some kind of good news.

"I'm in……" he started to say as he took a deep breath trying to find his words.

"Come on Dallas, spit it out." She replied getting more excited by the minute.

"I'm in love with you!" he blurted out really loud.

Everyone in the diner stopped what they were doing and looked over at the two of them. Shelby's mouth plummeted to the floor. This was not the good news she thought he was going to tell her. She had no clue as to what good news it might have been, but this was definitely not what she was expecting. This was twice in the last few days that two people she cared very much about laid a bomb in her lap and she had no idea how to deal with it. What is wrong with them, she thought to herself.

"Are you going to say anything? You're shocked aren't you?" he asked with a huge smile.

"Yeah…you could say that." She said shaking her head up and down as she took in a deep breath.

"Some things wrong though. I didn't expect to get that kind of reaction." He said. His smile disappeared.

She sat back in the booth and placed both hands over her face. She couldn't believe what was happening. How was she going to tell Dallas that Cole had just revealed the same declaration of love to her just a few days prior? The only way she knew how, just tell him the truth.

"I don't know how to tell you this, but Cole just told me the same thing a few days ago." she said as she pulled her hands off of her eyes to see Dallas's reaction.

"Cole told you two days ago that I was in love with you?" he asked in confusion.

"No, he told me that *he* was in love with me," she answered drawling out the word no.

"No he didn't. He couldn't have. No…he…did…not! You're joking right?" Dallas said as his voice got very angry and the look on his face completely changed.

"I'm not joking, Dallas. He just told me the very same thing the other day." she replied gritting her teeth as she did so.

"That back stabbing……he's supposed to be my best friend and this is what he does! I have to find him; NOW!" Dallas said as he got up from the table and headed for the door.

"Dallas, wait! Come back here so we can talk about this!" she yelled at his back trying to get him to stop.

It didn't make any difference. He flew out the door and she had no idea where he was going. She sat back down trying to figure out what was going on with these two. Why are they acting like this all of a sudden? Why are they telling her that they're in love her for starters? They've all been best friends for as long as she could remember.

The waitress walked up to her table with a grin shaking her head. "Honey, I don't know what you got going on, but I'd like to know your secret."

"What are you talking about?" Shelby asked shaking her head trying to play stupid.

"Oh, come on girl. This is the second guy that I've heard trying to spill his heart out to you in the matter of a few days. Those boys seem to have it bad for you." She replied with a slight laugh.

"Those *boys* have been my best friends since we were old enough to know what friends were. I don't know what's going on with them. I have to go." Shelby said as she stood from the table.

Shelby handed the waitress some money for the drinks and left. She had to see if I could find the two of them and find out what was going on. They all have to leave for school in a few more weeks; they couldn't go fighting like this; especially over something as stupid as her, she thought. They're going to the same college! They have the same dorm room! How is that going to work out?

A week went by and still nothing. Neither one of them would answer her calls. Every time she would go over to their houses, they were never home. This was about to drive her insane! CJ had talked to both of them and he wouldn't tell her a thing. She even threatened to beat the crap out of him and still nothing. This was not working in her favor.

Shelby's only solution came by convincing her parents to let her leave for college two weeks early. She couldn't stay at home and not doing anything, anymore. She thought if she left early then at least she could get settled at school and be ready when everything got started. She'd rather sit *there* doing nothing, then be at home where it was driving her crazy.

About a month after school started, CJ called her and said that everything with Cole and Dallas was fine. He told her that they had a huge fight and then were fine again. That was great for them but where did that leave her? They still wouldn't talk to her! The thing that aggravated her most was she didn't even do anything. CJ said that they made a pact between the two of them that they wouldn't let another girl come between them. Well that's great but she didn't do this to them. She didn't come between them! They came to her, not the other way around. Why was she being punished for their stupidity?

After some hard thinking, Shelby finally told herself that she was not going to let this bother her any more. If they want to act like idiots, that was fine. She was in college now. This was supposed to be one of the greatest experiences of her life, so she was going to make the very best of it all. At least for the most part, she was going to try.

Chapter 2

Two years came and went in no time since Shelby had left for college. She went home for just about every holiday. She was getting ready to go home right now for Christmas and she couldn't wait. The longer you were in college; the classes just seem to get harder and harder. She really needed this break. It'll be so good to be able to sleep in my own bed again, she thought to her self as her smile widened. She really looked forward to it every chance she got.

Shelby had everything packed and was just getting ready to walk out of her room when a friend stopped her. His name was Grant Summers. Grant's family moved to the United States from England when he was younger. She just loved to listen to him talk. His British accent was so cool. It also helped that he was dangerously good looking!

"Hey, Shelby, are you all packed to go?" Grant asked.

"Yep, I think I have everything. Now all I have to do is get it into the car and just drive." She replied with a huge sigh of relief rolling her hand out in front of her like a wave of the ocean.

"Cool, do you need some help?" he asked.

"Yeah, that would be great. Could you grab that bag over there?" She asked pointing to the huge bag that was sitting on her bed.

"No problem." He answered as he walked over to pick it up.

Grant grabbed the bag and Shelby had everything else. They walked out to the car and loaded everything into the trunk. He seemed to be acting kind of strange though. He seemed depressed for some reason. Shelby decided to press the issue and see if she could get some answers as to what was bothering him.

"So, do you have big plans for Christmas?" She asked casually.

"No not actually." He replied with a soft sigh.

"Aren't you going home?" She asked surprised.

"No, there won't be anyone there. My parents waited until the last minute to let me know that they're going to Italy for the holidays. I didn't see any point in going home to be there all by myself. It's just too depressing." He explained.

"I'm so sorry, Grant. That's horrible." She replied reaching her hand to his shoulder.

"Oh, it's alright. I'm used to it. It's not like it's the first time it's happened." He said slumping his shoulders and forcing a smile. "Listen I don't won't to hold you up any longer. You're family is probably waiting on you, so you had better hit the road."

As soon as he made that statement, Shelby's cell phone started ringing.

"You just hit the nail on the head. It's my mom calling. She most likely wants to know where I am." She told him as she let out a laugh.

"Ok then, I'll see you when you get back," he said turning to walk back toward the building.

"Ok, I'll see ya later." She replied.

Shelby climbed into the car and answered her phone. She told her Mom about Grant and his situation and her mother told her that she should bring him home for the holidays. She fought with her mother for a few minutes and finally had to agree with her; no one should be alone for Christmas. Shelby turned the car around and flew back to campus. Grant was just getting ready to walk into the building when she stopped him.

"Hey Grant, I have a question for you!" She shouted across the yard.

"What's that?" he asked curiously.

"How would you like to come home with me for Christmas?" She asked.

"I couldn't do that. I would be imposing on your family." He said.

"No not at all. We have a guest room and my mother said that I had better bring you. Like *she* said no one should be alone for Christmas." she answered shooting him a gleaming smile.

"Are you really sure?" he asked.

"I'm positive. Now stop arguing with me and go pack your stuff." She said pointing toward the stairs.

"I'll be back in ten minutes!" he answered in a panic and was gone.

Grant was back in less than ten minutes! He loaded his bag in the trunk and they were finally on their way. All the way home, he kept thanking Shelby for inviting him to stay with her family for the holidays. He was a really good guy, Shelby had to admit, and he was really cute too, but she liked him more in a friendly way.

When they got to her house, they parked out front and started getting the bags out of the trunk. Shelby's Mom and Dad came running out onto the porch just yelling and hollering like they always did. She could swear that the whole neighborhood had heard them. She sat one of the bags on the sidewalk and looked over at Cole's house. He was standing in the window looking out at them. She gave him a short smile and he walked away.

She reached into the trunk and grabbed another bag and handed it to her Dad. As she did, she could see Dallas's house. She looked and Dallas was standing in *his* window. She gave a slight wave with her pinky finger and he walked away. How long was this going to last? She was so sick of the two of them acting like five year olds!

Her Dad and Grant carried the bags into the house and her Mom caught her just as she was closing the trunk lid. She gave her one of her huge hugs like she always did when she came home for a visit.

"I'm so glad you're home. Did you have any problems on the way?" she asked.

"Nope, smooth sailing all the way here." she answered.

"So, what's with this Grant? He's very handsome. Why haven't I heard about him before?" she asked being very inquisitive.

"Yes, Mom, he *is* very handsome, and no, there's nothing going on. We're just friends. We have a lot of the same classes together, and yes, we hang out from time to time, but that's it; nothing more, nothing less. OK?" she answered with a serious glare.

"If you say so, I'm so glad you're home. I've missed you so much." She said hugging her again.

"Have you heard anything from the two guys next door?" Shelby asked with a fear of what she might hear.

"I talk to their mothers all the time but not anything really to tell you. I guess they're both doing really well with their football though. Your Dad was telling me that *their* Dad's were talking about scouts checking them out for the NFL. That's all I know." She explained.

"Yeah, well, I guess that's about as good as you can get then. Let's go in the house, it's freezing out here." Shelby replied rubbing her hands up and down the sides of her arms.

They walked into the house and her Dad was already grilling Grant about school. He wanted to know if she was doing well and if she was keeping out of trouble. Then he started on Grant and what all he was into. About that time, the front door flew open and someone was shouting. "I think someone had better get in here and give me a hug!"

"CJ's home," Shelby yelled!

She ran into the hall and there he stood. He was covered in snow and she didn't care. She jumped into his arms and wrapped her arms around him as tight as she could.

"I missed you!" she yelled into his ear.

"I missed you too!" he replied with as much enthusiasm.

"Why are you covered in snow?" She asked confused.

"I was over at the high school playing football with some of the guys." He replied.

"That explains it. You play all the time at school; don't you ever get tired of it?" she asked.

"Never! You know me, I can *never* get enough." He said as he began to laugh.

Just then Grant walked into the hall and CJ stood her back on the floor.

"Who's this?" CJ asked in confusion.

"Oh, this is Grant. Grant this is my twin brother, CJ." she said making the introductions.

"It's nice to meet you." Grant said to CJ holding his hand out to him.

"It's nice to meet you too." CJ replied with a confused look on his face. He looked at Shelby and then back to Grant. He reached over and shook Grants hand. Shelby shook her head at him and whispered in his ear that she would explain everything later.

They walked back into the living room and her mother asked if anyone wanted coffee. Of course every one said yes. Shelby told her that she would go get it. She walked into the kitchen and was standing at the sink when CJ came in. He did his usual hop up onto the counter to start grilling her on what was going on.

"So, what's with Grant? What's he doing here?" he asked picking up an apple and proceeding to take a bite out of it.

"He's just a friend from school. His parents decided they wanted to go to Italy for Christmas and left him high and dry. Mom thought it would be a good thing to bring him here." she explained.

"So, he's not a boy friend then?" he asked curiously.

18

"No, he's not a boy friend." she replied shaking her head repeatedly.

"So, that means I can aggravate the crap out of him?" he asked with a sly grin.

"No, leave him alone. Why do you have to be so terrible?" she asked playfully punching him in the arm.

"OW! Why do you have to be so mean?" he asked grabbing his arm.

"Boy, for someone who plays football all the time and can take hit after hit; you can't take a simple punch from your sister? What a wimp!" She said laughing at him.

"You're funny." He replied with a snickering grin wrinkling his nose at her.

"So, how are the other two doing?" She asked being nosy and not looking at CJ.

"You mean the neighbors?" he asked with a grin.

"Yes, the neighbors. Who else would I be asking about?" she said to him.

"They're doing alright. Why are you asking me? Why don't you go ask for yourself?" he replied in a smart way.

"Because even after two years they still won't talk to me. I feel so guilty and I didn't even do anything wrong. That's why." she answered.

"I know. The worst part of it all is that they know it to. Neither one of them can admit it though. They seem to think that if they both just stay away from you that they won't have anything to fight over. Stupid ain't it?" he replied still chomping on his apple.

"Yes it is. I don't understand you men. Why do you guys have to act that way?" She asked him.

"Hey, don't blame me! Not all men are the same. I'm still trying to figure out why they were fighting over you to begin with. That's just.........sick." He said as he made a squeamish movement and laughed.

"Just for that you deserve this!" She said punching him in the very same spot that she had hit him a few minutes before.

"Quit! Man that hurts!" he yelped.

Shelby stood back against the kitchen counter and laughed at him. Her brother might be a huge pain in her side, but she loved him more than anything. She didn't know what she would do if she didn't have him.

Just then, their mother came into the kitchen to see what all of the fuss was about. She could hear them all the way into the living room. They both told her that they were just trying to show their love and affection toward one another as usual. She burst out laughing and looked at CJ with sympathy. She said Shelby must have been beating on him again.

Once they had calmed down a bit; CJ carried the tray of coffee out to the living room with Shelby in tow with cups and condiments. As they drank their coffee, they answered questions Grant had about the family. Grant seemed to be amazed over the way they had grown up.

After supper that night, Shelby walked out onto the front porch. The snow was coming down again. She loved to watch the snow fall. The air was so still and there wasn't a noise around. She sat watching the snow until she heard a door shut. She looked to where the noise had come from and found Dallas standing on his porch. She wanted to walk over and talk to him but she just couldn't. Both of them stood still for a few seconds with their eyes locked on one another. Shelby was the first to turn her head away; she looked down at the ground. Dallas walked down the steps toward his car. She heard the door open and he stopped. He looked up at her again and she could hear him say under his breath "I'm so sorry, Shelby." Then he climbed into his car and left.

Shelby watched him drive away and her heart wrenched in pain. She wanted to break down and cry. Why did this bother her so much? Did it bother her because maybe deep down she did have feelings for these two guys? Could there be something there that she just hadn't seen or felt before? Had she been ignoring it all of this time? She didn't know and she definitely didn't have any answers. She didn't know what to think and she felt so confused and lost. She just didn't know what to do.

As she sat there thinking to herself for awhile, Grant walked out onto the porch. He asked if she was alright. She told him for the most part she was. He could see that something was really bothering her and she really, really didn't want to go into the details with him, but after a few more questions, she finally broke down and gave him the short story. He seemed to be shocked that her life was so interesting. That made her feel so much better, and by that, she was being completely sarcastic of course.

Their Christmas vacation went on and time seemed to shorten. Before they knew it, Christmas then New Years was over. Her parents really liked meeting Grant. They all got along exceptionally well. Shockingly enough, even CJ seemed to warm up to him. You would have thought they had been best friends forever. Then the day Shelby hated to see had come; it was time to go back to school. To a point, she was looking forward to it, but at the same time, she wasn't. With every visit she made home, she longed to be back permanently.

She and Grant loaded up the car once again and said their good byes to everyone. Grant hugged both of her parents and shook CJ's hand. They all told him that it was great to meet him and that they hoped to see him again. She gave them all big hugs and kisses and told them that she would see them again soon and after all was said and done, they were on the road once again.

Grant told her on the way back how much he loved hanging out with her family. He said that he wished his own family was like hers. He kept thanking her over and over for bringing him to her house for the holidays.

After thinking about it for awhile; she was glad that her mother had talked her into bringing him. Things worked out for the best and Grant didn't have to spend the holidays alone.

Chapter 3

It seemed after that holiday vacation, school went by really fast. Before Shelby knew it, the last two years had flown by. It was graduation time! Shelby could hardly wait to get her diploma. She finally had her degree and was already taking the first steps to getting her vets license. She was going to take a week or so when she got home to get things put together to start her own office.

Her parents and CJ made it for the graduation ceremony and it felt so good to know that when they went home, she was going right along with them; a college graduate none the less.

CJ was also in for some major changes. He had been drafted by an NFL team, right out of college. He wouldn't even be home for very long, they wanted him now! Shelby had made it to his graduation last week. Cole and Dallas have also been drafted. CJ is going all the way to San Francisco and Cole and Dallas were going to be close to home. There was a brand new expansion team in Ft. Wayne called the Wolves, that's where they were headed. The team had only been around for the last three years, but from what the media had said, they were moving up the ranks pretty quickly. Shelby was truly happy for them all.

After the graduation ceremony had finished and all of the pictures had been taken, Shelby and her mother went back to her dorm room to pack the rest of her belongings and ran into Grant in the hallway. They had a long chat and Shelby told him that just because college was over; he didn't have to be a stranger. He was welcome to visit any time. Grant was overjoyed at the invitation. He had really turned out to be a great friend after all.

Grant left them to go finish his own packing and Shelby and her mother were packing the last of her things when they heard a knock on the door. Shelby turned, and to her surprise, Cole was standing in the door way! Her mother stood there with a smile on her face, looking at him. She picked up one of Shelby's bags and said that she was going to take it to the car and give them some time to talk. She must have known he was there because as she walked past him in the door way; she placed her hand on his shoulder and just smiled.

"Can I come in?" Cole asked.

"Yeah, come in." Shelby replied as she watched him walk through the door way.

"How are you?" he asked.

"I'm not too bad, and you?" she answered in a stiff tone.

"I'm good." He said.

"What are you doing here?" she asked as she shook her head in disbelief.

"I had to come to your graduation. Was that Ok?" he asked.

"Yes, but I don't understand why. We haven't spoken to each other in four years. Why now?" She asked coldly.

"I know trust me, I'm really sorry about that." He replied looking down to the floor.

"You're sorry…you're sorry? I have been carrying this huge guilt trip for the last four years and all you can say is that you're sorry?" She replied as every word made her madder and madder and her voice went louder and louder.

"I know I can't say anything to change that. Can you please forgive me for acting the way I did? I've been a real jerk." he asked with a puppy dog pout on his face.

"You and Dallas are supposed to be my best friends and look what happened. I tried so hard to talk to the both of you and you just ignored me. I wouldn't even know where to start on forgiveness. You both have………"

Before Shelby could get out the rest of her sentence, Cole walked up to her, cradled her face in his hands and locked his lips with hers. Shelby's legs instantly felt like they were going to melt like hot butter. She fought against him to push him away and the harder she fought, the tighter Cole's grip held her. Shelby realized that he was not about to let go and finally gave in to his probing mouth. Relaxing her body against his, Shelby parted her mouth and let Cole and his wondrous tongue explore her mouth further while her tongue met his every move, his every thrust, his everything. He tasted like the peppermint gum he had been chewing when he walked into her dorm room. It was the sweetest peppermint she had ever tasted.

Shelby's head was in a whirlwind. She knew that this was so wrong, but at the same time, she couldn't stop herself. She didn't want to stop. Cole's body felt *so* good against her and her mind had lost all reasoning. His tongue fought against hers and as the kiss became more heated; he started to nip at her lip as his hands started to explore her body. They moved softly and smoothly across her back, over her back side, and back up brushing sensuously over her breasts.

Cole knew that if he continued like this, he was going to have Shelby flat on the bed in the next few seconds. She wasn't fighting against him anymore and that made him want her that much more. Once he realized it, for the moment, he had to know if *this* was what she really wanted. He had to know if *he* was what she wanted. After a few seconds that seemed like an eternity, Cole released her and backed away, breathing hard, he waited to see what her reaction was going to be.

Shelby opened her eyes slowly; her breathing was labored as well as she glared at him. Their eyes were locked on one another. She was mad. More than mad, she was ticked. At the same time, she knew that if she tried to take a step toward him, her legs were going to give way. As she glared at him, her eyes moved down to his lips. Those wonderful lips that just seconds ago, felt soft against hers and hot at the same time. Why does he keep doing that! She screamed in her mind to herself.

"This is like deja vu all over again. Can you please say something?" Cole asked with anticipation.

"Why did you do that?" She asked softly as she sat down on the edge of the bed.

"I had to do something to stop you from rambling. It was the first thing that came to mind; plus, the fact that I've wanted to do that again for the last four years." He replied and said the last part under his breath.

She sat still for a few more seconds while her brain caught up with its self considering her next move. That's when she realized that she had Cole's gum in her mouth! How the hell did I end up with his gum? She then realized that was a stupid question to be asking after the kiss they had just shared.

Pulling the gum out of her mouth and holding it on the tip of her finger, she looked at Cole and asked, "Do you want your gum back?"

Cole's face lit up at the realization that Shelby had ended up with *his* gum in *her* mouth. With a devious, crooked grin, he said to her, "Only if you give it back the same way you took it."

Without hesitation, Shelby started to blow up. "Cole, you have to stop throwing things like this at me! You're my best friend. I do love you but not the way you want me to. Will you *ever* realize that? You and Dallas mean the world to me and I *will not* let that be ruined by letting our friendships become a three ring circus. If we let it become more than friends, I'm scared to death that none of us will ever speak to each other again. Four years has been long enough, I don't want that to become forever. Don't you think so? Do you understand any of what I'm saying?" she explained to him as she reached for his hand, letting her temper cool some what.

"You really feel that way?" he asked with a solemn look.

"Yes, I do. I love the both of you too much to lose either one of you." she said smiling at him.

"I guess, I understand. I don't want to, but I will." He said finally, finally smiling back at her. A smile was going to have to be the best he could do for right now because even though he was agreeing with her reasoning, he wasn't about to give up just yet. Cole was bound and determined, more than ever, that he would win Shelby Russell's heart. It might take him awhile, maybe even years, but he was not giving up, and that was the vow he made to himself, right then and there.

"So, do we understand each other now?" she asked.

"Yeah, I think we do. I do have one more question though?" he asked knowing he had to change the subject to something a little more, light hearted.

"What's that?" she asked.

"Do you love Dallas more than me?" he asked with a snickering laugh.

"NO! Just for that......" she said punching him in the arm.

"OW! That hurt!" he yelped grabbing his arm.

"That's what you get for asking something stupid." she said to him. "Now, make your self useful and grab the rest of these bags so that we can go home, because right now, that's the only place I want to be." she said picking up some of the bags and boxes.

"You got it Shelby." Cole said with a chuckle.

She made one last pass through the room to make sure she had everything and closed the door behind her. They made their way down into the main hall and she turned in her dorm keys to the front office. She gave one last glance around and walked toward the car. This had been her home for the last four years and even though she was happy to be leaving it behind, she couldn't help but feel a little sad. She had met a lot of great people in her time here and learned a lot.

As they walked outside and down the walkway, suddenly, she heard someone yelling from behind them. She didn't even get the chance to turn around when he ran up on them. It was the other half of the story. She should have known that Dallas would be here too.

He was bouncing off the walls. She didn't think she had ever seen him so excited. He was carrying on something awful about how he was so glad that the gang was all back together again. He said that there was never going to be anything to get in their way ever again and after they had put all of her things in the trunk of her car, she had to turn and give him a big hug. Dallas was just the type of person you loved to hug on; he felt like an overgrown teddy bear.

Shelby looked around at her family and friends; she knew everything was going to be alright. Right now the only thing on her mind was going home. After four years; that was the only place she wanted to be.

Being home for about a week; Shelby was getting pretty antsy. She needed to get to work. Her and her father made their way around town looking for a building that would make a perfect office. Just by luck, they ran across an old doctor's office just on the edge of town. It was perfect. It had plenty of exam rooms, a nice size office for herself and enough room out behind for kennels, if she needed them. Since there were a lot of farms around the community, she was sure she'd be making a lot of house calls.

Once the location had been picked out; it was time to go talk to the bank. She had to have enough money to buy the building plus be able to buy enough supplies to get started. Her parents had told her that she could live with them for as long as she wanted but her dream was to find a house of her own as soon as possible. She had no problem living with her parents but to be truly on her own, she wanted a home of her own.

CJ left for San Francisco, and Cole and Dallas went to Ft. Wayne. Now she was the only one left so that gave her the opportunity to concentrate on whatever she needed to do.

With her mother and fathers help, she got the loan that was needed for the office. The next step was getting the building upgraded to handle animals instead of people. Some things had to be changed, but for the most part, it was just painting and cleaning.

The inspectors came in and approved everything. Shelby had thought they had done a pretty good job. Within a few days she had contacted a few vet suppliers and they came in with the supplies and medicines that were needed. She convinced her mother to help in the office a few days a week answering phones and helping with paper work.

There was only one thing left she had to do; flip the sign to open and wait for people to come in.

The very first person to come in was an older lady. The problem she had was that she had a splinter in her hand from her rose bushes. Yes, she thought that Shelby was running an actual doctor's office. It took Shelby almost half an hour to convince her that she was only a doctor for animals. The woman didn't believe her but Shelby did manage to get the splinter out of her hand.

"Sweetie, you did such a wonderful job. I'm going to tell the rest of my family and friends to come see you." The older lady said patting Shelby's hands.

"That would be just fine as long as they have animals that need tended to." She replied.

The little old lady looked at Shelby confused, smiled, patted her on the back and left the office.

No one else came in the rest of the day. Shelby knew this was going to be hard but she had at least expected a few more people than this. Then again, it was the first day she had been open, so maybe in a week or two, word would get around.

She prayed that it would.

Her father came in just as she was closing for the night and said that he had a surprise for her. He had a huge banner to hang on the front of the building. It said; Shelby Russell Veterinarian and had pictures of dogs and cats on it. It also had the address and phone number as well. She was still waiting on her business cards to come in and she was having fliers made up to hang around town for more advertising. Hopefully that would help.

Her Dad took his ladder out of the back of his pick up truck and climbed up to hang the banner. After he was finished, they walked out into the middle of the street to get a good look at it. Shelby had to admit; it looked pretty sharp. Her father had done a wonderful job. She gave him a big hug and told him thank you over and over again. She just couldn't believe that this was *her* office. That

Chapter 4

Now as Shelby sat looking through her high school year book, on her front porch swing, she couldn't believe what had happened over the last three years. She had to laugh again when she saw a sheet of crinkled notebook paper folded in half between the pages. There in front of her was the list of dreams she had made for freshman English class. She had written down five dreams; 1. Become a Veterinarian. 2. Own her own practice. 3. White picket fence. 4. Husband. 5. Kids. Grabbing a pen, "I guess I can check off the first three" Shelby said to herself. "Now, what to do about the last two?" she pondered. Shaking her head, she had no idea.

Looking back, Shelby realized destiny has a way of making it all come together. From the first day of her office opening, it had turned out to be a huge success. She had not only made enough money to pay off all of her loans but she also had bought an old farm house in the country and traded her car in for a pick up truck. She wasn't wealthy, but her business was a booming success and she had plenty of money put away in the bank. She was doing very, very well for herself and her name was traveling all over the country as one of the nations leading veterinarian doctors. Life could not get any better.

CJ was having a ball in San Francisco. He called her every time he had a game to see if she was watching. His team hadn't made it to a Super Bowl yet, but if she knew her brother well enough; they would in due time. He was very good at what he does. He's gotten such a good contract with his team that he sends their parents money *all* the time. It just about drives them nuts but they know why he does it. He loves them. Her mother puts the money away for him. She said that maybe one day he might need it and it would be there waiting for him. He sends Shelby things all the time. Shirts, footballs, clothes of all kinds, hats, anything you can think of.

These days she doesn't hear too much from Cole and Dallas. Every now and then she'll get a post card from one of them from another state where they've played. Their both still in Ft. Wayne with the Wolves. From what she had seen on TV, they were doing really well. She was so happy for both of them; they were doing exactly what they've always wanted to do; make it big in the NFL.

As she sat there sipping on her iced tea and thinking about her family, friends, and uncompleted dreams, the phone started to ring.

"Hi Mom." Shelby answered the phone.

"How did you know it was me?" her mother asked.

"How many times do I have to tell you, they have this thing called caller ID now. I usually know everyone that's calling these days." She answered.

"That's right, I forgot all about that. Well, anyhow, I was just calling to remind you about your trip to Ft. Wayne tomorrow. Did you find the list of things I left for you on your desk?" she asked.

"Yes I did and thank you. If you hadn't written that stuff down for me I probably would have only came back with half the stuff we need. See why I like having you working in the office?" Shelby asked with a slight laugh.

"My dear, as busy as you are these days, I'm surprised you can even think straight. It's my pleasure to be able to work with you." She replied with a tone of pride in her voice.

Shelby let out a slight yawn that she tried to stop but her mother heard it.

"It sounds like you need to get some sleep. I had better let you go for now. You be careful tomorrow and call me when you get home. I'll meet you at the office and help you unload the truck." She said.

"Yeah, I guess I should try to get a little sleep. It's been a long week and tomorrows errands won't get done if I'm half dead tired. I'll call you tomorrow night Mom." Shelby said as another yawn escaped her.

"Good night, dear." Her mother replied.

"Good night, Mom." She said and disconnected the call.

Shelby closed down the clinic one Saturday every month to go to Ft. Wayne to pick up supplies. One of her suppliers has a store there and if she gets into a pinch where she needs things quick, all she had to do was place an order and make the trip there to get them. That worked out really well. That was her plan for tomorrow; get up early and take care of that. Of course, while she was at it, it also gave her a chance to take some time for her self. There's a shopping center called Jefferson Point. It was the best place to get lost and spoil your self for a day. She couldn't wait. It was the one day out of the month that she had time for just her.

After she arrived in Ft. Wayne and picked up the supplies; Shelby headed straight for Jefferson Point. The first stop had to be Starbucks. Where she lived, you didn't hear about cappuccinos and lattes too often. She had to have coffee and lots of it. It's what kept her going most of the time.

Shelby sat for awhile drinking her coffee and reading the newspaper. She had to catch up with what was going on out in the world. After that, she thought about running over to the Rave and catching a movie. The only movies she had seen these days were whatever was on late night TV and most of the time she fell asleep within the first fifteen minutes.

Shelby left Starbucks and was walking toward the Rave when she started hearing this sound coming from behind her. She stopped to look but didn't see anything. When she started walking again, there it was. It sounded like it was getting closer and closer. Then she heard it again. It sounded like someone was calling her name. She thought, in a big city like this; I'm sure there are lots of people named Shelby. She just kept hearing Shelby over and over. She turned and looked behind her and off in the distance she could have sworn she saw Dallas. He was jumping up and down waving his hands in the air. She couldn't tell if it was him or not though, but it damn well looked like him.

The longer she watched the closer he got. She couldn't believe her eyes, sure enough, it was Dallas! She just couldn't believe it. What were the odds?

"I've been yelling at you for awhile!" he exclaimed with excitement half out of breath.

"I can't believe we ran into each other!" she replied with just as much excitement.

"What brings you to the big city?" he asked trying to catch his breath.

"I had to pick up some things in town. Forget about all of that, give me a hug!" she said reaching her arms out to him.

"I've missed you so much!" He exclaimed as he hugged her tight.

"Me too; this is so strange. I never expected to see *you* here." she replied.

"No kidding. Wow it's good to see you! You look good. I was just thinking about you the other day." He said.

"Oh no; I hope nothing bad." she said with a laugh.

"No, my Mom was telling me about how well your practice is doing." He replied.

"Yeah, it's doing really well. How about you? I've heard good things about you and Cole lately." she said.

"Yeah, we love it. This has turned out to be more than I ever expected. It's beyond my wildest dreams." He explained as he put his hands on top of his head.

"I'm so happy for you, I really am," she replied.

"So, what else are you doing? Were you getting ready to leave?" he asked.

"Well, I don't know. I was thinking about seeing a movie but since I've run into you; I don't know." she explained shrugging her shoulders.

"How about we go get some lunch and catch up on things? Sound like a plan?" he asked with that goofy look in his eye.

"That sounds awesome. I haven't had time to stop and eat yet." She replied. She was really thinking that she didn't want to eat because she was too excited from running into him.

They walked to a restaurant near by and sat for hours just talking and catching up. Nothing was ever brought up about what happened after high school. Thank God, Shelby thought to her self. She really didn't want to re-hash the past. All she could think about was how good it felt to sit here talking to him. It was like they had never been away from each other. They were just best friends as it was before.

"You know what? We should call Cole and see what he's doing. I bet it would shock him if he knew you were in town." He said.

"Sure, if you want to." She replied.

"Watch this. After I get him on the phone, I'll hand it to you." He said with that dirty grin he gets when he's about to be devious.

"Ok." she said with a grin.

"It's ringing. Hey dude. Where are you?" Dallas asked.

He had his phone on speaker so Shelby could hear what was being said.

"I'm over by the football field, where are you?" Cole asked.

"I'm over at Jefferson Point. Hey, I've got someone who wants to say hi." Dallas said.

"Come on Dallas. It had better not be one of those fans of yours again. Every time you're out in public, you call me with all of these people on the other end." Cole replied in a disappointed tone.

"No not this time." Dallas replied.

He slid the phone over closer to Shelby so that she could talk into it.

"Hi Cole, have any idea who this is?" She asked so softly it sounded sweet.

"No not actually......wait...Shelby is that you?" he asked.

"Boy, that didn't take you very long to figure out." She said with a laugh.

"Well, it's hard to forget a voice like that. Where are you?" he asked.

"I'm here in town having lunch with Dallas." she replied.

"Which restaurant; I'll be right there?" he asked with excitement.

They told him where they were and hung up the phone. It seemed like it didn't take any time at all when he was walking through the door.

For about two seconds, Shelby caught her self thinking things that she shouldn't be. As he walked toward them, she couldn't help but watch him; his black jeans were skin tight, his coal black hair and a smile that would make any woman's heart skip a few beats. She thought back to the two times in her life that he had kissed her; once in the diner after high school and once in her dorm room after she made it out of college. That struck her kind of funny. Both times he had kissed her it was right after they both had graduated from something. She felt a tingling sensation rush through her from her head to her toes.

"So, how did you guys hook up?" Cole asked as he gave her a snickering grin.

Busted! He caught me looking at him! Shelby thought.

"Sorry, what did you say?" she asked shaking the image from her mind.

"How did you two run into each other?" he asked slowly with a devious grin.

"I had just come out of Starbucks and I kept hearing someone calling my name. I turned and looked and there was Dallas jumping around like a chicken with its head cut off. It was pretty funny." she explained laughing and at the same time was trying to hide the flush of color that she knew had come across her cheeks.

"Yeah, when she figured out who it was; she looked like she had just seen a ghost." Dallas said while making goofy faces.

"Are you alright? You look a little......flushed." Cole asked with a devious grin looking straight at Shelby as he said it.

"I'm fine. It's just a little......warm in here, that's all." She said using her napkin like a fan to cool her self off a bit.

"You do look a little peeked. Are you sure you're alright?" Dallas asked as concern spread across his face.

"Dallas, why don't you go over to the bar and get her a cold glass of water. Maybe that will help." Cole said to him.

"Be right back." He answered jumping up from the table.

After Dallas walked away from the table, Cole leaned in closer to Shelby's ear and she turned her head away from him so that she wasn't looking at him.

"Why Shelby, I do believe you're blushing. Did I catch you checking me out when I walked in?" he whispered in her ear.

She spun around to look at him, "NO!" she said in a harsh whisper.

He narrowed his eyes at her and she looked as if she was blushing even more.

"It's that red hair of yours. I always said it was going to get you into trouble one of these days." He said as he winked at her just as Dallas walked back to their table.

Now she was even more embarrassed than she had been to start with. This was not a good thing.

"Here you go Shelby. What were you two talking about?" Dallas asked curiously.

"I was just asking Shelby what you guys were planning on doing after this." Cole said covering his tracks as fast as he could.

"Oh wow, look what time it is. I didn't realize we had been here for so long. I have to head home soon." Shelby said looking at her watch. Really she just wanted to get out of this situation as fast as she could.

"Oh, come on. You have to stay for awhile longer." Dallas begged.

"Really, I can't. I have a bunch of stuff in the back of my truck and I have to get back to the office." She explained hoping that would let her off the hook.

"Tomorrow is Sunday. Are you even open on Sundays?" Cole asked.

"Well no, but I do have things to get done before Monday," She replied.

"Come on, it would be awesome! It would be like old times again. You could stay with us," Dallas said as he was really begging now.

"Hold on a second. I don't know if that would be such a great idea," She said as she choked on her drink almost spitting it all over the table.

"What if you stayed in a hotel for the night?" Cole asked.

"That idea sounds better." She said then looked up at the ceiling shaking her head. She knew this idea was going to be a really stupid one. "Oh what the hell, I can deal with that. It's getting late and I really don't want to drive home in the dark anyhow," she explained.

"That settles it then. Dallas why don't you take her over to the hotel and I'll meet you guys there. I have some other things I have to take care of first." Cole said.

"Sounds good, see you in a bit," Dallas replied.

Cole left and Dallas and Shelby walked out to their cars. All that kept running through her head was; should I really be doing this? This has to be the most insane thing I've ever done. Well, I guess I'll just have to make the most of it now; I've done stuck my foot in it, she thought.

"If it would make you feel better I could get a room next to yours?" Dallas asked in one slick question.

"Dallas, why would you do that? You live right here in town. That makes no sense," She asked with a confused look shaking her head.

"Yeah, you're right; I thought you might feel weird being here by yourself is all." He explained with a look of disappointment.

"Besides that, I did spend four years away at college and I have my own house; I think I've learned to take care of myself by now. Don't ya think?" She asked with a giggle. "Still trying to be my big brother I see?"

"Hey, ya can't blame me for trying." He said with a laugh

When they got to the hotel, Dallas wouldn't let her pay for anything. He could be such a pain, she thought. As soon they had made it into the room he was like a kid in a candy store. He had to play with everything. Open all the cabinets, look in the fridge, and dig through the things in the bathroom. He couldn't leave anything alone. All Shelby could do was laugh at him.

About an hour later, Cole finally showed up. She didn't know where he had to go but he wasn't staring at her like he was at the restaurant. His attitude had changed some what.

They ordered food from room service and sat around talking about old times for hours more. Dallas even went and got a deck of cards. This was great and exactly what Shelby had needed.

Some time around two in the morning; Cole finally said that he had to go home and asked if they wanted to get together for breakfast in the morning. Shelby told him that as long as there was plenty of coffee flowing she was fine with it.

After Cole left, Dallas and Shelby sat around for awhile longer talking about all sorts of things. How life in college was, and how life was now. He told her stories about him and Cole and about different girls they had dated during school. He said life now was a whole lot different. Being in the big leagues, you really had to watch out who you hung out with. Most people only seemed to be around them because of the fame and money; not for who they really were.

Shelby was really proud of him. He loved to be in the spotlight during a football game, but in his personal time, he was no different then the next guy. That's what made him so special to her. He kept his feet on the ground that God gave him and not his head in the clouds. He didn't think he was better than anyone else. He still played the game because he loved it and that's the way she always wanted him to be. It's like he said "The money was good, but if you weren't in it for the love of the game, in the end it wasn't worth it. What was the point? Money didn't buy everything."

The last thing Shelby remembered was looking at the clock and it saying some where around five a.m. Now all she could hear was someone banging on the door. She sat up on the bed to try and get her eyes to focus and there laid Dallas beside her. They must have fallen asleep! She reached over and smacked him on the back and told him to go answer the door. He sat up and wiped his eyes trying to wake up.

"Dallas, go get the door!" She yelled at him.

"I'm going, just hang on." He replied in a groggy voice. If it had been any groggier, she would have thought he had swallowed a frog!

He stumbled over to the door rubbing his eyes as he opened it; there stood Cole.

"What are you still doing here? Did you sleep here last night?" Cole asked him in disbelief.

"Yeah, didn't you?" Dallas asked Cole.

"No, I went home, remember?" Cole asked.

"Didn't I?" Dallas asked in a state of confusion.

He started looking around the room as if he was lost.

"Dude you're still in the hotel with Shelby. Did you get drunk last night or something?" Cole asked with a worried reaction.

"No Cole; no one got drunk. We sat up late talking and must have fallen asleep." Shelby chimed in as she walked into the bathroom. Her hair was a mess and she looked like she hadn't slept in days.

She knew if she hadn't said something, Cole would have taken the situation completely wrong and given them the third degree.

"So you're telling me that he slept here…with you; and nothing happened?" he asked in disbelief shaking his head.

"Yes, that's what I'm saying. Look at Dallas; he's still wearing the same clothes from yesterday and so am I. They have not left my body, I swear," She said holding her hand up as if she was giving him an oath. He was really starting to rub her the wrong way. "What's with you?"

"Nothing; I'm sorry. I don't know what I was thinking." Cole replied hanging his head knowing he was in the wrong.

"Cheer up dude. I'm starved. You guys ready to go get something to eat?" Dallas asked as he grinned and held his stomach.

Dallas could eat like a horse. He had to have a very high metabolism for as much as he ate. Then again, he worked out a lot too.

"I am. I've got to get some coffee in me or I'll be crap for the rest of the day," Shelby stated.

"I'm ready if you two are?" Cole answered.

They left the hotel and headed for a near by restaurant and ate breakfast as if there were never a problem. They joked around and had a good time. As much as Shelby hated to break up the party, she knew she had to finally burst their bubble and told them she really had to get home. They didn't want her to go but she had to. She had things at home to take care of.

They stood out side of the restaurant saying their good byes and trying to figure out schedules to see when they all could hook up again. Shelby's schedule wasn't all that flexible but it was more than what theirs was. With their football season under way, they really didn't have much time for anything else. She told them that if they had any free time just to call her, and they would see what they could do from there. That was just going to have to do for now.

When Shelby finally got home, she was really in for it. She had forgotten to call her mom and tell her where she was last night. She was so mad at her right now. She had about fifty messages on her answering machine. Her mother must have known it was her calling because as soon as she answered the phone she started chewing her out. After about the first ten minutes or so, she finally had to stop for air; then Shelby got the chance to explain where she had been and what she had been doing.

Once her mother had calmed down, she was happy that she had gotten to hang out with the guys but when Shelby explained to her that she had stayed in a hotel room with Dallas, she freaked. Shelby explained over and over again how nothing had happened and that it was completely innocent. It took her about half an hour to get through to her but eventually she understood. At least Shelby thought she did. She really hoped she did anyhow.

Chapter 5

Two months had passed by before Shelby had even noticed. Business was booming and she felt like she hadn't had time to breathe let alone pay attention to how quickly time had passed before her.

CJ had called her last night to make sure she was keeping tabs on him. He was impressed with the way she had spouted off his season stats thus far. She also had to agitate him on how well Cole and Dallas were doing. CJ's team had lost five games and the Wolves had only lost one. What good was it to have a brother if you couldn't rub *some* things in his face from time to time? Shelby thought when she thought back to their conversation from the night before. That definitely brought a smile to her face.

It was Friday afternoon and her office phone had been ringing off the hook. Everyone knew that tomorrow was the Saturday she was taking off; so of course, they wanted to get things taken care of before the weekend hit. She couldn't believe how crazy it was around there.

The phone rang again and her mother yelled at her to pick it up.

"Hello?" she answered.

"Hi Shelby, whatchya doing?" the voice asked.

"Well, right now I'm working. What are you up to?" She asked. It was Cole.

"Nothing at the moment; I wanted to see if you had plans for this weekend?" Cole asked.

"Don't you have a game Sunday?" she asked confused.

"Yeah but it's at home. Coach gave us Saturday off to get some down time. We had practice today instead." He explained.

"Well, from the way things are looking around here, I might have to work this weekend. It seems there has been an outbreak of births this week. I haven't been this busy in awhile." she explained as her assistant placed another pile of folders on her desk. Frustration was starting to set in.

"Ok. Well, I was going to see if you could come up but it doesn't sound like you'll have the time." He said in a disappointed tone.

"Cole, right now it really doesn't look that way. If things keep going like this; I'm going to have to hire more help than I already have. Tomorrow was supposed to be my day off but it's not looking that way any more." She said digging through the stack of papers on her desk.

"Well then, I had probably better get off of here so you can get back to what you were doing. You sound really busy." He said.

"I'm sorry it won't work out this weekend. Try calling me later and I'll see what I can do for next weekend. That's about as much as I can promise you right now." she said trying to sound hopeful.

"No problem, I'll talk to you later." He said.

"Alright; Good luck with your game on Sunday." she said as they hung up.

He sounded kind of strange, she thought. He almost sounded depressed. I don't have time to think about that right now; I've got too much in front of me to deal with.

Later on that evening, Shelby was putting away some of her case files at the office and was getting ready to close up for the night when she heard the bell on the front door ring. She raised her hands to her head and started massaging her temples and shook her head in protest.

"Oh, not another one; I've been at this since five am this morning already. Now it's going on six at night. Well, this is what I wanted. This is what I got my self into. I wanted to be a vet. Heath problems don't go away just because I want to go home." She muttered to her self.

She grabbed a clipboard from her desk and walked out into the waiting room to see what her next case was going to be. To her surprise, Cole was standing in the middle of the room. She just looked at him dumbfounded.

"What are you doing here?" She asked with a smile on her face and a slight laugh.

"Well, hello to you to. Am I interrupting something?" he asked with a devious grin on his face that could make the stars in the heavens melt like a lit candle.

"No, not at all; I was just getting ready to close up for the night actually." She answered trying to keep her gaze away from that wicked smile of his.

"Well, you sounded like you were pretty swamped and needed an extra hand; I thought I would drive down and see if I could help." He explained.

"You actually came all this way to help out?" She asked in disbelief.

"Yep, I sure did. So you're done for the night?" he asked lifting one eyebrow as he looked at her more intensely.

"For now anyhow; unless the phone happens to ring or someone walks in before I can make it out the door. That actually happens quite a bit." She said jokingly.

"Do you have anything planned for the night?" he asked.

"Right now the only thing that comes to mind is a long hot bath and something to eat." She replied with a laugh.

Cole walked closer to her and placed his hands on her shoulders. At his very touch, Shelby's heart beat faster and her breath caught in her throat. Her body had never reacted like this before when she was around him. Why was it doing it now? The thought disappeared when he began to speak again.

"I think that can be arranged. I'll tell you what, how about I meet you at your place? You go on home and take that long hot bath. I'll cook you dinner. Would that be alright with you?" he asked with that wicked smile again.

Oh, heaven help me there's that smile. This can not be a good idea.

"I don't know, Cole. I'm afraid I don't have very much at home to cook; I'm not there long enough, plus I'm exhausted." She explained trying to get the really bad thoughts of what could happen if she were alone with him out of her head.

"Oh, come on. I'll run to the store and pick up some things. It'll give you time to get off your feet for awhile and relax. First you have to tell me where you live though. I have no idea where this big house you bought is." he said convincing her that the idea was more appealing with every word he spoke.

He was right. He hadn't been back to town for quite some time, so he really didn't know where she lived now.

"Do you remember where the old Carter farm is?" She asked him.

"Yeah it's out in the country a few roads out isn't it? Is that the farm you bought?" he asked.

"That's it," she replied.

"Ok, I know where that's at. You head home and I'll meet you there in a little while," he said as he released her and headed for the door.

"Alright; I'll leave the front door unlocked, just come on in when you get there." she explained. She wanted to hit that tub as soon as she got home.

"See you soon!" he said waving a hand in the air as he closed the door behind him.

Shelby grabbed her keys, finished locking up the office and then climbed into her truck. She wanted to get home before Cole had a chance to make it there. She was surprised that she didn't get a speeding ticket on the way; she was flying!

Turning into her drive way, she slid to a stop in front of her house. She jumped out of the truck, ran through the front door and sprinted up the stairs into her bedroom throwing clothes off as she went. As she headed toward the bathroom, she didn't have her jeans completely off her ankles and fell into the doorway. "That was just stupid!" She said out loud to the empty room. Gaining her composure, and pulling her jeans the rest of the way off her feet, she filled the bathtub and climbed in.

Shelby was in heaven! The steaming water was wonderful on her aching body.

After soaking in the tub for twenty minutes, she heard a car pull into the driveway. It was Cole! She heard the car door slam; then heard the front door open and shut. She had an old rickety wooden screen door on the front of the house; every time it opened and closed you definitely heard it. Then she heard Cole announce that it was him.

She sat in the tub for a few more minutes. She was so tired that she almost fell asleep; the only thing that kept her awake was the thought of why Cole was really there. She couldn't help but wonder if there was *more* to his visit than a casual appearance.

Just then, she was startled back to reality when she heard a knock on the bathroom door.

"Shelby, are you alright in there?" Cole asked.

"Yeah I'm fine. I'll be out in a few minutes!" she answered with a crackle to her voice.

"Ok. I was just checking," he answered.

She waited till she heard his foot steps move from the door before she made any movement. After they were a good distance away, she finished up and climbed out to get dried off. She wrapped a towel around her body and one around her hair, and then walked into her bedroom. Now she had to decide on what to wear.

She walked over to her dresser and as she walked by she realized that she had left her bedroom door wide open! Oh, crap! Just as she started to walk to the door and shut it, Cole walked by. He stopped dead in his tracks at the door as if he were about to ask a question and froze. Shelby immediately froze in her foot steps. They both just stared at each other.

How much more embarrassing can this get! She wanted to scream out loud.

"I am *so* sorry!" he exclaimed before he finally walked away from the door.

"No problem. It's my fault I forgot to shut the door!" she exclaimed as she hurried for the door and slammed it shut. She stood with her back against the door breathing like she had just finished a three mile run for her life!

By this point, she was completely horrified. That had to be one of the most embarrassing things that had ever happen to her. How stupid could I have been to leave the door wide open like that? Well, I didn't expect him to be walking around up here. He was supposed to be in the kitchen! Well one thing was for sure; at least I hadn't walked out of the bathroom naked. At least I had sense enough to have a towel on. Who am I kidding; that was just as bad! She argued with her self.

Finally, she heard foot steps going down the stairs. Now she could breathe a little bit better. She had to hurry and get dressed. She grabbed an old pair of faded jeans and a loose fitting t-shirt. She wanted clothes that didn't show more than she had already.

What she really wanted was not to have to go down there and face him but she had no choice.

She felt so humiliated.

After brushing out her hair and making sure she smelled good, she made her way down the stairs and slowly walked into the kitchen. Cole was standing over the stove stirring something in a pot. She could smell the aroma of garlic in the air. What ever he was cooking smelled wonderful.

She was trying to find the courage to say something when she heard him laughing to himself.

"What's so funny?" she asked amused.

When she said that, she must have startled him because he flipped the spoon he was stirring with right onto the floor.

"You scarred the tar out of me! I didn't hear you come down the stairs." He replied as he bent down to pick up the spoon. "What did you say?"

"I was asking what was so funny. You were laughing about something." She said with a slight giggle.

"I was just laughing about you." He said

"And just what is so funny about me?" She asked contemplating what his answer might be.

"The little embarrassing moment we just had a few minutes ago. I really caught you off guard didn't I?" he asked with a huge sneering smile.

"Yeah, you sure did. What were you doing up there? I thought you were down here cooking," She asked with a stern look propping her hands on her hips.

"I was, but I didn't hear any movement coming from upstairs, so I thought I had better check to see if you were still alive." He explained.

"I was doing just fine but even after you had checked on me, what else were you doing? Were you being nosy?" she asked with a devilish grin.

"You caught me! I was snooping around the rest of your house. This place is so big! I thought I'd look around while you were in the tub," He answered.

"Did you find anything interesting? Most of the other rooms don't have anything in them. I didn't have anything to put in there!" She said waiting to hear what he said next.

"You have some pretty big rooms for sure. What are you going to do with a house this big? It's just you living here." He asked knowing there was more in his meaning than just his obvious question.

"I don't know just yet. All I know is that when I saw it; I couldn't let it go. It has so many possibilities. Who knows, maybe if I don't meet the right guy one of these days, I might turn it into a bed and breakfast. So you really like it?" She asked.

"Yeah, I do. It's really a beautiful place. I really liked the master bedroom though. It seemed to have......" he stopped mid sentence and licked his lips, "a lot of possibilities." He finished as he batted his eye brows at her and smiled that wicked smile, again.

He is such a flirt!

"Stop it. I'm embarrassed enough as it is and you're not making it any easier by joking about it." She said jokingly.

His facial expression went flat and he cocked one eye brow looking her straight in the eye, "Who said I was joking?"

Her heart almost leapt out of her chest!

Now, she was really embarrassed! She could feel the heat start to rise in her cheeks. She knew she was blushing. Thank God there was a cool breeze out tonight, she thought. Shelby walked through the house opening some of the windows to let the air in because it was really starting to get hot in there now!

Cole finished cooking while Shelby set the table. He made spaghetti for dinner. She knew she had smelled garlic; it was the bread in the oven. They sat down at the kitchen table to eat and talked for a little while longer while they enjoyed their meal.

Cole jumped up from the table quickly and startled her.

"Do you have a stereo in the living room?" he asked.

"Yeah, why?" she asked confused.

"I thought that maybe some music would go good with dinner." He explained with a wry grin.

"It's over by the TV." She instructed.

Cole rushed out of the kitchen into the living room and found the stereo. He looked through her collection of CD's and found one of Stevie Ray Vaughan. He didn't know she was into blues? He popped the CD into the player and waited for the music to flow out of the floor model speakers that sat on opposite sides of the TV cabinet. The slow melody of a guitar in its bluesy strum filtered through the room.

Cole rejoined Shelby at the kitchen table.

"I didn't know you were into the blues." Cole said as he sat down.

"I love the blues. Stevie Ray has such a way with his guitar that makes you feel so calm and collected. I've feel asleep to his music more than once after a long day at the office." She explained.

"I know what you mean." He said not giving any explanation to his comment.

After they had finished eating, Shelby got up from the table to clean up and was surprised that Cole had jumped right in to help. For some reason, she just couldn't picture him as the domestic type. His life was about football and beautiful women, not cooking dinner and doing dishes.

She made a pot of coffee and asked him if he would like to sit on the front porch for awhile. They sat on the porch talking, enjoying their coffee, and listening to the soft music that filtered out through the windows. Even after all of the flirting and the intensity of how the evening had gone thus far, Shelby was glad that they could sit and talk just as they had done when we were younger.

By the time their conversation had dwindled, Shelby looked at her watch; it was after three o'clock in the morning.

Shelby let out a long drawn out yawn, "Oh, wow! I can't believe what time it is. I hadn't realized how fast time had flown by. I've to get some kind of sleep.

I've got rounds to make to a few farms in the morning. New babies need their check ups," she said to Cole while another yawn escaped her.

"No, I had no idea what time it was. I was going to stay at my parents' house tonight but as late as it is, I don't want to wake them." He said shrugging his shoulders.

Shelby thought long and hard about the aspect of him spending the night in her home. After some of the insinuations he had made earlier, the concept of Cole Parker spending the night was dangerous ground. Even after the friendship they had shared all of these years, she was finally ready to admit to her self that there really was a strong attraction between them and knew that he felt the same way.

Either way, she couldn't turn him out into the night alone. She did have a big house with lots of bedrooms. Just because he would be sleeping in one of them, didn't mean anything would happen, did it? She was trying to convince herself that it would be harmless if he stayed.

Before she could stop herself, she was blurting it out. "Well, in that case you have two options. The first would be to sleep on the couch; the second would be to sleep in one of the spare bedrooms. One of them actually has a bed in it. I'll have to go get some sheets and blankets for it." She silently prayed that he would pick the couch.

The extra bedroom she was referring to was right next to hers. That was stupid! I should have never given him options! She thought gravely to herself.

"The bed sounds a lot more comfortable than the couch, if it would be no trouble for you?" he answered with a grin.

"No, no problem at all." She said hesitantly "Give me a few minutes and I'll get you settled in."

She picked up their coffee mugs and walked into the house. She placed them in the sink and was headed for the stair case when he walked up behind her.

"I'll help." He said following her up the stairs.

Shelby was so nervous she could hardly breathe. This was a mistake; this is a huge mistake, her mind pleaded with her.

In the hallway between her bedroom and the bedroom Cole would be staying in, was a huge linen closet built into the wall. Shelby grabbed sheets, pillow cases and pillows and walked into the spare room. She handed Cole the pillows and cases while she put the sheets on the bed. They had it all put together when she realized that she had forgotten blankets.

45

"I have to go grab you a blanket and I'll be right back." She said walking toward the door.

"Ok." He replied.

Once out in the hallway, and out of his sight, she ran into her bedroom and grabbed a blanket off the rocking chair sitting in the corner. When she walked back into the spare room, he was already taking off his clothes. He had kicked off his shoes and was taking off his shirt. Shelby froze. He hadn't seen her walk through the door way. She was watching him undress.

Shelby didn't know what had come over her but she couldn't take her eyes off of him. He was facing away from her and she watched as he slipped his shirt over his head and watched as his coal black hair fluttered back into place.

If anyone had ever mistaken Cole for anything other than an athlete, they would sadly be mistaken, she thought. His lean body from what she could see of his back was chiseled with muscle from his hair line to the waist band of his jeans. He looked like a statue of a god that had been hand crafted out of beautiful marble.

He grabbed the button of his jeans and she could hear him slowly unzipping them. He slid his pants down to his ankles and pulled them across his feet. Just as he was straightening himself back up, he turned and was facing her.

Shelby had to cough the words out of her throat.

"I'm sorry!" she blurted out as she used the blanket to cover the embarrassment that was spreading across her face.

"Oh, I'm sorry. I always sleep in my underwear. Is that alright? If not, I can sleep with my jeans on." He said reaching for the pair of jeans lying on the bed that he had just discarded minutes before.

"No, if that's how you're comfortable sleeping, its fine with me. Here is your blanket. I'll just put it on the bed for you," She answered shaking her head.

Shelby walked over to the bed and laid the blanket out nice and neat. Now the bed was ready for him and she needed to make a quick exit.

As she backed away from the bed, Cole walked up behind her and put his hands on her shoulders.

"Thank you so much for tonight. It feels so good to be here with you." He said turning her to face him.

"You're welcome. I really should........." Shelby started to say when Cole pulled her closer to him and their lips were just inches from touching.

His lips moved softly across hers and before she could finish her sentence, he kissed her. She tried to struggle against him at first, but after a few seconds, she was lost to his touch. The longer he kissed her, he tightened his gripped. He deepened the kiss till she finally gave way and let him have what he so desperately wanted.

After minutes that had felt like hours, Shelby found enough energy to pull away. She took a few steps back and eyed him, catching her breath before she spoke.

"I was trying to say that we really should get to bed." She caught her self and blushed even more at the words that had just slipped out of her mouth. "I mean... *I* really should go to bed." She said looking deep into his beautiful deep blue eyes.

Cole stepped closer to her. His eyes were blazing with desire as he looked at her. Cole Parker had known all his life that he was in love with the woman that stood before him, and no matter what he had to do, he was going to make sure that tonight, she knew it.

He cocked one eye brow and gave her a devilish grin, not saying a word. He would wait till she made the first move. It didn't take long.

"To hell with it!" Shelby blurted out.

In one step, Shelby laced her hands around his neck and kissed him again! What has come over me? She thought as her brain tried to analyze what she was doing. She just couldn't help it. She knew that this was completely wrong, but it felt so right. She couldn't take the way he was looking at her any longer.

Cole wrapped his arms around her tighter and deepened their kiss. They both were thinking the exact same thing at the exact same time. Neither could help thinking how good they felt in each other's arms.

Alarm bells started blaring inside Shelby's head. What am I doing? I can't let this happen! She pushed away from him; again.

He stood completely stunned. This was exactly what he had been waiting for, but he was shocked at the way she had reacted. Then he began to smile. It wasn't a regular smile either. It was one of utter happiness. This is what he had longed for all of his life. *She* was what he wanted more than anything.

"I'm sorry. Oh god, I am so sorry. I shouldn't have done that." She said throwing her hands over her mouth in disbelief. She tried to run for the door.

"Shelby, what are you sorry for? I'm not sorry in the least bit." He said as he grabbed her arm.

He stopped her in the doorway and pulled her back to him. Her hands fell against his chest; his bare chest. She gasped for air just as his lips locked on hers once again.

This time a voice in her head screamed, "Stop this now before it goes too far!" but her body went limp with the very touch of his hands.

Without opening her eyes, she knew he was walking her to the bed. Softly, they both fell to the bed at the same time; still gripped together in each others arms. Never in her life had she thought of Cole the way she did at this very minute.

Shelby ran her fingers through his coal black hair, trembling with every touch and every kiss. His body was built like a brick but he felt like putty in her hands. He started pulling her clothes off when her conscience kicked in once more. Complete and utter fear rushed into her head.

If she let this continue; if she gave into the desire she felt right now; the want for him; his touch……this was truly the point of no return. Was she ready to sacrifice everything else?

"Cole stop, we can't do this." She blurted out with every fiber of her being as she pushed him off and struggled to breathe.

"What's wrong? Did I do something wrong?" he asked out of breath.

"No, but this is wrong." She replied sitting up and scooting over to the edge of the bed.

"Why, is this wrong? Shelby, I'm in love with you. I told you a long time ago how I feel. You didn't ever forget that did you?" he asked waiting for an answer.

"Cole, if we do this, it will change everything…forever. Are you ready to take that risk?" She asked gravely.

"Yeah, it would change for the better." He replied as he kissed her shoulder softly.

"I don't. I don't want something like this to screw up what we have. We have been friends for as long as I can remember. *Best friends*. If we let something like this happen, especially sex, I'm scarred to death that something will go wrong. We might not like each other so much after that. Can you understand what I'm trying to say?" She asked hoping he would understand her reasoning.

"I understand what you're saying but I don't see that happening. You have to know that this has been building for a very long time. I want you more now than I ever have." he replied holding his hands out waiting for her to reply.

"And what if it doesn't work out; what then? Can you honestly tell me that ending our friendship because of a bad break up wouldn't bother you?"

His face went blank. He didn't say anything for a few minutes. He was processing what she had said and it was starting to sink in. He knew that even as badly as he wanted her, he would never do anything again to jeopardize their relationship. It had happened once and if he had to sacrifice his feelings to make sure she was always a big part of his life, he would do it.

"I understand." He said as solemnly.

"Cole, it just can't happen. *Please* let things stay the way they are. I don't want something stupid to ruin this." She was begging for him to let it go.

There was one question he had to ask.

"Is there someone else in your life? Is there some other reason you don't want us to be together?" he asked skeptically.

"No! Who else would there be? I'm here all the time, by my self. I don't have time for anyone. I don't even have a social life!" she replied.

"Maybe Dallas; you guys seemed pretty comfy with each other the night you stayed in Ft. Wayne." he said softly knowing that was going to get her temper riled.

"How can you even ask that? Nothing has ever happened between Dallas and me. He has always been as much of a friend to me as you are. The only difference is that I've never kissed him." She answered. Her voice raised a decibel or two.

Now she was going from shock and confusion to mad and anger for him even suggesting such a thing.

"I seem to remember that before you left for college, I told you that I was in love with you. Do you remember that?" he asked.

"Yes, I remember and I've tried to forget it since." She said harshly.

"Well, didn't a few days later, Dallas tell you the same thing?" he asked pointing an accusing finger at her this time.

"How did you know about that? I never told anyone." she asked shocked by his question.

"No, but your buddy Dallas did. We got in a huge argument one night about you and it all came to a head. We almost got into a knock down drag out too. That's when we made the decision that we would *never* fight over you or any other woman again; *especially* you. You were to be completely off limits from that day on." He explained and his tone intensified.

"If that's the case, then what has changed? Why are you pushing this now? If I'm off limits to *BOTH* of you, why are you doing this? Does Dallas even know that you came here? Does he know you we're coming here? I'm sure he doesn't." She said almost to the point of yelling at him.

"Do you think I'm stupid? Why would I tell him I was coming here?" Cole stopped talking when he made that comment. His statement just smacked him between the eyes full force. "You're right. He doesn't know I'm here. He would be so pissed at me if he knew and what just about happened. Shelby, I am so stupid. I just can't believe how stupid I actually am." He said sitting down on the edge of the bed beside her. He propped his elbows on his knees and held his head in his hands.

"What are you talking about?" Shelby asked shaking her head in confusion and lowering her voice.

"Maybe you're right. We shouldn't do this. I was about to do the one thing that could cost me two of the most important people in my life; my best friend and my best girl. I *don't* want to take that risk. Can you please, please forgive me for being so stupid?" he asked with a calming tone. He could feel the sting of tears in his eyes.

How could I be so blind? He thought to himself.

Sitting next to Cole on the bed, Shelby placed her hand on his.

"Of course I forgive you. How could I not? Now do you understand why I said I don't want this to be complicated? I love you and Dallas way to much to ruin what we have. You guys mean the world to me. What would I do if I lost both of you over something like this?" She explained to him with compassion in her tone.

"I understand where you're coming from, now. I guess I just let my feelings get the better of me," He answered softly.

"Trust me; in the heat of the moment, I almost did the same. Parker you're a hell of a guy to resist and if I hadn't known you all of my life; it just might have happened." She said giving him a big smile and putting her arm around his shoulder.

"You had really better get some sleep. I'm sure the sun will be up soon." He said with half of a grin as he plopped his hand down on her leg. He was trying to reassure her that he understood now.

"Yeah, I better. Maybe I can get at least a couple hours of sleep." She replied. "Are you sure you're alright?"

"I'm fine. Go on and get to bed. I'll see you in the morning." He answered with no emotion.

Shelby put her arms around his shoulders and gave him a hug. She hoped that it would help a little bit.

Shelby left the room and went straight to her bedroom and closed the door. She could see the disappointment in Cole's eyes and knew he was upset. She hoped that they had finally reached an understanding in their relationship.

After she had climbed into bed, she laid staring at the ceiling. After their argument, she was so wired that it took her forever to finally fall asleep. She didn't think that it was the argument that had her tossing and turning but the fact that she almost; *almost* gave into one huge temptation that would have had indefinable consequences.

She had never realized how hot Cole actually was. She had known him her whole life and she had *never, ever* thought of him in that way. Right now, she did. He was gorgeous and any woman would be knocking the crap out of her this very moment for what she had just turned down.

Cole might feel stupid right now for what he could have messed up, but Shelby felt completely irritated for what she just let pass her by. Some women might give anything for a night of passion with the famous quarterback, but for Shelby it was much more. She didn't see a famous quarterback, she saw a man that she had grown up with and was *her* best friend. That was something a night of passion would never compare to.

Chapter 6

A few hours later, Shelby's alarm clock went off. How she hated the sound. She didn't want to hear that thing already. She knew she had to get up, get around and get the day started, as much as she hated to. She went into the bathroom to put her self together. She took a short shower, got dressed, fixed her hair and made sure she smelled nice.

When she was happy with the way she looked, she walked into the hallway and stood outside the bedroom door where Cole was sleeping. She wanted to see if he would like to join her in the kitchen for coffee.

She knocked quietly on the door and waited for an answer. Nothing. She knocked a little harder and the door opened a little. When she walked in, he wasn't there. The bed was made nice and neat and he was gone.

He had left a note on the pillow. He said that he had gotten a call from Dallas and that he had to get back to Ft. Wayne for practice. He said that he was sorry and that he would try to call her sometime this week and that was it; he was gone.

A few weeks had gone by and Shelby still hadn't heard from Cole; not one call. The thought of that night still played through her mind. She couldn't help but wonder how things might have been today if they *had* slept together.

That was another thing that had sent warning bells off in side her head that night. She was not only trying to protect her relationship with Cole but she was also trying to protect her own virtue. She had promised her self a long time ago, when she was a lot younger, that she would wait till she was married before she consummated her love to anyone. That night with Cole, she was a thread away from breaking that promise.

She had had relationships in the past and some started to get serious but she had always tried to keep her secret promise from them. The one time she had told another man what her promise was, he had laughed at her and dumped her on the spot. He told her that he was just looking for some action and that he was in no way interested in a long term commitment just for sex.

Now she couldn't help but think about Cole and why he still hadn't called her. He must have been a little more upset than she had thought. Still, his image and how it felt when he touched her sent shivers down her spine every time she thought about him. She had to stop thinking about him so much!

She really hoped that he would understand what she had tried to explain to him that night. I guess that just wasn't the case, she thought silently. She even tried leaving him voice mails on his cell phone but he never called back. Rubbing the temples on her head, she looked down at her desk, closed her eyes, and couldn't come up with one answer to fix the situation.

Oh, well, life goes on and it has as usual; work, work and more work. That's good though. It kept her mind off of things and it just went to show that her business was doing really well. She had people calling from other states now. Word of mouth can be really good for business, she thought.

Shelby began to think about the good news her mother had given her this morning. CJ has an away game in Ft. Wayne this weekend so they all would get to see him. It had been quite awhile since he had been home or even close to home. Her Mom and Dad were extremely excited. She was too but she didn't want to give him the satisfaction of knowing that.

His plane was coming in on Thursday and even though he would be arriving with the whole team, Shelby, her Mom, and Dad were going to meet him at the airport. She couldn't wait to see him. This should make for a really good football game to, she thought. CJ's team playing against Cole and Dallas; the only question was; who do you route for?

Before she knew it, Thursday was here and they had arrived at the airport a little early so that they could find out exactly where CJ's plane would unload. While they were waiting, Dallas showed up.

How odd was that; a rival coming to meet another rival. Shelby thought it was kind of ironic.

"Hey, Shelby; Hi Mr. and Mrs. Russell," Dallas said giving Shelby a hug and shaking her father's hand.

"What are you doing here?" Shelby asked narrowing her eyes at him in confusion.

"Hey, just because we have to play against each other doesn't mean we still can't be friends. Plus, this way I can rub it into him about how bad we're going to beat them on Sunday." Dallas replied with a laugh rubbing his hands together.

"You're terrible!" She said slapping him on the arm.

"OW! You know, even after all this time, you still hit like a boy." He said grabbing his arm and rubbing the spot where she had hit him.

She really didn't smack him that hard, she thought with a wry grin.

"Maybe if I hadn't grown up around all boys for the better part of my life, I wouldn't have to hit so hard or be so mean!" She said laughing at him.

"How is it you can take getting plowed over by the other guys on the field, but you flinch every time she hits you?" Shelby's Dad asked with a sly smirk on his face as he chuckled.

"Oh, he just got you good!" Shelby said pointing at Dallas.

"Well, I for one am happy to see that even though they have to play against each other, they can all still be friends." Her mother added.

They all laughed this time.

"We're going to walk over and get something to drink. Do you guys want anything?" Shelby asked her parents.

"Could you grab your father and me a cup of coffee?" Her mother asked.

"No problem. We'll be back in a few." Shelby answered pulling on Dallas's jacket signaling him to go with her.

They walked over to the little airport café and sat at the bar. Of course, he started asking her all sorts of questions.

"So, how have you been?" Dallas started the conversation nervously.

"Not too bad; just really busy with work. How about you? Staying out of trouble?" Shelby asked with a half crooked grin.

"Of course; you know I wouldn't be doing anything like that, would I?" he replied with a smirk as he rolled his eyes.

"Oh no, not you, how could I ever think such a thing?" she replied with a laugh.

"Man, I'm sorry I haven't called you in awhile. We have some huge games coming up and I've been focusing every thing on that. I've even been doing extra practices and spending double time in the gym to make sure I stay in shape and loose for these games." He said with a disappointing look.

"Dallas, don't worry about it. I know you're busy. With the play offs coming up soon, you have a lot of other things going on right now. Don't feel bad. I've been so busy lately, that once I get home, I just crash. Some times you just can't help it." she explained to him.

"I know, but it makes me feel like I'm not being too good of a friend these days. Even things with Cole have been really weird lately." He answered.

"What's going on with him?" she asked trying to see if Cole had said anything to Dallas about the night he had stayed at her house.

If he did, there would be a lot of questions to answer.

"I really don't know. He won't tell me any thing. He came home one weekend about six in the morning. I heard him come in but I didn't say any thing till later that day at practice. He just kept saying that he was some where he shouldn't have been. That's all he would tell me. Has he talked to you lately?" Dallas asked trying to see if she knew anything.

Shelby could see the worry in his eyes.

She did, but Dallas was the last person she wanted to tell what had happened that night. She new exactly where Cole had been.

"No, I haven't heard from him in at least three to four weeks." She replied looking away from him trying not to be too obvious.

She knew her cheeks had flushed at the very thought.

"I'm starting to wonder if he's mixed up in something really bad. He really *is* worrying me. It's not like him to act this way. I just don't know what to say to him anymore. I'm afraid that if I say the wrong thing he might bite my head off." Dallas said.

Shelby could tell by the look on his face that he was really concerned about Cole. More than she had previously thought.

"I honestly don't know what to tell you. I wish there was something that I could say or do. I don't think Cole would be into something that bad. He's smarter than that. Maybe it's just something that he has to work out on his own." she answered in a reassuring tone.

Shelby reached over to Dallas and pulled him to her. She thought if anything, maybe a good old fashioned hug from a friend might help cheer him up.

She held him for a few minutes then slowly started to pull away. Dallas stopped her; they were face to face. She smiled and told him that everything would be alright.

At that second, Dallas couldn't stand looking at Shelby any longer. He leaned forward to kiss her. He *had* to kiss her. He had been waiting for just a chance like this to come along. He had wanted to kiss her and feel her when they had stayed the night in the hotel but he couldn't bring himself to do it then. Shelby Russell had been his dream ever since he was in grade school and found out that girls weren't as gross as all the other kids had made them out to be.

Shelby looked into Dallas's eyes and knew he was about to kiss her. She didn't know what had come over her, but she decided she was going to let him. Why not? She had kissed Cole half a dozen times already. What would it be like to kiss Dallas?

Just before their lips touched, they heard someone talking behind their backs.

"Would someone like to explain to me why my best friend is about to kiss my sister right here in public?" The voice said in a gruesome tone.

Apparently CJ had made it off of his plane. They had gotten so lost in the moment, they both had forgotten all about him.

Shelby jerked away from Dallas, jumped off of the bar stool and ran over to CJ's arms. She gave him a huge hug. She was so excited to see him!

"Thanks Sis, but that still doesn't answer my question." He replied hugging her back. "Something going on with you two that no one has decided to fill me in on?" He whispered in her ear.

"No, there's nothing going on. Just one of those, get lost in the moment things." She whispered back. "Just let it go, ok?" she smiled at him.

"Dallas! Dude; am I glad to see you. How are things in your neck of the woods these days?" CJ asked Dallas letting Shelby go and hugging Dallas as well.

"Same old thing; we've been trying to keep up with you guys." Dallas replied giving CJ a high five.

Of course, now they were going into football mode. They talked about team stats and slammed each others teams. It had to be a jock thing, Shelby thought shaking her head.

"Where's Cole? I thought for sure he'd be here too." CJ asked.

"We're not really for sure where he's at. We don't see him much these days." Shelby answered looking to Dallas. They looked at each other and shrugged their shoulders.

"I guess I'll try to catch up to him at some point then. Let's get out of here. I want to get to the hotel and catch up with everyone before we have to head to practice." CJ replied.

"Do you have to ride to the hotel with the team or can you ride with us?" she asked CJ.

"No, I can ride with you." He answered.

"Well, why don't you ride with Dallas and I'll follow you guys with Mom and Dad. You know how they are about being in the big city. Dad can't stand to drive in the city." she said waiting for confirmation.

"Sounds good to me, how about you guys?" CJ said holding his hands up.

"I'll go get Mom and Dad and meet you guys there. We'll see you in a little bit." Shelby said and walked away.

As she left, she heard CJ talking to Dallas.

"Is she ok?" CJ asked.

"She's a girl, who knows." Dallas answered with a chuckle.

Shelby was tempted to go back and argue with them but she figured that was exactly what they were waiting for.

After she had rounded up her parents, they made their way out of the airport and found where they had parked the car. On the way to the hotel, they had a few questions of their own for Shelby.

"Where did you and Dallas disappear to?" Her mother asked.

"No where. We just went to the café to get coffee." she answered.

"That's funny, I never saw any coffee. Did you see any coffee?" Her Dad replied with a grin looking at her Mom.

"Ok you two; you can drop the dumb act. Before you go any further with this; there is nothing going on with Dallas and me. I know that will be the next question and CJ has already grilled me about it. Is that enough to answer your questions? Why can't everyone just get over it?" she said to the both of them.

"Ok, ok, you made your point. Are we there yet?" her Dad asked as if he were a little kid.

He was funny like that. Even though he was an older man, he still had his moments.

When they had finally made it to the hotel Dallas and CJ were waiting at the front desk for them. CJ had already checked in, so they all headed for the elevator and up to his room. When they walked in, there were foods of all kinds waiting for them.

"I guess we don't have to worry about dinner tonight." Her mother said looking around the room at the food.

CJ put his things in the bedroom and they all sat around for the next few hours talking about old times. Of course, when CJ and Dallas would tell their stories, they would have to get up and re-enact them just as it had happened. It was so funny to watch the two of them.

After more time had passed, and a few more stories; the phone rang. It was CJ's coach. He had to leave soon to go to a team meeting. After he hung up the phone there was a knock on the door.

"I'll get it." Shelby said pointing at CJ to sit back down.

When she opened the door, she found Cole standing on the other side. To a point, she was really hoping that he wouldn't show up.

"Hello Shelby." He said with a solemn tone.

At that moment, the night he had been at her house, flashed before her eyes again. She hadn't thought about it all day! The way he had looked at her, the way he had kissed her; she couldn't breathe.

What do I say to him? How do I act around him? No one has ever made me feel like this before. Could I really feel something for him? I'm still mad that he left without saying as much as good bye, but I can't say anything to him at this moment. What do I do? She contemplated in her mind. Her head felt like a spinning top.

"Hi Cole; are you here to see CJ?" Is all she could muster?

"Yeah, has he made it in?" he asked.

"Yep, come on in." she replied opening the door wider for him to walk in.

"Thanks." He said as he walked by.

His deep blue eyes seemed to peer straight into her soul.

Cole was thinking the same thing. He asked himself over and over why he had come here. He knew that she would be here with the rest of the family. It was killing him to even look at her. She had gotten into the very core of his soul.

Now that all three guys were together, they were carrying on like they hadn't seen each other in forever; everyone else sat back and watched as they told stories and acted them out as they went.

Shelby sat off to the side and watched. She shook her head from time to time or laughed at what ever it was they were talking about. At one point, her father even got in the middle of one of their re-enactments of a football game. Now that was hilarious! Shelby and her mother sat there and laughed so hard that their eyes started to water.

Again, the phone began to ring. CJ answered it and his coach was yelling at him this time. He said that he had better get to the meeting or else. CJ agreed and hung up the phone. He told everyone in the room he had to leave for awhile and that he wanted them all to stay put until he made it back. He said they still had *a lot* of stories to tell.

Cole sat and talked with Shelby's father while her mother cleaned up some of the mess left over from dinner. Dallas and Shelby sat at the table talking. "I'm sorry for that at the airport." He said laying his head on the table.

Shelby ran her fingers through his hair, took her hand and kind of shook his head and laughed.

"Don't worry about it Dally. Nothing happened." she replied with a grin.

"You haven't called me Dally in forever. What's up with that?" he said lifting his head slightly looking at her and grinned.

"I don't know. It's just what came out. I *haven't* called you that for awhile have I? That's funny." She said with a giggle when she realized what she had said.

"I have an idea, want to play pinochle?" he asked with a devious grin.

"Pinochle, where do you come up with these ideas?" she asked in amusement as she shook her head.

"I don't know. We haven't played it in years. Maybe now that I'm a big time football player, I might be able to beat you." He said pulling on his shirt to act as if he were a super star now.

He's so goofy, Shelby thought to her self.

"Alright, but you are forewarned. I haven't lost to you yet." she answered as she locked her fingers together and cracked them backwards.

Shelby lifted up her hands and waited for Dallas to lock his fingers into hers. He said on the count of three and began to count. She waited for him to get to two and flipped her hands down and bent his fingers backwards. He instantly stood from his chair and went down on his knees to the floor.

"Alright, alright, you can let go now!" he wailed waiting for her to release his fingers.

"That's not what you're supposed to say." She drawled waiting for him to say the magic word.

"Ok pinochle! I give up!" he blurted out.

Shelby let go of his hands and he sat flat on the floor moving his fingers back and forth to get the cramps out of them. All Shelby could do was laugh.

Her parents and Cole looked over at them as if they were nuts. Well, Cole had more of a scowl on his face then anything. From his reaction, Shelby could tell that he wasn't all too pleased with the way she and Dallas were acting.

"Are you beating on that boy again?" her mother asked.

"I told him that I could still beat him at pinochle! It's not my fault he didn't listen to me," Shelby said laughing.

"You cheated! I said on the count of three. You went on two. I want a rematch!" Dallas said as he stood from the floor and held out his hands.

"Now, Dally don't get mad; you knew what you were getting yourself into. Should you really be doing this anyhow?" she asked shaking her head.

"Why not, we used to play this all the time." He said with a dumbfounded look.

"Because you have a huge game on Sunday ding-a-ling; do you really want to take a chance on screwing up your hands before then? I'd like to see you try to explain that one to your coach. "Sorry coach but a girl broke my fingers." That would sound really good. Think about it." she explained as she lightly thumped him on the head.

"Yeah, that would be pretty bad. Ok, no more pinochle. One of these days *I will* get even with you," He said pinching her on the arm.

"Ok, we'll see about that," she said with a giggle and pinched him back. Shelby stood from the table and walked over to the door. "I'm gonna' go down stairs and get something to drink; does anyone want anything? She asked waiting for a reply.

No one did. She really didn't want anything her self, she just wanted to go for a walk. She needed to get some air. Cole's scowling eyes were driving her nuts! Well, maybe it was just his eyes that were driving her nuts.

She was actually shocked when no one offered to accompany her down to the lobby. That made her happy.

She took the elevator down to the lobby to where the pop machines were. Shelby stood for a few minutes looking at them trying to figure out what she wanted to drink when she heard a voice from behind her calling her name. It sounded familiar but she just couldn't place it. Who is that?

She turned around, looked, and was surprised to find a face from the past. She just couldn't believe her eyes. It was Grant Summers! He was the friend from college that she had brought home for Christmas one year. She was in complete shock!

"Oh…my…gosh! Grant is that you?" She asked in disbelief.

"In the flesh; I was hoping that you were the one standing here. I thought that if it wasn't, I would look like a complete idiot. How are you, Shelby?" he replied as he reached out his arms.

Shelby loved to listen to him talk. That British accent he has is just mesmerizing. She had actually missed hearing his voice.

Shelby reached out her arms, embraced Grant in a hug and said, "I'm great! I still can't believe it's you. What are you doing in this part of the country?"

"Well, there's a convention going on this weekend so that's why I'm here. How about yourself? What are you doing in a hotel? Don't you live close to here?" he asked with a confused look shaking his head.

"Yeah, I do. My brother is in town this weekend for a football game. He flew in this morning from San Francisco. My parents and I met him at the airport and now we're hanging out up in his room. I still can't get over you standing here in front of me right now." She said giving him another hug.

"I know. I really didn't expect to run into you. I was contemplating the idea of paying you a visit but this is even better." He said with excitement.

"Are you really busy right now?" She asked.

"No, actually I was just on my way back to my room. We finished for the day so I'm off to get some rest and maybe dinner." He explained.

"I'll tell you what; why don't you go put your things in your room and get changed. You can come and hang out with us for awhile." She said hoping he would agree.

"Are you sure? I don't want to impose on you and your family, especially if you haven't seen your brother in awhile." He said as if he might be in the way.

"Not at all, you've been around my family before. Here is the room number. Meet me there as soon as you get changed. Ok?" She said not giving him time to change his mind.

"Alright then, I'll see you in a few." He answered with a huge smile.

Grant walked to the elevator and Shelby finally grabbed a soda from the machine. She hopped on the next elevator and headed back to CJ's room. When she got there, everyone was still telling stories, laughing frantically and carrying on.

"What took you so long? I was beginning to think you got lost." her Dad asked.

"No, I just couldn't figure out what I wanted to drink. Plus, I have a surprise for you in a few minutes." She said as she sat down anticipating a knock on the door.

After about fifteen minutes the knock finally came.

"I'll get it!" She yelped jumping from her seat and running for the door.

"What on earth has her so jumpy?" Her Mother asked.

She flung the door open and sure enough, it was Grant.

"Mom, Dad do you remember when I brought a friend home from school for Christmas that one year?" Shelby asked with excitement.

"Yes, he was such a nice boy. What ever happened to him?" her mother asked.

"Well, it just so happens that I found him down in the lobby. Well, actually he found me. Come in Grant." She said to him softly.

"Oh, my heavens, what a surprise!" her mother said joyfully.

"It is nice to see you all again." Grant said to everyone in that beautiful British accent.

Shelby looked over to Dallas and Cole and they looked as if they had seen a ghost; both of their mouths where gaped open and they both seemed to be in shock.

"How did this happen?" her father asked standing to shake Grant's hand.

"I was down getting a soda from the machine in the lobby and I heard someone calling my name. I turned to look and there he stood. Trust me, I couldn't believe it myself." Shelby explained.

Grant went into the details about why he was in town. Everyone just kind of sat listening to him. Cole and Dallas never said a word the entire time. Then it hit her, she hadn't properly introduced Grant to them. So of course, she had to make the introductions.

Shelby got Grant's attention and told him that she had a couple of friends she wanted him to meet. He was a little leery first but she convinced him. Cole and Dallas were standing in the corner talking amongst them selves. It was more like whispering so that no one else could hear them.

"Guys, I would like for you to meet a friend of mine. We went to college together. This is Grant Summers. Grant this is Cole Parker and Dallas Smith. They are two of the best football players in the league *and* my best friends." She said. Shelby waited to see what they we're going to say.

"Are they the two guys that lived next door to you when you were younger?" Grant asked her in a slight whisper.

"Yes." She whispered back.

Cole and Dallas just looked at each other.

"Well, it is very nice to meet the two of you. Shelby has told me all about you guys." Grant said to them trying to get them to speak to him.

Cole and Dallas, at the same time, turned to look at Grant with devious smiles on their faces. Shelby knew exactly what that meant. They were going to give Grant the riot act.

"It's good to meet you too. So how good of a friend are you to our Shelly girl?" Dallas asked as he reached to shake Grants hand and give her a deathly glare.

Wow! Shelby hadn't expected him to be so direct. She did believe that she detected a bit of jealousy in the air. She had to stop this before they had a chance to pounce on an unaware Grant. Grant winced and she could tell that Dallas was already squeezing the life out of his hand.

"Grant, why don't you go over and talk with my parents, I need to have a quick conversation with these two." Shelby said pulling Grant's hand from Dallas.

"I think I'll do that." Grant said as he walked away gripping his hand with his other.

"Who the hell is that Shelby?" Cole started in.

"He's a friend from school, just a friend, just as the two of you are!" She said to them both in a very stern voice.

"What is he doing here?" Dallas asked.

"I asked him to come up. Now if you would prefer, I can go back to his room or you guys can deal with it and be nice to him *here* in *this* room. Better yet, I think I like the possibilities of going to his room. Then I won't have to get the third degree from you two and no one will know what's going on in there. How would you like that?" She asked with a hint of hostility.

She knew what the answer would be but she had to see what they would say.

"You wouldn't." Cole said. He was pissed.

"Watch me!" she said staring him dead in the eyes.

Both of them at the same time made it clear.

"No, no, no; he can stay here." They replied unison.

"Good, then we understand each other?" Shelby asked with a slight grin.

"Yes." They both replied.

"Now, can we get back to some kind of normalcy and enjoy the rest of the evening? I know I am." She said as she began to walk away.

Shelby heard them muttering something but she couldn't make out exactly what they were saying.

"Dude, I don't know if I can stay here and deal with this. I think it's time to bail." Cole said to Dallas.

"I know but we can't leave and not know what's going on. I think we had better stick around and keep an eye on him." Dallas replied.

"I'll stay for a little bit longer but I don't know how long." Cole answered.

"Do you know anything about this guy?" Dallas asked.

"I haven't got a clue. She said that she just ran into him in the lobby. She can't be serious about the guy, he's British." Cole said with confusion in his voice.

"I don't know dude, she seems pretty chummy with him. It could turn into something more." Dallas replied as he looked over at Shelby and Grant sitting next to each other on the sofa.

"I don't like this." Cole said.

They dropped the subject after that and kept an eagle eye on Grant.

On the inside, Shelby was laughing. Cole and Dallas stayed for a long time after their conversation. You would have thought that they were a couple of hawks stalking their next meal. They drove her insane but she loved them for it. To a point, she knew it wasn't funny, especially now that she knew how Cole felt about her and how strongly she was starting to feel something for him, but at the same time, it was still funny. She felt like she had two body guards.

Not too long after that, CJ came back. Thank god, Shelby thought to her self. The tension in the room was *really* starting to get thick. Of course with CJ there, now things were getting a little easier; except for the grilling she was about to get...again.

CJ pulled her off to the side and asked a million questions. She had to go through the whole story about how she had run into Grant down in the lobby. He wasn't too happy with her for inviting him up to the room but eventually she had gotten him to settle down. He was fine with it then.

After they had all told a few more hundred stories, her parents said that it was time to head back home. It was getting pretty late and they were getting tired. They all said their good byes and gave out hugs and kisses.

Shelby even had the decency to thank Cole and Dallas for behaving themselves and rewarded both of them with a peck on the cheek.

As Shelby and her parents were getting ready to walk out the door, CJ handed her four tickets for the game. He said he threw in the extra one just in case Grant would be around. She told him that he was very sweet to think of him but she wasn't for sure if Grant would be there Sunday.

Grant walked them down to their car while Cole and Dallas stayed behind with CJ. They had a lot of catching up to do.

When they had made it outside, Shelby asked Grant if he had any plans for

Sunday or if he had to get back home. She explained to him that she had an extra ticket to the game if he would like to join them. He said his plane didn't fly out until Monday morning so he would be happy to go to the game with her. She gave him a hug and told him that she would pick him up on Sunday. He told her that he couldn't wait.

On the drive home, Shelby's mother kept going on and on about what a wonderful man Grant was. Shelby couldn't help but think that she liked his accent more than she did. She agreed with her and they talked about how cute he was. Shelby also had to make sure that her mother understood that he was just a friend and no more.

That wasn't enough for her mother. "It could always develop into more than a friendship." She said keeping on the persistent side of things.

After so much, Shelby had to finally just ignore her. Her Dad got tired of listening to them and fell asleep. If she hadn't been driving, she would have done the same thing.

Shelby dropped her parents off at home and drove over to her office to check messages and on a few other things. After that, she went home, took a long hot shower, and crawled into bed. It had been a *very* long day.

Chapter 7

Sunday came and went. The game was awesome! Shelby thought to her self. CJ's team lost by one point; the score ended at 34-35. CJ was disappointed but said that if he had to lose to anyone; he was glad it was Cole and Dallas. Even though his team lost, everyone ended up back at the hotel for a huge party. Grant was there with them and Shelby thought he had had a pretty good time.

After all was said and done, they all had to part ways once again. Shelby gave Grant her phone number and address so that he could get a hold of her at any time. Even her parents told him not to be a stranger. That was nice of them, she thought. CJ had warmed up to Grant so much, that they had acted as if they had known each other all their lives.

Well, I guess it was time to get back to reality, Shelby thought wryly to her self.

Weeks passed and Shelby had been on the phone with Grant practically every day. He called her all the time and if she hadn't heard from him by the end of the day, she was on the phone calling him. Sometimes she really had to wonder; what am I doing? Did she want something to happen between her and Grant?

It was Friday afternoon and the phone in her office was ringing off the hook. Everyone knew that tomorrow was her day off to go to Ft. Wayne for supplies and it seemed that they all had last minute requests. It was like this every month. The phone rang again but her assistant was on the other line with a client, so of course, Shelby had to answer the phone.

To her surprise, it was Cole. She hadn't actually talked to him since the night at the hotel when CJ was in town.

"Shelby, is that you?" he asked in a confused tone.

"Hi Cole, yes it is. What can I do for you?" She asked dryly waiting for his reply.

"Do I have to call for anything in particular? I just thought I'd call and say hi." He replied.

"You usually *don't* call unless there's something else you want; so cut me some slack and just get to the point." She answered sternly.

"I'm sorry I guess I shouldn't have called you. I'll let you go and not bother you anymore." He said with a disappointed tone.

"No, Cole wait; I'm sorry. Things around here are really busy today and I'm trying to get things caught up so I can get out of here at a decent time tonight. I'm closed tomorrow so I can go to town for supplies and everyone *always* seems to hit me at the last minute." She explained to him.

"So, you're going to be in town tomorrow?" he asked. His voice was a happier tone.

"That's the plan, why?" She asked confused.

"Well, I was going to see if you might want to go out tonight." He said.

"You want me, to go out with you, tonight? Like as in a date?" She asked in complete and utter confusion. "Ok Parker, what do you have up your sleeve?" she asked with a wry grin of amusement.

"Here's the deal; I have a date tonight and I was hoping that you might want to come as a double date kind of thing. Would you be interested?" he asked with hesitation as he drew out the last question.

How stupid did he think she was? Why on earth would she want to go on a double date and watch him slobber all over some other girl? She might be crazy, but she was no where close to being that stupid! She thought about it for a few minutes.

"Cole did you just hear what you asked? How can I go on a double date with you when I don't have a date? Does that make any sense? Don't you have to have two couples to have a double date?" She asked.

The wheels in Shelby's head started to turn just then. If Cole wanted her to go with him on a double date, and not as *his* date, maybe he wasn't too serious about her after all. Maybe his confession of undying love from months earlier was wearing off. Shelby didn't know why, but that prospect bothered her. Why should she care if he went out with other women?

"Is Grant around?" Cole asked slowly as if he were fishing for Grant's whereabouts.

Ah, now she understood. He was trying to find out if she and Grant had been seeing each other.

"No, Grant is not around. I haven't seen Grant since the game. I've talked to him a lot on the phone, but I haven't actually *see* him." She answered.

Without skipping a beat, Cole asked, "What about Dallas? He could be your date for the night."

"Yeah, I could go with Dallas but………"

Before Shelby could finish her sentence, Cole went on to say, "Come on Shelby, its perfect! Today is his birthday. It would be like a favor to me and a surprise for him all at the same time. You know what I mean?"

"Oh crap it is! I forgot all about his birthday!" She exclaimed. The phone went deadly quiet as Shelby thought over his proposition.

"Shelby, are you still there?" Cole asked.

"Alright, I'll do it, but you have to let me get the rest of everything here finished, get home and clean up, and I'll head that way, alright? Will that make you happy?" She asked as the more she thought about it, the more aggravated she got.

After what had almost happened between the two of them, she couldn't believe he actually wanted her to go on a double date with him, not as *his* date. Re-thinking her earlier thought, Shelby figured he just wasn't into her as much as he had let on that night. That still kind of aggravated her, but at the same time, she felt like it was a relief; a huge relief as a matter of fact. She was starting to like this idea more and more, the more she thought about it. Maybe this was her chance to face facts and get the whole notion out of her head about her and Cole.

"Perfect! Call me when you get into town and I'll set you up with a hotel room for the night. How's that sound?" he said with excitement.

"That works for me because you owe me for this, Parker. I'll talk to you in a little bit." She replied and hung up the phone.

"Well, I guess I'm going to town a little earlier than expected. Beautiful!" Shelby said out loud as she looked up at the ceiling, closed her eyes and shook her head.

She finished at the office and drove home. The first thing she did was call Mom to let her know what she was doing. After the last time, she wasn't about to leave with out her knowing and for how long. She would kill her!

After she made her phone call, she took a shower, got dressed, packed a bag, and made sure all of the animals were fed, locked the door and jumped into her truck. She was on the road to Ft. Wayne. This should be a very interesting weekend, she thought.

When Shelby got into town, she called Cole on his cell phone. He said that he had already taken care of the hotel room and that she should go straight there, they would be there to pick her up shortly.

After she checked into the hotel, she went straight to her room to put her things away. She wanted to freshen up a bit and make sure she looked decent before Cole arrived.

Shelby's life didn't consist of too many opportunities where she could dress up but on occasion she did like to show off her femininity. Most of the time, her wardrobe consisted of jeans and t-shirts. Being a vet, she didn't think there had been a day that went by when she didn't get dirty. She owned at least two outfits that she considered dressy without revealing to much of her self. She tried on both to see which one would be the better choice. It was hard to decide because she had no idea what Cole had in mind for tonight.

Not seeing it when she had arrived, her question was answered for her. Lying on the bed was a silky black cocktail dress with nylons and shoes to match. She picked up the dress and held it in front of her astonished at how beautiful it was. There was a note lying on the bed next to it that said she was supposed to put the items on. Shelby was so excited; she grabbed everything and ran to the bathroom.

When Shelby walked out of the bathroom and stood in front of the full length mirror hanging on the wall of the bedroom, she couldn't believe what her eyes were seeing! It sure wasn't the woman she was used to seeing in the mirror everyday, which was for sure!

The front of the dress dipped a little lower than she liked and it showed the rounded tops of her breasts, while the back dipped *really* low giving anyone who looked, a clear view of her naked back.

"No wearing a bra with this outfit!" she said out loud to her self and giggled.

While she was in the bathroom finishing up her hair, the phone rang and liked to of scared her to death. Cole was on the phone to let her know they were waiting in front of the hotel in a limo. How cool is that? she thought. He must really be trying to impress his date. What did she care about that; she was getting to ride in style for once!

She took the elevator down to the lobby and found Dallas waiting for her. He was facing the elevator with his head hung down looking at the floor. As soon as she walked out of the elevator and it made a dinging sound, he looked up at her. She did believe he was completely stunned. His mouth dropped open as if it had hit the floor. Shelby was not one to wear dresses and no one else had ever seen her in one either.

She couldn't quite describe it but she felt like she was in the middle of a fairy tale or something truly unbelievable. Even Dallas looked like he was dressed to be prince charming. He had on black boots, snug black jeans, a white long sleeved button up shirt, and a black vest. While Shelby gazed at him, she had to correct herself; he looked like a country prince. Whatever you want to call it; all she knew was that he looked very, very, sexy. She had never seen him in this way before.

The longer she looked at him, the weaker in the knees she was getting. She really thought they were going to fall out from underneath her. She couldn't help her thoughts but…but…he's absolutely gorgeous!

What she didn't know was that he was thinking the exact same thing about *her*. Dallas couldn't take his eyes off of her. He had never before seen her dressed like this and it was taking all of his self control to keep himself from grabbing her up into his arms and marching right up to her room. In that instant, he wanted to kiss her, touch her, and feel her for the rest of his life. He vowed to himself that before the night was over, she would know *exactly* how much he loved her.

They stood in the middle of the lobby staring at each other for a few more minutes with huge smiles on their faces. Shelby blushed furiously when she finally found the strength in her legs again and started walking toward him. Dallas did the whole princely thing too. He put out his hand and she placed hers in his. He bent down and gently kissed it and then put out his arm. She wrapped her arm around his and they walked toward the door. She really had to be dreaming all of this, she thought quietly. There was no way this could be real!

As they walked, Dallas whispered into her ear.

"You look incredibly gorgeous tonight Miss Shelby."

"I have to say Mr. Smith, you look quite handsome yourself; by the way, happy birthday." She replied with a smile and a quick peck on the cheek.

Shelby wanted to tell him a lot more than that but she thought she had better bite her tongue. Oh, the thoughts that were running through her mind!

They walked through the doorway and there sat a long black limo waiting for them. Cole climbed out to hold the door open and Shelby thought she was getting the same reaction from him!

"No Way!" he exclaimed. His mouth dropped open and he didn't say another word.

He held the door open as she and Dallas climbed into the limo. Dallas went in first and she stopped and looked back at Cole.

"What's the matter Mr. Parker; cat got your tongue?" She cocked up one eye brow at him and said with a grin. Oh, this is too good to be true! She thought wildly.

"If I had known you were going to look *that* good in this dress, I would have never bought it for you." He answered still staring at her in disbelief.

"So, you're the one I owe the thanks to for my beautiful dress? Why, Mr. Parker, I do believe you're blushing." Shelby said with a devious grin as she ran one finger tip along his cheek. She could feel the heat radiating from the flush on his face.

As she climbed into the limo, she could hear him muttering under his breath, "Beautiful isn't the word I was even thinking. Sexy is more like it."

Cole climbed into the car and took his seat, still not saying a word. Shelby thought to her self that this was the first time she had ever seen Cole so speechless before. All she really wanted to do was bust out laughing but she knew she had to keep it together. This was *way* too good to be true and she was eating it up.

She sat beside Dallas and Cole was sitting beside another woman; she was assuming that this was his date. She's completely beautiful, Shelby thought. She had to be a supermodel with looks like that.

No one said anything for about twenty minutes. Dallas sat with his arm around Shelby and Cole just glared at them. Finally, Shelby decided that she had had enough and introduced her self to Cole's date.

"Hi, my name is Shelby Russell. It seems that these two want to be rude and not introduce us." She said to the woman.

"I know; I'm Lily Roberts." Lily replied elbowing Cole in the side.

"It's nice to meet you Lily. So do you have any idea of what these two have planned for us tonight?" Shelby asked trying to get some kind of conversation going.

"Not really. I heard them talking earlier about dinner and some club. I'm so sick of the club scene." Lily answered with disappointment while shaking her head.

"Do you go to clubs a lot?" Shelby asked hesitantly.

"Honey, when you're in my line of work; clubs are always the place to be." Lily answered snidely.

"Oh, well, what kind of work are you in?" She asked confused.

"You have no idea who I am? You really don't get out much do you, sweetie? I'm one of the top two supermodels in this country." Lily answered in shock that Shelby hadn't known who she was as she flipped her hair off to one side.

"I see." Shelby replied, dropping the subject quickly.

Shelby didn't think there was much more to say after that. She just sat back in her seat and Dallas put his arm around her again. This time she snuggled up to him as if he was her protector from the evil super model. She thought that if she had asked her anymore questions, Lily might bite her head off! Shelby kept looking over at her hands to see if she had actual nails or if they were claws.

Finally, they had arrived at the restaurant. The air in the limo was getting very thin and Shelby was thankful for the fresh air she would be stepping into. The driver opened the door and slowly they climbed out of the limo one by one. They walked into the restaurant and Cole told the hostess that he had reservations for four. The hostess immediately walked them to a table. Cole must really have the hook up, they didn't waste anytime, Shelby thought amusedly.

Both men pulled the chairs out for the women and waited for them to be seated before they took their own seats.

Shelby just couldn't get over the two of them. They had never behaved in this way. It was like someone hit them with a magic wand. As she sat there looking over the menu; she couldn't help but laugh a bit. She tried to keep it under her breath but everyone else heard her.

"What's so funny?" Cole asked with a grin as he looked from the menu toward her.

"Yeah, Shelby what's funny?" Dallas asked amused.

"Nothing, nothing; it was just a thought I had." she replied.

"Oh come on, you can share with us." Cole said with a slight chuckle.

"I'm sorry but I just can't get over the two of you," she said with a giggle.

"What are you talking about?" Dallas asked confused.

"I have never seen you guys like this before. You seem so grown up. So charming." she replied with a grin from ear to ear.

"What do you mean grown up? What did we seem like before, kids?" Dallas asked narrowing his eyes at her.

"No, but I've grown up with the two of you. I'm used to the rough housing and joking and just guys being guys. This side of you is something that I've never seen before. That's all I was saying. It's nice to see the two of you act like complete gentlemen." She said looking at Dallas and slowly ran her hand across his cheek.

"What about you?" Cole asked.

"What about me?" Shelby asked with a slight giggle.

"You've always been a tom-boy. You're just as rough as we are. Sometimes I think even rougher. Now you're sitting here in an elegant restaurant wearing a dress, no doubt. I've never, ever seen *you* dressed like a lady." He replied with an expression like he couldn't believe she could clean up so well.

Wow! I think I should have kept my mouth shut, Shelby thought ruefully. I should *really* bite my tongue because I've seen him in a lot less.

"I know and I realize that but look how I was raised. I didn't have other girls around. All there were was men. Dallas and his brother, you and your brothers, and of course I had a brother. And to make all that even better; almost all of you were sports junkies. Look at this; you, Dallas, and CJ are all pro football players. With all of our fathers pushing the issue, it's not like I had much of a chance being the only girl besides our moms. Look at what I had to deal with!" She explained to them with as serious of a look as she could.

"You're right; you were screwed from the start." Cole replied as he started to laugh.

"Yeah, so if anyone has a right to complain, it's me." Shelby said.

Dallas just burst out laughing. He thought it was hilarious.

"Now what are you laughing at?" Shelby asked as she looked at Dallas and started to laugh her self.

"She's right. Look at the crap we put her through. Dude, you had better be happy that she still puts up with us, *now*. We both had better be happy that she even talks to us!" he said laughing so hard that he almost fell out of his chair.

Lily looked around the table at the three of them as if she were disgusted. She placed one hand on her chest and the other on Shelby's arm and asked, "Did you really have to grow up with all of those guys?"

"Yep, up until we all left for college. I don't care about what any of us put each other through though; I wouldn't change a thing. I love these guys just the way they are; they're my boys." Shelby replied as she smiled at both of them.

"I just couldn't imagine having to deal with that much testosterone all the time. Did you ever have any problems with boyfriends?" Lily asked in astonishment.

"What boyfriends?" Cole popped off with a chuckle.

"Who needed boyfriends when I had these guys around? Besides that, every time I did start to get close to a guy; these jokers always found a way to screw it up for me." Shelby said with a laugh.

"Hey, we weren't the only ones that had a hand in that! Your brother was always the one that got us involved; well at least most of the time. Do you remember a certain diary or e-mails on your computer?" Cole asked with a devious grin.

"What's that got to do with anything?" She asked.

Like someone switching on a light bulb, his statement hit her full force.

"Maybe you should ask CJ about that?" Dallas chimed in with a sneering grin.

"He was going through my things? Oh that little pain in my......"

"You got it! He would read through your stuff when you weren't around and when he would find things about some boy you were interested in; he'd come to us. Between the three of us, we would make sure that the guy would steer clear of you. We were like the henchmen." Cole explained with in a tone of pure satisfaction.

"That makes so much sense! I can't believe it was you guys doing that!" Shelby was utterly shocked at this revelation.

"What makes sense about that?" Lily asked confused.

"In high school, I had a crush on this guy, and from what I had found out, he liked me too. He even asked me to the homecoming dance like a month ahead of time. As time went on and homecoming got closer, like two days before, he tells me that he can't take me. I tried to get him to tell me why but he just said that my brother's had made him sick. At first he had me confused because I only have one brother, but now, I know why. You guys are terrible!" Shelby said throwing her napkin across the table at Cole and jabbing Dallas in the ribs with her elbow.

"Yep, and that's how we took care of things!" Dallas said as he leaned over and gave Cole a high five holding his side.

"Why would he say that your brother's made him sick? Did he ever explain that to you?" Lily asked her.

Shelby sat back in her chair, crossed her arms over her chest and shook her head no looking to Dallas and Cole for an explanation.

"Well, we kind of told him that if he didn't stay away from Shelby, we would take care of him in gym class and he would never know it." Dallas answered.

"So, did you do anything to him?" Lily asked.

"He didn't listen to us at first; so we put itching powder in his shorts when he wasn't looking. The only problem was; we must have given him *way* too much because he ended up with such a rash that he missed almost two weeks of school." Cole explained laughing.

"You guys are horrible! I can't believe you would do such a thing! Can you imagine what he must have gone through?" Lily said angrily. She was really mad at the both of them.

"Hey, we're jocks not angels and he was messing with our best friend. We had to do *something* to make our point." Cole said still laughing.

"Well, I don't think it's very funny at all! If you will excuse me for a minute, I think I'll take a powder break." Lily said as she stood from the table and threw her napkin down onto her plate.

Cole stood as she did, watching her storm off to the bathroom. Shelby didn't think she liked hearing them tell their stories to well. She couldn't help but wonder which side of the tracks Lily had grown up on.

By the time Lily had made it back to the table, their food had come. She seemed to have settled down and had more of a grip on her composure. They all sat quietly eating while their conversations were a little lighter.

Dallas and Shelby sat picking and teasing each other as if they had been high school sweethearts or something. He would say something to her and she would reach over and tickled him in the rib cage. In the next moment, she would feel him pinching her leg. They were back and forth at each other for the rest of dinner. Dallas went to whisper something in her ear one time and actually licked it! Of course, Shelby had to get even so she pretended to whisper something into his ear and bit it. She thought he was going to jump out of his seat! She was laughing so hard that tears actually started to well in her eyes. Cole and his date just stared at them as if they were crazy.

Neither one of them had a care in the world. They were having too much fun.

Finally, Cole and Lily started talking to each other like they were actually on a date and not just company for one another. It was nice to see him enjoying himself, Shelby thought to herself. She and Dallas settled down a bit but every so often he would have to whisper something stupid to her and she would burst out laughing again. He whispered something to her again and it was so sweet, she had to kiss him on the cheek. He could be so sweet when he wasn't being ornery, she thought.

They finished eating and decided it was time to head to the club. Dallas said that it was time to have some *real* fun now. Cole stood and helped Lily put on her jacket and Dallas did the same for Shelby. As they walked out to the limo, Dallas grabbed Shelby's hand and they walked out side by side together. Cole and Lily were still inside the restaurant taking care of the bill.

As they waited for the limo to pull up; Dallas started whispering in Shelby's ear again. He was whispering all sorts of sweet nothings to her. Shelby froze where she was and felt her whole body tingle from head to foot. She had goose bumps all over. He might be goofy most of the time but boy did he have a way with words, she thought as his sensual words made his breath dance around her ear.

She pulled back from him just enough to be able to look deep into his blue eyes processing the thoughts of what he had just whispered into her ear. He had to be serious because she couldn't see one ounce of humor in his expression.

She had never really given it much thought till tonight, but damn if Dallas wasn't hot! These new feelings that had come over her, not only made her melt all over, but scared the hell out of her at the same time.

Shelby couldn't help but wonder what it would be like to kiss him. How would his lips feel against hers? How would he taste? Who the hell was she kidding? How could she even be thinking about something like this? Hadn't she just been through something so stupid not that long ago with Cole? Was she crazy to think of such a thing? Girl, are you that stupid? She argued with herself.

Then again……one kiss wouldn't hurt anything, would it? What the hell, why not.

After a few seconds of starring at him; Shelby gave him her most devious grin, leaned closer and Dallas gladly placed his lips on hers. For the fist few seconds, Dallas kissed her slowly and softly. Then as she parted her lips, he followed her lead and their kiss became more passionate.

Shelby's mind tried to reason with her insanity. Ok, maybe this was a bad idea after all. I don't know if I can stop myself! Her next thought was "To hell with this, let's just go home!" So, sue her, she couldn't help her self! Maybe, when she thought they had just been teasing each other during dinner, they were actually flirting more than anything. She didn't know what it was, but she was more than attracted to him right now and she could definitely tell that he felt the same way.

What has gotten into her? Could it be because she hadn't been with a man in a long time? It had been college the last time she had been serious about anyone; then there was the night she almost had broken her promise to herself with Cole. Maybe she was just tired of being alone, she thought as she tried to reason with her self.

Shelby didn't know how long they had been standing there kissing, but the next thing they heard was Lily talking. Shelby hadn't really comprehended what she was saying because she was a little preoccupied, but, she did make out part of it.

"I guess *they're* having a really good night." Lily said with disappointment as she folded her arms across her chest and looked at Cole.

"What the hell is going on?" Cole yelled as he threw his arms in the air. He was shocked at what he was witnessing.

Dallas and Shelby finally let go of each other and just stood frozen as if they had been busted by their parents. They both kind of hung their heads and then looked at each other. They both wanted to burst out laughing but they just couldn't take their eyes off of each other.

Shelby licked her lips and Dallas winked at her.

"Did I just see, what I think I saw?" Cole asked Shelby as if he were her father.

"Come on Cole, we just got a little carried away. Calm down; don't get your panties in a bunch." Dallas said as he started to laugh.

"Why are *you* so concerned about what *they're* doing? It's not like it's any of your business." Lily spoke up snidely.

She was right.

"Come on Cole, let's get to the club and have some fun. Don't look at me like that. It was the wine. I had too much wine, that's it." Shelby said walking toward Cole. Of course by the time she had finished her sentence, she was laughing again.

"Get in the car! Let's go!" Cole demanded as he pointed toward the limo. Dallas and Lily climbed in and as Shelby was about to; Cole grabbed her arm and stopped her.

"I want to talk to you later." He demanded.

"Yes Sir!" She replied with a salute. She knew exactly what he wanted to talk about.

She didn't think he thought her reply was too funny; he was glaring at her.

They all sat quietly in the limo, no one speaking a word. Dallas and Shelby sat holding each other. Neither one of them thought it would be a good idea if they started up where they had left off at the restaurant, at least not till they got to the club. Then they wouldn't have to worry about watching over their shoulders. If Cole was doing what he was supposed to be doing, and paying more attention to his own date; they wouldn't have to hide. Listen to me; I can't believe I am actually thinking these things, Shelby thought crazily.

Shelby glanced at Cole. He was still glaring at her. This was not good, she thought.

As soon as they arrived at the club, Dallas and Shelby made a bee line to the door. They didn't even give Cole and Lily a chance to catch up. They were gone! They didn't see hide or hair of them for at least three hours. Dallas and Shelby had a blast! They were all over the club dancing their hearts out. Of course when the music slowed down they were all over each other.

Believe me; this was not the night Shelby had expected. She had never dreamed she would find her self in this situation, let alone with Dallas; especially with Dallas.

Somewhere around four in the morning, they ran into Cole and Lily again. Lily was complaining that she was bored and wanted to go home. Poor, poor girl; I guess she just couldn't keep up, Shelby thought wryly.

After a quick discussion, they decided it was time to pack it in for the night. Cole said that they would drop Shelby off at the hotel first and then he and Dallas would see to it that Lily made it home. Shelby told them that that was fine with her. After all of this; she was completely exhausted and she had had *way* too much to drink.

When they arrived at the hotel, Dallas climbed out of the limo and was a gentleman by taking Shelby's hand and helping her out. He told Cole that he was going to walk her in. Cole told him not to take too long, snidely. They walked to the elevator and Shelby made sure she still had her room key.

"I want you to go straight up to your room, take some aspirin, drink a glass of water and go straight to bed." Dallas said to her with a heart warming smile.

"Yes sir!" Shelby said with a salute. "Do I have to do them in that exact order, Dr. Smith?" She replied with a giggle.

"No, you don't, but just make sure you do it. Or, I can come up with you and we can play doctor." He answered with a devilish grin as he pulled her closer to him.

With a slight slur, shaking her head, Shelby giggled and said, "Happy birthday Dally; I think I've had too much to drink."

"Thanks Shelby. After tonight, this has definitely been the best birthday I've ever had, and it's all thanks to you." He said. He then leaned down and kissed her.

It felt so good, Shelby thought as her head started to turn to mush. She wanted so badly to tell him to just forget about Cole and Lily and just come upstairs with her but she knew she couldn't. She thought they had already pushed the envelope far enough tonight. She just knew that she was going to end up regretting this night. At least, her head would.

"I'll see you tomorrow. How does breakfast sound?" She asked. Just then the elevator opened. She walked in and she heard him yell as it closed.

"Sounds good to me, now get some sleep!"

When Shelby got into her room, she slid out of her clothes and put on a robe. She had way too much to drink tonight. She really needed to get some sleep but she felt like she was floating on cloud nine. She hadn't felt this good in a very long time. She sat down on the couch and no longer than she had propped up her feet on the coffee table; someone was knocking on the door.

"Who in the world could that be?" she said out loud.

She walked over to the door and opened it. It was Dallas!

"What are you doing back here? I thought you left with Cole?" She asked giving him a confused look.

"I did, but I just couldn't stop thinking about you." He replied. "We dropped off his date and were on our way to the house and I told the driver to stop. I jumped out of the limo and ran straight back here."

"Yeah, I can tell, you're out of breath." she said. "Come in and sit down. I'll get you some water, just hang on a second."

Shelby walked over to the small fridge to get him a bottle of water; her head was still spinning from all of the alcohol that she'd consumed. She knew that

Dallas had followed right behind her. She turned to give him the bottle of water but he took it out of her hand and sat it down on the counter. She stared at him curiously, waiting for what his next move was going to be, for she knew he had come back to her room for the same thing that she was fantasizing about.

Dallas slowly slid his hands up the collar of her robe until his hands were touching her neck. Just touching her sent his entire body into a spiral. He looked deeply into her eyes as if he was waiting to see if she was going to tell him to stop. She gave him the same gleaming look and then a half crooked grin. He knew that was his sign giving him the green light. He leaned down and slowly started kissing her neck. Slowly he worked a line up to her cheek and moved to her lips. His lips softly touched hers and he could feel her body tremble all over.

The more time passed the more intense the kiss became. Shelby wanted to rip off his clothes and she wanted him to rip off her robe. She didn't know how much more of this torture she could take! For the first time in her life, she had never wanted anything more than she wanted Dallas right now, even if that meant breaking her promise.

Why is it that I just can't keep my hands off of him? She questioned herself. This is so wrong, I just know it, but I don't have the energy to stop it either! It feels so intense, but at the same time, it's the most intimate feeling. I didn't feel like this that night with Cole. That made me feel…guilty, but Dallas makes me feel so much more!

Dallas wrapped his arms around her and picked her up in one swift move. She wrapped her legs around his waist steadying her self so that she wouldn't slip out of his arms. He walked them into the bed room and laid her softly on the bed. She still had her robe on and she had taken half of his clothes off. All he had left was his jeans. She was in the process of undoing the button and reaching for the zipper when he stopped all of a sudden.

"What's the matter?" She asked breathing deeply.

"I have to go take care of something real quick." He answered with a sly grin.

"What could you possibly have to do?" She asked confused.

He picked up the do not disturb sign off of the night stand and shook it with a huge smile.

Shelby laughed as he walked away………

As she lay in bed; the sun was shining into the bedroom so bright, Shelby could hardly see. She stretched for a few seconds until her eyes adjusted to the light. That's when things started coming back to her; something didn't seem right; something didn't feel right at all. She sat up in bed and looked under the covers. Oh my god, where are my clothes? Oh, I'm really starting to freak out right now. What did I do last night? She was screaming inside her head.

Just then, Dallas walked out of the bathroom wearing only a towel wrapped around his waist and had another towel in his hand drying his hair. Gee, do ya think he just climbed out of the shower? She rationalized in her mind.

No, no, no, no! Oh, what did I do? I really, really, had too much to drink last night! The thoughts pounded through her head.

"What are you doing here?" She asked frantically.

"Are you alright?" he asked confused, narrowing his eyes at her.

"I…I think so. I'm not quite sure right now. What are you doing here?" She asked again.

"Don't you remember last night?" Dallas asked more confused, shaking his head.

"Uh…no…not really; what did I do? Um…Did I? Did we? Oh, this can't be happening." Shelby said as she sat holding her head in her hands, almost to the point of hyperventilating.

"Damn Shelby, it must have been pretty bad if you can't even remember." He answered. He had a very serious look on his face to.

"Oh…my…gosh; I am so sorry Dallas." She said shaking her head in disbelief.

She was so horrified right now. Shelby couldn't believe that she had had sex for the first time last night and couldn't even remember it!

Just then, Dallas burst out laughing. He was laughing so hard that Shelby thought he was going to fall on to the floor.

"What are you laughing at? I don't think this is very funny. I can't believe this. I can't believe your laughing about it!" Shelby yelled at him.

"What are you getting so worked up about?" he asked laughing even more.

"Well, I don't think it's that funny if we slept together last night and I can't even remember it! I don't think that goes to show too much for us! Don't you think?" She shouted. The more he laughed the madder she was getting.

Dallas could see it in her eyes. She had no idea what had happened last night and this was where he was going to use that fact to have some fun with her. She might kill him in the end, but it was going to be well worth it.

"You probably don't remember because you had way too much to drink last night." He said shaking his head up and down. He still had a sly grin on his face.

Something about the expression on his face had her baffled.

"Oh, you think so? I know this is going to sound completely stupid but I have to ask. Please don't get mad at me for asking either." She said pointing at him.

"Go ahead, I promise I won't get mad." He replied placing an X across his heart.

Now he had more of a devilish grin on his face. He must have known what she was about to ask.

"Was it any good?" Shelby asked as she buried her head in the blanket.

She was scared to death of what his answer was going to be.

It took everything in Dallas to keep a straight face. He wanted to laugh so badly but he knew he had to play this out. He walked slowly over to the bed and sat down on the edge. He just sat for a few minutes with this look as if he was trying to figure out what to say or how to explain it. After some deep thought he finally began to speak.

"Well, Shelby, you know, we have been friends for a very long time." He started.

"Oh, come on Dallas, if this is going to be some kind of long speech about your manhood, I don't want to hear it. Just answer my question so that I can sit here in misery and beat myself up some more." She blurted at him.

"Do you want the truth or......"

"Just tell me, damn it!" she lashed at him.

"It was awesome! It had to be; I'm still here ain't I? Girl you did things that I didn't even know existed." He answered rubbing his knuckles across his chest.

"This can not be happening......" Shelby groaned in disbelief. Then part of his statement hit her after she realized what he had said." Wait a minute; so you're telling me that if it had been bad for you, you would have left?"

"Yeah, that's what I do most of the time, so what." He said nonchalantly.

"And just how often does this happen to you?" She asked shaking her head. She was really starting to feel sick to her stomach. "You know what, don't even answer that."

"Just about every weekend, I think." He said with a grin as he shrugged his shoulders.

"You are a jerk!" She yelled.

She was so mad at him at this point that she took her foot and kicked him off the bed. When he hit the floor, with a loud thud, she got up from the bed, wrapped in the sheet and headed for the bathroom. She couldn't find her clothes in the bathroom so she started for the living room.

"Where the hell are my clothes?" She yelled.

Dallas was still lying on the bedroom floor laughing his ass off. This had gone better than he had pictured! Now was going to be the hard part. He had to tell her the truth and keep her from hating him for his little white lie.

"Shelby wait!" he yelled trying to get her to stop as he got to his feet.

"Wait for what; for you to stand there and explain to me about how you're a chauvinistic pig!" She yelled at him.

"Shelby, just stop and let me explain something to you!" he yelled back at her as he grabbed her by the arm.

"What else is there to explain? I thought we had really gotten close last night and now you're making it out to be just one of your weekend flings. A one night stand! I can't believe that *you* of all people would treat *ME* like this." She said as she jerked her arm away from him. By this point, she just wanted to lock herself in the bathroom and cry.

Before she could make it to the doorway, Dallas wrapped his arms around her from behind and told her that he wasn't going to let go until she listened to what he had to say.

"Fine, but I'm telling you right now; I've taken horses down bigger than you." She said through gritted teeth.

He let her go but made her turn to look at him.

"Shelby, nothing happened last night; you passed out before it had a chance to." He started to explain in a soft voice.

"Do you honestly expect me to believe that?" Looking into his eyes, Shelby could tell he was being serious. "So, now you're telling me that we didn't sleep together last night?" She asked as she shook her head no.

"No we didn't. I walked out to hang the do not disturb sign on the door and when I came back, you were passed out." He said.

"So, absolutely *nothing* happened?" She asked for reassurance as she shook her head again.

"Not a thing." He replied again.

"Then how did I end up in bed, with no clothes on?" She asked confused.

"All you had on last night was a robe when I got here. Maybe you took it off while you were sleeping." He answered.

"And the whole time I was asleep, you didn't try, anything? I just don't understand. Actually, I don't remember a damn thing. I do remember you going to the door with the sign but that's it." She replied in a dumbfounded tone.

A huge grin crept across his lips, "Trust me, you have no idea what was going through my head, but after I saw you lying there sleeping so peacefully; I knew that there was no way I was going to disturb you. You had way too much to drink last night and I wasn't about to take advantage of that. If we we're going to be together, in that way, I'd rather we both we're of sound mind and body. You mean too much to me, Shelby. If something like that happens between us, I want us both to enjoy it together and have no regrets. With that said; I pulled the blanket up over you and sat down beside you on the bed. I just sat there for awhile watching you sleep and caressing your hair. Then I got up; kissed you on the forehead and went out to sleep on the couch. That's it." He explained to her holding his hands in the air.

"Then what was all of that other stuff you told me?" She asked.

"When I walked out of the bathroom this morning and seen the reaction on your face; I just couldn't help myself. I knew you were going to freak out so I had to add to the fire a little bit. You know I love it when that red hair of yours flares up." He said with a chuckle.

"I should knock the slop out of you! That was a low down dirty thing to do; especially since you knew I wouldn't remember anything." She said to him punching him in the arm at the same time.

"OW! I know it was wrong but it *was* funny." He said laughing and holding his arm. "Do you forgive me? Please?" he said as he got on his knees and begged.

He looked like a lost little puppy dog and even with him begging, he set Shelby's body on fire; she was sober this time!

"Get up you dip-shit. Yes, I forgive you, now get up!" She said as she grabbed his arms to help him off of the floor.

"So, were ok?" he asked seriously.

"Yes, we're ok and thank you." she said with a sincerely.

"Thank you for what?" he asked.

"For being you; if I had been in this same situation with someone else; god only knows what would have happened. I think that's why I feel so safe and comfortable with you. I know that you would never do anything to hurt me." She answered. As she told him that, she wrapped her arms around him and gave him a big hug.

"You're right, I wouldn't. Shelby, I really have to tell you something" he replied.

"What is it Dally? Is something else wrong?" She asked staring up at his beautiful blue eyes.

"No, nothings wrong but I just need to say something to you, so please, let me get this out before I bust." He said seriously.

"What is it?" Shelby knew exactly what he was going to tell her.

"I'm in love with you! It's just as simple as that. I've been in love with you for as long as I can remember. I love you! There, I finally said it. I know I've said it in the past but I love you more now than ever." he answered.

As soon as Dallas finished talking, he leaned down and began to kiss her. A few minutes passed when he stopped to look at Shelby with a huge grin. She knew he was waiting for her to answer him.

She looked into his eyes. Could she actually tell him she loved him and mean it? This was all happening too quickly and she didn't know her self if she had fallen in love with him. What if she had been in love with him since they were younger and she had never considered it anything more than just having a crush on the boy next door?

"I......I......" was all she got out of her mouth.

Just as they were standing there, the door to the room flew open. Cole came bursting in ranting and raving about all sorts of things. Half of what he was saying Shelby didn't even understand because he was talking so fast. Then, all of a sudden, everything went deafening quite. He was standing in the door way of the bedroom staring at her and Dallas. He was getting a birds eye view too because she still had the sheet wrapped around her and Dallas was still sporting his towel, and they had their arms wrapped around each other.

Oh, I can just see how this must look to him, Shelby thought horrified. I know how it looks to me!

Cole never said a word. He just kept glaring at them. If looks could kill, both of them would be dead. The longer he looked at the sight before him, the redder his face got. He couldn't believe his eyes! Finally, he blew. He bolted straight for Dallas and slugged him square in the nose. Dallas fell back and hit the floor.

Shelby instantly went to Dallas to check on him. After she saw that he was alright, she went after Cole.

"What the hell is your problem?" She yelled at him shoving him in the back.

"You're unbelievable! Is this your way of making sure Dallas had a *very* good birthday?" he asked in a hateful tone. "I knew when he didn't come home last night, he had to of come back here but I kept telling myself; "No Dallas wouldn't do such a thing."

"Nothing happened and even if it did it's none of your business!" She yelled at him. "You had no right to punch him like that! How in the hell did you even get in here?"

"Oh, sure, you want to try and tell me another good story? If this is nothing then why are you both standing there half naked and kissing? Sure looks like a hell of a lot to me!" he yelled back ignoring her last question.

By this time Dallas had walked into the living room, he had his jeans on. He went straight after Cole. As soon as he got close enough Cole ended up with a bloody nose too.

"This is a bunch of bull Cole and you know it! What the hell is wrong with you man?" Dallas said while shaking his hand from hitting Cole. He hit him pretty hard.

Shelby ran into the bedroom and finally found her clothes. She threw them on and ran back to the living room to see if they had killed each other yet. What a mess this had turned out to be.

"You were supposed to be my best friend and this is what you do!" Cole said to Dallas.

"I *am* your best friend but what does that have to do with Shelby?" Dallas asked him.

"I told you years ago that I was in love with her and now here you are sticking your nose into it." He replied.

"Dude, you told me that, years ago, so what. If that was even the case; why haven't you done something about it? Instead here you are throwing a fit like a little kid when all along you've been dating some of the hottest women in the country, ever since you made it to the big time; you had no intentions toward Shelby." Dallas answered as he pointed at Cole.

"Oh really; then why don't you ask little miss innocent here about the night I spent at her house. Did she tell you about that?" Cole said with a snickering grin as he looked over at Shelby.

Cole knew that that little indiscretion that *almost* happened would destroy Dallas.

"Don't even try to play this game on me. You showed up at my office one night and you knew why you were there. It wasn't to help me get caught up on anything like you said either. That's why you didn't show up until I was closing that night." Shelby said to Cole. As she said it, she looked over at Dallas and he looked as if he had just been shot in the heart. His face paled.

"I might have had other intentions but you had no problem inviting me back to your house. We sat up all night talking and carrying on. You knew that I wouldn't be able to go back to my parent's house as late as it was, but yet, you made sure I had a bed to sleep in right next to your bedroom didn't you!. You knew that I wasn't going to sleep on the couch if I didn't have to. Come on Shelby, admit it; you wanted something to happen that night just as much as I did!" He yelled at her.

His words ripped through her like a knife. Shelby was completely mortified. She could see Dallas just start to wilt. She had just given him this big talk about not hurting her and she had just hurt him. She knew she should have said something to him about this. Secrets never help anyone.

"Fine you're right. Happy now! I might have wanted it to but I didn't let it, did I? I stopped it before it could go that far. At least I wasn't the one that snuck out that night and not even have the decency to tell me. You had to leave me a note. What a chicken shit that is!" She yelled at him.

By now, she knew that the last few hours that she'd spent with Dallas had been torn to pieces. She might as well of shoved a knife straight into his heart her self. There was no need to lie about what might have happened with Cole that night so she couldn't help but let those words fly out of her mouth.

"You left her a note? That's sad." Dallas said with a chuckle.

"Well, at least I didn't sleep with her! I bet you guys wouldn't have even told me about this would you?" Cole asked glaring at both of them.

"There's nothing to tell. Yeah we almost, and I said almost, slept together but it didn't happen." Shelby tried to explain to Cole.

"She shot you down too didn't she?" Cole asked snidely.

"No, actually, she passed out." Dallas answered. He looked over at Shelby with a half shot grin.

"And that makes everything so much better!" Cole yelled.

"You know what; it's none of your concern what happens between Dallas and me or any other guy for that matter. At least Dallas had the decency to stay here with me to make sure I was alright in the morning. At least he had the decency to stay here and explain to me what happened last night. He didn't take off in the middle of the night and leave me a note!" She replied strongly as she felt her whole body start to shake.

"Fine, you guys have it your way. I hope you enjoyed the room. I hope you had a wonderful birthday Dallas and I hope you *both* have a nice life because I won't be around to watch." Cole said as he bolted for the door.

"Cole, come on, can we please talk about this? Don't leave like this!" Shelby yelled to his retreating back.

"There's nothing left to say." He said as he slammed the door behind him.

"Oh, this is impossible! This is exactly why I have tried to avoid this for all of these years. I knew this was all going to come to a head one day but I sure the hell didn't expect it like this." Shelby blurted out loud.

Oh god! Stupid me, here I am ranting and raving and Dallas is sitting there like he's completely lost, she thought quietly to her self.

"Dallas, I am so sorry. I should have told you about him coming to see me but I didn't think it really mattered; nothing happened between us." She tried to explain.

"Now that I think about it, I do have to know one thing?" he started to ask.

"What is it?" She asked as she sat down beside him.

"With everything that went on last night; and I mean the dinner, the club everything; was that just a show to make Cole jealous?" he asked.

"No! No way! Dallas everything that happened between us last night was *us*. I had the most fun last night then I can ever remember. Everything I said last night *and* this morning I meant. Every kiss, every hug, everything that happened was from me to you. Nothing had a thing to do with Cole. Please don't think that way." She begged him. She grabbed his hands and held them as tight as she could; waiting for him to say something.

"I think I need to go. It looks like I need to go find another place to live. I can't see any way Cole and I can stay room mates after this." Dallas said pulling his hands away.

"I understand. I am so sorry Dallas. I never wanted any of this to happen." Shelby said looking down to the floor.

"What *do* you want Shelby?" He asked her with a serious stare. Then he went on to say, "Don't answer that; I need some time to think." He said shaking his head.

Dallas walked into the bedroom and put on the rest of his clothes. He couldn't believe that after last night and this morning, everything they had shared, had been for nothing. She had to have some kind of feelings for him but he couldn't help but wonder if there was more between her and Cole than he had ever thought. He walked out of the bedroom and to the front door. He opened the door and turned to look at her, one last time. As much as it hurt for him to walk away, he could feel the stinging of tears in his eyes and he knew Shelby could see it too.

"I'll try to call you in a few days." It was all Dallas had left to say. He hung his head looking to the floor and shut the door quietly behind him.

Shelby sat down on the couch and cried. She didn't think he believed anything she had said. Now, she sat crying her eyes out because she had just lost her two best friends, all over again. She didn't know if there would ever be anything to fix this catastrophe.

The question Dallas had asked her kept running through her head; what did she want? She had no clue.

After she had cried, till she couldn't cry no longer; Shelby finally got herself back together and grabbed her things. The only thing she could think about right now was getting back home and trying to deal with her work. That's all she really had left.

Chapter 8

Later in the day, after Shelby had finished her gruesome list of errands with a heavy heart, she had made her way back to Timberville. She dropped off her supplies at the clinic and drove to her house replaying the morning events over in her head. She was still in shock over the way things had turned out.

Carrying her bags into the house, Shelby let out a deep sigh as she sat the bags down on the living room floor. She looked over to the bar that separated the living room from the kitchen and saw that her answering machine was blinking; the number of messages was flashing twenty three.

"For crying out loud, I've only been gone for a day! Who in the world could have left me all of these massages?" She said out loud to her self.

A few were from her mother, a bunch from clients, and a few were from Grant. She had forgotten all about Grant! If he was going to be close to town this weekend they were going to get together for dinner and a movie. Shelby regretted her mistake of going to Ft. Wayne, but now, now she was starting to regret it even more. Maybe if she had stayed home and went out with Grant instead, maybe things would have turned out differently.

As she sat listening to the rest of her messages, the phone began to ring and made her jump out of her seat. She thought she was going to jump right out of her skin! One look at the caller ID told her who it was.

"Hi Mom, how are you?" She asked as she answered the phone.

"How did you know it was me?" Her mother asked.

"Mom, how many times do I have to tell you, they do have this thing called caller ID now; you just don't have it on your phone." Shelby reminded her jokingly.

"That's right, sorry. So, how was your night out with the boys? Did you have a good time?" She asked.

"Not actually. It was a really good night until this morning." Shelby replied.

"Yeah, I kind of heard a little bit about it." Mom said.

"I just got home; how did you hear anything already?" Shelby asked in shock.

"I guess Dallas came home to his parents' house and said that he and Cole had gotten into a huge fight and that he had to find a new place to live. She said that he was going to stay there for a few days until he could find something else. She also said that it had a lot to do with you and that he wouldn't go into any details about it." She explained.

"Mom, I think I really screwed up this time. Things with the three of us, I'm sure, will never be the same." Shelby said as the tears started to well in her eyes. She couldn't hold back any longer and started to cry and her Mom could hear her through the phone.

"Oh, honey, I'm sure it can't be that bad. Why don't you just go talk to him, he's in town." She said in a concerned tone.

"I can't, it's too soon for that. I'm just going to have to wait this out, you know? I just hope it doesn't take another four years for them to come to their senses." She replied.

"Why don't you come over for coffee or something and we can talk. Talking can always make things better." She said.

Her Mom's calming voice always helped, but this time, Shelby just wasn't up for it. She needed time alone.

"I can't right now. I need to go to the office and get all of my supplies put away. I haven't been home that long. I just stopped to check the machine and grab the mail. Can I have a rain check? I'll try to stop by later." Shelby explained to her.

"Ok, well, you know if you need anything just call; if nothing else just to stop over for a shoulder to cry on." Mom said reassuringly.

"Thank you. I love you and I'll talk to you later." Shelby answered.

"Ok honey; I love you too." Mom said and they hung up.

There was nothing for her at home to do but go stir crazy so Shelby decided to go to the office and straighten up a bit. It was a good thing she didn't live that far from her office; she'd hated to have too much time to think. Thinking was actually over rated; in the end, all you end up with was a head ache, she thought.

When Shelby got to the office, she unlocked the door and propped it open to let some fresh air in. The office had been closed up for two days and it needed aired out. She was standing in the middle of her office when she remembered she had left something in her truck. She walked out of the building and couldn't help but wonder if she would see Dallas anywhere. No such luck.

Shelby walked back into the building and locked the door behind her. She wasn't going to be open till Monday and she wasn't about to take any chances of being spotted until then. Then it dawned on her; she had left her truck parked right in front of the building.

"That was really smart. I'm asking for it now." She muttered.

She stood in the front window looking at her truck when she spotted Dallas walking into the hardware store. *Should I go try to talk to him? What would I say? Would another apology even help the situation?* She argued with herself. After giving the idea some more thought, she thought she had better not push her luck.

She was just getting ready to walk away from the window when he walked back out of the hardware store.

He spotted her truck in front of the building. She knew he did because he just stood there staring at it. He shook his head and flipped a set of keys in his hands. He stared at her truck and the building for a little while longer, then dropped his head and walked away.

It was definitely not the time to try to talk to him. He said he would call in a few days, so Shelby guessed she would just have to wait and see.

After two weeks had passed, Shelby had officially given up on a few days. In those two weeks, the only person she had heard from was Grant. He had passed through a few days ago, so Shelby had him stop to have lunch with her. He knew there was something bothering her from just the way she had acted; then again, she thought he had sensed something by the way she had sounded on the phone too the past few weeks.

Shelby finally had to explain the whole situation to Grant and how the worst weekend of her life had come about. By the time she had relayed the whole story to him, he had a very disappointed look on his face but he was very sweet about giving her advice. He asked her one question that she really couldn't answer. She didn't know how to answer it. She had never given it any thought until he said something.

Grant asked her flat out if there could very well be a chance that she *was* in love with Cole or Dallas. Was she?

Am I in love with one of them? She asked herself.

She knew that both of them had told her in the past that they were in love with *her*, *but*, could it be possible for her to be in love with one of *them*? She almost gave Dallas a reply in the hotel room that morning. Was she going to tell him that she loved him also or was she going to tell him that she loved him but not in that kind of way? Everything had happened so quickly that she had forgotten *what* she was going to say.

After her long conversation with Grant, Shelby *really* began to analyze the situation.

For years she had always thought of them like brothers. They just weren't guys that you fell in love with! There was a boundary there that was like they were off limits and she was more than happy to abide by that boundary. They were the guys next door. They were the best friends of her brother and eventually became *her* best friends. She had a lot of feelings for the both of them but was there really love there?

Was it the kind of love that would last forever, or the kind of love that you would have for your brother or family member? Was it that kind of love that all you had to do was look at this person and your knees wanted to buckle and you just melted to the floor? Was it that kind of love that when you're with this person you can see the two of you fifty or even seventy years down the road helping each other with your walkers and canes?

Shelby guessed she would be lying if she said that she hadn't day dreamed about it once or twice, and yes about both guys! What woman wouldn't? She thought. You know, it's those question that stew in everyone's mind; what if or what would it be like? Then after you have that dream you just kind of shake your head, laugh, and say no way; like that's ever going to happen.

Of course, after pondering all of these questions that were filling her head; Shelby was left with one more; *which one*? If she really could be in love with one of them; how would she know? How could she figure it out? How could she begin to choose between them?

Dallas was the one that she was the most comfortable and closest to, but Cole seemed to have some kind of pull on her that she just couldn't explain. The attraction between them was very strong. Just to hear him say her name at times made her blood boil all over.

Well, she reasoned, let's try a comparison between the two and see if she could find any answers that way. Dallas is fun loving, easy going, and doesn't seem to let anything bother him. He's a goofball and is just fun to be around. Plus add in the fact that he's really tall, built like a brick, and *very* good looking.

Then move over to Cole. He's the more serious one. He *can* be fun to be around when you catch him in the right mood. He's always really focused on his career. He's just a bit shorter than Dallas and he's *very* good looking too. Any girl in her right mind would do anything to have a guy like him.

Who was she kidding? *Any* girl in her right mind would give *anything* to be with either one of them!

What am I doing? She asked her self in disbelief. Sitting here comparing the two of them like this wasn't going to get her any where. This is just stupid; plus the fact that neither one of them want any thing to do with her at this point! What was she thinking?

Her mother called and asked if she wanted come over to the house on Sunday for dinner. She even said that if Grant was going to be close by that she should invite him as well. That was nice of her and as it turns out; he was going to be in town for the weekend. Shelby had even made up one of her spare bedrooms so that he had a place to stay. She took cautionary measures this time; she made sure it was one of the bedrooms down the hall and the furthest one away from her own bedroom. She had turned the room next to hers into an office at home so that she wouldn't have to worry about ever making that huge mistake again.

Grant showed up on Friday night and Shelby got him settled in his room. They had dinner and sat around talking about their jobs and families. They had a really good time. Then on Saturday, Shelby took Grant to work with her and he helped out with some of her cases. With him being a vet too, it was nice to have the extra hands. They had to drive out to some of the farms around the area to do check ups. He said that he really liked what she was doing. There weren't too many vets any more that would make house calls.

One of her clients even tried to give Grant a chicken for payment. He wasn't to sure on how to take that one. He was very gracious about it though. He handed the chicken back to her and thanked her for the thought. Shelby just laughed.

Sunday afternoon they sat watching a football game before they went to her parent's house. CJ's team was playing and she had to see who won. CJ's of course. After that was over they climbed into her truck and headed for her Mom and Dad's.

As soon as they pulled up in front of the house, her Mom came running out like she always did. It was just like when she had come home from college on the holidays. The only difference was that she just lived a few miles away now. It didn't matter to Shelby though. She knew that no matter what happened in her life, this was always home.

Shelby told them both to go on into the house; she had some desserts in the back of the truck she wanted to bring in. They both begged to help but she told them that she was fine and they needed to go in and catch up. Shelby thought Grant was just as excited as her mother was.

Shelby watched as the two of them made their way into the house. She couldn't help but smile at the way they got along. She grabbed what she needed out of the truck bed and was about to walk toward the house when she happened to glance over at Dallas's parent's house. She had to wonder what he had been doing since the last time they had saw each other. Just as she started to walk up the front steps, Dallas walked out onto the front porch.

Shelby froze instantly. He spotted her and their eyes locked on one another. They just stood staring at each other for a few minutes, never to say a word. Shelby heard his dad call for him, Dallas shook his head and looked down to the ground. He walked back into the house and Shelby went into her parents.

As she walked into the kitchen to set down the desserts it hit her. It was Sunday; didn't Dallas have a game today?

"Mom, I just saw Dallas next door; doesn't he have a game today?" She asked her with confusion.

"Oh, was he over there? Did you speak to him?" she asked as if she was trying to avoid the question.

"No," Shelby drawled out. "You know I haven't talked to him. You know something don't you?" She asked narrowing her eyes at her mother. She was acting funny and *really* had her curiosity going now.

"No, I don't know anything. Do you know something?" Mom replied suspiciously.

"Something's going on and you're not telling me. You had better spill it." Shelby said demandingly.

"Keep your voice down!" she said in a whisper. "Grant's right out in the other room. You shouldn't even be asking with your boyfriend in the next room."

"For one, he's just a friend and for two, what is going on?" Shelby asked impatiently waiting for a reply.

"I wasn't supposed to say anything but I'm surprised you haven't heard already." Her mother said still whispering.

"Heard about what?" Now Shelby was starting to get aggravated.

"Dallas won't be playing for the rest of the season. He was injured in a game after you guys had your falling out. The doctors said that he might never play again. His mother and I talk all of the time and she told me that he was very adamant that no one said anything to you unless you had heard it on TV first." Her mother explained.

"Why would he want that kept a secret from me? I don't understand." Shelby asked shaking her head in confusion.

"He was afraid that you would blame yourself for it because of what happened." She replied.

"Why would I blame myself? He knows the risks of playing football. Why would that have anything to do with me?" Shelby asked trying to figure out the reasoning for this.

"After what had happened between the three of you, Cole set Dallas up at the end of one of their games. He made sure that the ball went straight for Dallas and someone from the other team went straight for him and made sure he was knocked completely out. One of his legs was fractured in four places. Was he limping when you saw him?" Mom asked with both eye brows raised.

"Not that I could tell. He had just walked out the door. This doesn't make any sense though; how do they know that Cole set him up? I don't understand." Shelby asked more confused now than earlier.

"The guy from the other team was someone that Cole knew very well from college. I guess Cole and Dallas *both* knew him *and* Cole was seen talking to him right before the game, privately. There's a huge controversy going on about it right now. Cole has been put under suspension until the investigation is done. The guy that Cole had talked to, I guess, has even confessed to it." She explained.

"Oh, I can't believe this! I haven't heard a thing about it! I just watched CJ's game before we came over here and there wasn't a thing said about it. This is my entire fault! If I hadn't went to Ft. Wayne that night none of this would have ever happened. We all would still be friends and none of this would have happened!" Shelby exclaimed. The tears were already starting to well in her eyes.

Shelby tried to hold them back, but she started to cry. She just couldn't believe what she was hearing. This is insane! She screamed in her mind. She wanted to knock to holy living crap out of Cole for being such and jerk right now!

"This is why he didn't want you to know. There've only been a few things said about it on TV because Dallas has been fighting tooth and nail to keep it as quite as possible. He's been trying to protect *you*." Her mother said as she wrapped her arms around her.

"Why is he trying to protect me? He's the one that had the crap knocked out of him because of *my* stupid mistake. He might not have a career as a pro-football player ever again because of me! He must hate my guts after this. That's probably why he never called me. He can't stand the sight of me and I can't blame him for that." Shelby said as she began to cry even harder.

"Oh, honey, I can't believe you can't see what's in front of you. He's trying to protect you from what the media would do to you. If they knew that this whole thing was about two football players fighting over the same girl, well, they would just have a field day with that. I can see it in the papers now; "The love triangle of two of Indiana's pro-football players and their vet, news at eleven." Mom said holding her hand in the air as if she was showing the headlines. She was trying to be humorous.

Shelby laughed a little bit. She had to give her mother credit for trying.

"What am I going to do? I have Grant in the other room and then I find this out. I feel so lost; I'd feel so much better if I could just crawl under a rock and die. There's no way that I'll ever be able to talk to either one of them ever again. It just wouldn't be right." Shelby replied holding both arms up. She felt completely helpless.

"There will come a day when all will be forgiven. For right now, you'll just have to wait it out. Both of those boys love you too much for this feud to last forever. If that wasn't the case, then none of this would have ever happened to begin with. My poor baby is just stuck in the middle of it all." Mom said squeezing Shelby tighter before she let go.

"I just hope your right. I can't stand the thought of them not being in my life. I guess that's the biggest fear I have." Shelby said looking down to the floor.

"I know honey. Now, after all of this, do you think you can help me set the table because I know two other guys who will be very upset if they don't get their dinner pretty soon," Mom said with a laugh.

"No problem. What all needs carried out? Shelby asked as she laughed at her.

Shelby set the table and both women placed food in the middle. After she finished her task, she went to the bathroom to straighten her self up. Her face was a wreck and now she felt like crap. Her Mom always had a way of making her feel better but this time it really didn't work as good as she had hoped it would. It made her so mad that everyone kept this from her. Maybe it was a good thing that they did though. If she had heard about it sooner; she probably would have made an idiot out of her self by running straight to Dallas. She just couldn't believe that this had happened.

During dinner, they sat at the table conversing about anything and everything. In between conversations Shelby would catch her self drifting off though. One minute she would hear what the conversation was about, and the next, she would be thinking about Dallas and Cole. Cole must have been really ticked for him to pull such a dirty thing. What was he thinking? She thought to her self.

Of course, through all of dinner, her mother kept hinting about Christmas. Shelby thought that she wanted to get her bid in for Grant spending Christmas with them. Even her father was pushing for it. Grant told them that he would see where his schedule was at that time and maybe he might be able to fit it in. Shelby knew she would be here but Grant's whereabouts was always in question.

That brought Shelby to a point where she started asking her self another question. Where might Grant and I be by Christmas? We have been seeing a lot of each other lately. Could it grow into something more in a few months? She had no idea. She couldn't believe she was actually letting that concept run through her mind right now. She thought she would just have to wait and see but she was definitely not going to push the issue.

Little did Shelby know, her question was answered. It had been two and a half months since she and Grant had had dinner with her parents and now it was only two weeks from Christmas. She and Grant had seen each other just about every day since. As a matter of fact, he had practically moved in with her.

Mind you, they sleep in separate bedrooms though. His bedroom was filled with his things and even the bath room had his markings. This was the first time in Shelby's life that she had shared a house with a man that she was not related to, and the more she thought about it, the more she liked the idea. It was nice not to be alone any more, she thought happily as she looked around the bathroom at Grant's things.

They had decided to live together as roommates before they took their relationship to another level. They had grown really close and decided to take it as slow as possible for the time being. They didn't want to rush anything. Shelby knew that with everyday they had spent together, she was falling for him even more.

They both were really happy with the way things were right now. They go to work, come home, have dinner, and then curl up on the couch together and watch TV or a movie. Shelby's Dad even had Grant come over to the house from time to time to help him with projects that he was working on. It was so funny to watch the two of them together. It seemed to make up for the fact that CJ wasn't around to do these things with their dad. Shelby thought it was wonderful but she could tell by the look in her father's eyes that sometimes he wished he could be doing these things with CJ, and that made her sad.

CJ couldn't even make it home for Christmas this year! He has a game in Texas the day after Christmas. Even though their parent's were sad about it, he said that he would try to make it home for New Years. She really hoped he could, they all missed him terribly.

Chapter 9

Why did it seem that time flies by when you don't want it to? Shelby thought wryly. Two weeks have come and gone and Christmas is tomorrow.

"I guess I just wanted it to slow down because the New Year is fast approaching. Where has this year gone?" Shelby muttered under her breath.

There had been so many things that had happened to her in the past year; now Shelby just wanted to put it behind her. Then again, she thought about some of the things that she wished she could fix. This Christmas was going to be a little depressing for her. CJ wouldn't be home, Cole and Dallas still hate each other, *and me*. It just won't be the same, she thought.

Shelby couldn't help but notice that Grant had been acting really weird the past couple of days. He had been spending all of his extra time with her Dad. Shelby didn't have a clue what those two were up to but she bet it had something to do with Christmas, and her. Neither one of them would give her a clue as to what it might be. They were about to drive her crazy!

Grant would come home, eat dinner, kiss her on the forehead and out the door he would go. Not even a few minutes after he would leave; her Dad was on the phone wanting to know if Grant had left yet. She wished she knew what they were up to. Even her Mom was in on it; she had to be. Every time Shelby asked her something, she would tell her that she'd have to wait till Christmas. This was totally not fair!

For Christmas Eve, Shelby made a special dinner for Grant. She made all his favorites. They had to go over to her parents' house for Christmas night, so she thought it would be nice to have something for just the two of them alone. For once, he didn't have to rush off to meet her father. He was up stairs in the office while she was finishing up in the kitchen, when she heard a knock on the front door. She wasn't expecting anyone so she yelled for who ever it was to come in.

"I sure hope you made extra because I'm starved after the flight I had and that smells so good!" A man said.

"Well then, you had better brought an empty stomach because I have plenty to fill it." Shelby replied pulling a pie out of the oven. She recognized the voice immediately!

She sat the pie on the counter, turned and ran to him. It was CJ! She was so ecstatic that he was home that she jumped right into his arms!

"Wow, after a welcome like that, you act like you missed me or something." He said with chuckle.

"Are you crazy? Why would anyone miss you?" Shelby said with a laugh and snapped him with her dish towel.

She had to hug him again. She just couldn't believe that he was actually standing in her house. "What are you doing here; I thought you had a game the day after tomorrow?" She asked.

"No, I told Mom and Dad to tell you that so that it would be a surprise when I showed up." He answered.

"That it is! How long have you been home then?" She asked with a curious glare.

"Oh, since early this afternoon, I guess." He said shrugging his shoulders.

"Since this afternoon and you're just now coming to see me! Wait, I've talked to Mom half a dozen different times today and she never said a word. You just wait. I'm going to tell her that I'm taking her Christmas presents back!" Shelby said with a rueful laugh.

"Don't get mad. They thought it would be a good surprise for you. The look on your face was priceless." He said with a grin and chomped on a carrot.

"Well it is. I'm so glad you're home. Here I thought Mom and Dad were all depressed about you not coming home, and they knew all this time. *Man* they are really good actors." She replied.

"Where's your buddy? I heard he's living here now." CJ asked inquisitively.

"He's upstairs working on his paperwork. Hang on a sec." Shelby said as she walked over to the bottom of the stairs. "Hey Grant, you need to come down here! You'll never guess who's here!" she yelled up the stairs.

"Did CJ finally make it home?" he yelled back down the stairs.

"Don't you dare tell me that you're in on this too? Did you know he was coming home?" she yelled back up the stairs.

"Yeah, I kind of did. Your Dad told me, well let's see if I can remember his exact words; "I'll shoot your legs out from under you if you speak a word of this to Shelby!" I think that sums it up. After being told something like that, would *you* have said anything?" he asked. He was standing at the top of the stairs now with a devious grin across his face.

"You've been spending *way* too much time with my Dad. He's teaching you very bad things." she replied pointing up at him. He's just rotten, she thought as she walked back into the kitchen. She heard CJ and Grant talking.

"Hi CJ, glad to see you made it home." Grant said.

"It's good to see you too Grant. Thanks for keeping the secret" CJ replied.

They were both laughing at her, she just knew it! She knew things were getting bad when her own boyfriend was siding with her father and brother.

Shelby finished setting the table and yelled for the two of them to come and eat. CJ sat down and looked at her with a puppy dog pout about his face waiting for her to tell him that she wasn't mad at him anymore. She wasn't. Grant walked over and gave her a hug and asked her to forgive him. She did. She told him that she couldn't stay mad at him because it was such a good surprise.

Her brother was home for Christmas and the whole family was going to be together. God answered her prayers. What more could she ask for?

After dinner, Shelby informed the two conniving boys that their payback for tricking her was for them to do the dishes and clean up the kitchen. They weren't too happy about it but they eventually gave in humbly and agreed. They whined worse than two little kids, she thought with a giggle.

"I should have bought the two of you a bag of diapers for Christmas for pities sake. I've never heard two grown men whine as much as you two." She said jokingly. They couldn't find the humor in her statement. They didn't think it was very funny, at all.

Long after the two men finished in the kitchen, Shelby made coffee for them and they all sat in her living room talking for awhile. CJ told them all sorts of stories about football and where he lives. He told them about some of the girls he had met and went out with. Shelby asked him if any of them had any potential to be a long term thing and he said that he hadn't met any one like that yet. He told them that with his career going full bore he wasn't ready for anything serious. She couldn't blame him for that. These days, you never knew if someone really wanted you for you, or if it was just the fame and money they were after.

Of course after they had discussed CJ for some time, CJ turned the topic over to Shelby and Grant. CJ was curious of what lay ahead in his sister's future. Shelby and Grant sat next to each other on the couch holding hands and explained to CJ, for the time being, they were happy with the way things were. They were in no rush for anything and that's the way they liked it.

CJ looked at his watch and said that he thought it was time for him to head back to their Mom and Dads for the night. Grant went back upstairs to finish what he was working on and Shelby walked with CJ out onto the front porch.

He had a curious look in his eye as he turned to look at her, "Sis, I have to ask, what happened between you, Cole, and Dallas? I mean, if you don't want to talk about it, that's fine but I just wanted to hear you're side of the story." He asked with slight hesitation.

"I really don't know how to explain it. We got into a huge fight and now none of us speak to each other." Shelby answered placing her hands in her pockets and looked up into the dark sky.

"I only ask because I've talked to both of them and I knew you would tell me the real story. When I first heard about it, I wanted to kick both of their asses for treating my sister like that, but at the same time; I knew you would kick mine for sticking my nose into it. I heard that Dallas was out for the rest of the season. Have you talked to him at all?" he asked.

"No, I've seen him a couple of times around town and over at his parents' house, but I just can't bring myself to talk to him. To either one of them for that matter; especially after what I heard Cole did to Dallas. I mean, I understand that it's partly my fault; ok all my fault; for what happened between the three of us, but for Cole to go as far as he did is just wrong. Dallas didn't deserve that." She explained to him solemnly.

"It sounds like a real big mess. I wish there was something I could tell you but I've tried to talk to the both of them till I turn blue, I can't get through to either one. It's just going to take time, I guess." He replied.

"I know, I just wish I could fix it. Time will tell. You had better get going. You know Dad will lock the doors soon." Shelby said with a laugh.

"Do you think he would still do that?" CJ asked with a grin.

"I think he would just for old time's sake. You know that old man; he's just as ornery as he's ever been." She replied giggling as the thought of their father locking the doors of the house ran through her mind. She could just see him standing behind the door rubbing his hands together with a devious grin from ear to ear.

"Yep, you're right. I'll see ya tomorrow. Just remember, things will work themselves out eventually." He said giving her a hug.

After CJ left, Shelby walked back into the house and up the stairs to see what Grant was doing. She walked over to him and ran her fingers through his dark brown hair and asked him what he was working on. He pulled her around to him and had her sit on his lap.

"Actually, I'm all finished." He said. "Now all I need is my good night kiss before I head off to bed." He finished as he batted both eye brows at her.

Of course Shelby gladly obliged him.

As she sat on his lap looking deep into his emerald green eyes, Shelby really could see Grant as her future. He was so kind and caring. He always thought of her needs and never pushed for anything, even when it came to the subject of sex. There had been quite a few times that they had come very close but she would pull away every time. The most amazing thing was that he was fine with it. She would apologize over and over to him and every time he always told her that when the time was right and she was ready; he would still be there. That made her feel a lot better but she still had to wonder; how long will he wait? If marriage could be a possibility in their future, could he wait that long?

"Grant, can I ask you something?" She asked seriously, still sitting on his lap.

"You know you can ask me any thing." He replied.

"Would you sleep with me tonight?" She asked. Instantly, she thought she should have worded that differently. *That* was a loaded question.

"Sleep how? Do you mean.........or just sleep?" he asked with a stunned expression.

"I mean just sleep. I guess I should have phrased that a little differently. I want to lie in bed tonight with your arms wrapped around me. I want to fall asleep in your arms. I want to know that you're right there beside me instead of down the hallway. Am I asking for too much?" She asked wondering if she was going to get a response of "Are you crazy?"

"I would be honored. I have to confess something to you first." He replied.

"What's that?" Shelby asked confused.

"I was really hoping that you would ask me that. It's Christmas Eve and I can't think of spending it any other way." He said as his face lit up in a huge smile.

"Thank you." she answered and hugged him as tightly as she could.

Shelby jumped off his lap happier than she could ever imagine. She told him that she was going to go take a shower and put her pajamas on and that he could meet her in her bedroom in about forty five minutes. He said that was fine with him and that he needed to take a shower after she was finished.

Once Shelby finished in the shower and got dressed, she yelled to Grant to let him know the bathroom was open. When she heard the bathroom door close, she climbed into bed and waited for him. The longer he took in the shower, the more nervous she became. She couldn't believe she had actually had the guts to ask him to share her bed tonight, even though nothing else would come of it.

After some time, she heard the sound of the shower disappear, and the smell of soap and a men's cologne filled the air. It smelled so good! The soap smelled like Irish Spring and the cologne was a light scent of Stetson.

Grant walked to his room and put his clothes away. Before he walked into Shelby's bedroom, he couldn't help but wonder what had made her ask him to share her bed tonight. He had wanted Shelby Russell for his own since he had met her in college and now he was right where he wanted to be. If she only knew what he had in store for her tomorrow night at her parent's house? He couldn't wait! He just prayed that everything would go as planned. Admitting to himself, he loved Shelby more than humanly possible and he couldn't wait to here her speak those three precious words to him.

Her asking him to spend the night with her in her bed tonight was the icing on the cake. Her words had struck him to his very core. Knowing that she wanted to lie in his arms was the most intimate feeling he had ever had.

Grant walked into her bedroom and stood staring at her for a few seconds. God if she wasn't beautiful!

"Are you alright?" Shelby asked with concern.

"I'm fine. I was just taking in the view." He answered.

"Do you like what you see?" she asked flirtatiously.

"Very much." He answered.

Shelby flipped the covers down and said, "Then come to bed."

"Are you sure you want to do this?" he asked making sure one last time.

"Absolutely, Grant."

Grant walked to the side of the bed and lay down beside her. After he was comfortable, Shelby snuggled up next to him and made her self comfortable. Grant half cradled her between his arm and her head partially lay on his chest with her arm stretched across him. She felt so good next to him, he thought happily.

Shelby was thinking the exact same thing. Grant felt wonderful lying next to her. When he had walked into her bedroom only wearing a pair of pajama pants, he took her breath away. His bare feet, bare chest and freshly shaven face made every nerve ending in her body come to life, tingling all over. Oh, if you could just see the temptation running through my mind right now, she thought. He smelled so good!

Grant leaned his head down and Shelby craned her neck to him as their lips met for one last good night kiss. Grant reached to the side of the bed and flipped the light switch on the lamp that sat on the night stand beside her bed. The room was engulfed in darkness and he leaned down and kissed the top of her head.

"Good night, Shelby." He said.

"Good night, Grant." She answered.

They both laid silent in the darkness of Shelby's bedroom waiting for sleep to envelop them. Wrapped in each other's arms, neither one of them could think of another place in the world they would want to be at that very moment. They both felt safe, happy and content. Grant had finally found the woman he had always been looking for and Shelby thought she had finally found the man that would make her happy with out all of the melodrama. Admitting it to her self finally, Grant was what she wanted. She had been slightly attracted to him in college, but after spending the last few months with him, she had gotten closer to him than she ever thought she could with anyone. She was in love with the man that held her in his arms.

Shelby lay silent, almost ready to fall into the grips of deep sleep when she heard Grant whisper something.

"I love you."

She didn't give it a second thought when she whispered back, "I love you too."

The room stood silent again as both fell fast asleep with smiles from ear to ear across their faces.

Shelby awoke Christmas morning still wrapped in Grant's arms. She felt like she was flying high in the sky on cloud nine. Grant was in love with her and she hadn't felt this good since……well, since she didn't know when. She had no way of describing how happy she was either, ecstatic? There were no words, she was just happy.

Shelby got up and went to the bathroom and when she walked back into the bedroom; Grant was wide awake lying back against the head board of the bed, staring straight at her with a huge devilish grin. She stopped dead in her tracks and looked at him.

"What?" She asked with a grin.

"Nothing," He replied shaking his head.

"Why are you staring at me like that then?"

"Because, you're beautiful," He replied.

"Oh, yeah, I'm still in my pajamas and my hair is a wreck." She said looking down at her self.

"So what; that's what I love about you the most." He said, his grin deepening.

"So, I did hear you whisper something in my ear last night?" She asked teasingly

"So, you *did* hear me? I thought you might have been asleep." He said as he motioned for her to come over to the bed. She walked to the bed and sat down on the edge beside him.

"No, I wasn't asleep. I heard you." She answered shyly.

"I wasn't asleep when I heard you whispering either. Did I hear you right?" he asked with a half crooked grin.

"That depends. What did you hear?" she asked with a devious grin.

"Oh, that maybe you love me too." He said.

"Then I think your ears have served you well." she answered leaning in closer to him.

"Then would that make this a mutual agreement between us that we're in love?" he asked with a huge grin this time, leaning in closer to her.

"I do believe that would be a *very*, *very*, good assumption." She replied.

By this time they were so close to one another that their noses were touching and their lips were just barely brushing.

"Do you think this would be a good time for us to put a seal on the deal then?" he asked teasingly, waiting for her reply.

"I think it would be the perfect time." She answered.

Grant closed what little gap there was left between them and began to kiss Shelby slowly and softly. Shelby met his every movement. Within a few minutes, he wrapped his arms securely around her and rolled them both onto the bed, pinning Shelby underneath him. He was lying on top of her, with one of her legs pinned between his.

Grant gazed into Shelby's eyes and gave her a devious grin before his lips descended on hers once more. He couldn't believe how his life had changed in the time he had known her. As the thoughts swirled in his head, he began to kiss her more passionately, drawing his every breath from her. His heart began to beat faster against his rib cage and he could feel Shelby's own heart quicken as their kisses became more feverish. Oh, how he wanted this woman he held in his arms.

Shelby's breathing became more labored with every onslaught Grant's mouth possessed of her. He kissed her over and over, moving from her mouth at times, down her cheek, down her neck, and around to her ears. It sent shivers down her spine and into her inner core. Shelby parted her lips when Grant had once more reclaimed her mouth, inviting him to explore her every being. His tongue tangled with hers and she met his every move. She even went as far as trailing her tongue erotically around the soft curves of his lips. She heard him gasp for air as soft moans escaped from his throat. When Shelby heard his moans of pleasure, it sparked the flame inside of her to a whole new level.

Shelby moved her arms down Grant's back slowly and sensuously just barely touching him with her finger tips. She moved her fingers down to his waist, and slowly trailed her fingers around the waist band of his pajama pants. She heard him moan again with pleasure once more and it nearly pushed her over the edge. Grant had taken one of her breasts into his hand, caressing it softly, which in turn, made Shelby cry out moaning with pleasure as well.

Grant knew how turned on Shelby was and slowly started to move against her body to show her just how turned on he was too. His hips moved against her leg and as he ascended on her thigh, he pushed a little harder.

Shelby cried Grant's name as she felt his hardened manhood push against her. She cried out to him because as she felt him move against her, her head started to swim, wanting to know how his hard masculinity would feel deep inside of her. When that realization hit her, Shelby felt as if she had been slammed against a brick wall. They were going too far! But, at the same time, she didn't want it to stop. Her conscience was at war with its self as the warning bells blared inside her head. She wanted Grant to make love to her in every way, but she knew that it couldn't happen. If it did, she would be breaking her promise to her self, and that, she couldn't live with.

With luck, and just in the nick of time, Shelby's phone started to ring. Grant froze in his place and Shelby heard him let out a groan of "Urgh!" in

108

disapproval. Letting out a deep breath, Shelby thought it couldn't have rung at a better moment.

"I had better get that." She said to Grant in almost a whisper.

"Do you have to?" he whined rising up from her so that he could look into her eyes.

"It's probably my mother." Shelby said with a forced smile.

"You're probably right," he said groaning with disapproval once again as he rolled off Shelby to lie by her side giving her room to reach for the phone.

Shelby reached to the bed side table and plucked the phone from its cradle. Before she answered it, she heard Grant grumbling to him self, "There's nothing in this world to deflate a man quicker than getting a phone call from Mummy dearest."

"Grant!"

"Well, it's true!" He replied with a slight chuckle.

Before Shelby could protest further, Grant rolled onto his side, facing her, and started to tickle her. Shelby let out a gut wrenching laugh and realized she had better answer the still ringing phone she held in her hand.

"Hello?" she answered laughing.

"Shelby, its Mom. Are you alright?" She asked in a concerned tone.

"I'm fine Mom. How...are...you...this morning?" Shelby tried to ask as she let out another gut wrenching laugh. Grant was still tickling her relentlessly.

"I'm great, are you sure you're alright?"

"Yes, I'm fine, that is if Grant would stop tickling me." She said into the phone as she pointed at Grant with a stern but teasing look.

"Well, that explains it. I was just calling to wish you both a Merry Christmas." Her mother said with a slight giggle to Shelby's predicament.

"Merry Christmas to you to Mom, and pass that along to Dad and CJ as well." Shelby said with another laugh.

"I will and please tell Grant for us." She replied.

Shelby relayed the message to Grant and he put his mouth close to the phone and told her mother Merry Christmas. Her mother laughed at the excitement in Grant's voice.

Shelby told her mother that they would see them later on and after a few minutes more of discussing dinner plans, they hung up. Shelby didn't think she was ever going to get her off the phone! She loved her mother dearly but when she wanted to have a conversation, it was hard to stop her. As much as she hated to cut her off, she had to if she was going to get anything else done.

Shelby and Grant finally calmed down from their wrestling, slash torturing match, and decided that it was time to pull themselves together and get dressed for the day. Shelby had baking to finish and Grant; well, she wasn't for sure if he had anything to do. He corrected her on that. He said that there was something he had to go take care of for her father. She was beginning to wonder if it was actually for her father or for him. He acted really strange when she began questioning him about it. He just told her that she would have to wait till later to find out. What was he up to? She thought wryly.

Grant also informed her that, before he could do anything today, he now had to go take a cold shower to get his body temperature back to normal from their earlier moment of passion. As Shelby watched him walk toward the bathroom, she picked up a pillow from the bed and slung it at him, nailing him on his back side! Turning to look at her, Grant didn't retaliate, he just promised to make her pay for that later.

A few hours later, Grant had finally made it home. He explained to Shelby that they had to hurry up and get over to her parents' house because they were waiting on them. He was very adamant that they got moving, now! She kept asking him what the rush was but he wouldn't tell her anything. He was practically shoving her out the door without any of the things she needed to take with her. Finally she got him to calm down long enough to help her gather up the food and presents and haul them out to the truck. Shelby had to take one pie straight from the oven. This was fun holding on to while they raced over to the house.

When they pulled up in front of the house; her Dad had all of the Christmas lights lit up and there was a huge box sitting in the front yard that looked like a present. Shelby couldn't believe how huge it was. It was a *big* wooden box. It was made out of plywood! She asked her Dad where it came from because they had never had anything like that when they were younger. He said that it was something new that Grant had made for him. He turned his head, smiled at Grant, and gave him the thumbs up sign. These two were up to something and it was going to drive her nuts until she found out what it was!

Shelby stood staring at the big plywood present and Grant took hold of her hand. Her father insisted that they all head into the house for dinner. For some reason, they were in a hurry to get her away from that box, she thought to her self.

DESTINY HAS A WAY

They walked into the house and Shelby sat the food down in the kitchen. She walked to the hall closet and hung up her coat. CJ flew down the stairs and almost tripped on the way down. Apparently he hadn't seen her standing off to the side because he shouted out "Did she see it yet?"

Of course she had to ask him, "Did I see what?" Her mother quickly butted in and asked her if she would help with the rest of the food. She wanted to change the subject awfully quickly.

"What in the world is everyone up to?" Shelby asked as her mother dragged her swiftly into the kitchen.

"All in due time my dear, all in due time." Mom repeated.

"You know, I'm really starting to believe that you *all* have lost your minds." Shelby said shaking her head.

Once the table was set and all the food out, Mom called for everyone to come to the table and be seated. After everyone was settled her father said the prayer. They all began to make their plates and fill their bellies with the delicious food. There was ham, turkey, stuffing, mashed potatoes, sweet potatoes, cranberry sauce, corn, and biscuits. For dessert there was, sugar cream pie, pumpkin, banana pudding, cheese cake, and apple pie.

Dinner was excellent! Even though everyone had eaten way too much, it was well worth the belly ache later. Dinner was finished and all the plates were cleared; everyone moved to the living room to open presents. Dad played Santa Clause and passed the presents around to everyone with their names on them.

They opened their presents, laughed and had a good time. Shelby had gotten her mother a cordless phone with built in caller ID. Now the poor woman would know exactly who was calling her from now on. CJ of course, gave everyone football memorabilia from his team. That wasn't a bad thing though; in the future that stuff could be worth some money, but knowing her brother was a part of it, made them priceless to Shelby.

For their parents', CJ he had a *huge* surprise. CJ had really gone beyond his usual antics this year and he was bursting at the seams to give it to them. After everyone finished present time; CJ told Mom and Dad that he had a special present for them. He told everyone to grab their coats because they had to go outside for this. Walking them both over to the front door, he placed blindfolds on them. He asked Shelby to help walk their Mom as he took Dad and they walked them outside into the front yard, Grant following behind. They were almost standing on the sidewalk when a brand new Cadillac pulled up in

111

front of them with a big red bow on it. Shelby looked at CJ and dropped her jaw. He had a huge grin on his face and shook his head up and down and said, "OH YEAH!" Shelby was in complete awe of what he had done.

CJ told them that he was going to count to three and then they would pull off the blindfolds. He motioned to everyone to start counting and they started at 1, 2, and 3! The blindfolds came off and the look in their mother's face was one of utter shock. She stood with her hands on her cheeks and the longer she looked at the car; her face reddened and you could see tears start to well in her eyes. Dad was just speechless. This was the first time in Shelby's life that she had *ever* seen that man have no words.

Shelby walked over to CJ and gave him a *huge* hug. She was almost to the point of crying her self.

"Do you think I did well?" he whispered in her ear.

"Oh, I think you did more than well. I think you did excellent! Where's my car?" She asked with a goofy grin, throwing her hands into the air.

CJ finally walked over to Mom and Dad and they both hugged him at the same time. Mom was crying and Dad was sniffling. They could tell that he wanted to cry but he wouldn't. Dad tried to tell CJ that they couldn't accept a gift like that but CJ wouldn't have it. He started plugging his ears and bouncing up and down making noises like he couldn't hear him.

Grant walked up behind Shelby and wrapped his arms around her. By this time, the tears were falling down her cheeks. She just couldn't believe that her brother had done this for their parents'. She was so proud to have him as a brother. He was truly an amazing person after you got past his rough exterior.

After everyone pulled them selves together, they walked to the car to get a good look at it. This thing was so loaded; Dad said he would never be able to figure out what all of the buttons did. Mom said that she would be amazed if she could figure out how to shift it into drive. They all just started laughing.

When everyone had had a good look at the car, Dad went to Grant and told him that it was show time. Shelby asked her Mom what they were talking about but she wouldn't tell her anything. Grant approached Shelby and said that he had something else to give her. He walked her over to the huge box looking present that was sitting in the yard. Dad came from the house with a hammer in his hand and handed it to Grant; which in turn, Grant handed to Shelby.

"What am I supposed to do with this?" Shelby asked holding the hammer studying it.

"That's what I'm about to explain to you. Now, to be able to get to what lies in this box, you have to hit it with the hammer right here." He said as he pointed at the corner of the box.

"Ok." She replied curiously. Everyone waited patiently for her to take the first swing.

Shelby swung the hammer and hit the corner of the box on the first swing. After the hammer made contact, the four sides of the box fell and there was a smaller box inside of that. Grant walked over and lifted the top of the first box off and told her to swing at the corner of the next box. She did and it did just as the first had done. He walked over and lifted the top off of that one and told her to hit the corner of the next one. He had her do this four more times until she had gotten to a small box in the very center of them all. He told her to pick it up and hand it to him, so she did.

"I was trying to figure out a way to do this so that it would be something completely out of the ordinary. Your Dad helped me with it and I thought it was the perfect idea." He started to explain as he pulled the lid off of the last box that revealed a small, blue velvet ring box.

When Shelby saw it, she started trembling all over. Was he about to do what she thought he was going to do? She felt like hyperventilating at the very thought of it. She couldn't breathe!

Grant kneeled down on one knee and opened the blue box. There was a diamond ring that glittered instantly when the light hit it. It was so beautiful! Grant reached his hand out and Shelby placed her left hand in his.

"Shelby, I have been in love with you since the first day I laid eyes on you in college. I know that in the past few years, you've been dealing with some things that I didn't want to get in the middle of, but in the last few months, I haven't been able to think of any things else. Will you marry me?" he asked softly.

Grant looked as if he was about to pass out himself, Shelby thought.

"Grant, I don't know what to say! I knew you were up to something, but in my wildest dreams, I didn't expect this. It's absolutely beautiful!" Shelby replied shaking her head frantically.

"Not even a diamond can compare to you. You *could* start by saying yes. My legs are getting kind of numb kneeling in this snow." He said with a laugh looking deeply at her.

"Yes, of course, yes!" She shouted.

Grant jumped up from the ground and lifted her off the ground. He was so excited that he started swinging her around in circles. His perfect plan of making Shelby Russell his wife had went off with out a hitch. He was terrified that she would say no but he knew now that Shelby was as much in love with him as he was with her. This was the best day of his life!

"WOO HOO! I'm getting married!" he shouted at the top of his lungs.

Shelby's parents congratulated them and her Mom began to cry again. Dad shook Grants hand and whispered to him…"I told you that it would all work out."

"So, did you know all about this?" Shelby asked her Dad.

"Well, yeah, I might have had a little bit of involvement in it." He replied as he winked at her.

"I should have known." She said laughing as she gave him a hug.

"Grant asked me a few weeks ago if he could ask you to marry him and I gave him my blessing. I had to. Who could ask for a better son-in-law?" he explained giving Grant a huge grin of approval.

Grant and Shelby held each other and they both laughed at her Dad. CJ even gave them both his blessing and told Grant that he thought it would be awesome to have him as a brother-in-law. Shelby never thought that she could be so happy. This was definitely a Christmas she would never forget.

With all of the commotion going on outside, someone from over at Cole's parents' house came running out to their front porch. It was Cole's Mom. She wanted to know what was going on. Mom yelled at her and told her that Shelby was getting married. She started jumping up and down on her front porch clapping her hands with excitement and congratulating Grant and Shelby.

Then of course the next household was on their front porch to see what was going on. It was Dallas's parents. Grant and Shelby told them their good news and they were excited as well.

Once the excitement wore down and everyone went back into their houses; Grant and Shelby were still standing in the front yard. They were holding each other tightly and smiling at one another.

"Merry Christmas, Shelby, I love you so much." He whispered to her softly.

"Merry Christmas, Grant, and I love you too." Shelby replied as she leaned closer to kiss him.

Shelby cradled his face in her hands and kissed him with her whole heart. She couldn't help but think what a turn of events her life had taken this year.

It had been a tragedy one minute and the next she was in complete and utter bliss. She was in love with the man in front of her; he was her life, her future, her everything.

Shelby told Grant that they had better go back in the house before they both caught frost bite. He agreed and she told him to go on and that she was going to pick up some of the mess in the yard. After Grant had walked inside, Shelby held her left hand up to admire the glistening diamond that now rested on her ring finger. It was absolutely gorgeous, but not even the diamond she saw there could express what she felt in her heart.

She started to pick up some of the wood lying on the ground when she spotted Dallas walking toward his parents' front door. She had to wonder if he had seen anything that just happened. He must of, because as he walked through the door, she heard the door slam and it slammed so hard that she thought it was going to bust off of the hinges. "I guess maybe he did see the commotion." She muttered under her breath.

Chapter 10

Things couldn't be better right now for Shelby and Grant. Grant was officially moved in with her and on New Years Eve, they decided to have the wedding in early May. They didn't want a really long engagement but they didn't want to get married right away either. They thought a spring wedding would be perfect. Five months should give them plenty of time to get everything planned out the way they wanted it.

Shelby's mother on the other hand, had been going insane. She seemed to think that five months was not near long enough to plan a wedding. She wanted it to be this big spectacular event and they were pulling tooth and nail to convince her otherwise. It didn't have to be a huge wedding. They just wanted their family and close friends to be there. It wasn't like they had three to four hundred people coming. This town couldn't handle that many. Between Grant and her; she didn't think they even knew that many people.

Shelby did need to make a trip though. She had talked with Grant's parents' on the phone quite a bit but she still hadn't actually met them. Grant's family lived in New Hampshire and from what Grant had told her; his father was left a lot of money from his grand father when he was very young. His grand father had bought into a lot of stocks a long, long time ago and over the years the stocks from these companies had made quite a bit of money. Of course, when the companies made it big, the stocks went through the roof. Grant had told her when they were in college that his family was well off, but at the time, Shelby hadn't paid much attention to it. It made sense now why they were always gone to another country during the holidays.

Shelby was so nervous about meeting them. She was scared to death that they wouldn't like her. Grant told her that she was crazy to think that way. He loved her and they were going to love her just as much. They both took a long weekend so that they could fly up to see them. Shelby hated flying but it was the quickest way to travel in the short time they had.

When they had landed at the airport in New Hampshire, Shelby thought that they would have to rent a car to get to his parents' house. Boy was she surprised. After they had collected their luggage and walked to the entrance of the airport, there was a man standing with a sign that had Grant's name on it. His dad had sent a car and driver to pick them up. This was just like something you would see in a movie. How exciting is that! Shelby thought to her self.

Grant knew the man right away. He introduced Shelby to him and he told her that his name was Carl. Carl had worked for Grant's parents for many years. He had worked for them for so long that he was like one of the family. He was such a sweet man. He kept calling Shelby, Miss Russell. She had to remind him over and over that he could just call her Shelby. She thought that when you're so formal with people for so long, it had to become a habit.

It wasn't too far of a drive to the house. Shelby wasn't for sure if she should even call it a house. It was huge! When they turned off the road and onto the driveway, she was speechless. There was a long drive up a winding road to the house. The yard was so manicured and green. The place was like something out of a fairytale. No, better than that, it was like a place you envision in England when read out of a historical novel, Shelby thought. There were statues and bushes that were cut like figures. There were some that were cut like animals, and some like people, and even some cut like buildings. This place was magnificent. After seeing what the outside looked like; Shelby couldn't wait to see what the inside.

The car pulled up in front of the house and there was a bit of a sigh from Grant. He told her that this was the part he liked the most about her family. When ever they pulled up in front of her parents' house, they always came out to greet them. His parents' *never* do that. Being raised in England for most of his life, Shelby thought that his parents still lived some of the ways of old.

Carl climbed out of the car and opened the door for them. Grant got out and held his hand out for Shelby, to help her out of the car. He was such a gentleman, she thought. Both men grabbed the luggage out of the trunk and they walked to the two enormous front doors. They looked as if they had been taken off of a medieval castle in England and shipped to America for this house. For all Shelby knew, that's most likely where they came from.

Grant chose to ring the door bell instead of using the huge lion head door knocker. A few seconds later, a man opened the door. It was Grants father.

He seemed to be happy to see Grant but he really didn't show any emotion or too much excitement.

He greeted them and said that he was happy they had made it and told Carl to go put their things in their rooms. Shelby's first thought was rooms? Did they actually have to sleep in separate rooms? She thought it wasn't a bad thing but she hadn't expected it either. That explained why Grant didn't have a problem with it at her house when he first started staying with her. It made perfect sense now.

As they walked through the long entrance of the house, off in another room they could hear someone playing a piano. It sounded beautiful. Between the sound of the piano and looking around at all of the detail of the house; Shelby was lost in admiration. She loved to look at old houses. This place was so gorgeous! What it must have been like to grow up in a house like this, she thought to herself. It was definitely designed after an old castle but it still had the amenities of the modern age.

"I take it that Tabitha is home as well?" Grant asked his father.

"Yeah, she's playing as usual." He answered.

So, she was the one playing the piano in the other room, Shelby realized.

"How's Mum?" Grant asked.

"She's doing very well. She's excited about meeting your fiancé. Let's go and see if we can find her, shall we?" His father replied as he smiled at Shelby.

They walked quietly through the room and into another room where the music from the piano was coming from. There was a girl sitting at the piano and another woman sitting on a huge sofa across the room from there. Shelby was guessing that this beautiful woman was Grant's mother. She was a remarkable woman. She seemed to be so poised and proper, just like the English people Shelby had watched in movies and read about in books. Graceful, was the word that came to mind.

"Grant, you've finally made it! I have been so excited to see you. This must be Shelby. Oh, let me look at you. You are such an exquisite looking girl. Grant you have done quite well for yourself." She said with excitement. She was smiling from ear to ear after she gave Shelby the full inspection.

"It is very nice to meet you Mrs. Summers." Shelby said politely as she held out her hand to the woman.

"Nonsense child, if we are to be family, only a hug will do." She said to Shelby holding out both arms to her.

Shelby took the woman's embrace as a good sign; so far, so good.
"Mother, I have to say that you look incredible. I just can't get over this, you're absolutely radiant." Grant said in amazement.

Grants mother had been fighting cancer and has had a real battle with it. He had told Shelby about it before they had came, but from the way she looked; she had really fought it well. Shelby couldn't tell that she had any health problems at all. Grant had said that she had gotten really bad at one time and they didn't think she was going to make it. He said that with all of the money that they had; they made sure she had the best doctors in the country helping her. It must have paid off because she was in excellent health now and the cancer was in remission.

"Tabitha, come and meet you brothers' fiancé. She will be your sister-in-law in a few months. Come and make nice my dear." Grants mother called to Tabitha.

"Yeah, Tabby where is my hug?" Grant asked her.

"Hello brother dear, it is nice to see you again." Tabitha said dryly.

"It's good to see you too my sister. I would like you to meet Shelby. Shelby this is my little sister Tabitha." Grant said as he introduced the two of them.

"It's very nice to meet you Tabitha. How are you?" Shelby asked as she tried to shake her hand.

"I might be Grants' little sister but I am much smarter than he, and very fine thank you." Tabitha replied snootily as she turned and walked away.

Tabitha was Grants little sister and she didn't take to well to people she did not know. She was twenty one years old and thought she had the world by the horns. She had spent the better part of her life at boarding schools and prep schools. Her biggest problem was that she's *very* smart. She's just border line of being a genius. Her parent's praise her on that. She can never do any wrong and she gets everything she wants. Shelby thought it was going to be very hard to become friends with her.

After all of the introductions and everyone had gotten acquainted, they all sat and chatted; as they say. Grants' father announced that it was time for dinner. Grants' mother told him and Shelby to go freshen up a bit before they ate; so, Grant took Shelby up to their rooms to change. Oh, how Shelby wanted to go home. There was no way she would ever be able to fit into these peoples lives. She knew that she was definitely not what they had expected for their son.

Grant showed Shelby to her room and explained where everything was. Even though they had to sleep in separate rooms it was nice that the bathroom was right in between the two. This was cool because they had to share and they could walk back and forth between the two rooms with out anyone else knowing.

Grant and Shelby had been sleeping in the same room at home since they had gotten engaged, but they still hadn't let it go any further than that. They both decided that they would wait until they were married so that they could consummate it the right way. Shelby had finally gotten the nerve one night to tell Grant about her secret promise to herself that she would not give herself to any man unless he was her husband. She had thought at the time that Grant might tease her about it. To her astonishment, Grant had smiled brightly at her and admitted that he had made the same oath to himself.

He did tell her that there had been plenty of opportunities in the past, as did she, but none of them had ever made it all the way. He just couldn't bring himself to go through with it. He knew that out there somewhere, he would find his soul mate and that he had when he met Shelby.

Shelby had known that she was in love with Grant before that discussion, but after his confession, she knew now, more than ever, that she loved him more than anything in this world. He had been completely honest with her and that was a turn on more than anything else.

It was still hard for Shelby to picture Grant not being with a woman. *Ever.* He was every woman's dream. He was tall, muscular, and absolutely gorgeous; his dark brown hair, emerald green eyes, and a smile to die for. His English accent made his whole mystique that much more desirable. How could he not have women falling to his feet? Wait a minute, Shelby thought. What am I talking about? He's *my* man now, who cares about other women? She had to shake that thought from her mind real quick.

They had gone this long without it so a few more months weren't going to hurt anything. She had gotten so used to having him right beside her that now; it was going to be hard to sleep by her self for a few days. You never know; maybe he could sneak into her room or she could sneak into his, she thought wantonly.

"Grant, I have to ask; is your family always like this?" Shelby asked hesitantly.

"I knew that was coming." He replied.

"I wasn't trying to be mean or sarcastic. Please don't take it the wrong way. I just feel like they really don't like me. I'm not as prim and proper as they are. I think they were expecting someone a little different. Someone a little more like…" Shelby tried to explain.

"Them? To answer your question; yes they have always been like this, and no, I didn't take it the wrong way. I do think it will take them some time to get to know you though. I just didn't expect to see them put on such a good act. I have always told them that they should have been in the theater." He replied with a laugh.

"Stop joking, I'm trying to be serious." Shelby said jabbing him in the shoulder.

"Ok, ok I'm sorry. Come here and sit with me." He said as he sat on the edge of the bed.

Shelby did as he said and he put his arm around her shoulder and flipped them both back on the bed. Shelby rolled over on her side to look at him and Grant rolled over to her.

"We might get caught if we lay here like this." She said with a teasing grin.

"I know, wouldn't that be fun." He said with a chuckle.

"Shouldn't we get back down there? I don't want to be disrespectful." She asked.

"No, I think we should let them stew on it for awhile. Knowing my mum and Tabitha they're dreaming up all kinds of reasons why we haven't made it back yet." He said batting both eye brows at her. "Now come here because I haven't had a hug or a kiss since we've been here." He said holding out his arms.

Shelby leaned over and wrapped her arms around him and kissed him passionately. They laid there for a few minutes kissing and then were abruptly interrupted.

"What are you doing?" his mother shouted through the doorway.

Grant and Shelby jumped straight off the bed. Shelby felt like she was a little kid getting caught stealing a piece of candy or something.

"Nothing mother; we were just having a moment alone." Grant replied in a calm voice.

"Well there won't be any of *that* going on in this house! You two should know better. It's probably too late but you should have waited till you were married. Grant, I thought I taught you better than that. Shelby, I thought you at least would have had the dignity and self respect to wait." She started ranting.

"Mother, listen to me." Grant tried to say.

"The two of you will not……" she started as Grant cut her off.

"Mother!" Grant said in a louder tone.

"What?" she asked.

Shelby looked over at Grant and shook her head to tell him not to say anything. She knew this was her chance to redeem her self.

"Mrs. Summers, I know exactly what you mean." Shelby said to her.

"How could you have a clue as to what I mean?" she asked grimly.

"I know because Grant and I haven't let our relationship go that far. We love each other very much but we both made the decision to let sex wait until we were married." Shelby started to explain.

"You actually expect me to believe that? You kids these days could care less who you're sleeping with and how many people you've slept with." She began to lecture them looking to Grant then back to Shelby.

"Mother, it's true. Shelby and I sleep in the same bed at home, but that's as far as it goes. We *are* waiting until we're married. We want this to be special. As a matter of fact, you should be pleased to know that neither one of us has, well, you know, lost our virtue. "Grant explained to her as he walked to Shelby and wrapped his arms around her and smiled.

"How can this be? I can't see the two of you sleeping in the same bed without…well…something else." She replied waving her arm through the air in disbelief.

"It's true. When Grant first started staying with me, I made him sleep in a different room. When Christmas came around, I asked him if he would sleep in my room with me. Nothing else but just holding each other and sleep; that's the way it's been ever since. Trust me, it has been very hard to keep it that way; you have a very handsome son; but if we get to close to going over the edge, we both put the brakes on. It's a tough thing to do but we manage quite well." Shelby explained to her.

"I am truly amazed. I didn't think this could be possible in this day and age. Most people these days could care less about, pardon me, virtue or their virginity. My son has found a true gem. I'm so happy that he has you. You really do have a good head on those shoulders. You had better listen to her son. She will take good care of you." She said to Grant. This time she had a smile on her face when she placed her hand on Shelby's shoulder in approval.

Shelby let go of Grant and gave his mother a big hug. She stood completely still for a second or two as if she were stunned. Shelby didn't think she expected that. As Shelby stood hugging her, Grant gave her a thumbs up signal. He knew that that was exactly what she needed to hear.

When that was all settled, they went down to the dinning room for dinner. Mrs. Summer's whole attitude toward Shelby had changed. Mr. Summers and Tabitha had picked up on her attitude as well and they too seemed to be acting differently toward her. Shelby thought she had found her edge to fitting into this family. Well, maybe not fit but be accepted at least. This was a true accomplishment, she thought happily to herself.

The rest of the weekend flew by before they knew it. They had such a great time. Grant's family gave her the grand tour of the house and gave her the history of it all. They went all over town shopping and taking in the sites. This was truly a beautiful place. It was filled with so much history. Shelby was completely amazed the entire weekend.

Grant and Shelby spent the rest of the weekend just soaking in one another. Grant had been around her family for quite some time and had gotten to know them really well. Now that she had seen him with his family; she felt like she knew him so much more. She felt so much closer to him. Of course they did end up sleeping apart. Shelby respected his mother so much for her beliefs. Now, she could see why Grant had no problem with it when he first started living with her.

After everything was said and done, it was time for them to head home. Shelby loved being here but home was really starting to sound so good. They said their good byes and hugged everyone. Grant's parents kept repeating over and over how much it would mean to them if they could pay for the wedding. Grant explained that the two of them had everything under control and that everything would be fine. All they had to do was be there. They finally gave up and said they wouldn't miss it for the world. They were truly great people.

The car pulled up in front of the house; Grant and Carl loaded the luggage into the trunk. They said their final good byes and climbed into the car. They were off to the airport once again. Shelby just couldn't keep from thinking about home. For only being gone for four days, she felt like she had been gone forever.

On the plane, Grant told Shelby that he just couldn't get over the turn about his mother had made. He explained to her that in the past, when he had serious relationships and would bring them home to meet his parents'; things never worked the way they had this weekend. He explained that his mother and sister would put on this huge act, as if they were better than everyone else, and make his girlfriends feel like they were at the bottom of the chain. It drove him nuts because usually when that happened; not to long after they would split up. Once they had met the family; then it was pretty much over

Not this time. Shelby must have made some kind of impact, because you would have thought she was already one of the family. Grant was so relieved that everything went the way it did. He was a little apprehensive about taking her there because of the past, but he was relieved that she had stood up for her self to his mother. If she hadn't, things probably wouldn't have gone as good. I think she did quite well, Grant thought to himself. They loved her, what could he say?

The plane landed in Ft. Wayne and Grant went out to get the truck. Shelby stayed inside to locate their luggage. As she was standing at the baggage claim, she could hear someone talking behind her. She knew that voice. It sounded just like Cole's voice. She stood completely still trying to ignore it. He was talking to some woman. Then she heard him tell her that he would be right back; he had seen an old friend.

Please don't let it be me. Please, please, please, don't let it be me; oh, too late, Shelby pleaded quietly in her mind.

"Shelby, is that you?" Cole asked behind her.

Shelby spun around to look at him. "Yep, it's me. How are you, Cole?" She asked with hesitation.

"I'm good, how are you?" he asked.

"I'm doing very well. So, what are you doing here?" She asked calmly.

Why is he even talking to me? He hasn't talked to me in forever. She argued with her self.

"I just flew in from Hawaii. I took a long vacation. I had to get away from here for a while. Where are you coming from?" He asked curiously.

"New Hampshire. Grant and I just made it back from his parents' house." She replied.

"Oh, that's right. I heard you were getting married, congratulations. Have you guys set a date yet?" he asked.

"Yeah, it's going to be the first weekend in May. How about you? Have you found someone to settle down with yet?" Shelby asked looking around him at the woman he had been talking to before.

"You mean her? No, no, no, I don't think so. Well maybe; I don't know. She has a lot of potential but she's also a model. Sometimes they aren't ready for something like marriage just yet. She's focused on her career right now. I can't blame her for that. She looks really good on the beach though." He answered with a huge grin.

I guess I should have seen that one coming, Shelby thought wryly.

"Well, here are our bags, so, I guess I had better get going." she said hoping that that would end their conversation.

"Yeah, I guess I had better get going too. It was good to see you again." He replied.

"Yeah, you too; take care." Shelby answered.

"Could I at least get a hug? I don't expect to get an invitation to your wedding but a hug would at least do." He asked holding out both arms.

"Sure, why not," She said as she sat the bags on the floor.

Shelby reached her arms out and hugged him. Cole had his arms wrapped around her so tightly she thought he was going to break her in half. Before she pulled away he whispered something in her ear.

"That should be me standing next to you in May." He said as he pulled away with a smile.

Shelby was completely dumbfounded.

As she watched him walk away, he turned back toward her and pointed, he said, "Don't ever forget me."

In the blink of an eye, he was gone.

Shelby hadn't even had enough time to give a reply. She was completely in shock. She looked down at the floor and put her hands on her head. When she had looked back up; he was gone. It was like he had vanished into thin air. Did that really just happen? She asked her self. Maybe she was just hallucinating. Why did this keep happening to her? She stood there for a little while longer. She just kept looking aimlessly around the airport. People must have thought she was nuts! She thought for sure that after that; Dallas was going to pop up out of nowhere too. He didn't, thank god. Usually when something like this happens with one of them; the other one wasn't too far behind. At least it hadn't been that way this time.

Shelby grabbed the bags and headed out the front doors to find Grant. She wanted to get home *really* bad now. She wanted away from this airport and home. As a matter of fact, she didn't ever want to leave home again. That's the way it could stay for the rest of her life and she would be happy.

For the rest of the drive home, Shelby really didn't say much. She just kept thinking about Cole.

When they got to the house; her Mom came running out yelling with joy. She was so excited about them being home. You would have thought that they had been gone for years.

"Oh, my goodness, I'm so happy to see you two!" she belted out with glee.

"Calm down Mom. We weren't gone that long. Are you ok? Is everything alright?" Shelby asked because of the way she was acting.

"Everything is great! Why, are you alright?" Mom asked and her tone changed.

"Everything is fine with us. I just haven't seen you this happy in awhile. I think it's funny." Shelby replied with a slight giggle.

"Oh, you're funny. Come in, I made you a pie." She answered.

"You made us a pie; in our house?" Shelby asked.

"I hope that's ok. I didn't think you would mind." Mom answered.

"Mom, that's absolutely fine. You know you're welcome any time. After Grant and I are married though, that might be a different subject. Well, the any time part anyhow." Shelby said with a laugh.

After unloading the bags from the truck, the three of them walked into the house and sat the bags down on the floor. Shelby was in no hurry to unpack just yet. The answering machine was slammed full of messages, again. She wasn't even in a rush to listen to them either. She just wanted to sit down and relax; have a cup of coffee and a piece of Mom's pie. That sounded so good right now.

Mom gave Grant a big hug and told him how much she missed him. He in turn replied the same. Grant carried the bags upstairs and joined the women in the kitchen a few moments later. Mom gave them the run down on everything that transpired over the weekend; which really wasn't that much.

Mom told Grant that when he had time; Dad had some project he was working on and needed his help. Grant loved helping her Dad with things. He told Shelby one time, that with the way he had grown up; he had never really learned how to do some things. He wasn't too handy around the house. When he helped her father, he was teaching him how to do these things. What better way of bonding could you get than that; men working on manly things, Shelby thought. They cracked her up with their antics.

No longer than they had had their coffee and pie, Grant jumped from the table, and bolted for the front door. He wanted to find out what Shelby's father was working on now. Grant told the ladies that he didn't want her Dad to feel like he had left him alone. He acted like a kid in a candy store. He couldn't wait to get out of the house. He told Shelby he wouldn't be gone for long and that he would be back as soon as he could. He gave her a kiss, told Mom thanks for the pie, and ran out the door.

"He is so funny." Shelby said to her mother.

After Grant had left, Shelby put the dishes in the sink and her Mom could tell that some thing was bothering her.

"So, how was your trip? Was Grant's family nice?" Her mother asked her.

"They were great. At first, things were a little rocky though. I had to be my usual charming self and make my feelings known about a few things; then after that it was smooth sailing." Shelby answered with a giggle.

"I bet they just fell in love with you." Her mother said.

"I hope so. After you get past the "stereo typical" name tags; they are really nice people." she answered.

"What do you mean by "stereo typical"?" Mom asked.

"How do I explain this? They have money, I mean; they have lots of money. We don't have lots of money but I think we all do pretty well for our selves. They just have lots of money, and of course with that said; they know how to live like that too. After you strip all of that away though; they're down to earth people just like us. His Mom likes to throw her weight around and his sister follows right behind her. His father on the other hand tries to do as they do, but he can't pull it off as easily. He's just as big of a character as Dad. I can't wait for you all to meet them. When the time comes; don't be intimidated by them. Just give them a little bit of time to settle and they'll fit right in." Shelby explained.

"It sounds like you really like them. I'm so happy things are going so well for you, Shelby." Mom said to her.

"Yeah, I just wished the past would stop haunting me." She replied with a big sigh.

"Why do you say that?" Mom asked.

"When we got to the airport in Ft. Wayne, I ran into Cole."

"Oh, I see. Did he say anything to you?" she asked.

"Yeah, he made a point of it." Shelby replied as she explained the whole story to her about what was said.

"Well, if that's the case, you might not want to listen to the messages on your machine either." Mom said with slight hesitation.

"Who's on there?" Shelby asked heading for the living room.

"I was going to erase it but I thought I had better let you deal with it on your own." Mom replied.

Shelby stood in front of the answering machine debating on whether or not she should push the play button. Did she really want to hear what might be on there? She asked her self. She had to. Shelby put the tip of her finger over the play button and hesitated. Finally, she pushed the button. The first dozen messages were from clients wanting to know when her office was going to be open. Another message was from an old friend of hers from high school. She said that she was going to be in town for a few months and wanted to catch up. Last, but not least, the last message was from Dallas.

As soon as she heard his voice, she pushed the stop button. Did she really want to hear what he had to say? Mom just looked at her and she knew she had to listen. Shelby pushed the play button again. He sounded like he was three sheets to the wind. He was drunk! He was slurring his words and Shelby couldn't tell what he was saying half the time. For the most part, she put it together. He was ranting about how if she married Grant; it would be the worst mistake she had ever made. He told her how much he loved her and that nothing would ever change that; not even if she *was* married to someone else. After all of that he finally said that he had to go to sleep and the phone went dead.

Wow!

"I knew it! I knew it!" Shelby started yelling.

"Shelby what is it?" Mom asked.

"Every time I have a run in with one of them; the other isn't too far behind. Why is that? Why can't they just leave me to my life and go on with theirs? I can't stand this!" She exclaimed as she slammed her fists on the table.

"Honey, I honestly don't know what to tell you. I've never in my life been put in a situation like this. His mom told me that he has been like this since he found out that you were engaged. They just don't know what to do with him." Mom answered, wrapping her arms around her. By this time, Shelby was bawling.

"That's the hardest part about all of this. I feel like it's my entire fault and there isn't anything I can do about it. How long do I have to be the bad guy?

How long do I have to pay for this?" Shelby asked wiping her eyes with the backs of her hands.

"It can't be easy having three men in love with you; especially when two of them have loved you for most of your life. I really wish there was something I could say or do to help you." Mom replied full of concern.

Shelby had a brilliant idea strike her. "I know what I can do. After Grant and I are married, we'll up root everything and move far away from here. Maybe we can move to San Francisco with CJ. This way I can still have family around but be far away from the other two." She said with some kind of enthusiasm. "That could work!"

"Now, let's not go to extremes here. I think *that* would be a huge mistake. Look at what you have built here. You have a thriving business and your family; it would be a terrible, terrible mistake to up root that." Mom replied quickly to stop her in her tracks.

"I know how stupid that would be. I'm just talking out of my head. It's an idea though, you have to admit." Shelby replied.

"Yeah, let's just leave it at a thought and move on to something else." Mom said.

"That sounds like a good idea. Looks like I need to call Leah. It'll be so good to see her. I haven't seen her in so long; high school, I think." Shelby said to her mother.

"Now that sounds like a good idea. I'm going to head home and see what your father has Grant doing. Why don't you go make your phone call and take a long hot bath? I bet that will help to ease your stress. With all of this set aside; we need to start planning a wedding. We can't forget about that." Mom said with a warm smile as she waved her finger teasingly at Shelby.

Where did she even begin to start? Shelby thought hopelessly. She grabbed a note pad and started making out a list of things that she knew were going to be needed. She grabbed the phone and walked up the stairs. She started filling the bath tub while she dialed the number Leah had left on her answering machine.

Leah was so excited to hear from her. She explained to Shelby all about what she had been up to over the years since high school and what she was doing now. Shelby in turn gave her the run down of what she had done with her life and the predicament she was in now, trying to plan a wedding. Leah's words were music in Shelby's ears. She had just gotten married a few months ago and said that she could help her with all of the arrangements. The two made plans to meet at the diner in town tomorrow to talk about it some more before they hung up.

While Shelby was in the tub, Grant finally made it home. She finished and climbed out. She was anxious to hear what kind of adventure he and her Dad had tonight. She walked into the bedroom to put on her pajamas while Grant explained. He wanted to take a shower also and as he did, he was talking the entire time. Just listening to his tale about him and her father warmed her heart. She was so happy that the two of them got along so well.

Chapter 11

"Hey, there stranger, long time no see." Shelby said to Leah as she walked toward the table where she was sitting.

"Well, hello to you to. You look good. How have you been these days?" Leah asked giving Shelby a quick hug.

"I'm doing really well, how about your self?" Shelby asked as she sat down.

"Enjoying marital bliss I must say! I can't believe how happy I am. I never thought in a million years that I would be this happy. So, let's hear all about you. I need some details so that I can figure out just how I can help you." Leah said excitedly.

"Wow, you get right to work. Well, I guess I should tell you a little about Grant." Shelby started and Leah cut her off with a quick hand in the air.

"Grant? Who's Grant?" Leah asked confused.

"Grant's my fiancé. Why did you react like that? Were you expecting something else?" Shelby asked. Leah seemed to be in shock.

"I wasn't expecting to hear the name Grant. I'm sorry Shelby; I thought I was going to hear Cole or Dallas." She answered.

"Why would you think that?" Shelby asked narrowing her eyes at Leah.

"I just assumed that if you ever got married, it would be to one of them. With the way you guys were in high school, I always thought that one day you would end up with one of them. I said something wrong. I'm so sorry. I still have that problem where my mouth opens before my brain reacts." She said as she tried to apologize.

"Leah its fine; I think this whole town expected that. The only one that never saw it was me. If you wouldn't mind, I would really like to get back to the wedding and not the subject at hand, if that's alright with you?" Shelby said.

"No problem. Maybe some day you can explain it to me but for right now, I won't push the issue. So, tell me about Grant." She said with anticipation.

"Well, I met Grant in college, he's British. We were in a lot of the same classes and over time, we became friends. I brought him home for Christmas one year because his family was out of the country and my parents' fell in love with him." Shelby explained.

"So you guys have been together ever since?" Leah asked.

"No, it wasn't until a year ago or so that we started seeing each other. After college we kind of lost contact and then we ran into each other again. That's when things started coming together for us. He was staying with me and on Christmas he proposed." She explained.

"Wow that sounds pretty juicy." Leah said.

"There hasn't been too much that's been juicy; as you call it. We just took it slow and fell in love. CJ took awhile to get used to him but now you would swear that they were brothers. They get along so good." Shelby replied.

"Speaking of CJ; how is your brother?" Leah asked sheepishly.

"I was wondering how long it would take for that subject to come along. He's doing really well. He loves his football. You know that." Shelby answered.

"Where did he end up going?" Leah asked.

"He was drafted by a team in San Francisco. He loves it out there. He said the only thing that he doesn't like was how much it rains." Shelby said with a grin.

"Is he going to be coming back for the wedding?" Leah asked with hesitation.

"Yes, he is as a matter of fact. Why are you asking? I thought you were happily married?" She asked inquisitively.

"I am! It doesn't hurt to check up on old friends does it?" Leah asked with a devious grin.

"No, not at all, but is that as old friends or old flames?" Shelby asked with a slight laugh.

"Oh, you're funny. Ok, on to the next subject please. We need to make a list of things you want for the wedding. Now the first thing is to figure out where it's going to take place. The venue is everything. Do you have an idea for that?" she asked.

"I was thinking about the big hall down by the park. If the weather is nice, I would like to have the ceremony outside. If the weather turns bad, we can move it into the hall with the reception taking place right after. How does that sound?" Shelby asked about her idea.

"That actually sounds really good. We need to call the hall and get it reserved and tell them what we would like to do with the park. If we have to move it into the hall, we could still do some kind of decorations in the park. This would help to make the event stand out more. Sound good so far?" she asked. Leah was getting very excited about this.

"That sounds great! So, now that we have that part figured out what's next?" Shelby asked.

"For now, that's it. Once we have the hall and park secured; we can start on everything else. You need to get the invitations laid out, and make out a guest list. With the list we can tell the hall about how many people we will be expecting." She said.

"That's what I'll get started on then. You know, you seem to have this down pat pretty well. Have you ever thought about being a professional wedding planner? I think you would be really good at it." Shelby pointed out.

"You know, that sounds pretty good; Leah Palmer, wedding planner extraordinaire. I like the sound of that. Now you've given me something to think about. Thanks!" Leah replied excitedly.

"I didn't realize how much time had gone by. I have to get back to the office. Do you have the hall under control?" Shelby asked as she stood from the table.

"Yep, just let me take care of that. You get back to work and I'll give you a call later." Leah replied.

"Sounds good, I'll talk to you in a bit." Shelby answered as she walked away.

Leah is going to be a *huge* help. Between her and her mother; they should have everything pretty much taken care of. Now, Shelby was getting really excited! Planning all of this is going to be so much fun!

That night when Shelby got home, she told Grant all about her meeting with Leah. Grant said that what ever she wanted; do not hesitate to get it. If there was anything she needed his advice on, just ask. Wasn't he great! He was so laid back and calm about everything.

Leah called later that night to let Shelby know that she had the hall reserved. She said she had to fight with the owner on the date but after she told him that money was no object; it was theirs. Shelby made sure to tell her not to be telling everyone that money was no object. If she did that; this wedding was going to cost a fortune! Grant had never had a problem with money but Shelby would rather keep the cost to a minimum. She was not one to blow it all on something; even if it was her own wedding.

A month passed and the wedding was getting closer. Everything seemed to be coming together quite nicely. They have figured on having at least a hundred people attending. They didn't expect that many; mainly friends and close family but they wanted to make sure they had extra for just in case purposes.

Grant and Shelby had to make a trip to the bakery and order the cake. Shelby was just happy that the bakery here in town made beautiful wedding cakes. Both of them were trying to keep as much of the planning locally so that the community could prosper from their big day as well. It might not be much, but every little bit helped. As they were standing in the bakery looking at all of the cakes; someone walked in the door behind them.

"You had better order something really good. That's the only reason I'm coming to this wedding in this first place. It's just for the cake; and the food; well maybe a hot girl or two!" A man said with a laugh.

"I should've known that you would find us where the food was!" Shelby answered back. It was CJ! "What are you doing home so early?" she asked.

"Mom told me that poor Grant here was stuck with all these women planning your wedding. I thought maybe I had better get back here and save the poor bloke." CJ replied with a laugh as he put his arm around Grant.

"I should've known. He isn't going anywhere until he helps me with this cake." She replied pointing at Grant and giving him a teasing evil glare.

"Hey, don't point at me." Grant said holding his hands in the air in defeat.

"That's no problem, but as soon as you're done; we're out of here." CJ answered with a grin.

Grant and Shelby finally agreed on the flavor, icing, and decorations on the cake. It will be a four tier, vanilla cake with raspberry filling. It will have vanilla frosting with red roses and a lighted fountain on the bottom cake. It was so gorgeous, Shelby thought. Even her brother said that it sounded good.

Of course as soon as they were done, CJ kidnapped Grant and they took off. Shelby had no idea what he was up to. She really didn't know if she wanted to either. It couldn't be a bachelor party. They still had a few weeks left. Male bonding seems to come to mind, she thought laughing to her self.

Shelby walked out of the bakery and decided to walk down the street to her office. The weather was shaping up nicely and it was a beautiful spring day for a walk. As she walked along the street, she took in the sights and sounds of the town. She listened to the birds singing and saw that some of the trees had the beginnings of buds growing. If the weather stayed like this; her wedding should turn out quite nicely.

She walked along a little further down the street when she heard the door to the corner bar open. She happened to glance across the street to find Dallas being shoved against the wall of the bar by some woman. He started laughing then wrapped his arm around her. He was walking like he was stoned drunk. He stumbled a few more times until he finally fell to the ground. The longer Shelby watched them, the madder she got. She had to do something! She couldn't stand to watch this go on. It was turning her stomach with every second that passed. Shelby grabbed her cell phone and tried calling CJ. She thought if anyone might be able to get him home in one piece, it would be him. Damn voice mail! God only knows where he is! She thought helplessly.

"I guess I'll have to do this my self." She muttered.

Shelby half walked and half jogged back to her office where her truck was parked out behind. She fired it up and drove down the street to where Dallas was lying on the sidewalk slumped half way up the side of the building. When she stopped in front of him, she slammed on the brakes and slid the truck sideways. The woman that was with him started yelling at her for acting like an idiot. She sounded as drunk as Dallas acted.

"Give him to me!" Shelby yelled at her as she wrapped her arm around him to lift him from the ground.

"Wha-da-ya tink you doin'?" The woman asked mumbling her words with a slur.

"I'm taking him home. Get out of the way!" Shelby yelled at her again.

"He's goin' home whif me! He's goin' to teach me how to… (Hiccup)…pay football." She replied between burps and hiccups.

"I don't think so! Not tonight or any other night as far as I'm concerned." Shelby blurted as she pushed Dallas up into the truck.

"Who-da-ya tink you are? Ya can't juss take him away from me." The woman said pulling on the back of Shelby's jacket.

"Watch me! Get off!" Shelby said pushing her away. "I'm a good friend that is going to make sure he makes it home and you should do the same."

"Hey, I know you. Ya're the girl that broke his heart. He showed me pitcures of you." She said pointing at Shelby and almost stumbling to the ground.

That was enough! Shelby poked her head inside the door of the bar and yelled for someone to come get the drunken woman. She had no idea who she was and she had never seen her around here before. Jason, one of the guys Shelby went to high school with was working; thank god, she thought.

"Jason, have you ever seen this woman before?" Shelby asked him when he came to her aid.

"Not till today. Dallas seems to bring in a different woman every day lately; probably from Ft. Wayne." He replied trying to steady the drunken woman.

"Why didn't you cut them off?" Shelby asked.

"Shelby, they're paying customers; until my boss says otherwise, I have to keep serving them; my hands are tied." He explained.

"Can you figure out where she lives or something; I have to get him out of here." She asked Jason.

"Go, I'll find some way of getting her home even if I have to call the town cop." Jason answered.

"Thank you."

"Not a problem and by the way; congratulations, I heard you were getting married." He said politely with a smile.

"Thanks." Shelby said as she walked around the front of her truck. "Maybe I'll send you an invitation."

"Please do. I'll be there." He answered with a wave good bye.

Shelby climbed into the truck and shifted it into drive. She headed straight for Dallas's parents house. It was the only place she could think of to take him. She had no idea of where he had been staying or what he had been doing as of late. Now she had a really bad idea of *what* he had been doing. Along the way, he started talking but she knew he had no idea what he was saying.

"I don't know who you are, but you must be an angel. You look just like my angel Shelby. Are you Shelby?" he asked before he passed out again.

Shelby didn't answer him. Thank the good Lord that she had electric locks in her truck. He kept trying to open the door as she drove down the street! She had to get him home and fast. She pulled into his parents' driveway and didn't see their car anywhere. She did see CJ's blazer sitting in front of Mom and Dad's.

Shelby jumped out of the truck and made sure she took the keys with her. She ran next door and found CJ and Grant.

"CJ, you have to help me." Shelby said in a panic, breathlessly.

"What's wrong?" He asked with a look of confusion.

"Dallas is next door in my truck in his parents' driveway. He's drunk as a skunk. I need you to help me get him into the house." She explained.

"Let's go! Grant, come give me a hand." CJ shouted to Grant as he ran out of the house.

The three of them ran for Shelby's truck, and somehow, Dallas had managed to get the door open. He fell out and was lying on the ground trying to crawl across the yard. CJ told Shelby where the spare key was hidden for the house and told her to get the door opened. CJ and Grant picked Dallas up off of the ground and dragged him into the house. As soon as they had made it through the door; Dallas said that he had to throw up. CJ and Grant made a bee line for the bathroom and planted his face over the toilet. Shelby had to walk back outside. She couldn't stand to see him like this.

CJ yelled for her and told her to fill the kitchen sink full of ice cold water and make a full pot of coffee. When they had finished with Dallas in the bathroom they drug him into the kitchen.

"Both of you stand back." CJ said after he and Grant had Dallas positioned over the kitchen sink.

"What are you going to do to him?" Shelby asked frantically.

"I'm going to wake him up real quick and he's going to jerk." He explained.

Shelby stood off to the side trying to get the coffee started but she was shaking so badly that she could hardly hold onto the pot.

CJ grabbed the back of Dallas's head and plunged it into the ice cold water. All of a sudden, they heard him yell and someone hit the floor. Shelby spun around to find Dallas lying on the floor. CJ told Grant to help him get Dallas back up so that he could do it again.

They did this about three more times before they could finally get him to come around. CJ and Grant sat him at the kitchen table, and by this time, Shelby had the coffee made. CJ tried to get him to drink a mug full. Shelby was so scared. She thought for sure that they were going to have to take him to the hospital for alcohol poising. After a few minutes, he finally started drinking the coffee. CJ said he would stay with him until someone came home. Shelby had never seen someone that bad off before.

Shelby and Grant were getting ready to leave when CJ stopped her at the front door.

"He wants to talk to you." He said her.

"CJ, he's in no shape to talk to anyone." Shelby replied.

"I agree, but just go talk to him." CJ said.

"Fine."

Shelby walked into the kitchen not knowing what she would see. She just wanted to die. She couldn't believe this was Dallas. She could tell that he had been drinking for a long time now. He wasn't that big, muscular football player she had known for most of her life. Not anymore. It made her sick to her stomach.

He was slumped over the table with his hands just barely holding onto the coffee mug in front of him. He smelled like a brewery and his face was pale and sunken. His hair looked as if it hadn't been brushed in days.

"CJ said that you wanted to see me?" She asked in a low tone.

"I just wanted to say thank you." Dallas said lifting his head from the table to look at her. His eyes were blood shot.

"You're welcome. I hope you feel better." Shelby replied softly.

"I don't think that's going to happen any time soon." He said with a deep sigh.

"I wish there was something I could do to help you. I'm sure you'll feel better after you get some rest." she answered sympathetically.

"Maybe, who knows? Shelby, I miss you. Can you fix that for me?" Dallas asked with tears in his eyes as he wiped at his face.

"Dallas; please don't. You're not in any condition to get into this conversation right now and I don't have the strength to." Shelby answered.

Shelby wanted to cry right then and there. She could feel the tears start to well in her eyes.

"You're right; you *are* right. I think I need to go lay down now. I'm not feeling so good." He replied laying his head back down on the table.

"I think that would be best. You don't look good at all." She said. He didn't; he looked almost green.

Shelby called for CJ to come get him and lay him down on the couch. She knew this way he would be close enough to the bathroom and CJ could keep a better eye on him. Grant and Shelby walked out to her truck and pulled it over to her Mom and Dad's.

"I want to hang out here for awhile until CJ comes home." She said to Grant.

"That's fine." He replied putting his arm around her.

When they got into the house, Mom and Dad wanted to know what was going on. Shelby explained the whole situation to them and how she had found Dallas in the shape he was. At first, she was a little worried that Grant might be upset over it all but he was really supportive. He told her that she did the right thing. She sure hoped he was right.

After pacing the floor in the living room for about an hour, CJ finally came home.

"How is he? Is he ok?" Shelby asked with concern.

"He's alright. His mom is watching over him right now. That poor woman is beside herself. She just doesn't know what to do with him anymore." CJ replied as he shook his head in disbelief.

"I just don't understand how he let himself get like this. I would've never pictured Dallas like this." Shelby said.

"Come on Shelby; we all know why he's like this." CJ said snidely as he looked her dead in the eye.

"Now you wait one damn minute!" Shelby shouted at CJ, immediately going on the defensive. "I'm sick of everyone blaming me. Dallas is how old? He's not a little kid. He's done this to himself because of his own stupidity, not me. He needs to grow up!" She replied, her voice rising. She was getting madder by the second.

"She's right CJ. None of this is her fault. Dallas is a big boy and can take care of himself. It's just a shame to see him do it like this. Is he even going to be able to play football next year?" Mom asked.

"From what I've heard; his injuries have healed. He wasn't able to finish the season but he should be able to play this year. The only problem is, if he keeps going down the path he's on now, they'll cancel his contract for sure. The league has enough problems with players dealing with drugs and alcohol; they sure don't want anymore. They're getting stricter about that every year." CJ explained.

"Maybe it was a good thing that Shelby found him tonight then." Mom started to say.

"Why do you say that?" Shelby asked her.

"Maybe he'll be so embarrassed because of the shape you found him in; he'll wake up. Some times that's all it takes." She explained.

"I think it's going to take a miracle for him to get back to where he was." Shelby replied.

"You never know, honey. The Lord works in mysterious ways. Maybe *you* finding him; was just the miracle he needed. Only time will tell." Mom answered.

"I hope you're right." She replied.

After their discussion and knowing Dallas was going to be alright, Grant and Shelby left for home. She wanted to go home and get some sleep. With work, the wedding planning and now Dallas tonight; she thought she had as much as she could take for one day.

"You really care about him don't you?" Grant asked her quietly.

"Who? Dallas?" She asked confused.

"Who else would I be talking about?" he asked with a hint of jealousy.

"He's my friend; of course I worry about him." Shelby replied.

"I wonder sometimes if it's more than just worry." He said dryly.

"Grant, I've explained everything to you before. There is nothing else I can tell you. Dallas is a very dear friend to me, and yes, I do care very much about what happens to him; but you have to stop and think about something else; I'm engaged to you. We're getting married in just a few more weeks. How much more reassurance do you need then that? I love *you*." She explained.

She knew exactly where he was going with this and now he was starting to aggravate her.

"I know and I'm sorry. I know that you guys have a lot of history, and from time to time, it just gets the best of me. Please forgive me for being an idiot," he replied as he knelt down on the floor on his knees begging for forgiveness.

"Why do you have to be such a goof? Get up. This is just one of the many things I love about you." Shelby said with a laugh.

"What's that?" he asked as he stood up.

"Even in a terrible situation; you always know how to make me laugh." She replied.

"Oh, yeah, well I do have other talents as well." He said.

"And what would that be?" She asked with a devious grin.

"I know how to make you melt." He replied wrapping his arms around her.

Grant knew the only way to take her mind off of Dallas was to put her mind on him. He pulled her tightly against him, leaned his head down, and gave her a very soft, slow, passionate kiss.

She hated it when he was right!

"I think that worked." She said with a smile as she pulled away.

"I knew it would." He replied with a grin. "Alright, I think we had better get some sleep now *or* I might do something I'll regret."

"We wouldn't want anything like that to happen, now would we." Shelby answered with a teasing smile.

They walked upstairs to the bedroom and changed for bed. After they both were settled, Shelby kissed him good night and turned off the lights. Within a few minutes, Grant was lying there snoring softly. As for Shelby, she tossed and turned all night. She just couldn't sleep. She had way too much on her mind. One minute she would be thinking about Dallas, the next about wedding plans, and the next thought would be about work. She was ready to pull her hair out!

Please, just let me fall asleep! She pleaded with her self.

After a few hours of fighting it, she finally decided to go to the kitchen and make some tea. She really didn't like tea that much but a cup here or there was good for the nerves. Leah had told her that she started drinking *a lot* of tea when she was doing all of her planning. It helped her immensely. At this point, Shelby was ready to try anything.

She poured water into the tea kettle and sat it on the stove. While that was heating, she looked through the fridge and cabinets trying to find something to snack on. As she dug through one of the cabinets, she ran across an old photo. How in the world did this get here? She thought to her self. It was a picture of her, CJ, Dallas, and Cole. It was a graduation picture from high school.

She stared intently at the picture and started to think back to that day. She could remember it like it was yesterday. That had been one of the best days of her life.

About that time, the tea kettle began to whistle. She was so lost in thought that it scared her half to death! She even jumped.

Shelby shut the burner off and poured water into her coffee cup. She placed a tea bag into the hot steaming water and walked over to the table and sat down. She was still looking at the picture. They were all standing beside each other with their arms over one another's shoulders laughing. They were in front of the high school in their caps and gowns. Things were so much simpler back then. Well, at least she thought they were.

Shelby sat at the table sipping her tea and studying the picture when she felt a hand touch her shoulder. She turned her head to find Grant standing there.

"Why didn't you say some thing? You scared the hell out of me!" She yelped at him.

"I'm sorry; I didn't mean to scare you. I heard a noise down here so I came to investigate." He said calmly.

"Its fine, I'm sorry, I shouldn't have yelled at you like that. You just startled me; that's all." She said catching her breath.

"What are you doing down here so late? What's that that you're looking at?" he asked inquisitively looking at the picture she held.

"I couldn't sleep so I thought some tea might help. I found this picture up in the cabinet. I'm still trying to figure out how it got there." She answered.

"Can I see it?" he asked.

"Sure, it's a picture from when I graduated from high school." She replied handing him the picture.

"Wow, you guys must have really had fun back then." He said looking at the picture.

"Yeah, we had some good times." She said as she walked to the sink to put her cup down. Grant laid the picture down on the table.

"Are you ready to come back to bed?" he asked.

"Yeah, I feel a little sleepier now. Hopefully the tea did the trick." She answered.

The two of them walked upstairs and went back to bed. It must have worked because Shelby was asleep in no time.

Chapter 12

From that night on, the days flew by in a haze. The wedding was coming down to the wire now. They only had three days left. There were still all sorts of little details left to finish and Grant had to be in Ft. Wayne at midnight tomorrow to pick up his family at the airport.

In other news, from what Shelby had heard; Dallas was doing a lot better. He was getting his life straightened out. She had been told that after his last incident, it finally scared him half to death. He still didn't remember anything from that night. That's what scared him the most. Shelby really hoped that he got his life back on track now, for his own sake.

Leah and Shelby had to be at the hall later today to finish what little needed to be done. They hadn't really had much to do. Leah has over seen most of it and the caterers have taken care of the rest. Of course, Mom was there all of the time making sure that they were putting everything together the way it was supposed to be. She's been watching over everyone like a hawk. Nothing was going to go wrong if Shelby's mother had anything to do with it.

So far the weather forecast was holding out. The temperature is supposed to be high seventies to low eighties for the big day. Grant and Shelby decided that as long as it stayed that way, they would have the wedding ceremony in the park and then move to the hall for the reception. So far, everything has gone exactly as planned.

CJ has big plans tonight for Grants bachelor party. Shelby couldn't even begin to imagine what he had up his sleeve. Thank God his parents weren't flying in till tomorrow night. Knowing her brother; Grant wasn't going to be in any shape to go anywhere in the morning. This should be very interesting, Shelby thought coyly.

Leah and Shelby's mother threw her a big bridal shower the other day. It was amazing. They went to a little restaurant here in town. They had champagne and a beautiful cake. The food was just out of this world! Friends from all over town were there. The presents ranged from perfumes all the way to lingerie. Half of the clothes made Shelby blush just looking at them. Her face had turned the same color as her hair! To be honest; she didn't think that she and Grant would have any problems on their wedding night. Even thinking about it now was causing her cheeks to flush.

It couldn't get here fast enough, Shelby thought. The sexual tension between them was getting worse every passing day. Shelby really didn't know how they were going to be able to hold out till then. The other day, things in the kitchen got heated so much that they had made it as far as getting all of their clothes off, down to their underwear before they finally stopped; well, Grant had the sense to stop it. Shelby didn't think she could have.

"Shelby, come on, you know we have to wait till after the wedding." Grant pleaded with her breathing hard.

"Grant, I can't wait that long! I can't take this anymore!" She pleaded with him breathlessly.

"I promise you, as soon as the ceremony is over; we're sneaking off somewhere and we're *not* waiting. I don't care if we have to consummate this marriage in a limo!" he said breathing even harder.

"How; the reception is right were the wedding is being held?" She asked confused.

"Trust me; there'll be so much going on, no one will miss us for awhile." He replied putting his clothes back on.

"Is that a promise?" She asked with a deep breath.

"That is *definitely* a promise." He said kissing her again.

That was two days ago.

Well, everything in town had been accomplished as much as they were going to be, for the time being. The only things left now were for the caterers to bring in the food on Saturday and the cake to be delivered. The hall was set, the park was set, and now, Shelby's nerves were stating to run wild. She was so excited but at the same time; she felt like she was about to jump out of her skin!

This was really happening. In less than forty eight hours, she was getting married. She would be Mrs. Grant Summers. Oh, the more she thought about it; the more she couldn't breathe. The anticipation of Grant's promise of what would take place after the wedding was the only thing that kept her sane right now.

The list was gone over and over, making sure they hadn't missed a thing. Shelby went home so that she could see Grant for a few minutes before CJ came to pick him up for his bachelor party.

"I see you finally made it home." Grant when Shelby walked into the house.

"Yep, here I am." Shelby replied wrapping her arms around him.

"Did you have a productive day?" he asked.

"I think so. Everything should be perfect as long as there are no last minute problems popping up." she answered.

"Good, there won't be. Our day will be spectacular, you'll see." He said as he kissed her.

"I don't know, that didn't really convince me. I think you had better try again." She said with a sly grin.

"Oh, you need more?" he replied with a big smile kissing her again. They kissed for a few minutes longer when Shelby heard someone pull into the driveway.

"He really has bad timing. Couldn't he have waited for at least a few more minutes?" She asked with a sigh. She knew that it was CJ.

"It'll be ok. Just think about this; in forty eight hours we will be able to do this for the rest of our lives." Grant said comforting her.

"I know, I know, but it feels *so* good right now." She answered with a whine to her voice.

"Are you sure you're ok with this?" Grant asked.

"Sure, why wouldn't I be?" She asked.

"Some women don't like the thought of bachelor parties."

"Well then, you had better be glad that I'm not some of those women." She replied kissing him again. About that time, CJ walked in.

"Oh, come on you two. Can't you guys wait till you're married? I mean, there are other people in the room." CJ said as if he was disgusted. They both just laughed at him.

"It's our house. You could walk back out on the porch if you don't like what you see." Shelby said to him with a laugh.

"Dude, are you ready? I don't think I can take much more of this." CJ asked Grant shaking his head.

"Yeah, just let me grab my jacket." He said to CJ. "I'll see *you* tomorrow. Don't sit up worrying either. Take tonight and relax." Grant said to Shelby.

"I won't, I trust you." She said giving him a hug and a very passionate kiss. "CJ, are you sure we have to go? I think I can have just as much fun here. I love you!" Grant said as CJ pulled him out the door.

"I love you too!" Shelby yelled out the door.

She stood in the doorway watching the two of them leave. She couldn't help but laugh. Her life couldn't possibly get any better than this. She had a brother that she loved very much and that would do anything for her; and a man that loved her to no end. She loved him just as much. She never knew that one person could have feelings like this for another. She had always dreamed of what it would be like, but until you actually experienced it for yourself; there was no way to describe it.

Although, Shelby thought she had felt like this one other time in her life; maybe not as intense, but the memory of Cole and the night he had stayed in her house and what almost happened between them, flooded her mind like someone had blown out a dam in her brain. Then there was the night in the hotel with Dallas. Shaking the memories from her mind, Shelby couldn't think about that right now, not ever again.

She was marring Grant, not Cole or Dallas. Thinking about them and what might have happened, didn't matter anymore. Grant was the only man that mattered. Grant was going to be her husband.

Now, Shelby had to figure out what to do for the rest of the night. She had some left over food in the fridge from lunch today and she thought she would go take a very long hot bubble bath. She poured her self a glass of wine and walked up to the bathroom to start the tub. She poured some bubble bath into the tub and let it fill. She lit candles and turned off the lights. She went to the bedroom, took off her clothes, and put on her robe; then the phone rang. Her first thought was that it was CJ or Grant calling. She looked at the caller ID and it said unknown. She wondered who it could be.

She answered the phone but there was no one there. She could hear someone breathing but they wouldn't say anything. She kept saying hello over and over until the line finally went dead. That was strange, she thought. She never got calls from an unknown number. Well, if it's something important, they'll call back.

Shelby walked back into the bathroom and climbed into the tub. Wow, she had really gotten the water hot! If this didn't help her to relax, nothing would. After she settled in, she went over every detail that was left for the wedding. So far, she couldn't come up with anything that had been forgotten.

For some reason, her mind started to drift. She started to think back on the night that she, Cole, and Dallas were in Ft. Wayne together. She just kept seeing Coles face. She thought she hadn't seen it then, but now, she remembered the look he had in his eyes that night. He really didn't pay much attention to his date. He was always looking at her. Why didn't she catch it that night? She asked her self.

While she thought about it, the next thing she remember hearing was the phone ringing again. She woke up to the water being ice cold. Gee, I guess I fell asleep, she thought stupidly. She was more exhausted than she thought. She looked at the phone and it was that unknown again. She answered and of course there was no one there. She said into the phone that if they had nothing better to do than make prank calls they had might as well give it up; the line went dead.

"That just goes to show that some people have nothing better to do." She said out loud to her self.

Shelby climbed out of the ice cold water, dried off and got dressed. She blew out all of the candles went to bed. The next couple of days were going to be very hectic so she definitely needed to get a good night of sleep for once. It didn't take long till she was out like a light.

What Shelby didn't know was that across town, at a gas station, a man had called her house from a pay phone wanting desperately to hear her voice. In forty eight hours, Shelby was going to marry another man, and he was going to lose her forever. Hanging the phone up for the last time, tears filled his eyes, and Dallas knew that no matter who Shelby was with, he would love her for the rest of his life and the sound of her voice would be all that he had left of her.

When Shelby woke up the next morning, she noticed that Grant hadn't made it home. She wondered if they might have stayed in Ft. Wayne last night. Maybe she had better go check the answering machine. They might have called and left her a message. You would think that if they had called, she would've heard the phone ring. "Who am I kidding?" She said to her self. After she hit the bed last night, she was dead to the world. She wouldn't have heard a bomb go off!

She got out of bed and slipped on her robe. She walked down to the living room to check the machine and got the crap scared out of her. To her surprise, there laid Grant sprawled out across the couch! He still had his shoes and his jacket on. He also had a garter wrapped around his head and a note pinned to his jacket. He looked like a kid that had been sent home from kindergarten with a note stuck to him so that his parents would get it.

Shelby slowly crept over and slid the note from his jacket. She was trying to be as quite as possible so that she wouldn't wake him. After she had the note in her hand, she tip toed into the kitchen to read it. It was from CJ and it read:

> *Sis,*
> *Grant was out of it by the time we made it home so I put him on the couch. There was no way, I was about to carry him up the stairs. Don't worry, he might look worse than what he is. He'll definitely need something for a hang over. He had a good time and yes he was a good boy. See ya later.*
> *Love, CJ*

This had to be the funniest thing she had ever witnessed! This was just too good to be true. Well, I guess he won't be up for awhile, she thought, laughing to her self. She had to go over to Mom and Dad's and see if CJ was awake. This should be a *really* interesting story.

Shelby ran up the stairs to get changed and snuck out of the house as quietly as she could. She didn't want to wake Grant as she left. She climbed into the truck and let it coast out of the driveway. She drove straight to her parents' house. Parking in front of the house, she snuck around to the back door. When she walked into the kitchen, Mom was already pouring cups of coffee. Before Shelby had a chance to say a word, Mom sat the cups down on the table, looked at her and grinned.

"I thought you might want this."

"How did you know it was me? You had your back turned when I came in the door." Shelby asked confused.

"Haven't you ever heard the expression that mothers have eyes in the back of their heads? Besides, I heard your truck slide to a stop in front of the house." Mom answered with a laugh.

"Oh, well, that explains it. Is CJ awake yet?" Shelby asked anxiously.

"No not yet. I'd say he'll probably be asleep for awhile. I think he came in around six this morning." She replied sitting down at the table.

"I was hoping he was awake. He left me this note that he stuck to Grant. I had to hear what all had happened." Shelby said as she handed the note to Mom.

"I bet that was a site to see when you got up this morning." Mom said with a chuckle.

"It was. I wanted to burst out laughing so badly. I knew if I did though, I'd probably wake him up. That's why I snuck out of the house and came here." Shelby answered.

"Well, I'm sure your brother didn't let things get out of control. About the first time he caught Grant doing something stupid, the poor boy would get his bell rang for sure." She said with a giggle.

"I know; I wasn't worried. I trust Grant. He wouldn't do anything to hurt me. I thought I might get to hear a good story though." Shelby replied.

"I don't think that boy has a bad bone in his body. You two will have a very happy life together; I'm sure of it. I just feel sorry for him." Mom said solemnly.

"What do you mean by that?" She asked.

Shelby thought she was talking about her.

"Because, only god knows what your brother put the boy through last night. I guess you could say that he has been officially *initiated* into the family." Mom answered with a joking laugh.

"I never thought of that. Oh, dear lord, he might not wake up for three days!" Shelby said laughing.

"Can you see all of us trying to explain to the guests why the wedding has been postponed for a couple of extra days; *I'm sorry, but the groom is in a slight coma at the moment. He needs to sleep off his bachelor party and we assume he should be raring to go in about three days. Please feel free to come back at that time.*" Mom said. The more she talked; the more Shelby laughed. She thought she was going to fall out of her chair!

"Oh, no, I don't think he really knew what he was getting himself into! Now *I'm* starting to feel sorry for him and *I'm* the one marring him." Shelby said laughing even harder now.

"Oh, honey, I don't think you could have found a better person. Your Dad and I are so proud to have Grant for a son-in-law. He is such a fine man. I have to be honest though; at one point in time, I thought you were going to end up marrying one of the local boys. That was something that scared me." Mom said becoming more serious.

"If something like that would have happened; why would that scare you? I know who you're talking about. Would one of them have really been that bad?" Shelby asked soberly.

Mom was talking about Cole and Dallas and Shelby wanted to know her honest opinion about them.

"Don't get me wrong, their not bad boys. That's not what concerns me. What does, on the other hand, is what they have done with their lives. They both have become really big football stars and with that, fame comes with it. I just don't think with the way all of you had grown up, if it would have lasted. Sometimes being such an influence in the public eye can put a huge strain on a marriage like that. We see it everyday, in the papers and on TV. I never wanted to see you put through that kind of situation." Mom explained to her.

"I understand. Well, that's one thing you won't have to worry about. Have you heard anything about either one of them lately? Every now and then I feel a little bit better if I know their doing ok. Does that make any sense?" Shelby asked with a hint of concern.

"Of course it does. You wouldn't be you if you weren't keeping an eye on your friends. The last thing I heard about Dallas was that he was doing really well. He quit drinking and hanging out in bars. He's been back in training so that he can get ready for the new football season in the fall." She started explaining.

"Well that's good. I'm glad to hear it." Shelby said.

"As for Cole, I guess after the investigation, he was fined by the league and has to sit out the first three games of the season." Mom said.

"Wow, I wondered what ever happened with that." Shelby replied.

"Plus, there's something else. I didn't know if you had heard anything about this or not." Mom started to say.

"I haven't heard anything about anyone in awhile."

"From what his mom told me, he's due to get married in about three months." She said watching the expression on Shelby's face change.

Shelby had just taken a mouth full of her coffee and spit it all over the table.

"What!" She yelped in shock.

"I knew that was going to shock you." Mom replied.

"Holy crap; I wasn't expecting that! Oh wow! I don't know what to say.

I always thought that between him and Dallas, Dallas would be the first one to get married. I guess I was wrong. When did you find this out?" Shelby asked with curiosity.

"Actually, I found out about it not long after you had come back from meeting Grant's parents. I think it was just a couple of weeks after that." Mom answered sipping from her coffee mug studying Shelby over the rim of her cup.

The first thought that popped into Shelby's mind......Is he doing this because *she* was getting married? It was too much of a coincidence that he got engaged right after she had run into him at the airport. Shelby was speechless.

Mom couldn't help but wonder what was running through her daughter's mind. She could tell from the expression on her face that this news was disturbing her. What she really wanted to know was; how did she feel about it?

"How does that make you feel?" Mom asked cautiously.

Shelby stood up from the table and looked out the kitchen window that faced Cole's parents' house. At the moment, she didn't know how she felt.

"I'm happy for him, I guess. I'm surprised, but if he's happy, that's all that matters, doesn't it?" Shelby replied looking down at the diamond engagement ring on her finger.

"Does it make you have second thoughts?"

"No. I love Grant more than words can ever begin to express. It does make me realize, looking back at the past, if I had wanted to be with Cole, I could have. I'm happy with the direction my life has taken. If things in the past had never happened, I might not have met Grant and I might not be where I am today." Shelby said.

"And where is that?" Mom asked not only to reassure her self but for Shelby's sake as well.

"In twenty four hours, I will be Mrs. Grant Summers and I would not change that for anything in this world. That's exactly where I *will* be and exactly where I *want* to be." Shelby said as she turned to look at her mother.

"I'm happy to hear you say that. Grant's a very lucky man." Mom replied as she stood from the table and hugged Shelby.

Both women sat back down at the table to finish their coffee.

"I still can't get over this though. Who's the woman he's marring?" Shelby asked curiously.

"I guess some model or maybe she's an actress. I'm not sure but she has something to do with Hollywood." Mom answered shaking her head.

"What does his parent's say about all of this?" Shelby asked.

"His dad thinks it's just the greatest thing. Of course, he's a man, he would. His mom on the other hand is very skeptical about it. She thinks it's just a publicity thing to get over the investigation. Plus, the fact that she said she can't stand the girl. Who knows why but all we can do is pray that it works out for them; you know?" she explained.

"Isn't that something? Well, I guess it's all good news then. They both seem to have their lives back in order." Shelby said with a forced smile.

About that time, CJ was standing in the kitchen doorway. "What are you two in here yakking about?" CJ said as he walked into the kitchen.

"Just stuff; what are you doing awake? I thought you would sleep all day." Shelby asked with a giggle.

"I was trying to until I heard the two you down here laughing. What was so funny?" He asked trying to wipe the sleep from his eyes.

"We were just talking about what poor Grant must have gone through last night," Mom said with a giggle.

"What poor Grant went through? I'll tell the both of you right now; that man's an animal." CJ replied.

"Why, what did he do?" Shelby asked.

"Oh, no you don't; you're not going to hound me about your soon-to-be husband's activities last night. As the old saying goes; what happens at a bachelor party, stays at the bachelor party. If you want details you'll have to talk to him." CJ said holding his hands up.

"Can you at least tell me if there was anything bad that I *should* know about?" Shelby asked glaring at him.

"I know what you're implying and no there wasn't anything like that. We just had fun." CJ answered.

"That's all the details I need to know. I trust Grant." Shelby answered.

"That's one thing for sure; he's a really good guy." CJ said. Coming from her brother, that means a lot.

"Well, I guess I should call Leah and see what's on the agenda for today. Do you know of anything, Mom?" Shelby asked her.

"There shouldn't be too much. Your dress is hanging in your old room upstairs. You *are* coming back here to stay for the night aren't you?" Mom asked.

"Yeah I am; I have to get some things from the house first. Are you staying at my house tonight with Grant, CJ? He has to go to the airport tonight to pick up his parents'." Shelby asked.

"As far as I know that's where I'll be. What time does he have to be at the airport?" he asked.

"I think he has to be there at midnight." She answered.

"I have some other things I have to do tonight, but after that; I'll be at your house. I won't be able to go with him to the airport though." He replied.

"That's fine; he knows his way around pretty well now. He shouldn't have any problems getting there. Well, I guess that's it for now. I'm going to head back to the house and see if he's alive yet. I will see you guys later." Shelby said as she stood from the table and put her jacket on.

Shelby parked in front of her house and stared at it for a few minutes. She loved this house. She had bought it with her own hard earned money and now it was going to belong to her and her husband. She had to smile when she thought about the idea. She had bought this house with the intentions that one day she would have her own family to raise in it. In twenty four hours, she would be taking the first step in making that dream a reality. She would have the husband that she loved with all her heart and the thought of having kids with Grant made her dream even better.

When Shelby walked into the house, there was a message on the answering machine. It was Grant's mother calling to let them know that their flight had been delayed and that they wouldn't be getting into Ft. Wayne until three a.m. instead of midnight. Grant was still passed out on the couch. She put her ear down to his face to make sure he was still breathing. She didn't think he had moved an inch since the time she had left till the time she had came home.

Shelby went to her bedroom and gathered up the things she would need to take with her to her parent's house for the night. She wanted to get that taken care of before anything else happened to come along. She had everything packed into her suitcase and carried it down to the living room. She sat it beside the front door and heard a noise come from the kitchen. It must be Grant because he wasn't lying on the couch anymore.

"I see you finally decided to come back to the living!" Shelby yelled as loud as she could.

"Oh, *please* don't do that!" he said as he threw his hands over his ears. She thought she had scared the crap out of him at the same time.

"What's the matter; do you have a headache?" Shelby asked with a pouted look.

"Yes, I do. I take that back; I don't think I even have a head left. It hurts so much." He replied holding his head in his hands.

"Come here, I'll kiss it and see if that makes it feel better." She said holding her arms out to him.

"Do you think that will do the trick?" he asked with a crooked grin.

"I don't know, but I can try." She replied kissing him on the forehead.

"As much as that felt good; it didn't help." He said shaking his head.

"Wow, you need to go take a shower! You smell like brewery." she exclaimed.

"Yeah, the guys decided that I hadn't had enough to drink, so they dumped a bucket of beer on me. I found out that it takes a long time for beer to dry on clothing." He replied sniffing his shirt.

"Well, then, I think we had better get you into the bath tub. That might help you feel better too." Shelby said.

"What ever you think is best, dear." He said with a chuckle. "Do we have some kind of pain medicine? That just might help my head from pounding as hard as my heart is." Grant asked.

"Yeah, I have some in the medicine cabinet in the bathroom." She answered.

Shelby grabbed his arm and led him up the stairs. He was coherent but he was still a little bit out of it. She walked him to the bathroom and sat him down on the toilet. She turned the bath tub on so that it could fill while she helped him get out of his clothes. She got everything off except his underwear. After the tub had finished filling, she told him that she would leave the last article of clothing for him to take care of.

"Aren't you going to help me with these too?" he asked looking down at him self. Now, she knew he was just being ornery.

"No, you can do that and get yourself into the tub." She answered with a slight giggle.

"But I can't get in the tub with these on." He pleaded.

"You can if you want to, I don't care either way but I'm not taking them off of you!" She hollered at him. She wanted to laugh so badly.

"You never know; you might like what you see!" he said as he started laughing and moving in a goofy dance.

"I'm sure I will, but we'll save that for tomorrow *after* the wedding; remember?" Shelby reminded him.

"Ok, but you don't know what you're missing!" he said with a pouted expression.

Shelby walked into the bedroom and shut the bathroom door behind her. She had to laugh. She laughed so hard that her stomach started to hurt. This was a side of Grant she had never seen before and it was comical! After a few minutes, she could hear water sloshing around so she knew he had made it into the tub. She put in plenty of bubble bath so that if she did have to walk in there, no body parts would be seen. All of a sudden, she heard Grant call for her.

"What do you need Grant?" She asked through the closed door.

"I want you to come here for a minute." He answered.

Shelby opened the door and walked into the bathroom. He was lying safely covered in the tub.

"What's the matter?" She asked.

"Come here and sit with me." He said patting his hand on the side of the tub. Water and soap slopped over the side and onto the floor.

Shelby sat down on the tub just like he asked.

"Ok, now what..........." She started to say when he grabbed her arm and she slid into the tub with him.

"I just wanted to tell you how much I missed you." He replied.

"Are you crazy? Now I'm soaked!" She yelped.

"Yes I am; I'm crazy in love with you!" he exclaimed.

"What am I going to do with you?" Shelby asked with a big smile.

"What ever you want, I'm yours for the taking." He said as he waggled his eye brows at her.

She picked up a hand full of bubbles and blew them at him.

"For starters, you can kiss me. After that, you can tell me how much you love me, and after tomorrow, we can spend the rest of our lives being crazy together." He said. How could she argue with something like that?

Shelby leaned toward him and kissed him and again and again and again; you get the point. She went to move and her arm and it slipped down behind his back. Whoops, but she discovered something she hadn't expected!

"Grant, did you finish getting undressed before you climbed in here?" She asked curiously.

"Do you mean my last article of clothing?" He asked with a smile and a wink.

"Yes, that's exactly what I mean. Did you leave on your underwear?" She asked with a grin.

"Yes, I did. You see; I knew I was going to con you into getting in here with me, *so*, I didn't think it would be right if I was completely naked." He answered as he shook his head.

"Oh, you did, did you? Well, I guess it worked because here I am." She replied with a laugh.

"Yes, you are." He said as he kissed her again.

Grant pulled her over him so that her legs were straddling over his thighs and she was sitting on his lap. He pulled her closer and wrapped his arms around her, crushing her breasts against his chest. Her body felt so good against his. He kissed her and ran his hands along her back, caressing her, loving her. He wanted her so badly right now it hurt.

Shelby could feel *other* body parts awaken. Grant was as aroused as she was! She wanted this man so much it felt like she would die if she didn't have him now. What did it matter if they consummated their love a day early? The longer time went on, things were getting heated more and more by the minute; ok a lot heated. Time seemed to stand still.

"We had better stop." Grant said gasping for air.

"No." Shelby whispered against his lips.

"Are you sure you want to do this now?" he asked.

"Yes." She said pulling off her shirt.

"You're absolutely, positively sure?" he asked again.

"Do you want me or are you going to keep talking?" She asked looking him in the eyes. "We're going to be married in less than twenty four hours, what difference does it make if it's just a little earlier?"

"I haven't wanted anything more than the way I want you right now…but…"

"But what?" She asked sliding to the back of the bath tub.

That had to be one of the worst turn offs, Shelby thought, the word "but."

"Don't get mad. I want to wait till tomorrow after we've taken that last step and we're husband and wife forever." Grant explained.

Shelby thought about his statement for a few seconds. "Well, when you put it that way, I guess I can't argue. You really love me that much?" She asked taking a deep breath to calm her lungs.

"It's because I love you that much that I have the will power to stop, before we go that far." He replied with those big green eyes; forcing a smile while he tried to keep from looking too disappointed.

Shelby climbed out of the tub and grabbed a towel to dry off what she could. She walked back to Grant and gave him another kiss and left the bathroom to change her clothes. Her whole body ached with wanting. She wanted to feel Grant's body next to hers so badly that it was about to drive her crazy! She knew he was right but it still didn't help the need to feel him.

Grant pulled the plug in the tub and turned on the shower. Cold water was the only thing that was going to get his blood to cool down now. Tomorrow could not come fast enough! He wanted to feel Shelby's naked body next to his now more than ever. He stepped into the cold water and let out a yelp when the water splashed across his body. "This is what I get for being a bloody good boy." He muttered wryly to him self.

While Grant was finishing in the shower, Shelby heard his yelp. She ran to the door and asked him if he was alright. He said that the water from the shower was just a tad bit cold. She guessed he had to cool off some how.

Shelby went down to the kitchen to get something to drink. After Grant had gotten dressed, he met her there. She apologized to him for getting so carried away. It wasn't right for her to do that, but at the same time, he hadn't helped the situation either. He admitted he was partially to blame also and every thing was alright. Tomorrow they would make up for it. She told him that he had better believe they would.

Grant wrapped his arms around Shelby and told her tomorrow couldn't come fast enough. She agreed whole heartedly. Now was the hard part. Shelby had to go to her parents' house for the night and Grant was going to stay here. They were trying to do this the traditional way where the groom wouldn't see his bride until she walked down the isle to him.

Shelby remembered to give Grant the message from his mother. It worked out better, in a way, since Grant had planned on taking a short nap before he left for the airport to pick up his family. Shelby also explained that CJ and her Dad would be over later as well.

They gave each other a final kiss and made sure it was enough to last for the night. Shelby also told him to make sure he called her before it got to late to say good night.

When Shelby arrived at her Mom and Dad's, she carried her things up to her room and sat them on the bed. Her dress was hanging on the front of the closet door and her shoes were sitting on the dresser. After the interlude, back at the house with Grant, she was getting more anxious by the minute.

The nervousness and fear had left and now she just couldn't wait to walk down the isle. She was so in love with him; so much that she felt like she was about to explode from so much happiness.

Shelby found her Mom in the kitchen making dinner. She had made a big dinner so that CJ, Dad and Grant would have plenty to eat tonight while they were alone at Shelby's house.

Mom and Shelby were the only ones left in the house. After they had eaten, Shelby poured a cup of coffee and walked out onto the porch. The weather had warmed up so much. It was a beautiful night. As she sat gazing at the stars, she caught a glimpse of a shooting star streaming across the sky. She believed *that* was very good luck.

Shelby's mind began to wonder how many other people were sitting under this very sky watching that same star shoot across the dark night. How many of them might be in love as mach as she was and waiting for their wedding the very next day? She couldn't help but wonder if Cole or Dallas might have seen it too. Could they be looking at the very same thing she was?

It was getting late and Mom called for Shelby to come back in. Grant was on the phone. Shelby knew he would be calling anytime now. He told her how much he missed her and she told him the same. Thank god this was only for one night, Shelby thought. They talked about the wedding and a few other things before Grant said he was going to lie down for a little bit before going to the airport. He told her he loved her and Shelby told him how much she loved him too. Shelby also told him to be careful on his way to Ft. Wayne and on the way home. He said he would and that he couldn't wait to see her tomorrow.

Once they had hung up; Shelby kissed her mother good night and went up to bed. She was so excited she could hardly sleep. She just kept thinking about the wedding over and over. She drifted off to sleep and woke up again about an hour later. She tossed and turned all night. Not being able to stand it any longer, Shelby found her Mom and explained how she was feeling. She was so anxious her adrenaline was shooting off the charts. Her mother gave her a sleeping pill to help her sleep and to calm her nerves. *That* helped a lot; she was out before she knew what hit her.

Chapter 13

The next morning, Shelby awoke to being shaken frantically by her mother. She was hysterical. She just kept saying that she had to get down stairs, now! She was scaring the hell out of Shelby! Shelby kept asking what was wrong but she wouldn't tell her anything.

Shelby made her way down to the living room and found CJ standing in the middle of the room with a grim look on his face. His face was pale white and he looked as if he had just seen a ghost.

"What's going on with you guys?" Shelby asked holding her hands in the air waiting for a reply.

"Shelby, Grant never came home this morning." CJ said grimly.

"What do you mean? He had to pick up his parents'. They should be here by now." She replied looking to the clock on the wall. It was eight in the morning, they should have been at the house long before now, she thought.

"His father called your house about twenty minutes ago. He said Grant never showed up at the airport. His dad said they waited and waited before they wanted to call you. Shelby, he's no where to be found. They've tried calling his cell phone but they just keep getting voice mail." CJ answered.

"Where are they now?" Shelby asked placing her hands on top of her head.

"I told them I was coming to get you and he said they were going to a hotel until we could make it there. Grant's mom is really worried something might have happened to him. She said this is not like him." CJ said.

"It's not; was his car gone when you left?" She asked.

"Yeah, I heard him leave the house around two this morning, so, I know he wasn't there." He replied.

"No one else has called the house?" Shelby asked trying to think of what they should do. Her mind was reeling.

"No one; I don't know what we should do." CJ said. "You don't think he skipped out, do you?"

"I don't think Grant's that type of person." Mom said to CJ.

"I……oh…um……I can't breathe." Shelby said fanning her face with her hands. Pointing toward the stair well, she said, "Let me go get my clothes changed and we'll head to Ft. Wayne. Did you get his parents' cell number? Maybe we should check the hospitals or call the state patrol and see if there were any accidents this morning or…………I don't know!" Shelby answered becoming more frantic with every breath she took.

"Shelby, just calm down and take a deep breath. Getting worked up right now isn't going to help you find Grant. Get changed and go meet his parents. I'll stay here and I'll have your father stay at your house for the time being in case he turns up." Mom said to Shelby wrapping her arms around her trying to comfort her.

Shelby shook her head yes and ran up the stairs to change. With in minutes, her and CJ had jumped into his blazer and headed for Ft. Wayne. She called Grant's parents to see if they had heard anything. They told her where they were and said they hadn't yet.

Shelby was really starting to freak. This couldn't be happening! Where could he be? Is he alright? Why didn't he answer his phone? She argued in her mind. She wanted to cry, but at the same time, she wanted to scream!

As soon as they got into Ft. Wayne, they drove straight to the hotel where Grant's parents had checked in. They went up the elevator to their room and knocked on the door. Mr. Summers answered and Shelby could hear Mrs. Summers in the back ground crying. Even Grant's sister Tabitha was bawling her eyes out. The scene was not looking good at all.

"Come in." Mr. Summers said to them holding the door open.

"What's going on? Have you heard anything?" Shelby asked hesitantly.

Mrs. Summers started crying even harder when Shelby asked what was wrong.

"Shelby, you had better come over here and have a seat." Mr. Summers said guiding Shelby toward a chair.

"I'm not going to like this am I? Oh…my…god, what has happened?" Shelby asked as she looked at Tabitha then to Mrs. Summers.

Tabitha was crying so hard that Shelby could already see the answer in her eyes.

"The state patrol called just a few minutes before you knocked on the door. They said Grant was in a very bad car accident this morning." He tried to say holding back the emotions clouding his face.

"*Please* don't say what I think you're about to say." Shelby said shaking her head in disbelief. "I know what it's going to be; *please* don't say it!" Shelby said as she fell to the floor on her knees crying.

CJ stood in silence with his hands over his mouth in shock.

"They found his cell phone and that was how they found our number. Shelby, he's gone. My son is gone!" Mr. Summers blurted as he began to cry. He couldn't hold back his pain any longer.

Shelby couldn't say anything. She just sat on the floor crying. Every time she would try to say something, she cried that much more. CJ sat down beside her and wrapped his arms around her as tight as he could. She cried even harder. This couldn't be real, she thought to herself. This had to be some kind of a cruel joke! She felt lost. She felt mad. Shelby didn't know what to feel because she was feeling so many different things at once. Why is this happening?! She screamed in her mind.

After crying their hearts out and dealing with the shock, they all sat in silence for a long while, not knowing what to say. Was there anything they really could say? The hard part now was to try and pull together and figure out what to do next.

Shelby walked over to Mrs. Summers and put her arms around her. They both began to cry again. She hugged Tabitha and Mr. Summers and tried to comfort them, but under the circumstances, it was not an easy task.

"Did the officer say where they had taken him?" Shelby asked Mr. Summers sniffling.

"He said the ambulance had taken him to a Lutheran hospital. Do you know where that is?" he asked.

"Yeah, I know where it is." CJ said quietly.

"I'm so sorry; everyone this is my brother CJ. CJ this is Mr. Summers, Mrs. Summers and Tabitha. This is Grant's family." Shelby said as she made the introductions.

"It's nice to meet all of you." CJ said sympathetically.

"It's nice to meet you as well, CJ." Mr. Summers replied.

"I'm going to go call Mom and Dad and let them know what's going on. I'm sure Mom is going out of her mind right now." CJ said to Shelby.

"Ok, tell her we'll keep her informed when we know more." Shelby replied.

CJ left the room and Mr. and Mrs. Summers began to talk.

"Well, what should we do from here?" Mrs. Summers asked.

"I guess we should go to the hospital and make arrangements to have him flown home." Mr. Summers answered.

"Did they say what had happened?" Shelby asked.

"Only that Grant was driving down the road when another car pulled out in front of him. Grant t-boned the car and it caused Grants car to flip into the air. The officer said that it looked like he had flipped four or five times. When the car landed on the last flip, it crushed him." Mr. Summers explained trying to hold his composure. "He had vital signs for awhile but they just couldn't save him. His injuries were too severe."

Shelby sat with her head in her hands staring at the floor. She couldn't even begin to imagine what he must have of gone through. She felt so guilty. She was up half the night worrying about the wedding and Grant was in a car some where dying. CJ came back into the room and sat down beside her.

"Our parent's said to tell you, if there is anything they can do, please let them know." CJ said to Grant's family.

"Tell them thank you for us." Mr. Summers replied.

"I guess we had better go to the hospital and see what needs to be done." Mrs. Summers said. "Did you say that you knew where the hospital was, CJ?"

"I sure do. Would you like for me to take you there?" CJ asked.

"Yeah, we had better start getting this figured out." Mr. Summers replied.

"Why don't you go down and pull the blazer around front. I'll bring them down and meet you there." Shelby said to CJ.

"Alright, take your time." CJ replied as he laid his hand on her shoulder.

They left the hotel and headed for the hospital. At the information desk, a woman gave them directions to the morgue; Shelby never dreamed in a million years that she would be spending her wedding day in a morgue; *their wedding day.*

When they had made their way there, Mr. and Mrs. Summers went to talk to someone about arrangements for Grant's body to be transported back to New Hampshire for burial. They also had to identify his body to make sure that it *was* him. They asked Shelby if she wanted to be included but she just couldn't do it. Even as they asked, she began to break down again.

The arrangements had been made for Grant's body to be flown home the day after tomorrow. It was the soonest flight they could get. Mr. and Mrs. Summers invited Shelby and her family to fly home with them for the funeral. Shelby thanked them for including her but she couldn't. It was taking everything in her power to keep from having a complete meltdown and she didn't know if she could with stand watching Grant being entombed in the earth for eternity. It was just too painful.

Shelby did ask if it would be ok for her to have a memorial service back in her home town. She explained to them how much everyone in town loved Grant. He was loved by the whole town and she knew they all would miss him very much. Mrs. Summers said that would be a wonderful thing for them to do.

Right before they were getting ready to leave, Shelby asked if she could see Grant one last time. His parents showed her where he was. CJ wanted to go in with her, but Shelby told him this was something she had to do for her self, alone.

As she walked through the door, she took a deep breath. Was she actually going to be able to do this? She asked her self.

A man walked Shelby to one of the tables and slowly pulled back a sheet that was lying over a body. Shelby couldn't look at first and then she slowly turned her head. It was Grant for sure. He had a few scrapes on his head, but for the most part, he looked peaceful, Shelby thought. She looked at him intently for a few more minutes and started to pray. As the tears started to fall, Shelby bent down and kissed him on the forehead one last time. Under her breath, she whispered to him that they would meet again one day in heaven. That's all she could take. She had to get out of there.

They left the hospital in silence and drove back to the hotel. Shelby invited Grants parents' to stay with her until they had to fly home. At first they weren't to sure about the idea but eventually they thought it would be alright. Shelby explained that they could see where Grant had been living and meet some of the people that had grown to love him.

CJ and Mr. Summers gathered up the luggage and carried it down to the blazer. Mrs. Summers and Shelby sat down and had a talk while the guys were gone.

"This must be so hard for you." Mrs. Summers said.

"It's very hard. I just don't know what to feel. Right now, I feel numb. I feel like this can't be real." Shelby explained as she shook her head in disbelief.

"I know what you mean. He's my only son and now he's gone. I've loved him since the day he was conceived and even now, I still love him. It's very hard for me to except this but I can't imagine what it must be like for you. This is supposed to be the happiest day of your life, and now it has to be horrific for you." She said as she started to cry again.

"I never dreamed that I would wake up today and find out the man I love was not going to be here anymore. I would give anything to be able to change that. I wouldn't have cared if we would have never gotten married if it meant he would still be alive." Shelby replied.

"I can't help but feel this is our fault." Mrs. Summers said as she turned her head away from Shelby.

"How could this possibly be your fault? It's not like you were the one that hit him." Shelby replied trying to understand why she would say such a thing.

"If our flight hadn't been delayed, it might have made all difference in the world. He wouldn't have been driving that early in the morning; he would have already picked us up." She explained sniffling.

"You can't place that kind of blame on yourself. No one could have known this was going to happen." Shelby replied trying to comfort her.

"I know, but I can't help thinking like that; he's my son and I'm going to miss him so much." She said weeping again.

"I am too." Shelby answered holding her in her arms.

"You're not upset at us for taking him home to be buried are you?" she asked Shelby.

"No not at all. I understand that you want him home where he belongs. If we would have been married, it would be a different story. I would want my husband to be close to me, and the same if I was to go before he did. I guess I'll never have to be in that situation though." Shelby explained as her eyes started to tear up again.

"You're right. If the two of you had been married, I wouldn't have interfered with what you wanted. I know that it's not something you want to think about right now, but someday there *will* be another man in your life. Take your time and let yourself heal from this tragedy and there will be love for you again." Mrs. Summers said forcing a smile.

"That's the furthest thing from my mind. I see myself, now, growing old alone. After feeling like this; there's no way I want to ever live with the thought of having to lose someone else. It's bad enough that I know some day my parents' will be gone and I can always lose my brother. I don't want to deal with this. It's way too hard." Shelby explained to her.

"I know my dear, I know."

Mrs. Summers wrapped her arms around Shelby and held her when she started to cry again. She kept telling her to let it all out. She explained that if she kept it all bottled up, it would only do her more harm then good.

Mr. Summers called from the front lobby to let them know he and CJ were ready and waiting. The women gathered themselves together and took the elevator down. CJ was a gentleman about everything. He helped them get into the blazer and made sure their doors were shut.

On the way to Shelby's, Mr. and Mrs. Summers started talking about things Grant had done when he was really little. Then they started talking about the day he called them to let them know he had finally found the woman he wanted to marry. They were a little shocked at first but then realized he was finally going to settle down and start a family. They weren't happy he was going to be living so far away but it would also give them a reason to go on vacation somewhere besides out of the country. The atmosphere in the car was silent after that.

When they arrived at Shelby's house, Mom and Dad were already there waiting on them. Mom had coffee, tea and pie waiting just in case. Shelby could tell that she had been crying. Her face was flushed and streaked red, and she was sniffling a bit. Dad and CJ grabbed the luggage from the back of the blazer while Shelby made introductions. Mrs. Summers seemed to hit it off with her mother right off the bat. Shelby thought to herself that it was such a shame that they weren't going to be family. She missed Grant so much. This entire situation still seemed to be one huge nightmare.

Once everyone was settled, Mom and Mrs. Summers sat at the kitchen table discussing a memorial for Grant. Mom thought maybe it could be held at the hall since there were all of the things meant for the wedding. Shelby told her it was a nice thought but she didn't know if she could handle it since that was where they were supposed to be married. Her mother agreed; bad idea.

While the parents carried on the discussion, Shelby decided to go up to her bedroom and lie down for a few minutes. She just needed to be alone and try to make sense of it all. When she walked into the room, the bed wasn't made and some of Grants clothes were lying on the floor. She picked up one of his shirts and sat down on the bed looking at it. Then, she could smell it. It smelled just like Grant. She could smell his cologne all over it. She lay back on the bed and held onto it for dear life. The longer she smelled it, the harder she began to cry. She couldn't believe that she was never going to see him again!

After awhile, she must have cried her self to sleep because the next thing she heard was Mrs. Summers calling her name. She had walked into her room.

"I have to say Shelby; you really do have a beautiful home. It's so big. It would have been perfect for raising a family." She said to her.

"Thank you. I've always had a soft spot for big farm houses. They have so much potential. Grant loved the architecture of it. I always teased him that he was only marring me for my house. Then again, it was *our* house; at least for a little while." Shelby said to her as she looked down to the floor.

"I could see that. He always was one for beautiful things." She said. "Just look at you. My son had exquisite taste." Mrs. Summers said as she stroked Shelby's long red hair.

"Yes, he did. I miss him so much." Shelby said to her. She was trying to keep from crying again but it was really hard not to.

"Shelby, could I ask you something?"

"Sure."

"It's kind of a personal question." She said.

"You can ask me anything. You should know that by now." Shelby replied as she wiped tears from her eyes.

"Did you and Grant ever break the promise the two of you had told me about back in New Hampshire?" she asked with a strange look, hesitating.

"Are you talking about the sleeping together thing?" Shelby asked confused.

Why in the world would she be asking me something like that? Shelby thought, especially at a time like this.

"Yes." She answered bluntly.

"Mrs. Summers, please forgive me, but I think that's a little too personal for you to be asking. Grant has died; why would you ask about such a thing?" Shelby asked in a defensive tone walking away from her.

"Oh my heavens, I wasn't asking in the way that you think I am. I should have worded the question a little differently. I'm so sorry Shelby." She said trying to apologize.

"Then what else could you mean by that and why would you want to know about such a thing?" Shelby asked completely confused now.

"I was hoping...if you two had broken that promise; maybe there might be a part of Grant growing inside of you at this very minute. I know it's just wishful thinking. That's such a stupid thing to be thinking right now. I'm sorry for implying something that outrageous." Mrs. Summers explained as she started to weep again. She shook her head trying to rid her self of the thought.

"I understand what you're asking now. I wish I could say that we did, but unfortunately we did not. I'll tell you one thing; we came very close to it last night and knowing what I know now; I wished we had. I know that's a little more information about you're son then you needed to know, but now, I really regret it." Shelby explained as she hugged Mrs. Summers.

"Thank you for being honest with me. I can see why my son loved you so much. Now, if you'll excuse me, I'm not feeling that well. I think I'll go lie down for a bit. I think your Mom and friend Leah; I think that's what she said her name was; has everything under control for tomorrow." Mrs. Summers said as she started to leave.

"Is Leah down stairs right now?" Shelby asked.

"Yes, she is. She's a very nice girl. I'll see you in a little bit." She replied leaving the room.

Shelby put Grants shirt on and walked down to the kitchen. Leah wrapped her arms around her and hugged her as if she was never going to see her again. She told Shelby how sorry she was to hear about what had happened to Grant. Shelby thanked her and thanked her again for helping with the memorial. She also thanked her for everything she had done for the wedding. It would have been a really beautiful wedding.

The next morning, the family was busy with the arrangements for Grant's memorial service. The preacher that was going to marry Grant and Shelby agreed to hold the service at his church. He was another person that liked Grant very much. Shelby spent most of the morning searching through what pictures she had of Grant. She had to see which one would be the best to have at the service. Finally, she found one of him sitting on the front porch banister. Even though he was being goofy when she had taken the picture; it turned out to be a really good one of him.

After she had finished with that, she thought she had better pack up some of his things for his parents' to take home with them. The biggest problem she had was; where did she start? She knew she wanted to keep a few things but which things did she keep? Shelby finally gave up on figuring it out by her self and called for his mother to help her.

Mrs. Summers helped a lot. She saw some things that right off the bat she knew she wanted to take home. She left everything else to Shelby. Shelby knew it sounded crazy, but she put all of his things away just where they were supposed to be, as if he was going to come home someday. Right now, she just needed for things to be this way. It gave her some sort of comfort. She didn't even bother to wash his clothes.

Later that afternoon, everyone gathered at the church for the memorial service. Leah, once again, did an incredible job. She had Grant's pictures sitting around with all of the flowers everyone had sent. They took their seats and the preacher said some words about Grant and then gave a short prayer. He then asked if anyone else wanted to say something about Grant. Grant's family one by one walked up to the podium and spoke. Shelby's parents' and CJ took their turn; then a few people from town said some remarkable things about Grant.

As Shelby sat listening to every ones kind words, CJ reached over and tapped her on the shoulder. She looked at him and he moved his head motioning for her to look to the back of the church. Shelby turned slightly to see where he was looking, and to her surprise, there sat Dallas and Cole. Not together of course. Cole was sitting on one side of the church and Dallas on the other. They both were staring right at her.

Shelby leaned toward CJ and whispered in his ear, "What are they doing here?"

"I'd say they're here for you." He answered.

"Who told them?" Shelby asked.

"Shelby, it's all over town. How could they not know? Besides, I might have said something." He replied.

"Why would you do that?" she asked.

"Hey, they're still *my* friends and they worry about *you*. I told them both that if they showed up they had better not cause any problems." He answered.

"As soon as this is over, would you *please* head them off at the pass? I'm not ready to deal with them. I can't right now." Shelby begged him.

"No problem; I'll take care of it. I just wanted you to know that they were here, for you." He replied.

Shelby put the two men from her mind and after the last person finished speaking, the preacher asked if there was anyone else that would like to say a few words. No one stood, but everyone looked at Shelby. She didn't know if she could do this, she thought to her self. Shelby took a deep breath and stood from her seat. She walked to the front of the church to the pulpit. As she walked, she kept her eyes focused on Grants picture. When she was standing in front of it, she kissed the tips of her fingers and placed them over Grant's lips in the picture. She kept telling herself to breathe and take it slow. She stood behind the pulpit; still for a few minutes before she started to speak, and just as she started to open her mouth, her head became dizzy and everything went black. She had fainted.

Shelby didn't know how long she was out, but when she came to, everyone was standing over her. They wanted to know if she needed water, if she was alright, did her head hurt; all sorts of questions were flying at her. She told them she just needed to sit down and breathe. CJ helped her back to her seat and everyone else settled down. The preacher said another prayer and concluded the service.

CJ and Leah gathered the flowers and pictures to take back to Shelby's house. When they had gotten home, people were starting to come in with food, flowers, cards, and anything they thought might be comforting to the family. Mrs. Summers told Shelby she was glad they had the service for Grant. Now she understood why everyone in town loved him so much. She admitted he would have had a very good life here. Shelby smiled at her and gave her a big hug.

Later on, as people started to thin out, Shelby went upstairs to rest for awhile. She shut her bedroom door and lay down on the bed. She curled up with Grants shirt and fell asleep.

Mom came into the room and woke her up at some point.

"Shelby, there's someone here to see you."

"Who is it?" Shelby asked groggily.

"It's Cole. He wanted to check in on you. Should I send him in?" she asked.

"Mom, please don't let him in here. Just tell him to eat some food or something. Better yet, just tell him to go away. I can't do this right now." Shelby answered.

"Honey, I'm sure he means well. He's just concerned about you." Mom said.

"I know, but not right now. I just want to be left alone for awhile. I'm not ready to talk to anyone yet." Shelby explained.

"Ok, I'll tell him. If you need anything, just let me know. I'll be down stairs." She said as she shut the door quietly behind her.

For the rest of the night, people came and went, but Shelby stayed in bed.

She couldn't bring her self to listen to everyone's condolences and how sorry they were. She knew tomorrow was going to be another bad day. Grant's family would be flying back to New Hampshire and burying him. She had to go to the airport to see them off. Shelby really didn't want to leave the house but she knew it was the right thing to do.

Shelby woke to the smell of coffee brewing and the smell of bacon frying. Mom must be downstairs cooking breakfast for everyone, she thought to her self. Sometimes she really had to wonder where that woman got her energy. Not delaying the inevitable any longer, Shelby pried her self out of bed and walked to the bathroom. Maybe a long hot shower would help. It might help her body at least but it sure wasn't going to fix her soul.

As she stood in the shower with the hot water running over her shoulders and back, Shelby started to think back to the last night she saw Grant. He was sitting in this very tub in his underwear. She started laughing over the image, but the longer she laughed, the more she began to cry.

How stupid am I? She scolded her self. Why did I let Grant stop me that night? Why did I let him talk me out of it? I should have pushed him for it. I should have made love to him right here in this bath tub. I should have told him that I wouldn't marry him unless we did!

Bringing her self back to reality, Shelby knew she could ask *why* a thousand times over but it still wouldn't change the fact that Grant was gone.

Shelby stood in the shower until the water turned cold. She dried off and dressed her self and went down to the kitchen. Everyone was sitting at the table and Mr. Summers was carrying their luggage out to the front porch. They would have to leave for the airport soon; another grim reality that this nightmare was really happening.

Mom had a big spread of food sat out. She had made everything from pancakes, bacon, sausage, muffins, biscuits, gravy; the whole shebang. Shelby didn't think she had forgotten anything. She explained that she wasn't sure what everyone would like, so, she made everything she could find.

Shelby poured a cup of coffee and tried to eat something. It made her half sick to eat, but her stomach was telling her it needed it. She thought starving her self wouldn't help anything.

Once breakfast was over, Shelby started to straighten up the kitchen but her mother stopped her. She said she would take care of it while she and CJ took the Summers to the airport. CJ wanted to go with her because he didn't think she was in any no shape to be driving. He was right. Shelby started to think about how much she loved her brother. He had been great through all of this. Never once had he made fun or tried to joke about anything. That had always been his way of cheering her up in the past. He could always make her laugh.

Grant could make her laugh.

Mr. Summers had loaded the last of their things into the back of CJ's blazer once again. Shelby's parents' hugged everyone and shook their hands and said their good byes. They all agreed and wished they had met under better circumstances as they were supposed to in the first place. None the less, they were all glad they had had the opportunity to meet.

Shelby and CJ told Mom and Dad they would be back in a little bit before they drove off. On the way to the airport they chit chatted about different things, but for the most part, it was quiet. It had been a solemn ending to what was supposed to be an extraordinary weekend.

At the airport, Shelby said good bye to everyone. CJ told them all how happy he was to have met them and to have a safe trip home. As they were ready to board the plane, Shelby happened to look down at her hands and realized one last thing.

"Mrs. Summers!" She yelled for her.

"What is it my dear?" she asked turning back to Shelby.

"I just realized I still have Grants ring. Do you want it to put with his things?" Shelby asked out of breath.

Mrs. Summers took one look at her ring finger and placed her hand over her mouth.

"Like I said before, Grant always did have good taste. You keep it my dear. He gave this to you because of his love for you. You should never forget that." She explained.

"I don't feel right wearing it with him being gone." Shelby said as a tear rolled down her face.

"No one said that you had to take it off at this very moment. One day there will come a time when you have the courage, but for now if it gives you comfort; I would wear it for as long as you need to." She answered as she hugged Shelby one last time.

"Thank you so much." Shelby replied with a smile.

"You're welcome. Now don't forget what I said. Any time you want to come for a visit, you just call me. I would love to see you again." Mrs. Summers said as she walked down the hall waving good bye.

Shelby waved back to her until she turned the corner. CJ walked with her to the window and watched as everyone boarded the plane. As they watched, Shelby happened to see a man pushing a casket out to the plane to be loaded. She knew instantly that it was Grant. That's when she lost it.

CJ wrapped his arms tightly around her and held on as best he could. He decided that it was time to go. He had to get her out of there. He didn't want her to watch anymore.

Once CJ had Shelby out of the airport, she calmed down and caught her breath. She felt like someone had their hands wrapped around her lungs and were squeezing the life out of them. It hurt so badly. The rest of the way home she didn't remember; she had fallen asleep.

CJ had to wake her up when they got back to the house. Mom and Dad were still there. Shelby thanked god for her family. If it hadn't been for them, she thought she would have been a bigger mess than she was.

Shelby's next obstacle was to figure out how to start a new life. She and Grant had been together for awhile now. How was she supposed to get used to being alone again? How did she get used to sleeping alone? She didn't know how she was going to deal with it all. All she knew right now was that she wanted to sleep. Everything else could wait till tomorrow.

For the next week, Shelby hardly left her bedroom. She would come out long enough to go to the bathroom or to get something to drink and that was about it. Mom came over every day to try and get her to eat. Some days she would and other days she just felt sick to her stomach. Mom tried her best to get her out of the bedroom.

"CJ, I just don't know what to do with her. She won't even come down here to eat. I'm scared that she's going to slip into such a deep depression that there might not be any helping her at all." Mom said to CJ with great concern.

"I know; I've tried everything too. Sometimes I try to push her hard enough that she'll get mad and want to knock the slop out of me, like she always did when we were kids. Not even that's working. I don't know what else to do." He replied shaking his head.

"I found someone to come in and look over her office for a little while but her clients are starting to get worried. Every time I run into someone they're all asking when she's coming back. I just tell them, when she feels better. That's only going to last for so long." Mom said.

"I guess the only thing we can do is give her a little while longer. Maybe after she comes to terms with everything, she'll start to come out of it. We'll just have to keep praying right now." CJ replied.

"I hope you're right; I just hope you're right, son." Mom said as she shook her head.

Chapter 14

Three more weeks passed since Shelby had overheard the conversation her mother had had with her brother. So far, there hasn't been as much traffic in her house either. Mom still stopped by to check on her at least once a day, but other than that; no one else. At some point in time, she really did need to get back to work. Maybe that would help her stay busy and not think about Grant so much. At least she hoped it would.

Not putting it off any longer, Shelby got out of bed and walked to the bedroom door. She had her hand on the door knob staring at it. She was wondering if she really wanted to open it. Do I really want to walk downstairs? She asked her self. Standing here wasn't going to answer any questions.

She turned the handle, opened the door and got the ever living day lights scared out of her! Cole was sitting on the floor with his back against the door. When she had opened it, he fell back and was lying on the floor looking up at her.

"Hi."

"What are you doing here?" Shelby asked in confusion.

"I stopped by last night and your mom said that you were sleeping. She said she needed to go home and take care of some things, so, I told her that I would stay for a while and keep an eye on you." He said with a forced smile.

"I don't need anyone to baby sit me. Get off the floor. You've been here since last night?" Shelby asked as she reached out her hand to help him up.

"I slept on the couch, and just a little bit ago, I sat down here on the floor. I wanted to knock on the door but I was scared to. Please don't be mad. I promised your mom and I would hate for her to be mad at me for not keeping my promise." Cole answered with a sheepish grin.

Shelby was shocked. She didn't know what to say to him, so she said the first thing that came to mind.

"I want some coffee. Do you want some?" She asked as she walked past him and down the stairs.

"Sure, I already made some just in case you might get up." He replied.

"Thanks, I guess." she answered.

They walked into the kitchen and Shelby poured them both a cup. They sat at the table drinking their coffee without really saying anything to one another. It was awkward. She didn't know what to say to him. She was still mad over the stunt he had pulled on Dallas and didn't know how to deal with him just yet. Shelby watched him through squinted eyes as she taped her spoon on the table.

Cole couldn't take the silence any longer, or the way she was glaring at him. He broke the silence first.

"So, do you think you'll be going back to work soon?" he asked.

"I don't know yet; maybe next week. It just depends on how I feel." Shelby replied shortly.

"I see you're still wearing your ring." He said looking at her hand.

"Yeah, I just can't seem to take it off. It's not for the lack of trying. I think I've tried about half a dozen times now, but I just can't do it." She said as she looked at her left hand.

"I bet it's a hard decision to make."

"Yes it is. I know there isn't a reason to wear it anymore, but I'm just not ready to let go. Oh, by the way; I hear there should be congratulations to you as well." Shelby said with a half crooked grin.

"For what?" he asked confused.

"I was told that you were engaged. Did I hear wrong?" Shelby asked dryly. She dropped the spoon onto the table. It landed with a loud clink.

"Oh, yeah, I am. Thank you," Cole said.

"Well, who is she? You don't seem to be too enthused about it." Shelby asked.

"She's a great person. Do you remember when we ran into each other in the airport?" he asked.

"Yeah, was that her?"

"Yep, that's her."

"Well, tell me a little about her. What's her name? What's she like? How did you two meet? You know; all the good juicy stuff." Shelby asked trying to find out just how in love with this girl he was.

Truthfully, she didn't even know why she was asking. She could care less. She was ready to bite nails.

"Her name is Tiffany and she's a super model." Cole quickly held up his hands to stop Shelby from going off the handle. "I know what you're thinking too. She's not like that whole stereo typical model hype that you hear about either. She's really down to earth. We met at a photo shoot I was doing with the team. We started talking and after that we started dating. That's pretty much it. About a week after I had run into you I finally asked her to marry me." He explained.

"You didn't ask her just because we ran into each other; did you?" Shelby asked with hesitation.

"No, it had nothing to do with you in particularly. It was more of what you said. I finally realized that you were right; I need to settle down and get my head straight. Tiffany helped me with that. She makes me happy and I haven't been this happy in a *very* long time." He explained.

Cole suddenly had a huge smile on his face and Shelby could tell by the look in his eyes that the realization of what he had just stated sank in. He looked very happy.

Shelby's nerves began to calm down and now she didn't feel so mad at him any more.

"Wow, that's something. I never pictured you this way. Someone has finally stolen your heart. I'm *really* happy for you." She said to him.

She really was trying hard to be happy for him but at the same time, her own heart was still in so much pain.

I miss Grant.

"Thank you; that coming from you means more than you'll ever know. Shelby, I want to apologize to you for all of the stupid things I did in the past. I wanted......" Shelby cut him off before he could say another word.

"Cole, please don't; just stop before you go any further. I have wanted to rip your head off for so long for what you pulled on me and what you did to Dallas. Even just now, it was taking everything inside of me to keep from coming across this table and squeezing your neck in two." She started explaining to him. He looked as if he was ready to bolt out of the front door.

"I don't feel that way any more. After what I've been through; I realize that I just want to forget the past and try to find some way to move on with my life. I think the first step in doing that would be to forgive everything that's happened, starting with you."

"You really do forgive me for being such an idiot?" He asked.

"Yes, I do, but only if you can forgive me for being such a bad friend?" She asked him.

"There isn't anything to forgive you for. You've never done anything wrong. It's always been me and my stupid jealousy." He said solemnly.

"Yeah there is. We should have had this conversation a long time ago but I let my anger keep it from happening. I should have confronted you from the start and I didn't. We've been friends since before I can remember and we should have never let things get this bad. We should always be able to talk things out." Shelby answered.

"I was the one that let it go to far. I let my jealousy get the best of me. I always thought that you had more feelings for Dallas then you did me. How stupid could I have been?" He asked him self, shaking his head.

"That's the worst part of all; I love you both the same. Dallas and I always have fun together because that's just the way he is. He's a fun guy. You're always so serious about every thing. You know how to have fun too, but, most of the time you're just too serious to do so. You need to let go and have a little fun from time to time." Shelby replied with a laugh.

"I know, I know. If you only knew how many people tell me that? Even half the team says the same thing. I don't know why I'm this way; I guess it's just who I am." He said as he started to laugh then went serious again.

"I'm sure that some day you'll find a balance between the two. You'll have to if you want your marriage to work with Tiffany." She said.

"I know. We get into little arguments every now and then about it. She's always telling me to lighten up. I guess she's right." He replied.

"I only have one question left then." Shelby started to ask.

"What's that; or do I really want to answer it?" he asked with a grin.

"What are you doing here? Why aren't you with her?" Shelby asked with a smile shaking her head.

"I know what you're saying; I just wanted to make sure that my *best friend* was alright. And to make sure I still had a best friend." He answered.

"I'm ok and I'll be a lot better once I get things back on track. I just need a little more time to deal with everything. I will for awhile, but, I'm sure things will work themselves out eventually." She said with a smile patting his hand that was resting on the table.

"I'm sure they will. I know you'll find a way. Now can I at least get a hug?" He asked with a laugh.

"Yeah, I think I can handle that." Shelby answered standing from her chair.

They stood from the table and hugged each other. It felt so good to know that we had finally buried the hatchet between us, Shelby thought as she hugged Cole. She knew things would never be quite the same as it was when they were a lot younger, but at least now she knew that they were still good friends. That's all that mattered to her.

Cole grabbed his jacket and walked to the front door to leave. Before he walked out he had one last thing to say.

"Grant *would* have been a very lucky man." He said as he turned and looked at Shelby with a smile.

"Why do you say that?" Shelby asked curiously.

"He would have been married to a very special woman." He replied.

"Well, Tiffany *will* be one lucky lady." Shelby said with a grin.

"Why do you say that?" Cole asked curiously with a crooked grin.

"Because, she'll be married to my best friend and he's one special guy." She replied.

Cole smiled at her with that big dimpled smile of his and Shelby could feel her heart start to warm again. He shook his head and walked out the door. Shelby watched him leave and she realized that she was starting to feel a little bit better. She thought the conversation with Cole helped her to realize that even though she had lost Grant; she still had a lot of life to live. She had her family, her job and her friends. She may find love again someday, but for right now, she just needed to focus on finding her self again.

It will all come in due time, she thought happily to her self.

Shelby felt so good after that, that she ran up the stairs, jumped in the shower, got dressed and ran out of the house. She drove straight to her parents' house. When she got there, she slowly walked into the kitchen and scared her Mom half to death. She definitely wasn't expecting to see her.

"My heavens girl, what are you doing here?" Mom squealed.

"I thought I would surprise you." Shelby said to her with a smile.

"Well, you accomplished that. Are you ok? Do you feel alright?" she asked with concern as she placed her hand on Shelby's forehead.

"I feel great! How would you guys like to go out to dinner?" Shelby asked.

"Are you sure you're alright? I don't think you need to be going anywhere just yet." Mom replied.

"No, I *need* to get out of the house. I've kept myself there for long enough. What has it been, three, four weeks now?" Shelby asked.

"I think so. Are you sure about that? You seem…not…like yourself." Mom said hesitantly.

"I'm fine. Is Dad and CJ home?" Shelby asked.

"Yeah, their in the living room, I think." Mom answered slowly.

"Dad, CJ come in here!" Shelby yelled for them.

Within seconds, both men burst through the kitchen door way.

"What in the world is going on?" Dad asked.

"Would you guys like to go out to dinner tonight? It's my treat." Shelby asked them both.

"Sis, are you alright? You're acting weird." CJ asked her.

"I'm fine! Now, will you guys *please* give me an answer or will I have to go find someone else to eat with me?" she said.

"I'm in." CJ replied without hesitation.

"If that's what you want my dear." Dad answered.

"Ok, then it's settled. You guys go get ready and we'll go eat." Shelby said to them.

"Now that they have left, do you want to tell me what's really going on?" Mom asked with one eye brow raised.

"I just had a long talk with Cole and I finally realized that I needed to get myself out of the slump I'm in." Shelby answered her.

"So, he was still there this morning? What did he do?" she asked protectively.

"He didn't do anything. We talked about his life and mine. As much as I loved Grant, I know he would want me to be happy and not moping around the house for the rest of my life." Shelby started to explain.

"Happy with Cole; you're really confusing me." Mom replied shaking her head in confusion.

"No not with Cole. Just to be happy with my life. He wouldn't want me feeling sorry about him being gone from my life and this world. I made a mends with Cole and we settled a few things. I'm trying to make a fresh start and the next step will be to fix things with Dallas. I'm sure that won't happen to soon but eventually I'll find a way." Shelby explained.

"Well, in that case, I'm glad I told him to stay with you. It seems the boy did wonders. I'm so happy to see you up and out of the house. Come here and give me a hug. I was so worried about you." Mom said as she almost started to cry.

"Mom, I'm going to be fine. It's just a hard lesson in life to learn. I thought that Grant and I would be married right now but I guess God has other plans for him *and* me. I don't know what my plan is as of yet, but I'm sure in time He will show me the way. Right now I just have to have faith that one day I *will* get my happy ending," Shelby said to Mom as she hugged her.

"You just keep your faith and good things will come. I love you so much and I'm so happy to see that you're doing better," Mom said with a huge smile.

"Thank you so much for taking care of me. Between you, Dad, and CJ, you guys have been amazing. I love you all so much." Shelby said as a few stray tears trickled down her cheeks.

"Oh no, you're crying again. What's wrong now?" CJ said as he walked back into the kitchen and saw the sight before him.

Shelby let out a laugh.

"It's ok, I'm just happy. I love you," Shelby said to him as she gave him a hug.

"I love you too." He replied hugging her back.

Dad walked in about that time too.

"I love you, Dad," Shelby said wrapping her arms around him.

"Well, I love you too, Shelby," He replied with a strange look.

"I'm ok you guys, really. I just wanted you all to know that I love you and thank you for what all you have done for me. I couldn't have dealt with all of this if it hadn't have been for you. You guys mean the world to me and I just want you all to know that. Now before I break down and really cry, can we please go get something to eat? I feel like I could eat a horse," Shelby said with a laugh as she wiped the tears from her eyes.

"Well, in your profession, I don't think that would be a good idea, so how about a steak?" Dad asked with a laugh.

"Sounds great; let's go!" Shelby replied.

They left the house and headed downtown to the local steak house. They serve the best steaks in town. Shelby was a little worried that if she ran into people they would ask her all sorts of questions. How are you? Are you doing alright? Do you need anything? Can we help you in any way? Things like that. She knew that they all meant well but sometimes a person just needed to be left alone. She was sure it would be fine though. As a community, they would, do anything for one another. That was one of the reasons Shelby had wanted to have her business here. Plus, buy a house and start a family here. So far, most of her plan had worked out that way; the marriage and kids would be later on in the future now.

Being as it was a Friday night, Shelby noted right away how busy the restaurant was. Timberville was limited to only a few restaurants and it seemed the whole town had turned out for a bite to eat. She at once was bombarded with the questions she had feared. Surprisingly though, Shelby was quite comfortable answering them. To her amazement, it actually made her feel better to let them all know that she was coping well. She was glad to once again be out in public talking with people.

Once they were seated and perusing over the menu, Dallas and his parents' had come in. Mom and Dad being the courteous people that they were, asked if they would like to join them. They did of course and the waiter pulled over another table. The parents sat at one end, while CJ, Dallas, and Shelby sat at the other end.

Not knowing how to act toward Dallas, Shelby pretty much ignored him for the most part. It was a good thing that CJ was sitting right across from her because every now and then, she would hear him say something and she would kick him under the table. He kept getting mad at her, but she didn't care. She didn't want to be included in whatever conversation he and Dallas were in the middle of.

She hated to act that way! She knew that eventually she would try to make a mends between her and Dallas, but right now she didn't know if it was the right time. It was better for the time being, to just nod her head and force a smile when needed.

It had turned out to be a great night. The food was ordered and after everyone had eaten their fill, the dirty dishes were cleared away. Shelby and Dallas never spoke to each other. They would give sideward glances from time to time but nothing was ever said. Mom and Dad said they were going to stay for a bit and talk with the Smiths over coffee and dessert. Shelby went to the front counter and paid the bill. CJ met her at the front door.

"Do you want me to take you home?" he asked.

"No, not yet; I think I want to go for a walk. Do you want to come with me?" She asked motioning toward the door.

"Sure, would it be alright if I asked Dallas to tag along?" he asked with hesitation.

"Yes, that's fine." she replied.

"If it's too much for you to deal with I won't. I just think he needs some friends around right now too." CJ said.

"I know he does. CJ its fine, go ask him. I'll meet you outside." She answered.

CJ turned and walked back toward the dinning room while Shelby walked outside. The evening breeze felt wonderful as it drifted across her face. The air was so crisp and clean. It was a beautiful, perfect night for a walk, Shelby thought lazily.

Shelby took in a deep breath of fresh air as CJ and Dallas walked out of the restaurant. Dallas gave her a quick shrugging smile and the three of them walked lazily down the sidewalk. Shelby thought it would be neat to walk to the park like they all used to do when they were still in school. The three of them had spent a lot of time there back then.

As they walked along, Dallas and CJ started acting like they were playing football. It would have been more entertaining if they would have had an actual football, but, pretending to have one, made the scene much more comical, Shelby thought as a laugh escaped her.

She couldn't believe how good it felt to laugh.

The three of them had walked about four blocks when they heard a woman calling to CJ from across the street. She wanted to know if he would join her for a drink at the bar. Shelby gave him a warm, devious smile before she started hounding him about the unknown woman. CJ explained that she was just a friend and they had been hanging out together for awhile now.

"So, why haven't I heard about her before now?" Shelby asked with a grin.

"I wanted to see what might happen." He replied sheepishly.

"So, could this be something serious?" She asked.

"I don't know, it might, it might not. I'm still weighing my options. Besides that, I have to be back in California in a couple of weeks; me and long distance relationships don't work out; you know that." He answered with a chuckle.

"Go on; go have a drink with her." Shelby said shooing him toward the curb of the street.

"Are you sure? I told Mom and Dad I would make sure you made it home alright." He explained.

"CJ, I'm a big girl. I think I can find my way home." She said.

"I'll make sure she gets there." Dallas spoke up.

"You'll be ok with Dallas won't you?" CJ asked slightly hesitating.

"I'm sure I'll be fine. Now go see your girl." Shelby replied pretending to kick him in the rump.

"Thanks dude, I'll see ya later." CJ said to Dallas as he ran across the street backwards.

He was such a goof, Shelby thought with a satisfied smile.

Shelby and Dallas kept walking toward the park still not saying anything to one another. When they had gotten to the park, Shelby went to the swing set and sat down in one of the swings. Dallas sat down on the one next to her and they just sat for awhile.

Not being able to take the tension any longer, they both looked at each other at the same time and said, "How are you?"

Surprised that they both were thinking the same thing at the same time, they looked at each other for a moment longer, and then started laughing out load.

"How are you really doing?" Dallas asked.

"It's been hard but I'm doing a lot better now. How about you? How are you doing these days? Better I hope?" Shelby asked as she lifted one eye brow looking at him.

"I'm getting there, I guess; it's been a long road but I'm handling things better day by day." He replied.

"I'm glad to hear it. I was really worried about you for awhile." She said.

"I wanted to thank you for what you did the night you found me by the bar. I think that was the worst night of my life." He said looking down at the ground.

"You don't have to thank me for anything. That's what friends are for, aren't they?" She asked with a grin.

"Yeah, but I didn't ever want you to see me that way. I can look back now and see what an idiot I was. I thought I could drown all of my problems in alcohol but it just made them worse. I had already lost my two best friends and was well on the way to losing my career too. With the injury to my leg, I thought I was done for sure." He explained.

"I guess we both have had a pretty rotten year so far." She said solemnly.

"Yeah, we have. Have you heard anything from Cole or is he still not talking to you either?" he asked.

"Actually, I talked to him this morning. It was weird. I woke up and he was sitting out side my bedroom door on the floor." She answered shaking her head.

"Oh. I see. Did you guys work everything out?" he asked fishing for what had happened between them.

"Yeah, we had a long talk. In the end everything turned out pretty good." She smiled happily.

"So, I guess that means that you two have finally worked things out and are together now?" Dallas asked disappointedly as he hung his head toward the ground.

"What are you talking about?" Shelby asked confused.

"Cole always said that one day you two would be together. He told me he didn't care if it took a life time, one way or another; he was going to marry you." He answered.

"Oh, he did? Well that's news to me!" Shelby said surprised.

"Isn't that what he talked to you about this morning?" he asked.

"No, it's not. We talked about his engagement and us being friends again. That was it." She answered.

"He's engaged; to who?" Dallas asked in shock.

"Some girl named Tiffany. She's a model that he met at some photo shoot. He seems really happy." She explained.

"Boy was I off base. I thought for sure you were going to tell me…never mind." He said shaking the thought from his mind. "Well that explains a lot. She must be the girl that was always hanging around at practice. He was happy about it?" he asked still in shock.

"Yes, he was. He sat at my kitchen table talking about her and the expression on his face just kept changing. You could tell that he's really in love with her. I was impressed." Shelby explained.

"I'll be damned. I can't get over it. Cole finally found someone else. I guess I'm happy for him to." Dallas replied with a smile.

"I should get home. I have *so* many things I need to sort out. I feel better today but I know I still have a lot in front of me." Shelby said looking down at her hands.

"Do you want me to walk you home?" he asked.

"You could walk me to my parents' house. My truck is parked there. That is, if you wouldn't mind?" She asked smiling from ear to ear.

"It would be no problem." He replied with a huge grin.

Dallas and Shelby walked through town toward her parents' house. They talked non stop and finally the subject of their friendship came around. She and Dallas came to the same understanding that she and Cole had come to earlier in the day. Their friendship meant everything and they weren't about to let the past destroy it.

By the time they made it to Shelby's truck, they were laughing and having fun again. Shelby needed this *so* much. She hadn't laughed in so long that she had almost forgotten what it was like. Laughter definitely soothed the soul, she thought to her self

"Well, thank you for walking me home kind sir." Shelby said with a grin and a curtsy.

"You are very welcome my lady." Dallas replied bowing.

"I'll see you around?" She asked with a crooked grin cocking one eye brow up.

"You bet!" he said as he shut her truck door with a smile that lit up his face. He stepped back from the truck to watch her leave.

Shelby started the truck and drove away. On her way home, she felt better than she had in a long time. Today was a very good day, she thought ruefully. She had finally gotten to talk to both of her best friends and make a mends. Now if she could only get them talking to *each other* again. She guessed that was something that she would just have to pray for; it might take a very long time though.

Chapter 15

Two years later…

Shelby still thought about Grant from time to time even though it had been two years since his death. It seemed she thought about him less and less with every day that passed. She would never forget him. She needed to let him go all the more. She knew she could never fully move on with her life till she let go of him for good. It took her a year before she could finally pry his engagement ring off of her finger!

Getting over Grant's death had been one of the hardest things Shelby had ever done, but in the last two years, a lot of good things had happed. Cole did marry Tiffany. They were married about a year ago and Shelby had even been invited to their wedding. It was a huge event and it was held in Ft. Wayne. They had spared no expense. It was as beautiful as anything Shelby had ever read about in a fairy tale.

She thought back to that day and the dance she had shared with Cole. He had held her tightly in his arms and the gorgeous smile that he had given her still made her week in the knees when she thought about it. She could see the happiness in his eyes when he talked about his new wife. She was *so* happy that he had finally found the happiness that he had been looking for.

Rumor has it now; they have a baby on the way.

From what Shelby had been told as of lately; Dallas had gotten engaged. She thought out of everything that had happened in the last couple of years; that was the biggest shock of all. To tell the truth, as long as he was happy, that's what mattered to her the most. Cole and Dallas had been *her* boys ever since they were in diapers, and to see them *both* happy, meant the world to her. She did wish them both, every happiness in this world. Life was too short and no one ever knew when it could be taken away. Shelby knew all too well first hand.

Another shock came when CJ had called her out of the blue and explained that he had finally found a woman of his own. She lives right here in town! He was actually making a long distant relationship work. That fact made her so very proud of him. He tells her all of the time that this girl is definitely the one. Shelby hoped against the odds that everything would work out for the two of them. She really is a sweet girl and Shelby would be more than happy to have her for a sister-in-law.

As for Shelby......other than work, there hadn't been much of a change. She did start dating again about six months ago. Leah, her best friend that she is, had set her up on half a dozen dates or so. None of them had been great. Well, maybe one. His name was Tyler Martin and he had just moved back into town. Shelby had gone to high school with Tyler but he graduated the year before her.

She really like hanging out with him but there was one thing that scared her about him. He had just gotten out of a *very* long relationship. He was engaged for four years and about two months ago, they split up. Things were no where close to being serious between Tyler and Shelby, but she couldn't help but think of the rebound aspect of the situation. He was very good looking and he made her laugh, a lot. He was fun to be around. They would go to the movies or dinner and sometimes on the weekends; he helped her at the office. They had a pretty good time together, but Shelby didn't think she was ready for anything serious yet. She didn't think he was either.

Mom called Shelby a little while ago and wanted her to come over for dinner tonight. Shelby didn't have anything else to do. After she finished at the office, she drove to her parents' house and pulled up out front like usual. She was climbing out of the truck when Dallas pulled into his parent's driveway. He had a woman with him. Shelby wondered if this was *her*, his fiancé.

Shelby pretended not to see them but as she walked up the side walk, he yelled for her to wait a minute. Shelby stopped dead in her tracks, slumped her shoulders and knew he was about to introduce her to his future wife.

"Shelby, I have someone I want you to meet!" he yelled across the yard. Shelby stood still watching them walk across the yard.

"Shelby, this is Sara; my fiancé. Sara, this is Shelby; one of my closest friends." He said as he introduced them.

After his introduction, Dallas couldn't bring himself to look Shelby in the eye.

"Hi Sara, it's nice to meet you." Shelby replied offering her hand to her. She was beautiful, Shelby thought to her self.

"It's nice to finally meet you. I've heard so much about you. For awhile, when Dallas would talk about you, I thought he was talking about his sister. I was surprised when he informed me that he didn't have a sister." Sara answered with a slight giggle.

Giggly. Shelby couldn't stand giggly people.

"Well, I hope what you've heard has been good things. Dallas here can be quite the character when he wants to be." Shelby said with a slight laugh as she looked at him.

"Oh. Yes, nothing bad." Sara said with a smile.

She's a blond. Shelby thought.

"I had heard that you had gotten engaged; I'm so happy for you." Shelby said to Dallas holding her arms out to him for a hug.

At that moment, her stomach felt like it was in knots. She felt like she could throw up at any second. Why did she feel sick all of a sudden? Shelby asked her self.

Whispering into Shelby's ear, Dallas asked, "Do you really mean that?"

"Why wouldn't I?" She asked narrowing her eyes in confusion.

"Thank you, that means a lot." He said as he stood back from her.

"So, have you two set a date yet?" Shelby asked.

"So far, I think we're shooting for a late summer or fall wedding. I just wish we could find someone to help us plan it all." Sara said with a look of disappointment.

"Well, in that case, I have someone that can help you with that. Call this woman. She helped me with my wedding and she did a great job." Shelby said digging through her purse to find one of Leah's cards. She handed the card to Sara.

"I thought Dallas said that you weren't married?" Sara asked in confusion.

"I'm not; my fiancé was killed in a car accident the morning of our wedding." Shelby answered looking down at the ground.

"I am so sorry! If I had known, I wouldn't have said anything." Sara said. She was very sincere and glared at Dallas for not telling her.

"It's fine. That was over two years ago, so, we can move on to another subject?" Shelby asked forcing a smile.

Dallas took care of that when he said, "Well, we had better get over to Mom and Dad's, Sara. They're waiting on us for dinner."

"It was nice to finally meet you and again, I'm so sorry." Sara said as she apologized once more.

"Its fine; don't worry about it. You guys enjoy your night." Shelby said to them both waving good bye.

"I'll see you around, Shelby." Dallas said.

"Yep, see you later." Shelby replied as she turned to walk to the house.

When she had walked onto the porch, she took a sideways glace toward Dallas and she saw him mouth something with his lips. He said he was sorry as he held out his hands shrugged his shoulders as if he was asking for forgiveness. Shelby shook her head that it was alright and waved him on.

Shelby walked on into the house and yelled to her Mom and Dad that she was there. She had no idea what her mother was cooking, but she could smell it as soon as she walked in. It smelled wonderful! Her Mom yelled back, letting her know that she was in the kitchen.

"I heard you pull up, where were you?" Mom asked when Shelby walked through the kitchen door way.

"I was outside meeting Dallas's fiancé." Shelby replied dryly.

"So, you finally met her? What was she like?" she asked.

"Beautiful, of course; she seems alright; I don't know." Shelby answered as she went to pour her self a cup of coffee.

"What do you mean by "I don't know"? Did she act funny or say something you didn't like?" Mom asked curiously.

"No, there's just something that doesn't sit right with me about her. My stomach started to turn as I was talking to her. Maybe it's just in my head."

"Is it in your head or maybe your heart?" Mom asked as she looked her in the eyes.

"Oh, Mom, don't even go there. You know that there is *no* possible way for that to even be a possibility. It never has. I just don't feel that way about him." Shelby answered in an aggravated tone.

It almost was a possibility a few years ago. She thought to her self. Where did that thought come from?

"Ok, ok, I was just thinking outside my head again; I'm sorry." Mom said holding up her hand in defeat.

"Don't worry about it, its fine. So, how have you been?" Shelby asked.

"Fine, I just saw you a few hours ago, Shelby." She said smiling. She knew her daughter was changing the subject quickly.

"I know. I was just trying to find a way to change the subject." Shelby said with a laugh.

They went on to talk about other things after that. Dad walked into the kitchen and was telling Shelby about having to have their car worked on and talking to CJ on the phone. He told her CJ had asked him his opinion about asking his girlfriend to marry him. Shelby almost lost it! CJ was finally getting serious about someone; *really* serious! Her brother getting married; what was this world coming to?

After supper was over, Shelby helped Mom do up the dishes and kissed them both good night. It was time for her to head home for another night alone. Maybe Mom was right about one thing; she *was* tired of being alone. Everyone around her was getting married or has gotten married and she would be the only one left.

When she had gotten home, she changed into her comfy clothes. Ok, they were her pajamas. Shelby poured her self a glass of wine and curled up on the couch with a blanket. It was Friday night and she felt it was a good night for a movie. The movie had started when she heard a knock on the door.

Who in the world is here this late? She asked her self.

She answered the door, it was Tyler.

"What are you doing here this late?" Shelby asked him confused.

"I was sitting at home alone and I thought of you. I thought maybe we could keep each other company." He answered with a half crooked grin.

"I guess we could. I was just starting a movie. Come in." She said as she opened the door wider.

"Are you sure it's alright. If I'm bothering you just let me know." He said.

"No, it's completely fine. I was just sitting here thinking about how lonely it was to watch a movie by my self." Shelby answered with a smile.

"Well, then I'm your man! Look, I even brought popcorn." He said with a laugh waving a box of microwave popcorn in front of her.

The two of them walked to the kitchen and Tyler started the popcorn in the microwave. Shelby poured him a glass of wine and they sat down on the couch together. This is a nice surprise, Shelby thought happily. They had only been seeing each other for a few weeks but Tyler always seemed to have a way of cheering her up

As they sat watching the movie, three fourths of the way through it, Shelby heard him snoring. One minute he was talking away and the next he was out like a light. He must have worn himself out today. Shelby wondered what he had done. What did she do now?

Shelby finished watching the movie and decided she had better go to bed. She grabbed a blanket off the back of the couch and covered Tyler with it. She snuck up the stairs trying to stay quite so that she wouldn't wake him. It was kind of cool having someone sleeping in the house besides her self for once. That hadn't happened in a *very* long time.

The next morning, Shelby woke up to the smell coffee brewing and something cooking in the kitchen. At first, she was scared to death. She thought something was on fire. She wasn't used to having anyone else in the house. Sure enough, it had ended up being her second thought; Tyler was cooking breakfast.

"Hey sleepy head, you're awake. I didn't wake you, did I?" he asked in a happy mood.

"No not at all. You didn't have to do this." Shelby said trying to get her brain to focus.

"I thought it was the least I could do for you letting me crash on your couch last night. Thank you." He replied as he handed her a cup of coffee.

"It's no problem. I figured you were pretty tired so I let you sleep. Was that ok?" Shelby asked waiting to see what he would say.

"It was more than ok. I'm glad you did." He answered with a smile from ear to ear.

His smile made her blush because in that instant her cheeks felt like they were on fire.

"Did you sleep well?" She asked ignoring the fire in her face.

"I slept like a baby. You have a very comfortable couch." He said as he sat down at the table.

The two of them ate their breakfast and talked for awhile. Tyler wanted to know what she had planned for the day. Today was the first time, in a long time; she really didn't have anything to do. Shelby just realized that she actually had the day off. She had nothing scheduled for today. Tyler told her he had a few things to take care of but later they should get together and go do something. Shelby told him that was fine with her.

Shelby gathered up the breakfast dishes and started to wash them. Tyler helped to dry and she explained to him where they were to be put away. Shelby was rinsing out the sink when Tyler walked up behind her and placed a hand on each side of her, resting them on the sink. She had her back to him.

Shelby froze.

His mouth was right behind her ear. She could feel his breath. It moved across her ear, down her cheek, along her neck. A shiver coursed down her spine and goose bumps appeared down her arms. Her heart began to beat faster. Her mind began to fog. Her heart was drumming so hard against her ribs she actually thought they might break.

"Do you know how much I like being around you?" he asked softly in her ear.

"I think, I might, have an idea." She replied trying to keep a straight face as her breath caught in her throat.

"You are such a beautiful woman." He said as he slid her hair to one side.

"Thank you." Shelby answered trying to keep her bearings.

She didn't know what else to say! She could feel his breathe against her neck as he moved.

He started to slowly kiss the back of her neck and worked his way around the side to her ear. She couldn't breathe. She stood completely frozen in place as he turned her slowly to face him. Tyler wrapped his arms around her. As she looked at him, his eyes held a serious glare and slowly, his face lit up with a smile. His smile made her whole insides melt. He slowly leaned in to kiss her and Shelby didn't stop him. His lips brushed hers, waiting, to see if she would stop him. She didn't.

Tyler's mouth locked with hers. Shelby could instantly feel the heat she felt in her own body, radiating from him. Within seconds, she opened to him and their tongues were at war with each other. She met his movement, every step of the way. They stood at the kitchen sink, kissing, for at least twenty minutes. Tyler never pushed for anything more than just this kiss. No groping or grabbing; just passionate kisses. With each kiss, he stirred feelings Shelby had not felt in a very long time.

Tyler pulled back and took a step away from Shelby. She finally opened her eyes to look at him. She couldn't help but wonder what he was thinking. As if reading her mind, he licked his lips seductively and smiled.

Shelby was breathless.

"I'll be back around six to pick you up. Is that ok?" he asked with a shallow breath.

"That would be fine." She coughed out the words. Her head swam with other thoughts.

No it's not; stay here and finish what you started! Shelby screamed in her mind.

She was also thinking that someone needed to bring her an oxygen tank because she couldn't breathe right now!

"I'll see you in a little bit. Make sure you're ready. Wear something...sexy." Tyler said as he walked toward the front door.

"OK." Shelby drawled. She didn't know if she owned anything sexy.

Tyler shut the door behind him and Shelby waited until she heard his car pull out of the driveway. As soon as he was out of sight, she slid down the front of the kitchen cabinets in front of the sink and sat on the floor trying to catch her breath.

"What just happened? Oh...my...god, he is so hot!" She said out loud to the empty kitchen. Standing, it took everything she had to keep her legs from giving out on her. They felt like rubber bands!

Shelby couldn't believe how good she felt right now. She hadn't felt this way in so long; she really didn't know what she was feeling. She was happy, excited, scared to death, she...she...she was alive!

"That's what it is; I feel alive again!" She shouted through the kitchen.

She spent the rest of the day cleaning her house and trying to figure out what she had to wear that would even come close to sexy. She had lots of nice clothes but she had no idea *what* Tyler had in mind.

Then she saw it. The little black dress she had worn the night she stayed in Ft. Wayne with Cole and Dallas. She couldn't believe she still had the dress. It was hanging in the back of her closet behind everything else. She thought she had thrown it away after that night. Well, it had turned out to be disastrous that night, maybe it would bring her good luck tonight.

Did that make sense? She thought it did.

Shelby finished with the house and looked at the clock. She only had an hour and a half to get ready! She ran up the stairs and flew into the shower. After the shower, she dried off and started on her hair. She dressed, finished all of the little things and took extra care to make sure she smelled nice. By the time she had finished, she could hear someone pulling into the driveway. She looked out of her bedroom window and sure enough, it was Tyler. Talk about just in the nick of time, she thought taking in a deep breath and letting it out.

Shelby heard Tyler knocking on the door so she yelled down the stairs for him to come in. She told him she would be down in a few minutes; all she had to do was slip on her shoes.

Shelby started down the stairs and Tyler was waiting for her. He was shocked to his very core. His whole body ached with desire at the sight of her. She had a black dress that fit snuggly to her entire body, clinging to every curve; black silk stockings and high heeled shoes. She was a dream come true! He thought to himself.

"Wow!" he said with a look of shock on his face and a low whistle.

Shelby slowly turned in front of him so that he could see the ensemble.

"What's the matter Tyler, cat got your tongue?" She asked with a devious smile.

"I'm impressed; you clean up *very* well." He said almost in a growl.

"Well, I would have to say the same for you. You look very handsome." She replied with a half crooked grin.

Handsome was an understatement. Sexy all the way! Shelby thought. He was dressed in a dark navy blue pin stripped suit that made his blue eyes sparkle.

"Well then, I think it's time for us to hit the town, don't you?" he asked holding his arm out to her. Shelby wrapped her arm around his and Tyler gave her a quick wink of the eye.

"Let's do it." Shelby answered.

They walked out of the house and out to his car. Just like a gentleman, Tyler opened her door and closed it after she had climbed in. Once inside the car as well, Tyler explained that they were going to a very romantic restaurant in Ft. Wayne.

Shelby thought happily that this was going to be a wonderful night.

After arriving at the restaurant, Tyler and Shelby were seated and handed menus. A young waiter asked what they would like to drink when Tyler spotted someone sitting across the room.

"Hey, do you see whose sitting over there?" he asked Shelby in disbelief.

"Where?" She asked looking around the room.

"Right over there, by the wall. Do you see them?" he asked shyly pointing toward another table in the corner of the room.

"No, where are you pointing?" She asked still trying to see who he was looking at.

"Right…over…there." He replied whispering.

Shelby kept searching until she finally spotted where his finger had been pointing. To her surprise, she spotted Cole and Tiffany. Her face lit up in a smile from ear to ear.

"Isn't that Cole Parker and his wife?" Tyler asked.

"I do believe it is." Shelby replied nonchalantly looking back to her menu.

"Man, I would give *anything* to meet him. He has got to be one of the best football players in the league." He said.

"Oh, you would?" Shelby asked teasingly. This could be kind of fun. "Why don't you go over and say hi? Maybe he'll give you an autograph." She said with a grin.

"Yeah right; he probably gets hounded by people every where he goes. I'm sure he's too busy for that." Tyler replied sitting back in his seat looking at the menu once again. He was disappointed.

Shelby let Tyler stew on the thought for a few minutes before she asked, "What if I could introduce you?" She asked slyly.

"Like I'm sure you could do that." Tyler said disbelieving her. Then he asked a second later, "Can you do that? How?" he asked in confusion.

"Just give me a few minutes and I'll bet you, I can get him to come right to our table." Shelby said as she laid her menu on the table.

"Yeah, right, I have to see this to believe it. There's no way! What makes you think he'll come over here?" He asked still not believing that she could do it.

If he only knew, she thought wryly. Shelby almost felt guilty for deceiving the poor guy.

Shelby gave Tyler a devilish grin then turned to look toward Cole's table. She watched Cole and Tiffany intently for a few minutes. Cole was talking to Tiffany and then he put his cell phone up to his ear. As he talked on the phone, he looked across the restaurant and right at Shelby; as soon as their eyes locked and he figured out who he was looking at, his face immediately lit up in a huge smile. He sat for a few more seconds staring at her, then, laid his phone down on the table.

Cole and Shelby looked at each other for a short while and Shelby slowly raised her hand to give him a quick wave with her fingers. His smile widened, he said something to Tiffany, and stood from their table.

The entire time Shelby was pulling this off, she was eating it up. Tyler looked as if he was ready to go out of his mind! This was so awesome! She thought. She had never pulled a stunt as good as this before.

I guess it *does* pay to have friends in high places after all, she though ruefully.

Shelby and Tyler kept their eyes glued to Cole. He walked right across the room and straight to their table. Tyler's mouth hung to the floor. This was *so* priceless!

Cole bent down and gave Shelby a peck on the cheek.

"Hi Shelby, it's good to see you. I thought that was you when I looked over here." Cole said as he sat down beside her.

"*You know him?*" Tyler asked more shocked now than he had been before Shelby had made the challenge.

"Yeah, we kind of go way back. How have you been Cole?" She asked with a slight laugh.

"I can't believe you know him! Why didn't you tell me that to begin with?" Tyler said in disbelief.

"I thought it would be way cooler this way. I got ya good didn't I?" She asked Tyler.

"What's your name dude?" Cole asked Tyler as he extended his hand to him.

"Tyler Martin, it's an honor to meet you." Tyler said choking on his words as he shook Cole's hand.

"You seem familiar to me. Have we met before?" Cole asked him.

"It was probably in high school. Tyler graduated a year before us." Shelby explained to Cole.

"That's it; you played football too, didn't you?" Cole asked.

"Yeah, I was the quarterback until I got injured. That pretty much ended my football career." Tyler answered.

"I came in and took over for you." Cole replied.

"No way; you were the one?" Tyler said in shock.

"Yep, it was me. Hey, why don't you guys come over to our table and join us. We always sit in the corner so that not too many people see us." Cole asked them.

Shelby wanted to stay where they were, but Tyler being so infatuated with Cole, wasn't going to happen. They walked over to Cole's table and Cole said to Tiffany, "Look who I found, Honey."

"Hi Shelby, how are you?" Tiffany asked snidely as Shelby and Tyler sat down.

"I'm good and you?" Shelby asked nicely.

"I'd be a lot better if I had this baby already." She replied as she stood to show Shelby her swollen belly.

"Wow, I can see that. When are you due?" Shelby asked trying to make her feel a little better.

"In a couple more months; I can't wait for it to be over. I am in complete misery." Tiffany replied as she gave Cole a cold look.

"Oh, by the way, this is my date, Tyler Martin." Shelby said as she introduced Tiffany to Tyler.

"It's nice to meet you." Tiffany said to Tyler as she shook his hand.

For the most part, the four of them ate dinner and talked most of the night. Cole and Tyler talked non stop about football and every now and then, Tiffany would make some kind of snide comment. Shelby bet, that if she wasn't pregnant, she would have drunk herself silly. She was not at all happy.

Finally, Tyler brought up the subject of how Cole and Shelby knew each other and wanted to know all the details. Shelby was hoping to avoid the subject but she had a feeling eventually it would have come up any how.

"Well, we grew up together. He lived in the house right next to mine and Dallas Smith lived in the house on the other side of me." Shelby started to explain.

"You lived right in between the two of them?" Tyler asked in shock once again.

"Yes I did." Shelby replied.

"Were you friends with both of them?" he asked.

"Yep, she sure was; still is." Cole said winking at her. "Back then we were known as the three musketeers through out high school. We were inseparable. The three of us went everywhere together." Cole explained with a far away look in his eyes.

"Isn't that a big surprise?" Tiffany mumbled dryly under her breath.

Tyler, sensing the jealousy in Tiffany's voice, shifted the subject and asked how she and Cole had met. Now that was something she was more than willing to talk about.

Shelby decided this was the opportune time to take a break and head for the ladies room. She excused her self and told them she would be right back. What she really needed was to catch her breath and get some air away from them all. When she walked out of the bathroom, Cole was standing by the door waiting on her. He scared her half to death!

"What are you doing?" Shelby asked him holding her hand over her chest.

"I just wanted to talk to you for a few minutes." He replied quietly looking down at the floor.

"Ok, what is it?" Shelby asked confused.

"Nothing in particular, I just need someone to talk to besides Tiffany." He answered.

"Cole, is everything alright? You really don't seem like yourself." She asked with concern.

"I'm *so* glad I ran into you tonight. I need a friendly face." He replied.

"Are you going to tell me what's wrong?" Shelby asked folding her arms across her chest.

"In short; my marriage is crap, my career is going down the tubes, and I'm just not happy anymore." He explained.

"What's changed?"

"Let's go sit at the bar and I'll try to give you the short story." He said.

"Won't your wife get mad?" She asked.

"She's telling Tyler her whole life story by now, so, she'll be busy for awhile." He replied dryly.

The two of them walked to the restaurant bar and sat down. Shelby ordered a glass of wine because it seemed like they might be there for awhile.

"I'm going to tell you something but you have to promise that you won't ever tell anyone. You have to promise me Shelby, I mean it." Cole said straight faced with a serious tone.

"Cole, you know I wouldn't repeat anything you said to me." Shelby replied.

"Tiffany and I really got married, because at the time, she was pregnant. We were just in the middle of splitting up when she told me. Trust me, my parents' don't even know about this." He started explaining.

"She's pregnant now, so what happened? I don't understand." Shelby asked confused.

"About two months after we got married she had a miscarriage. She told me the stress of her career and dealing with mine was just too much for her to handle and that's what caused it. I stood by her through it all because it was really hard on her. It was for me too. I was so happy about becoming a father that I just let everything else fade out of my mind. By the time we had settled everything and decided to call it quits; she came along and said she was pregnant again." He explained.

"Cole, I'm so sorry. I didn't realize you had been dealing with so much. I wish there was something I could do." Shelby said as she placed her hand on his.

"Just listening to me talk is enough. I've been holding all of this in for so long; it feels good to be able to tell someone; especially someone that I can trust." He said as he squeezed her hand and gave her an appreciative smile.

Shelby realized what they were doing and quickly pulled her hand back, shaking her head at him.

"I'm sorry, I shouldn't have done that." Cole apologized.

"No, you shouldn't. You're out in public and if you don't want any other problems, I suggest that you watch your every move." Shelby replied.

"Yeah, your right; the last thing I need running through the media would be an affair. Then again, if it was with you; I don't think I would mind the press so much." He answered with a wink, laughing.

Shelby thought that had been the first time she had seen him laugh all night.

"So, what are you going to do?" She asked.

"I'm going to do what I had intended on doing the first time. I'm going to be a father and a husband; that's all I *can* do. I'm going to love my child with all of my heart and love my wife for as much as she'll let me. I'm hoping that after the baby's born, things will change. I do love her but after everything that's happened; she just keeps pushing me away. Sometimes she doesn't even *want* to have a baby. When she gets into one of those moods it really scares me." Cole went on to say.

"I really wish there was something I could do for you guys. I really thought you were happy." Shelby said.

"I was at one point in time, but I guess this is just the way life is. Well, enough of my problems; how have you been? We haven't had a chance to talk in a long time. I see you're dating again; that must be good." He said as he took a drink of his wine.

"Yeah, I guess it is. I've had a few dates but Tyler seems to be the one that's stuck around the longest. It's nothing serious yet; but you never know." Shelby replied shrugging her shoulders.

"He seems like a good guy. Do you want it to get serious?" He asked with hesitation.

"After what I went through with Grant; I'm really scared to get close to someone again. On the other hand, I'm tired of being alone. It would be nice to have someone lying beside me again when I fall asleep and wake up to them being there in the morning. It just really scares me to get too close and have them taken away all over again." She explained.

"You really loved Grant, didn't you?" He asked.

"I really did. He meant the world to me. I never thought I could *ever* feel that way about someone." Shelby answered as she played with the rim of her glass.

"Even though things haven't been the greatest between us; I'm truly sorry for what happened to Grant. I didn't know if I had ever told you that before." He said apologetic.

"I know you are, but hey, I just have to move on with my life now. Thank you for being concerned though; that means a lot. I know you were just trying to help that day I found you on my hall way floor." She replied with a laugh.

"Yeah, that was kind of stupid wasn't it?" he asked with a chuckle.

"No not at all. It just showed me that you were worried about me and that you care. It makes me very happy to know I have friends like you and Dallas yet." Shelby said as she gave him a peck on the cheek.

"So, I take it that you still talk to Dallas?" he asked as he placed his hand on his cheek and rested his elbow on the bar.

"Not too often. I see him from time to time in town, but it was funny, that day that you were at my house, my family and his ended up having dinner together that night. I talked to him for awhile after dinner and we straightened some things out just like you and I have. I just wish that the two of you would talk again." She answered with a crooked grin.

"Well, for your information, we do at least say hi to each other on occasion these days. We're still not talking in conversations but we do acknowledge each other." He replied.

"I guess that's a start. I don't expect the two of you to become best friends again overnight, *but*, I would at least like to see you on speaking terms. Even after everything that has happened; the two of you still mean the world to me. The two of you are my boys, my guys; I miss that." She replied swatting him on the shoulder.

"Maybe someday, right now, I don't even know what's going to happen with my own life at this point. I guess we'll have to wait and see." He answered.

"Right now, I think maybe we had better get back to our table. I think we've been gone long enough and they might be looking for us." Shelby said to him.

"Your right; Tiffany has no problem creating a scene. It would just give her something else to rant about. Grab your wine and let's go." He said as he helped her down from the bar stool.

When they had gotten back to the table, Tiffany was still going on about her and Cole and her career. Poor Tyler looked like he was bored out of his mind. "Well, look who decided to join us once again. Did the two of you have a nice little chit chat?" Tiffany asked in a suggestive tone.

"I am so sorry it took so long. I ran into an old friend and he was so drunk that we had to help him into a cab. He was in no shape to be by himself. Thankfully, Cole was there to help me. You are so lucky to have a husband like him. He's so thoughtful of others." Shelby said to Tiffany. She was lying the whole time but it was the first thing that came to mind. She had to cover for Cole some how.

Tiffany's expression changed instantly.

"Did you really help that man?" Tiffany asked Cole.

"Yeah......I did." He answered with a slight hesitation.

"Oh, you are such a good person! I love you so much." She said as she gave him a big hug. Cole looked at Shelby in disbelief.

"Oh, now I have to make a trip to the ladies room. I'll be right back." Tiffany said as she stood from the table.

Shelby wanted to laugh but she kept her composure. When Tiffany stood, both men stood. Tyler watched her as she walked away and Cole looked at Shelby with another quick glance. He moved his lips and said thank you without saying a word. Shelby smiled at him, then, both men sat back down.

"Boy, she's quite a talker, isn't she?" Tyler said with a chuckle.

"Yeah, that's my girl. How far did she get on her life story?" Cole asked with a smirk.

"I think she was up to your wedding. She's had some life." Tyler replied.

"That, she has." Cole answered with a grin.

"Well, I guess we should probably head home. It's a long drive and it's getting pretty late." Tyler said to Shelby.

"Yeah, I guess we should. It's been nice to see you again." Shelby said to Cole.

About that time, Tiffany came back to the table as Tyler and Shelby stood.

"Are you guys leaving? I haven't finished my story. I'm sure Tyler would like to hear the rest of it." She said in despair.

"I'm sure you can tell me the rest another time. I'm sure we'll run into each other again now that I know Shelby is good friends with the two of you." Tyler said trying to get away from her.

"It was really good to see you guys. Maybe we can get together another time." Shelby said to them.

"I'm going to go get the car." Tyler said to Shelby.

"Alright, I'll be there in a minute." She replied.

"I'll walk you out. Honey, I'll be back in a second." Cole said to Tiffany.

Cole walked with Shelby out to the front door of the restaurant. They had just a few minutes before Tyler would drive up with the car.

"Thank you so much for listening; plus what you told Tiffany at the table. She would have lit into me by the time we had gotten home. How did you come up with that story so quickly?" He asked in amazement.

"I don't know. When I saw the look on her face, it just kind of rolled off my tongue. I don't know where it came from. At least I was able to help in some way." Shelby said with a laugh.

"No matter what has happened you've always been the one constant thing in my life; whether it's been good *or* bad. You're always right around the corner. I can really see why Dallas and I always fought over you, now. I'm happy that we didn't lose you forever." He said softly kissing her forehead.

"Well, I'm glad at least something good has come from it all. If you ever need to talk, you know where to find me; or call for that matter. I might not be able to help but I can always listen." She said to him.

"Just always remember; if *you* ever need anything, just let *me* know." He replied.

"I will, now go take care of your wife." Shelby said with a slight laugh.

Tyler drove up in front of them and Cole opened her door. Shelby climbed in and said good bye to Cole. He shut her door and her and Tyler drove away.

On the way back to Shelby's house, Tyler kept thanking her over and over for introducing him to Cole. He never thought, in his wildest dreams, he would meet someone like him. Then he went on to tell her some interesting things about Tiffany. She was a real piece of work. She had told him the only reason she wanted to marry Cole, in the first place, was to further her career. She would get better modeling jobs if she were married to a pro athlete. That might have been the case, at one time, but Shelby knew the *real* reason why they had gotten married.

Once Tyler and Shelby had made it to her house, Tyler opened her car door and walked her to the front door. He asked if she had had a good time and wanted to know if she wanted to go out again next weekend. He would be gone this week on a business trip but would call her when he got back. Shelby told him that would be fine and she would be waiting to hear from him. Tyler gave her a long kiss good night and went on his way.

For the next week, Shelby felt like she had been dancing on a cloud. She had a little more bounce in her step and just felt really good all around. She once again had someone in her life that wanted to be with her. Of course, she had to tell Mom all about it. She was happy for her but warned that she had better not rush into anything to fast. Shelby explained that she was taking it slow and cautiously. She was happy about that.

Sunday afternoon rolled around and Shelby still hadn't heard from Tyler. She was beginning to wonder if he'd even made it back from his trip yet.

Later that evening, he finally showed up at her house. The two of them ate dinner together and watched a movie but Shelby noticed something just didn't seem right about him. He seemed like he was somewhere else most of the time. His mind kept wondering and she would have to repeat things to him because he wouldn't hear her the first time. Shelby asked him if there was anything wrong but he said he was working on a big deal and was concentrating on that. He kept apologizing but there just seemed to be more to it. Shelby didn't push the issue and let it go. She was starting to get worried.

That week Tyler had gone out of town again. He was gone a lot lately. She knew there had to be something else going on but Shelby was too scared to pry. She guessed she would have to wait and see if he told her what the problem was.

Chapter 16

Shelby received a phone call from Cole today giving her an update on him and Tiffany. Since that night at the restaurant, everything had been ten times better between them. They hadn't fought anything like they had before. Shelby told him she was happy for them and she hoped everything worked out. He deserved to be happy, even if she thought he didn't at one point in time. Well, the phones were ringing off the hook again; Shelby thought she had better see who it was. It was her mother.

"Hi Mom, how are you; even though I just saw you a couple of hours ago." Shelby started the conversation.

"Shelby, you might want to hear about this. Dallas's father is in the hospital." Mom said nervously.

"What happened? Is he ok?" She asked.

"They think he either had a heart attack or a stroke. They're not for sure yet. They've just taken him to the hospital; whatever it is, he's not doing very well at all." Mom explained.

"Are you guys going over there?" Shelby asked.

"Yeah, do you want to come with us?" Mom asked.

"Should I; yeah I should. I'll be there in a few minutes. Let me wrap things up here." She replied.

"Ok, I'll see you in a bit." Mom said as they hung up the phone.

Shelby gave her assistant instructions to cancel the rest of the day's appointments and close up the office. She grabbed her keys and ran out to her truck. She started it, put it in drive and headed for her parents' house. When she got there, Mom and Dad were already waiting for her in their car. She parked the truck and jumped into the car with them. She didn't think she had ever seen her father drive this fast! He and her mother both were very concerned about Mr. Smith. They all had been such good friends for years; way before any of the kids had been born, if she understood the stories right.

Mr. Smith had been taken to Lutheran Hospital in Ft. Wayne because they have one of the best heart facilities in the state. When they had gotten there, Mom and Dad went straight to the information desk. They found out where the Smith family was and headed straight to that floor.

Once they had found the right area, they found Dallas and his fiancé sitting in the waiting room and Mrs. Smith was pacing the hall way. Mom hugged Mrs. Smith and told her they had gotten there as fast as they could. Mrs. Smith kept thanking them all for coming. The doctors hadn't been out to tell her anything yet and they were still working on Mr. Smith.

Mrs. Smith was a wreck. She was so upset and crying. Mom kept trying to comfort her but until someone tells her something, Shelby was afraid that no amount of comforting was going to help. Shelby walked into the waiting room where Dallas was.

"We came as soon as we heard. Has there been any news yet?" Shelby asked wrapping her arms around him.

She knew there hadn't been but she wanted to get Dallas to talk.

"Thanks for coming. We haven't heard from anyone yet. I just wish they would tell us something. It's been over an hour now!" Dallas said as he let her go.

"Hopefully everything's alright. I'm sure they're doing everything they can. What happened?" Shelby asked trying to find out what he *did* know.

"Sara and I went over to the house for dinner, and while Dad and I were standing in the living room talking, he grabbed his chest and hit the floor. He just kept saying how bad it hurt. I screamed for Mom to call the 911 and when they got there, they loaded him up in the ambulance and he and Mom came straight here. Sara and I drove right behind them." He explained.

Sara stood from her seat and asked, "I'm going to go get some coffee. Can I get anything for anyone else?"

Everyone shook their heads no and she told Dallas to hang in there, she'd be right back.

Shelby sat down with Dallas for a little bit hoping that someone would come and tell them something soon. Finally they did. The doctor came through the doors and Shelby could tell by the look on his face what he was going to say.

"I'm looking for the Smith family." The doctor said.

"I'm Mrs. Smith. How is my husband?" She asked with tears in her eyes.

"We did everything we could but his heart was in really bad condition." The doctor explained.

"NO!" Mrs. Smith yelled as she hit the floor.

Dallas grabbed a hold of her and tried to pick her up from the floor. He tried to get her to sit in one of the chairs.

"I don't understand, I was standing there talking to him and he just collapsed. What caused it?" Dallas asked in disbelief.

"He had a massive heart attack. We got it going again but the damage was to severe; it just gave out. I'm so sorry that there wasn't anything else we could do. I'm truly sorry for your loss." The doctor answered.

Dallas sat beside his Mom trying to comfort her and calm her down. It was so hard for him because there was no one there to comfort him. Dad went to talk to the nurse to find out what they needed to do and Mom tried to help Mrs. Smith the best she could.

"I'm so sorry Dallas." Shelby said to him in a soft whisper.

"I just don't know what to do. This can't be happening, can it?" he asked in a lost tone while tears began to fall from his eyes.

"I'm afraid it is." Shelby replied as she wrapped her arms around him as tight as she could. The more he began to cry, Shelby started crying. He was hurting so badly and Shelby knew how he felt. Her thoughts instantly flashed back to Grant. She just stood holding him and she wasn't about to let go until he wanted her to. Dallas held her so tightly against him; she thought he might break in half.

Sara walked into the waiting room a few minutes later and dropped her coffee to the floor when she saw the scene before her. Shelby and Dallas spun around at the sound of the cup hitting the floor. From the expression on Sara's face, she knew that something bad had happened.

Shelby let go of Dallas and turned to Sara, "You need to take care of him right now. I'll clean it up." She said as she wiped tears from her eyes.

"I can clean it up." Sara replied almost in tears.

"NO, go take care of him!" Shelby said forcefully, pointing toward Dallas.

Shelby bent down on her knees to clean up the spilt coffee. Her eyes still tearing up with every sob she heard in the waiting room. She began to pray that God would help this family through the difficult time before them and give them all the strength to deal with their loss; they needed it more than ever right now.

She picked up the rest of the towels and threw them away. Shelby couldn't take much more and walked into the hallway and began to cry again. She loved Mr. Smith very much. He was more like an uncle to her than a next door neighbor. Her heart was breaking for Dallas and his family.

Mom asked Mrs. Smith if anyone had called Luke. Luke was Dallas's younger brother. Dallas said he had called him on his way to the hospital. Just at that moment, Luke came running down the hall.

"I got here as fast as I could! What happened?" he said trying to catch his breath.

Dallas and his mom pulled Luke off to the side and told him everything. Luke sat down and started to cry as well. He just couldn't believe that their father was gone. The three of them sat together, embraced in their grief.

Mom, Dad, and Shelby walked into the hallway to give them some time to themselves. Sara walked out with them saying she thought it would be better if she left them alone. A nurse had come into the room to talk to them about making the preparations for Mr. Smith.

After a little while, the Smiths' came out of the waiting room and Dallas said the nurse had taken them to see his father so they could say their good byes. Shelby hated this! Shelby hated more than anything to see a family go through such a tragedy. She knew their pain and she was beginning to hate hospitals even more. Just the smell of the place was a constant reminder of what she had experienced with Grant's death.

Both families walked down to their cars to get ready to go home. Mrs. Smith kept thanking them for coming to the hospital and for their support. They explained; if she needed anything, or, any help in any way, to make sure she called them. She said she would. Shelby's parents had already decided they were going to keep a close eye on her anyhow.

Mom and Dad followed Dallas all the way back to Timberville. Once they were home, Shelby decided to go in and have a cup of coffee before going back to her house. The three of them sat at the kitchen table talking when it dawned on Mom that someone had better call CJ and let him know what had happened. Dad walked into the living room to call him right away.

As Mom and Shelby sat talking, Shelby's cell phone started to ring.

"Hello?" Shelby answered.

"Shelby it's Cole. Did I just hear the news right? Did Dallas's Dad pass away tonight?" Cole asked with concern.

"Yes, he did. He had a massive heart attack. We just got back from the hospital." Shelby explained.

"Mr. Smith was a great man. I can't believe he's gone." Cole said solemnly.

"Yes, he was."

"Is there anything I can do?" he asked.

"I don't think there's anything anyone can do right now except keep them in your prayers." Shelby said.

"I will. Will you call me and let me know what the funeral arrangements are? I'd like to be there." Cole asked.

"As soon as I know, you'll be the first one I call."

"If you happen to talk to Dallas, tell him my prayers are with him and his family. I'll talk to you later." He said.

"Alright Cole, I will, bye." Shelby said as she hung up her phone.

Shelby's mother looked at her with surprise in her eyes.

"So, are the two of you talking frequently now?" Mom asked with a goofy grin.

"Yes, from time to time. He calls me every now and then just to catch up." Shelby answered.

"How are you getting along?" she asked with the same look.

"Not too bad these days. He's married and has a baby due soon. He seems to finally be happy with his life and that makes me happy. Why?" Shelby asked sipping her coffee.

"I was just curious. I'm glad that you two are talking again." Mom answered with a crooked grin.

"CJ is on the first plane he can get. He said he'll call when he gets to Ft. Wayne. We can pick him up or he'll just rent a car." Dad told them when he walked back into the kitchen.

"Well, I guess for now I'm going to head home. If there's anything that needs to be done or anyone needs anything, call me. I don't care if it's the middle of the night; call me." Shelby said to both of them.

Shelby hugged them both and left the house. Before she climbed into her truck, she stood looking at the Smith house. The lights were on and she just couldn't help but wonder what they must be going though right now. She knew how she felt, but she couldn't imagine how they did. They were such a great family and she hated that they had to go through this. They were a big part of her own family and she loved them *all* very much.

Over the next few days, Shelby's family spent most of their time helping the Smiths with the funeral. Mrs. Smith was in no condition to do very much. Dallas and Luke stayed with her most of the time. If one would leave the other was there with her. They were taking shifts. Shelby would go over and check on her from time to time as well. She was in bad shape and it was completely understandable.

CJ got home yesterday and has been spending most of his time with Dallas and Luke. CJ being home has helped out a lot. He could talk to them and try to comfort them a little bit better than Shelby could; at least from a man's point of view.

Mom decided to cook dinner for everyone tonight and invited the Smiths over. She thought it would be good for them to get away from the house for a bit; even though it was right next door. She made a big feast and everyone sat in the dinning room. There was a little bit of conversation, but for the most part, it was a solemn mood.

After dinner, CJ and Shelby cleaned up while Mom and Dad sat at the table talking to Mrs. Smith. After Shelby had finished, she decided to sit on the porch for awhile and have a cup of coffee. The fresh air was nice. The house was just too stuffy. It was kind of humid and Shelby felt as if she were being suffocated. Maybe it was just her, she thought.

Shelby reasoned that it brought back to many memories of Grant and what a hard time she had. She just hated to see someone else going through the same kind of situation. The worst part was; she and Grant hadn't even gotten married yet. Mr. and Mrs. Smith had been married for years and now he was going to be buried in the morning.

Shelby sat pondering these thoughts when Dallas walked out of the house.

"Is it alright if I sit with you for awhile?" he asked.

"Of course you can; have a seat." She replied sliding him a chair.

"At least it's a half decent night out. The breeze is a little chilly though." He said as he sat down.

"Yeah, it's not too bad." She answered.

"You know, to a point, I can't wait for this to be over. I hate seeing Mom like this. It's killing me inside, but I know she's carrying the weight of it all. She's trying to be so strong for us boys but she's hurting so much herself." He explained.

"How are *you* doing? I know that everyone has been concerned with your Mom, but has anyone asked you how *you* are?" Shelby asked with concern.

"No, not actually; you've been the first. I'm hanging in there, I guess. I loved my Dad so much; I just can't believe he's gone." Dallas replied as the tears started to fall.

"I know it's hard, but just remember, you have all of us here. If you need someone to talk to or just someone to give you a hug; I'm always here." Shelby said as she wrapped her arms around him.

"I know, trust me, you have no idea how much that means. I think that's what I need the most right now, a friend to tell me that everything will be alright." He answered holding on to her tightly as the tears fell in earnest.

"Eventually it will be. It takes a long time but you'll make it through. All of you will make it through this. It's hard to deal with, trust me, I know first hand, but at some point in time you'll be able to get past it. I know your Dad wouldn't want you to grieve forever." She said tightening her grip on him.

The tighter Shelby held him, the more she just wanted to tell him she would take care of him and help him get through this. It was tearing her up inside. She knew that she couldn't do that though. He had someone else to take care of him. He has a fiancé for pities sake, she thought stupidly to her self.

"I don't know what I would do if you weren't here." He replied.

Shelby knew this was her opportunity to shift the subject.

"Speaking of that, and I'm not trying to change the subject, where is Sara?" She asked confused.

It dawned on her that she hadn't seen her all day.

"She said she had some things to take care of. Actually, she hasn't been around much lately." He said letting go of Shelby and wiped his eyes.

"Is everything alright between the two of you?" She asked.

"Recently, it hasn't been. For about the last month she just seems to be distant from me. Anytime I bring it up, she flies off the handle and leaves. I'm really starting to think things aren't going to work for us." He explained.

"I thought the two of you were happy."

"I thought so too. The more I think about it, I thought we were so much a like, you know? Now I see how totally different we are. I'm trying to hold out and see if things work themselves out, but it gets harder everyday. I really don't know what's going to happen." He replied looking down to the floor.

"I'm so sorry, Dallas. I had no idea what you were going through and now you're Dad. I just can't imagine dealing with all of this at one time." Shelby said to him as she held one of his hands.

"That's why I said I didn't know what I would do if it wasn't for you. You're the only one I can talk to that makes me feel a little bit better." He replied with a slight smile.

"Well, you know I would do anything I could for you." She answered with a smile.

"I know and I appreciate it a lot." He said.

They sat for a little while longer in silence, watching as traffic passed by.

When everything was calm and quite, the air was still. It was peaceful. Of course until her cell phone started going off in her pocket. Shelby pulled the phone out and looked at it. It was Tyler. Perfect timing, she thought wryly. She answered it and he explained that he was back in town. He wanted to have dinner tomorrow night and he had some things he wanted to tell her. As long as he's been gone, she hoped it was something good. Shelby told him she would see him tomorrow and hung up the phone.

"Was that your boyfriend?" Dallas asked with a grin.

"Yes, it was. How did you know?" She asked sheepishly.

"Did you forget that this is a small town and word travels fast?" he said with a chuckle.

"I don't think it's a case of small town syndrome; it's more like my Mom said something to your Mom, didn't she?" Shelby laughed.

"Yeah, I think that's what it was. Well, I had better go check on Mom. Hopefully she's feeling a little better by now." He said as he stood up.

"Ok, well, I will see you in the morning then." Shelby said as she stood with him.

"I'll see you in the morning." He said with one last smile.

The smile he gave her was one of those smiles she remembered from the past. It was one of those smiles that brought you to your knees with just one glance. Dallas had a gorgeous smile, Shelby thought to her self.

She couldn't be thinking like that right now. *I can't think about Dallas like that!* Shelby had to get away from him and back to the safety of her home. If she let past feelings creep up on her now, she didn't know *what* stupid thing she might do. She reasoned she was feeling like this, right now, because she was caught up in the emotions of what Dallas was going through with the loss of his father. That had to be it, she thought.

Dallas held the front door open for her and they both walked back into the house. Shelby told Mom and Dad that she was going home for the night. Mom pulled her off to the side and asked how Dallas was doing. Shelby explained he was fine and that at least she had him smiling. Everyone was concerned that maybe after his father dying; he might go back to drinking again. That was one of the reasons Shelby was trying to keep a close eye on him. After what he had explained to her about his girlfriend, she worried a little more. All of this might be just enough to push him over the edge, Shelby thought helplessly.

When Shelby had made it home, she took one look around her house. It was such a mess right now. She thought, for as much as she was gone, it wouldn't be like this. If she wasn't at work, she was at Mom and Dad's. She guessed when she came home long enough to shower and change, things could become a little messy. Well, if Tyler was coming for dinner tomorrow, she thought she had better get the place cleaned up. She had to be at the funeral in the morning and she had patients to take care of all afternoon.

The next morning, the funeral came and went. The ceremony was beautiful and everyone that spoke about Mr. Smith had wonderful things to say about him. After it had finished, everyone gathered back at the Smith house for dinner but Shelby didn't go. She had so many house calls to make; she knew if she didn't get them done now, she would never be able to get home at a descent time tonight.

Shelby was in for a very long day. She had only gotten a few calls done when more poured in. She didn't think she was ever going to get done. It was like all hell had broken loose in the animal kingdom. Thank the Lord some of the calls were just simple things. Some of them she really didn't have to go to, but, to be a good doc, you must check out every call.

By the time she had made it home, it was so late; Tyler was sitting on the front steps of her house waiting for her. He had a bouquet of flowers in his hands and Shelby was covered in mud. It had definitely been a long day.

Tyler handed her the flowers and apologized for not being around much the past few weeks. Shelby thanked him and invited him to come into the house. She had to get cleaned up and change her clothes. Tyler graciously told her to do whatever she needed and take her time.

Shelby took the stairs two at a time heading straight for the bathroom, throwing her clothes off as she went. She took a quick shower, got dressed, and brushed her hair *and* her teeth. Then she walked subtly down to the kitchen.

Tyler was sitting at the table looking very nervous about some thing.

"Are you alright? You seem out of sorts." Shelby asked trying to figure out what was wrong.

"I'm alright but I think you had better sit down. There are some things I have to tell you." He said as he shook his leg up and down in a nervous twitch.

"Ok, now you're scaring me. Some thing is wrong, isn't there?" Shelby asked with confusion as she sat down at the table.

"The last month or so that we've spent together has been great, *but*, something happened and…oh, I really don't know how to explain this…you see, remember when we first started seeing each other and I told you that I had just gotten out of a really long relationship?" Tyler asked getting more nervous by the second.

"Yeah, I can recall that conversation." Shelby answered nodding her head.

Right then, Shelby knew what he was trying to tell her, this conversation had some thing to do with another woman.

"Well, when I was gone on one of my business trips, I got a call from her. It just so happened that I was in the same city as her when she called. Anyway, she told me that she wanted to meet me for a drink; she had some things that we needed to talk about because she was having a hard time moving on with her life." He started explaining.

"Ok, so, what happened?" Shelby asked.

"We met and we talked about what had gone wrong with our relationship; the longer we talked, the more we started to understand each other. Of course, with that, we both came to the same conclusion that we couldn't move on with our lives because we didn't have each other to do that with. Is all of this making any sense to you?" Tyler asked with hesitation.

"So, does this mean the two of you are back together? Is that what you're trying to tell me?" Shelby asked calmly. She already knew the answer to the question.

"*Please*, don't hate me for this. I understand if you do, but you really have to understand where I'm coming from. We had a *very* long relationship and after sharing that much of your life with one person; in the back of your head, you really never get over them. You understand, don't you?" He pleaded with her. It was as if he were begging for forgiveness.

"Why didn't you just tell me this over the phone? You didn't have to come here to tell me, Tyler. It's not like we were in that serious of a relationship." Shelby replied shaking her head.

"I know, but I'm not that kind of person. I started something with you and I couldn't just leave you hang like that. Even if I thought I would get my head knocked off; I had to talk to you face to face. Trust me, I never thought this would happen, but it did. I thought she was out of my life forever!" He explained.

"Let me ask you this; do you *really, truly* love her?"

"With all of my heart; I would give my life for her." He answered truthfully.

"Then that's all I need to know."

Tyler was in shock. It couldn't be this easy, he thought. Then he asked, "You're not mad at me?"

"No not at all. I know what it's like to lose someone you love. I also know what it's like to be with someone when your heart belongs to another." She answered.

As those words rolled off her tongue, she saw someone's face flash before her. The words, "when your heart belongs to another," reverberated through her head. At that moment, Shelby realized that her heart *did* belong to someone. Why hadn't she seen this before? She asked her self. Suddenly, she felt a burning feeling through out her entire body at that very moment.

I am in love with someone!.

"So, you do know what I'm talking about?" Tyler asked confused.

"Yes I do, I just never knew it until now. Thank you Tyler, you have just opened my eyes to something! Thank you for being honest with me. It took a lot for you to come here and tell me this." Shelby said to him as she kissed him on the cheek.

"You're welcome, and in that case, I think I'll leave now." he said as he started for the front door.

"Ok, I hope the two of you have a great life together!" Shelby shouted to him as he shut the door.

Oh no! Shelby began to argue with her self. She just had the biggest revelation of her life and she couldn't do a thing about it. Her heart did belong to someone else, but he was with *someone* right now! What should she do?

Shelby thought about the possibilities and the consequences over and over in her head. She finally came to the realization, right now, she couldn't do a thing. She couldn't disrupt someone else's life because she was an idiot and *just* realized it. She had had so many chances in the past and had blown them all. She couldn't do this to him; only time would tell now and she would have to sit back and wait. She couldn't stand this feeling! It wasn't fair!

The days seemed to drag on forever. Days became weeks and weeks became months. Shelby still had no idea what she was going to do about her problem. She was in love and she couldn't tell him how she felt. This had to be true torture.

Shelby did what she always did though; she sank her self into her work. It's all she had. There was a big convention going on for a whole week she was considering going to. It would get her away for awhile. She called her mother and ran the idea past her. She told her it sounded like a great idea. Shelby gave in and made arrangements for someone to cover the office for her while she was gone.

Even though the trip was work related, it would be like taking a vacation. It would feel so good to get away, Shelby thought happily. The best part about the convention was it was in Florida! White sandy beaches here I come! Shelby yelled to her self. She was packed and ready to go when her Mom and Dad stopped by to see her off. Shelby was driving her self to the airport and leaving her truck there for when she came home. Shelby hugged her parents' and kissed them both, before she climbed into her truck and told them good bye.

Shelby couldn't get to the airport fast enough!

The plane ride was perfect and the hotel was gorgeous. As soon as she had gotten to her room, she threw everything down and leapt onto the bed. This was going to be a great week! After she settled into her room, Shelby changed her clothes and headed down to the restaurant for something to eat. She thought she would relax a little bit before all of the commotion of tomorrow's events.

Once Shelby was seated at a table and was looking over the menu, a gentleman walked up to her table. He asked if she was here for the veterinarian convention too. Of course, she explained she was and he asked if he could join her. He sat down and once he and Shelby got acquainted with each other, he went on to tell her all about him self. *That* was the first problem. He boasted about himself the entire time! Shelby couldn't get a word in edgewise while he just went on and on.

Ok, maybe this wasn't such a good idea after all. *Someone help please!* Shelby screamed in her head. He wasn't that attractive of a man either. He was tall and scrawny and a bit older than Shelby. His head was partially bald and he wore thick glasses over his eyes. He was dressed neatly in a dark grey colored suit and his pant legs were hiked up over his ankles. He talked *so* much; Shelby couldn't even remember his name. She didn't know if she wanted to either. All Shelby knew right now; she wanted away from the man as soon as she could!

By the time dinner had finished, Shelby couldn't wait to get back to her room. This man was insane! He wanted to walk her back to her room! She lost him before he could get that far. As soon as she caught him with his head turned, she snuck off. She hoped like hell she didn't run into him again.

The next day, she spent the entire day going from lecture to lecture learning new techniques and handling procedures for different animals. It was really educational and helpful, but after so long, it became boring. It seemed every class was just about the same. Shelby was so worn out by the time they had finished for the day; she went back to her room, order room service and fell asleep.

By the time Wednesday rolled around, Shelby was ready to go home. This wasn't half the fun she thought it would be. She was so tired by the time the classes were over; she hadn't even had the energy to enjoy the beach yet. She still had two more days to go!

Oh no, that strange man was heading her way again. What am I going to do? She asked herself squirming in her seat. This time he didn't even ask if he could sit down; he just did! Shelby sat listening to him ramble on and on. It all went in one ear and right back out the other. How could she get rid of him?

Her question was about to be answered.

"Hello my darling, I wondered where you got off too." A man said as he sat down at the table in the seat next to her. He leaned closer to her and kissed her on the cheek.

"I was just sitting here trying to cool off, dear." Shelby replied trying to keep a straight face. She was in complete shock!

It was Cole to the rescue!

Cole gave the man sitting across the table a deathly glare and he caught the hint real quick; he left the table. Shelby sat back in her seat and looked at Cole in complete shock.

"What are you doing here?" She shouted as she hugged him.

"I was about to ask you the same question, well, that was until I saw that you were in trouble." He replied with a laugh.

"I can't believe your here! This is so amazing. I had to come down for a convention. What are you doing here?" She asked again with amazement.

"Tiff and I decided we needed a vacation before football season started up.

We thought this would be the perfect time to show our daughter off in front of the media." He answered.

"Oh, my gosh, you have a daughter?" She yelped in shock for a second time.

"Yep and she is gorgeous." He replied with absolute pride.

Just then, Tiffany walked up to the table with a baby in her arms wrapped in a thin blanket. Cole was right; she was absolutely beautiful. Shelby couldn't believe Cole was a father now! Well, she knew it would be soon but she didn't know that she had already been born. She was utterly flabbergasted.

"Congratulations you guys! I am so happy for you. She is just adorable. I just can't believe it; you're a daddy now. This is so amazing!" Shelby exclaimed with excitement as she clapped her hands together.

"I know what you mean. I can't get over it myself. This has been the best thing to ever happen to me; of course besides you, my dear." He replied as he kissed Tiffany on the cheek.

Shelby could see how much they loved each other. Babies did strange things to people. Ok, wonderful things, Shelby thought happily.

"Well, I'm so happy for the two of you. You guys deserve it." Shelby said. She gave them both a hug.

"Honey, I'm going to go take her up to the room. She's getting a little fussy." Tiffany said to Cole.

"Alright, I'll be up in a little bit. I want to catch up with Shelby for a few minutes." He said to her.

"That's fine; take your time." She answered with a smile. "It's nice to see you again Shelby."

"It's good to see you too Tiffany and again, congratulations."

"Thank you." She said as she walked away.

"How crazy is this; we ended up in the same place at the same time?" Cole asked in amazement.

"I know, isn't that weird?" Shelby replied.

"So, what do you think?" Cole asked as he looked toward Tiffany's retreating back.

"I have to admit Parker; you make a beautiful baby." Shelby replied with a laugh.

"Yeah, I thought so." He said rubbing his knuckles on his chest smiling.

"It looks like everything worked out for you two."

"I never would have dreamed it would turn out this way. After Shelly was born; Tiffany did a whole one eighty. She's a completely different person now." he explained.

"You named the baby Shelly?" Shelby asked confused.

"Yeah, you kind of inspired that. You've always been a big part of my life even when we weren't talking. I wanted there to be some part of you in there." He replied with a warm smile.

"Well, I'm honored. Thank you very much; that means a lot."

"So, what have you been up to these days? You still seeing that Tyler guy?" he asked.

"No not actually. That's ancient history now. He found his long lost soul mate and decided he wanted to give that another try. So, I'm back to just me again." She explained.

"Well, you know, we could always have a hot affair once a year." Cole said with a huge grin batting both eye brows at her.

"You're funny! As much as I would like to take you up on that offer; I think I'll have to pass." She said wrinkling her nose at him as she hit him in the arm.

"I was just joking; but if you ever feel the need, you just let me know." He replied with another wink.

"You're terrible!" She said with a giggle.

"I know. So how's everyone else been in that neck of the woods? Hey, how's Dallas? I know losing his father must have been hard on him." He asked with concern.

"It was. As far as I know, he's been doing alright. I haven't spoken to him really since the funeral. Last I heard, he was getting married soon, I think." Shelby answered disappointedly.

"Yeah, I heard that too. I heard CJ was going to be walking too. What do you think about that?" he asked.

"The girl he's engaged to is a real sweet person. I've know her for quite awhile and I think they'll be good together. As long as he's happy, that's all that matters." She explained to him.

"And what about you; are you happy?" he asked with a serious look.

"I guess. I'm as happy as I'll ever be. I know someday, something will happen for me, but right now, it just doesn't seem to be in the cards." Shelby replied with a sigh. She wasn't about to tell him what she was *really* feeling and about who.

"Can I ask you about something, with out you getting mad about it?" he asked.

"Sure and I'll try not to."

"Do you remember back when we had that big blow out at the hotel in Ft. Wayne?" he asked.

"Yes. Do we really have to re-hash that?" She asked hoping he would drop it.

"What really happened between you and Dallas that night?" he asked with a dead stare.

"Just what I told you; nothing; something might have if I hadn't passed out though. I won't lie to you about that." Shelby said shaking her head.

"Did you want something to?" he asked.

"Maybe."

Yes.

Tears started to fill Shelby's eyes. She picked up a pen and started flicking it against the table. She always did when she started to get nervous. Cole had already figured it out.

"Can I give you my opinion?" he asked.

Shelby nodded and Cole went on.

"Shelby, I think that all of these years, you've had feelings for Dallas and you've spent so much time trying to fight it that you never saw it before. Am I right?" he asked seriously.

"As much as I hate to admit it; especially to you; you're absolutely right. I realized it when his dad passed away. I wanted to hold him so close and tell him that I would take care of him so badly, but I just couldn't do it." She answered looking down at the table.

"Why the hell not?" he blurted out.

"He's engaged!"

"What's that got to do with it? It's not like he's married yet. What the hell are you doing here? Why aren't you at home going after him; before it's too late?" Cole asked as he grabbed her hands.

"I can't put myself in the middle. He's made his choice and if he doesn't go through with the wedding, *then*, that's his decision. I can't be the one to make it for him." She answered.

"Have you ever told him how you feel?" he asked.

"No, I haven't, because I didn't know myself till recently." Shelby replied whipping her eyes.

"Do you love him?"

Shelby hesitated.

"Come on, Shelby. Do…you…love him?" Cole asked again.

"Yes."

"I'll tell you one thing right now; if you walked up to him and told him that you loved him; that boy would drop the world for you. I think that's one of the reasons why I fell in love with you in the first place. It wasn't so much me; it was that I was jealous of the two of you. You guys have a bond that's so much deeper then the two of us could ever have had. I wanted that *so* much that I let my brains take over before I let my heart. Don't get me wrong; I *was* in love with you; but eventually, I came to terms that I wasn't ever going to have you the way that Dallas did." He explained to her.

Shelby slumped back in her chair and asked, "Cole, what am I going to do? I have been so stupid for so long."

"Do what anyone else in your shoes would do; go home!" He replied.

"What if it doesn't work out that way?"

"Then he's a bigger goof than I thought and we can still have our affair once a year!" He exclaimed with a laugh.

"Oh, get over yourself! Thank you so much for this. I really didn't want to answer you when you asked, but I'm tired of replaying this in my head over and over. I have felt horrible for so long, but you've helped me figure out at least some thing. For that; I do love you." Shelby said as she stood from the table to hug him.

"I knew one day I'd get you to say it!" he shouted.

"Say what?" She asked confused.

"That you love me, of course." He replied with a laugh.

"I don't know what I would do with out you."

"I know; so what's the game plan?" he asked.

"I have to finish the next two days here and then I'm on a plane straight home. I guess I'll never find out until I try." She replied shrugging her shoulders.

"Sounds like a plan to me. I had better check on Tiffany and the baby. She probably needs a break by now. Let me know what's going on and maybe we can have dinner before you fly home." He answered.

"Alright; I'll see you later and Cole; thanks again."

"Don't worry about it. It'll work out, you'll see." He said with a smile as he walked away.

Great, just a couple of more days and I'll be home, Shelby thought nervously. She just hoped she could find the guts to do this when she got there. What would she say to him? How will he react? Am I making a huge mistake? I think I'm starting to get a headache. The thought of the possibility of holding Dallas in her arms forever made her head swim. She had to get home.

Chapter 17

Friday afternoon had arrived and Shelby couldn't take it anymore. She got the first flight she could find and called her Mom to tell her she would be home soon. Shelby was shaking all over. The anticipation was about to drive her crazy! It was late night before her plane landed in Ft. Wayne and she talked to her mother practically the whole way home.

Mom bugged her all the way there as to what was the matter. Shelby finally broke down and told her the whole story.

Mom was happy Shelby had finally came to that realization, but Dallas had been out of town this week and wasn't due to be back until tomorrow morning. Great, now she had to wait another night. Maybe this was a sign and she wasn't really supposed to do this. Who was she trying to kid?

Shelby made it home in record time and thanked her mother for helping to keep her awake while she drove home. Weird enough, Mom told her not to get her hopes up too soon. She was keeping tight lipped about something. For the life of her, Shelby couldn't get her to spill it. Mom said she was just over reacting. *What* did she know? Shelby asked her self.

Later that night, Shelby sat twiddling her thumbs not knowing what to do. She picked up the phone and called Leah to see what she was up to. She thought maybe she might want to get a drink or something. Sitting in her house, doing nothing was driving her insane!

"Hey, Leah what are you up to?" Shelby asked when Leah answered.

"At this moment nothing; how was your trip?" she asked.

"It wasn't' too bad. Would you want to go out for a drink? I need to get out for awhile." Shelby asked her.

"Shelby, I'd like to but I have a really big wedding I'm working on for tomorrow." She replied.

"Oh, I see. I didn't know anyone was getting married this weekend. Is it here in town?" Shelby asked curiously.

"Yeah, haven't you heard?" Leah asked in a confused tone.

"No, who is it?"

"Dallas and Sara; I thought you knew." She replied.

"They're getting married tomorrow! They can't be! This can't be happening. When did this come about? I thought they weren't getting married till this fall." Shelby shouted into the phone.

"Well, they weren't supposed to, but at the last minute, I got a call from Sara saying they didn't want to wait any longer. So, they decided to do it this weekend. Trust me, trying to get this entire thing put together in just a week has been hell. Thank God for my quick thinking, or otherwise, I wouldn't even be close to being ready." Leah answered.

"Leah, I have to let you go. Something just came up......I'll talk to you later." Shelby said frantically.

"Ok, well, call me." She replied.

"Ok." Shelby said as she hung up the phone.

What am I going to do now? They're getting married tomorrow afternoon! This can't be happening! This must be what Mom wasn't telling me. If the wedding is tomorrow and Dallas will be back in the morning; maybe I can catch him then. Yeah that's what I'll do; I'll track him down first thing in the morning, Shelby thought helplessly.

She stared out the window trying to put a plan of action together in her head. The longer she stood there thinking; the more she thought about how stupid she was being. Who was she kidding? She couldn't go through with this. If he wanted to get married so quickly, it just goes to show *this* is what he really wants. Who was she to stand in the way of that? She couldn't do this to him; it wasn't right. It's just not fair, she thought hopelessly.

Shelby awoke the next morning with a pounding head ache. She had drunk a whole bottle of wine last night just trying to fall asleep. She kept replaying the situation over and over in her head. She couldn't find one reason to go through with it except for her own gain. She had the biggest head ache she ever had in her life. It was pounding so badly right now. She walked down to the kitchen to get something for it when she heard the phone ringing. That made it worse. She didn't ever remember the phone being that loud.

"Hello?" she asked.

"Hey, what's happened? Did you tell him?" the voice asked.

It was Cole.

"No I didn't and I'm not going to." She answered.

"Why the hell not?" he yelled.

"Stop yelling; my head hurts bad enough as it is. He's getting married this afternoon. I just can't do it."

"He's getting married this afternoon? Wow, that was fast! Shelby you have to tell him. What if he gets married and regrets it for the rest of his life? You're going to regret it for the rest of *your* life if you don't. Trust me, I know Dallas, probably better than anyone else; you have to do this!" Cole exclaimed.

"Cole, what if I do and he still wants to marry her? I'll feel like such a jerk for trying to stop what he *really* wants." Shelby pleaded with Cole.

"That's a risk you're going to have to take. You'll never know if you don't. If you *truly* love him; you have to tell him." He answered.

"I know, I know, I know! I have to let you go. I need to call someone and find out where the wedding is." She said to Cole.

"That's my girl! I knew you couldn't give up that easily. You just needed a good old fashioned pep talk." He said with a laugh.

"Alright, I'll talk to you later." She replied holding her head.

"Alright and you had better call me and let me know what happens. Bye." He said.

"I will; bye." She answered hanging up the phone.

Shelby popped a couple of pain pills for her head and ran up the stairs to change her clothes. She grabbed the phone and called Leah to find out what time the wedding was. Leah asked if she was going to be there and Shelby told her she would. Shelby just wasn't about to tell her why; at least not yet. She said it was at two and it was twelve thirty now. She didn't have much time! Shelby told Leah that if she wasn't there before it started; stall. Leah really started freaking out then. Before she got too far, Shelby hung up the phone.

She ran out to her truck, staring at the steering wheel trying to figure out where to start. What was she going to say to him? As she drove down the road it dawned on her; what church is it being held at? Oh crap! Shelby didn't ask Leah which church it was. Oh no! She kept trying to call Leah back but she wasn't answering her phone. God how she hated voice mail!

Shelby spent most of the time driving from church to church. So far there was none with a wedding. Finally, she found one with a bunch of cars parked around it and there was one car that said just married across the back wind shield. This had to be it.

Shelby jumped out of the truck and ran through the doors. She could hear the wedding music playing, so she knew they were just getting ready to start. She ran into the main part of the church and there was a man and a woman standing in front of the preacher, at the altar. Shelby yelled at the top of her lungs...

"STOP; YOU CAN'T GO THROUGH WITH THIS!"

Everything went deadly silent and everyone turned to look at her. Much to her surprise, this was not the wedding she was looking for! She heard the bride ask the groom if he knew who she was. He of course said no and he had never seen her before in his life. Shelby told him he was right and she was at the wrong wedding. She apologized to everyone, told the bride she looked beautiful, and slowly walked away. As she was leaving, she heard someone say they felt sorry for who ever she *was* looking for.

Shelby was humiliated. *That* had to be the most embarrassing thing she had ever done. She walked back to her truck and climbed in. She started to cry. This was the last church she could think of. She had no idea where else to look. It was ten after two and she just knew they had started by now. Leah wasn't going to delay the wedding. She had a job to do and Shelby knew she wouldn't jeopardize her reputation for *her* and she didn't blame her for that.

Shelby was starting the truck when it hit her. There's one more church out on the west side of town! It was out in the country a bit. It would be just like Dallas to want a country wedding. Shelby shifted the truck into drive and drove as fast as she could; pedal to the floor.

Have you ever been in one of those situations where you're in a huge hurry and everyone else seems to be in slow motion? That was her predicament *right now*. She had to of run across every slow moving vehicle she could find. She knew she was too late. It was two thirty. She would be lucky if there was anyone there, let alone trying to stop a wedding!

Sure enough, when she pulled into the parking lot of the church; there was only one car left. It didn't look familiar so she bet it was the preachers. She had to go in and see for her self.

As she walked through the doors, the whole church was decorated with flowers and pretty little bells. No one was here. A wedding had taken place and she was too late. I'm *way* too late, Shelby thought.

Shelby stood in the middle of the isle trying to imagine what it must have been like. The only difference was; she imagined it was her walking down this very isle and Dallas was waiting for *her*. She heard a noise come from down one of the hallways and her dream vanished. Shelby walked to the altar, knelt on her knees and began to pray. She thought since she hadn't made it in time, the least she could do was say a prayer for them. She prayed for them to have a wonderful life together and love each other always.

As Shelby stood back up, she heard someone cough from behind her. She spun around to see who it was. It was the preacher.

"Can I help you, Miss?" he asked politely.

He was an older man. He had to be pushing at least eighty.

"No, I don't believe you can. I see I've already missed the wedding." She replied quietly.

"Yes, you have, probably by about ten, fifteen minutes I'd say."

"Thank you." Shelby said as she walked away.

"It was a beautiful ceremony." He said as she let the door slide out of her hand.

Game over, she was too late.

Shelby crawled back into her truck and laid her head against the steering wheel. After a few minutes of crying to her self, she finally started the truck and put it in gear. There was nothing left for her to do but go home to her empty house.

When she got home the answering machine was blinking. She pushed the play button and Mom had left her frantic messages.

The first message; "Shelby, are you home? Pick up the phone! Call me as soon as you get this."

The Second message; "Shelby where are you? I need you to call me as soon as possible."

The third message; "Shelby, I don't know where in the world you are but you better call home immediately!"

What in the world was going on over there? She thought confused.

Shelby picked up the phone and dialed their number.

"Hello?" Mom answered.

"Mom, what's going on? I just got your messages."

"Shelby, you need to get over here fast; something's terribly wrong." She said in a panic.

"What is it?" She asked more confused

"I don't want to talk about it over the phone; you just need to get here now!" Mom said as she hung the phone up on Shelby.

Something must be wrong with Dad! Shelby thought in a panic.

She jumped back into the truck and flew to their house. Shelby slid the truck sideways in front of the house and bolted for the front door.

"Mom, what is it? Is Dad alright? Are you alright?" She yelled through the house.

"Your Dad and I are fine." Mom said calmly.

"Then what's all the fuss? I didn't come screeching down the street for nothing." Shelby said trying to catch her breath.

Dad was standing at the bottom of the stairs and Mom gave him a sneaky smile. They both walked up the stairs and left her standing in the middle of the living room by herself.

"What *is* going on?" Shelby said out loud to herself flinging her arms in the air. What is wrong with these people?

Shelby turned to look out the door and Dallas was standing in the doorway. Dumbfounded and in shock, she couldn't say anything at first. She just stared at him.

"What are you doing here?" Shelby whispered and placed her hands over her mouth when she finally found her voice again.

"I have some unfinished business to take care of." He said with a crooked grin.

"Shouldn't you be on your way to your honeymoon or something?"

"That's what I'm *supposed* to be doing, but it didn't seem to happen that way." He answered.

"I don't understand?" Shelby asked confused while shaking her head.

"Everyone was at the church; Sara walked down the isle; and while I was lifting the veil over her head; I looked into her eyes and I couldn't go through with it. With one look; I knew I couldn't do it." He answered.

Shelby's breath caught in her throat. Her voice cracked when she asked, "Why?"

"Because, I realized at that moment; she's not the one that I'm truly in love with. I loved her, yes, but I wasn't *in* love with her. So, are you going to tell me why you've been running all over the county side looking for me?" He asked with a grin as he took a step toward her.

"Where did you hear that?" She asked.

"Oh, a little birdie told me." He said with a chuckle as he took another step toward her.

Cole!

"I don't suppose that little birdie might have been Cole?" Shelby asked.

"Maybe, so, are you going to tell me why you were trying to find me?" he asked as he took another step toward her.

Shelby's feet were cemented to the ground. She couldn't move. If Cole had told him that she was looking for him, he must have told him why. Shelby wasn't for sure about anything anymore, but Dallas was one thing she was positive about. Here goes nothing, she thought.

"I realized that the man I'm in love with was about to make the biggest mistake of his life." Shelby answered shyly with a straight face.

Dallas stood for a second with a confused look and then looked around the room.

"I don't see anyone else here. Just when did you know that you were in love with this man?" He asked teasingly taking another step toward her.

"I knew when we spent this amazing night together in a hotel once. He treated me like a queen and at that moment, I knew. I was just too stupid and scared to realize it at the time." Shelby explained as a tear rolled from her eye. After thinking long and hard about it last night, Shelby had realized that she had fallen in love with Dallas that night. She almost told him so the next morning when Cole had burst through the door and everything else had blown up.

"So, what took you so long?" he asked as the smile on his face grew bigger and tears started to well in his eyes. Dallas took another step closer. "Why didn't you tell him then?" he asked.

"Because when I was about to, we were interrupted. Now years have passed. Things have changed, *we* have changed. He was with someone and I had to give it some time to see if *who* he was with; was what he *really* wanted." She replied.

"And what about now; is your mind made up?" he asked.

Hell yes it is!

Dallas was standing right in front of her now. He was so close and all Shelby wanted to do was lock her arms around him and kiss him with everything she had. She wanted him to know just how much she was in love with him. First, she couldn't help but tease him; just like he had tormented her in the hotel room.

"I don't know. I think I might need some more time to think about it. I'll get back to you on that." Shelby answered when she turned to walk away from him as if she were going to leave.

Dallas threw his head back and laughed but as soon as Shelby turned; he grabbed her by the arm, spun her around and wrapped his arms around her as tightly as he could. The two of them stood looking at each other; everything was just as it should be. Dallas bent his head closer to her just to the point of their lips brushing. They paused for a second; giving each other a slight smile; and finally kissed. At that very moment Shelby knew; this was exactly where she wanted to be; in his arms for the rest of her life.

"I love you so much." Shelby said to Dallas; her voice cracked.

"If you only knew how long I have waited to hear you say that." He said with a smile as he kissed her again.

"I can't believe it took me this long to tell you. Did Cole actually call you and tell you that I was looking for you?" She asked.

"After I called off the wedding and Sara almost knocked my head off; my phone rang and it was him." Dallas started to explain.

"What did he say?"

"Well, first off, I wasn't even going to answer it. When I did, he told me that if I went through with the wedding, I would be making the biggest mistake of my life. I hadn't even told him yet that I had already called it off. I asked him why and he asked me one simple question." Dallas explained.

"What was his question?" Shelby asked inquisitively.

"What was the one thing in this world that I wanted more than anything?"

"What did you tell him?" She asked with a devious grin.

"I told him that he knew the answer to that question. Cole then went on to tell me you were probably out searching for me somewhere. Before everyone had left the church, I asked if anyone had seen you and no one had. I waited at the church for awhile, but when you never showed, I figured the next place to look was here." He answered.

"You're right. I checked every church around. I asked Leah what time the wedding was, but forgot the biggest question; where was it being held? That was kind of stupid. That's what took me so long. I found it, but I thought I was too late. I just thank God you didn't go through with it." Shelby said kissing him again.

"You and me both; I just can't get over how today has ended up. I was supposed to be married this afternoon; and here I am with the woman I love instead. How crazy is that?" He replied.

"Well, you know what they say; God works in mysterious ways."

"That, I do believe. So, how did Cole know about all of this?" he asked.

"*That* is a very long story and I'll tell you all about later. Right now, I just want to talk about us. What do we do now?" She asked.

"That's the best part of all; whatever we want." Dallas said as he picked her up and spun her around.

"I wonder if we should call Cole and give him the good news. I bet he's pulled all of his hair out by now." Shelby said with a chuckle.

"I bet he has. Call him and tell him you got there too late." Dallas said with a laugh.

Shelby shook her head and started dialing Cole's number on her cell phone. He knew it was her as soon as he answered.

"It's about time you called. What happened?" Cole asked.

"I was too late. He already went through with the wedding." Shelby said in a depressed tone.

"You have got to be kidding me! So, even though I called him; he still didn't listen? I'm going to knock his head in. I should've known he wouldn't listen to me! How can he be so stupid?" Cole ranted through the phone.

Dallas and Shelby held their breath trying not to laugh out loud.

"Cole, what do I do now?" Shelby asked doing her damndest not to laugh.

"Well, we can always do what I suggested in Florida." Cole said.

Dallas narrowed his eyes at Shelby with a funny look as to what Cole had said. She held up one finger to tell him to wait a second.

"What was that?" Shelby asked Cole.

"We can still have that hot affair." He answered.

Dallas took the phone out of her hand.

"Hey dude; I don't think so; that just isn't gonna' happen! If you think it will, I'll hang up on you right now!" Dallas blurted at Cole through the phone.

"Dallas is that you? I knew you were there! I knew if anything would get you going that would be it!" Cole shouted through the phone. "So, are both of you happy now?"

"Yeah, we are!" Dallas and Shelby said simultaneously into the phone as they looked deeply into each other's eyes.

"So, are you two together now or what?" Cole asked.

"Yes, we are and always will be." They both replied.

"Good, now go on with your lives so I don't have to worry about you anymore, and don't forget to send me an invitation to the wedding!" Cole said before he hung up on them.

The two of them burst out laughing.

"So, what's this about an affair?" Dallas asked Shelby confused with half a grin.

"It was Cole's way, at the time, of cheering me up. I had just told him how I felt about you and he knew saying something like that would make me laugh, and it did." Shelby replied.

"Well, I'm glad he told you to come after me." Dallas said as he cupped her chin in his hand.

"You and me both," Shelby answered as she kissed him, again.

"Do you think we should tell your parents?" Dallas asked as he held her in his arms.

"How much do you want to bet, we don't have to?" Shelby asked with a devious grin.

"What do you mean?" he asked confused.

"Watch this," Shelby said as she walked to the bottom of the stairs. "Mom, Dad, can you come down here?"

Within seconds, Shelby's parents were down the stairs. Shelby couldn't help but laugh at their reactions.

"So, how much of our conversation did the two of you overhear?" She asked them with a crooked grin narrowing her eyes at them.

They gave each other a look and looked at Shelby and Dallas holding each other before Shelby's mother spoke up shyly saying, "All of it."

"And what do the two of you think?" Shelby asked them.

"It took you long enough." Her father said as he slowly began to chuckle. Shelby's mouth gapped open. She couldn't believe her father had said that.

"What?" Shelby said in shock.

"You heard me. I'll admit, I liked Grant, but I've been rooting for Dallas for years. I saw it when the two of you were still in high school. You're Daddy ain't no dummy. I just can't believe it took *you* this long to see and it took almost losing him for you to realize it!" Shelby's father explained.

"Thank you, sir." Dallas said as he extended his hand to her Dad.

"What am I, the middle of a conspiracy around here?" Shelby asked disbelievingly.

"No, honey, we all just love you and we knew a long time ago that Dallas loved you too." Shelby's mother said as she hugged her.

Shelby's cell phone started to ring.

"Hello?" She answered.

"Are the rumors true?" CJ asked.

"What rumors?" She asked.

"About you and Dallas; are the two of you finally together?"

"Yes but how…let me guess, Cole called you too?" Shelby asked him.

"Yes, he did, thank God, now the three ring circus is over! Sis, by the way, I'm happy for you and will you please pass that along to Dallas as well?" CJ asked.

"I will and CJ, thank you. I love you." Shelby said to him.

"I love you too, Sis." CJ said as he hung up.

Did everyone around her realize there was something between her and Dallas all of these years but her? Shelby asked her self. What difference did it make now, *she* had him and that was the *only* thing that mattered.

Chapter 18

Dallas moved in with Shelby after the first week. The only problem they had was sleeping arrangements. Shelby had no problem with Dallas sleeping with her as long as they restrained themselves from making love till they were married. That was one particular subject Shelby was adamant about. Dallas didn't understand at first, but as long as he could wake up every morning with his beautiful red head beside him, he felt celibacy, for the moment, was worth the torture. Shelby had explained to him, even when she was engaged to Grant; *that* had been the one request she would not back down from.

Dallas prodded her for awhile about the subject but Shelby found she was too embarrassed to tell Dallas the truth. She knew Dallas was already experienced in the ways of making love and sex, but for her, she didn't want him to know that she herself, was still a virgin. She wanted her first time to be special and how more special could it be than waiting for the night of her wedding with the man she had loved since childhood.

Shelby was worried about one thing though. Now that she and Dallas were finally together, everyone, including themselves, we're assuming they were going to be married. She and Dallas discussed it all the time, *but*, he had still not actually proposed to her and put an engagement ring on her finger. Was that something she needed to worry about? Or, was Dallas planning something and he was waiting for just the right time?

For the next few months, they were practically inseparable. They were never far away from away each other, if they could help it. Football season was approaching fast and they both knew there would be times they would have to be away from each other. Up to this point, Shelby even went with him from time to time to practice. She could guarantee, for all of his home games; she was going to be there. Everyone knew *not* to get a hold of her on those Sundays.

Life could not be any better. It was everything Shelby had dreamed of and more. Both of them were happier then they had ever been. Shelby's parents' weren't surprised at the turn of events; but none the less happy as could be. Mom had told her that she thought Shelby would end up with one of the neighbor boys along time ago and to this day, Shelby still couldn't believe how right she had been; even though her mother had been scared of the idea back then. Shelby thought she had definitely changed her opinion about that now.

The first football game of the season was about to start and Dallas had invited everyone to come. He gave out tickets to everyone in town. He was up to something, Shelby just knew it, but at the same time, she thought he was just excited about the new season. A lot had happened to both of them since last season, so maybe that's what it was.

It was so cool because Dallas had reserved Shelby's family and his, VIP box seats. This was so awesome! Shelby screamed inside her head.

Before the game started; everyone in the stadium rose to their feet for the national anthem. Then the team captains from both teams met on the fifty yard line for the coin toss. Right before kick off, the announcer came across the intercoms and said with this being the first game of the season, there would be a special half time show. The crowd was hyped up so loud; no one could hear themselves think.

This is so amazing! Shelby thought excitedly. She had been to plenty of games in the past, but this time, it is *so* much better. She guessed it was all due to the fact this time, she watching *her* man down on the field. She still felt like she was living in a dream but she loved it!

By the time half time rolled around, the Wolves were down by fourteen points. That wasn't the greatest way to start a new season but they still had the second half of the game to go. As Shelby sat watching both teams run off the field to the locker room, she could swear she heard someone calling her name. She listened for a few minutes and didn't hear anything. After a few more minutes, she heard it again. It was the announcers; they were calling out her name! Why would they be calling my name? She thought confused. She kept hearing "Shelby Russell; you are wanted on the field. Please report to mid field at this time."

Shelby looked at her mother and she shrugged her shoulders confused as much as Shelby was. Shelby walked out of the box and there was a security guard standing at the door. He told her to follow him and he would show her where to go. "What is this all about?" She asked her self under her breath. The guard walked her down to the field and instructed her to stand in the middle of the field on the fifty yard line.

Had she won some kind of contest? She asked in the back of her mind.

As Shelby waited, one of the announcers came across the PA speakers again. He was talking to Shelby and instructing her on what she was supposed to do. He told her to stand and face toward the crowd; so she did. Shelby looked up to the box where she had just been sitting. This was so embarrassing. Why am I standing here? She asked her self.

All of a sudden, music began to play and the crowd in the stadium went quiet. The song playing was "You're My Better Half" by Keith Urban the country singer. After a few minutes of the song playing, the crowd became one huge billboard. Everyone had a huge square board and as they held them up together it spelled out something.

In the first round, there was a huge smiley face. The next round spelled SHELBY, then RUSSELL. The next round was WILL, then YOU, then MARRY, then ME? Then LOVE and finally DALLAS.

Shelby stood completely still for a few minutes, then her hands flew over her mouth when the reality of what the message said finally hit her. It said; Shelby Russell will you marry me, love Dallas. She was in complete shock! Tears started to fall silently down her face; she couldn't stop her self from crying. She was crying because she was so utterly happy!

About that time, the crowd began to roar. Shelby turned to look behind her and found Dallas standing behind her with a small red velvet box in his hand. Standing there in his uniform without his helmet, Shelby couldn't help but think how damn sexy he looked.

As the tears rolled down her face, Shelby ran toward him and jumped into his arms wrapping her legs around his waist. She kissed him over and over and over again. She couldn't believe he had done all of this for her. Dallas had a microphone hooked to his jersey and after he set her feet back on the field, he knelt down on one knee.

"Well, Shelby, what do you say to making it forever?" he asked with a huge smile as he opened the red velvet box exposing a beautiful diamond engagement ring.

"There's only one thing to say, yes! Yes, yes, yes!" Shelby yelled.

Everything that was said between them was blasted over all of the speakers in the entire stadium.

Dallas took the ring out of the little red velvet box and slipped it onto Shelby's ring finger. He stood back up and they started kissing again. The crowd went crazy and after a few minutes, his coach walked out on the field.

"We do still have a game to finish; and by the way congratulations." He said to the both of them as he shook Dallas's hand and winked at Shelby.

"Thanks coach." Dallas replied.

They ran off the field and Shelby gave Dallas a few more kisses. Shelby went back to her seat and he went back to work on the field. Shelby's Mom and Dad knew all along what was going to happen. Even CJ called her on her cell phone to congratulate her. "It's about time!" he yelled through the phone.

Everyone knew but her and it was the best surprise she could have ever received.

By the end of the game, the Wolves won by twenty one points. Shelby thought with what had happened at half time; it gave everyone a little extra "ump" in their step. It had been an awesome game and an awesome day!

Dallas and Shelby decided to wait till after football season was over to get married. The Wolves ended their season with a 14-2 record and went all the way to the Super Bowl and won.

Realizing that all of her dreams were coming true, one more dream had come true as well. Dallas and Cole had finally made up and were friends once again.

Dallas and Shelby's wedding came soon after. Cole was his best man.

The look in Dallas's eye as Shelby walked with her father down the isle of the church made her weak in the knees. She was going to spend the rest of her life with this man, and as she looked at him, a tear started to fall from her eye. She was bursting was so much joy, she was overwhelmed.

She and Dallas took each other's hands after her father handed his daughter over to Dallas. The preacher started the ceremony. Dallas and Shelby exchanged vows, exchanged rings and with tears in both their eyes, kissed each other happily when the preacher told Dallas to kiss his bride.

"I give you, Mr. and Mrs. Dallas Smith!" The preacher exclaimed once they had stopped kissing and turned toward the congregation seated in the church. Everyone stood and applauded relentlessly.

At the reception, everyone had a blast. Shelby watched as Dallas, Cole and CJ took over the dance floor. She wasn't exactly for sure what they were trying to do, but it looked as if they were trying to break dance. She stood off to the side of the dance floor clapping her hands and moving back and forth to the beat of the music watching the men in her life. It felt like it had taken them a life time to get here, but, she couldn't have made it through any of it if it hadn't been for her boys.

"*Me and my boys*," Shelby said quietly to her self as she watched them with a smile from ear to ear. They might not be considered the three musketeers any longer, but they always knew they could count on each other. No matter what life would throw their way, they were still family and in the end, that mattered more than anything else.

Her life was complete.

Almost

Once the reception started to die down, Dallas and Shelby made their exit. Not telling anyone else what they had planned to do, they went back to *their* house. They were leaving in the morning for their honeymoon in Hawaii, but tonight, tonight was the night Shelby had dreamed about since her and Dallas had finally gotten together. Neither one of them could wait to make their marriage complete.

As soon as they had walked onto the front porch, Dallas swooped Shelby up in his arms to carry her across the thresh hold.

Winking at her, he said, "Welcome home, Mrs. Smith."

"Welcome home, Mr. Smith." Shelby said as she kissed him.

Dallas walked them through the door and didn't stop to put Shelby's feet back on solid ground. He took her straight up the stairs to their bedroom. Dallas laid her gently down on the bed that had been covered with rose petals. Candles were lit through out the entire room illuminating the ceiling with sparkling prisms that reminded Shelby of sparkling champagne.

"Did you do all of this?" Shelby asked as she looked around the room in amazement.

"Do you like it?" he asked staring down at her.

"It's beautiful."

"Not half as beautiful as you," he said as he leaned his head down to her.

Dallas kissed her with so much passion that Shelby thought she was going to drown. When he pulled back, Shelby was swimming with desire. Her entire body felt as if it were on fire. She looked up into his gorgeous blue eyes and smiled contently.

"You do know you're going to have to help me with this dress." She said seductively.

"It would be my pleasure." Dallas replied as he took hold of her hands and pulled her up to stand.

Shelby turned her back to him as he started to unbutton the back of her wedding dress. Shelby was thankful the dress was sleeveless and strapless. Once Dallas had unbuttoned the last button, he pushed the back of the dress open and slowly let it slip out of his hands and slide to the floor.

He turned Shelby to face him looking up and down the length of her body. Damn was she beautiful, he thought to himself and every inch of her was his. He still couldn't believe that Shelby Russell, correction, Shelby Smith was his wife. His dream had come true and now, she stood in front of him wearing only her sexy underwear and a strapless bra. He reached for her hair, pulling the pins out that were holding her hair, letting it free from their confinement to cascade down her around and over her shoulders. She had the most beautiful red hair he had ever seen.

She took his breath away.

Shelby watched Dallas intently as he looked at her. She was half naked and she felt more comfortable than she thought she ever would. Now, it was her turn to undress him. She was nervous beyond belief because she knew she was about to be educated in something she had never experienced in her life before now. Would Dallas be disappointed that she had never made love before? She asked her self in the back of her mind.

Shelby slid her hands underneath Dallas's tux jacket and up over his shoulders. His jacket slid down his shoulders, down his arms and fell to the floor. She unbuttoned his shirt and repeated the same movements she had made with his jacket. His chest was hard muscled and he looked like a Greek God that had been chiseled out of marble. Nervously, she slid her hands to the waist band of his pants and fumbled with the button. Once she had it undone, she slowly unzipped the zipper. She was shaking all over.

Dallas took hold of her hands when he saw how she was reacting and said, "You're shaking all over. Are you alright?"

"I'm fine, just a little nervous is all." She said when he cupped her chin in his hand and turned her to face him.

"Are you sure?" he asked with concern. He knew there had to be something wrong.

"No." Shelby said knowing this was her moment of truth." I have a confession to make."

"What is it? You're starting to scare me." Dallas said as he held her hands looking at her confused.

Shelby looked into his deep blue eyes and he could see fear staring straight back at him.

"I've never done this before." She said quietly looking down to the floor.

"Never done what?"

"I've never been...intimate...with a man before." She explained.

Dallas's eye brows came together as he became more confused about what she was talking about. Then, as if a light bulb went off inside his head, it hit him.

"You've never made love before?" he asked in shock.

"No."

"Never? Are you sure? How is that possible?" he asked confused.

"Dallas, I think I would know if I had ever had sex before." She said to him agitated at his questions.

"No, that's not what I meant. Please forgive me. I'm just surprised, is all. Shelby, you're a beautiful woman, I just assumed that you had before. After all, you were engaged once. Why have you waited for so long?" Dallas asked trying to understand her reasoning.

"I promised my self, when I was younger, that I would wait and save my self for the man that I would marry." She explained shyly.

Dallas smiled at her. He understood so much now. "That explains everything."

"What?"

"I didn't understand why you wanted to sleep in the same bed together but never wanted it to go further than that. Now, I understand. Why didn't you tell me this before?" He asked.

"I was embarrassed. Are you disappointed in me?" Shelby asked.

"Disappointed, are you crazy? Shelby, I love you more than anything in this world. To know you have saved yourself all these years, makes me love you even more. I'm your husband, and knowing that I will be the first and *only* man to make sweet passionate love to you for the rest of *our* lives; that makes me the luckiest man alive." He said as he pulled her close to him and wrapped his arms around her tightly. He was so happy that tears started to well in his eyes.

"Dallas, I love you so much." Shelby said as she held him tighter. Her fears were swept away with the understanding he had given her.

"I love you too." He said as his lips claimed hers.

Shelby pulled back after a few seconds and looked deeply into his eyes. She had one more question and knew she could ask with out feeling embarrassed, "Will you make love to me?"

Dallas's heart wanted to leap from his chest. How could he be so lucky to have such a beautiful, untouched woman? Life with Shelby was going to be *so much more* than he ever dreamed.

In that instant, he was more aroused than he had ever been in his life! "I can do better than that. I'll make love *with* you," he said. His voice was husky and filled with desire. He lifted her from the floor and carried her to the bed.

Taking his time, Dallas unfastened her bra and discarded it to the floor. Teasing her body with his hands, he slid his hand down to her underwear sliding them slowly down her hips, down her legs and over her feet.

Shelby was completely naked and she didn't care. In Dallas's arms, nothing bothered her and her embarrassment was gone. All she knew right now, was she wanted him more than ever. She wanted to know how their naked bodies felt against each other. She wanted to know how it would feel when they were joined together making them man and wife forever. With every movement and every kiss he showered across her body, she felt the fire build inside her.

Shelby moved her arm to caress his back when she brushed her hand across his hard arousal. At first, she felt some what embarrassed but when she heard him moan with pleasure, she couldn't help her self. She slowly felt every inch of him with her hand. Her body tingled with the sensation from her finger tips straight to her inner core.

Dallas couldn't take anymore. She was driving him wild with her caressing his very manhood. He moved him self away from her and raised himself above her positioning him self between her thighs.

Shelby looked up at him and he could see the desire burning in her eyes.

"Dallas," she said between labored breaths, "Please."

"This might hurt for a few seconds, but that's all." He said trying to reassure her of the pain she might feel when he entered her.

"I don't care," Shelby gasped. "I want to feel you."

Dallas started to slide into her and Shelby could feel him pushing slowly. He wasn't all the way in and it was about to drive her insane. She wanted all of him and now! Not giving him the chance, Shelby lifted against him, pushing him all the way inside her. She let out a shallow scream allowing the pain to course through her entire body.

Dallas didn't move. She needed time to cope with the pain and let her body adjust to the length of him that filled her every being.

"Are you alright?" he asked gasping for air.

"Don't......stop." Shelby uttered.

Dallas started to move slowly with in her. He rose gently and moved back into her. With his every move, Shelby moved in unison with him. The pain had gone and now all she felt was pleasure. At her urging, they began to move faster. Shelby lifted her hips, wrapping her legs around Dallas tighter. He slid into her deeper. She let out a soft moan the farther he went until there was no more space between the tip of him and the very core of her womanhood. The faster Shelby moved the harder Dallas thrust into her until they both screamed with pleasured release.

Dallas, keeping him self inside her, collapsed on top of her. He rained kisses all over her until his lips finally met hers. He held her tightly against his body.

"God, I love you." He said still trying to catch his breath.

"I love you more than you'll ever know." Shelby replied kissing him again. "If I had know that making love was like this…I would have done it along time ago."

Dallas threw his head back and laughed, "I'm glad you didn't!"

"Me too, I can't imagine making love to anyone but you." Shelby said as she hugged him to her.

They made love three more times during the night. Shelby couldn't get enough of him. This was one experience she was glad she had waited until she was married to experience. Exhausted beyond belief, the two of them finally fell asleep in each others arms.

Dallas awoke the next morning to the feeling of Shelby's finger tips sliding sensually up and down his chest; neither one of them had had much sleep and she was already teasing his body, telling him she was ready to go again.

"Good morning, Mr. Smith." Shelby said seductively.

"Good morning, Mrs. Smith." Dallas replied with a chuckle.

Dallas gladly gave in and made love to her again. He could make love to her for the rest of his life. Wait a minute, he thought, I do get to do this for the rest of our lives!

"You do know that if we keep this up, we're going to miss our plane." He said to her nibbling on her ear.

"And your point is?" she asked teasingly.

"My point is, my sexy little vixen, is that we do have a honeymoon to get to."

"I'd much rather stay here like this." Shelby said as she kissed the tip of his nose.

"Ok then, think about this. Imagine lying on a secluded beach in Hawaii, completely naked, making love under the stars while the ocean waves crash against the white sand." Dallas said arching both eye brows quickly at her.

"Hawaii it is!" Shelby said as she jumped from the bed and ran toward the bathroom to take a shower.

Dallas shook his head and laughed.

Then he wondered how she might like to make love in the shower. Boy, if he didn't have a lot to teach her! He thought ruefully to himself as he crossed the bedroom toward the bathroom with a crooked devious grin.

Chapter 19

Two years later...

It was the fourth of July and everyone had gathered at Shelby and Dallas's house for a barbeque. Dallas had built on a huge deck to the back of the house that made gatherings even better. Cole, Tiffany, and their little girl Shelly was there; Shelby's parents, Dallas's mom and his brother Luke, CJ and his wife Cara. Leah and her husband Troy had even shown up with their two kids, Ginger and Steven.

Life had been good to them all. CJ had gotten married and now he and his wife were expecting twins. Twins! Shelby could hardly believe it when they told her the news. CJ had even worked a deal to be traded to the Ft. Wayne Wolves so that he could live closer to home.

Shelby stood at the kitchen sink watching through the window at all of the people who had gathered in her back yard. She was awe struck with the happiness she felt. She had never dreamed that her life could be this fulfilling. Everyone she loved was having fun in her back yard. She had her veterinarian practice, which had been more profitable than she had ever dreamed, and the man that she would love till her dying day beside her always. She couldn't ask for more.

Bringing her out of her thoughts, she heard Dallas calling her name through the kitchen screen door.

"Shelby, are you finished yet?"

"Just one more second!" she called back.

Shelby picked up the birthday cake she had been placing candles on and waddled toward the back door. Using her rear, she bumped the door open and proceeded out onto the deck where everyone else was waiting. Setting the cake down on the picnic table, she looked around for the birthday boy.

She looked to Dallas and said, "Where is he?"

Dallas wrapped his arms around her and with a devious grin, he said, "In the barn with Uncle Cole playing with the puppies."

"Dallas, he's going to be filthy!" Shelby exclaimed trying to push away from him.

"He'll be just fine. We live on a farm; you're supposed to get dirty." He said as he wrinkled his nose at her teasingly.

"I'll go get them." Shelby said as she gave him one quick peck on the cheek and waddled down the deck stairs.

Walking to the entrance of the barn and being careful to not be seen, Shelby watched as Cole sat on the dirt covered floor with puppies scattered about and the most beautiful blue eyed, dusty blond headed little boy she had ever laid eyes upon. His name was Cody and he was all hers. Today was his first birthday.

"Are you trying to steal my son?" Shelby asked Cole when she finally made her presence known.

"Yep, I'm gonna' run away with this little guy." Cole said as he stood and tossed Cody playfully into the air. Cody erupted in laughter.

"I think you might have a fight with his father over that. Well, you'd have to get through me first." Shelby said laughing.

Cole walked up to Shelby and wrapped his arm around her shoulders, "I can't believe how big he's gotten. We just might make a football player out of him yet."

"Now, just slow down there bub; let's just get him onto kindergarten first. Don't be getting too far ahead of yourself. You sound like his father. My little man can be anything he wants to be." Shelby said as she took Cody's hand in hers and kissed it.

"What's going on in here? Are you hitting on my wife again?" Dallas asked teasingly as he walked into the barn.

Cole let out a long drawn out sigh and said, "I keep trying. I tell her all the time that she should have that affair with me, but for some reason, she says she loves that husband of hers." Cole said shaking his head in disapproval.

"Husband, huh? Is this husband of yours the jealous type?" Dallas asked giving her a side ways glance.

Shelby gave him a seductive grin and that was all Dallas needed. He wrapped his arms around her waist and leaned down to kiss her.

244

"I'll just take Cody back to the house." Cole said quickly and left the barn.

Once outside, Dallas and Shelby heard Cole talking to Cody saying, "I do believe that if your mommy and daddy keep this up, you'll have a house full of brothers' and sisters."

Dallas and Shelby both chuckled at Coles comment. Dallas started to kiss her again and cupped her behind in his hands.

"Dallas! In the barn?" Shelby asked in shock.

"Why not, we've christened everything else around this farm." He replied with a devious grin of his own.

Shelby pulled him closer to her and began to kiss him. As she did, she felt a slight thump against her belly. Dallas jerked back quickly to look at her.

"Did you feel that?" Shelby asked him with a grin from ear to ear.

Dallas placed his hand on Shelby's protruding belly and smiled, "I believe our little girl is letting us know she's in there."

"I believe you're right." Shelby said as she placed her hand on top of Dallas's.

Dallas wrapped his arm around her waist and walked with her to the entrance of the barn. Neither one of them could believe that in another three months, they were going to be parents again; this time to a little girl they would name Allison.

Dallas and Shelby watched their friends and family enjoying themselves and both of them were happier than could ever be. Dallas had his Shelly girl and Shelby had her Dally. There was nothing in this world they could want more, than each other. Dallas turned to look at Shelby and Shelby turned to look at Dallas.

"I love you *so* much, Shelby Smith."

"And I love you *more* than that, Dallas Smith." Shelby answered winking at him.